# Skull Water

# Skull Water

HEINZ INSU FENKL

*Spiegel*
*and Grau*

Spiegel & Grau, New York
www.spiegelandgrau.com

Copyright © 2023 by Heinz Insu Fenkl

This book is a work of fiction. All characters, names, incidents, and places
are products of the author's imagination or are used fictitiously.

Jacket design by Strick & Williams; Jacket illustration by Carson Ellis;
Interior design by Meighan Cavanaugh

Library of Congress Cataloging-in-Publication Data Available Upon Request

ISBN 978-1-954118-19-5 (HC)
ISBN 978-1-954118-20-1 (ebook)

Printed in the United States of America

First Edition

10  9  8  7  6  5  4  3  2  1

*For Big Uncle,*

*and for my family,*

*past, present,*

*&*

*future*

# Contents

## III

# The Train to Pusan

## IV

# Three Days That Summer

## V

# Twilight

## VI

# Time & the River

I

# One Big Word

# One Big Word

## 1974

The shadow of the 707 rippled like a giant black egret as the hilly contours below us became the flat green expanse of the rice paddies around Kimpo Air Base. I could not imagine what power it took to keep these tons of alloy and steel in the air, to keep the plane from simply plummeting like a stone into the fertile earth below. We were falling at more than two hundred miles an hour, and yet the landscape moved lazily until the plane slowed, just before touching the runway, and then everything seemed to accelerate with a dizzying speed. The world lurched and the air grew suddenly thick with the roar of the jet engines, and we could feel the sudden roughness of the tarmac through the landing gear, right through the bottoms of our seats, as the earth ground itself up into our spines.

As the airplane braked to a near stop, everything outside looked at once too large and yet oddly too small. I glanced over my little sister's head to the aisle seat and saw my mother's eyes brim with tears of joy at being back in our homeland.

Korea. 1974. Early summer in the Year of the Tiger.

THE TAXI DRIVER from Kimpo said he could take the new highway, but my mother asked him to take the old road that had been the route for the U.S. Army buses we used to ride. Through mile after mile of chain-link fences, the American and Korean military posts we drove past were just as I remembered them. Where the road used to turn to gravel, the odd Purina Chows sign in English was still there, its red-and-white checkered squares faded, the lower right corner burnt—scars of a year's weathering.

We were going to live in Kisu's house, in the same neighborhood where we had lived before leaving for Germany, and when the taxi pulled up outside the wooden gate with its faded tri-color *t'aeguk* symbol next to the tailor shop, I felt a strange mix of ease and fatigue.

At first, Kisu's house appeared exactly the same as when I had last seen it a year earlier. And yet during our first day back I realized that the house had aged just as Kisu's grandmother Halmoni had; she had grown lighter and more shriveled, like a dried gourd that will rattle in the wind. It was a ramshackle house nearly a hundred years old now, built decades before the Japanese occupation, and since then, as the tiny village by the stream had grown into Pupyong, it had sheltered four generations of Changs. The original building was wood and whitewashed plaster, but now the roof beams were full of dry rot and the *kidung* posts were warped and tilted. When I walked across the wooden *maru* with the added weight of my year away, the floor creaked in spots I didn't recall, and the compacted dirt of the courtyard, which had always seemed as hard as baked clay, seemed to have become softer, dustlike. The black dirt floor of the kitchen was special—people from the neighborhood would visit from time to time to scoop up a few spoonfuls of it to make medicine pellets, which they would take with foul-smelling concoctions of Chinese herbs. Now, though I had grown taller, it seemed somehow even lower than before.

For the first few months after our return to Korea, we would live in this house in Pupyong in the old neighborhood of Tatagumi, which still bore its Japanese name, in the very same rooms we had occupied before; my mother, my sister An-na, and I all slept in the room where I had been born.

The first morning I stepped outside the front gate, I was startled by the red cock that guarded the tailor shop next door. It stood alert, jerking its head this way and that, clucking deep within its throat. Seeing me, it aimed its gaze, which was no less sharp than its knife-sharp beak. I retreated slowly, and suddenly I felt as if I were back in time. When we were last here, there had been a cock just like this one, with the same twitchy movements, the same red-black-and-orange sheen to its feathers. Perhaps this was the son or the grandson of that one— surely it could not have been the same bird. My cousin Yongsu had once come home with a small sack of rice from the corner store and the cock had attacked him for daring to pass without feeding him. Yongsu had nearly lost an eye that time, and forever after that he and I made sure to toss a clump of dried rice or a crust of old sandwich bread to distract the bird when we left or returned to the house. Kisu's mother joked that they had never been burglarized since the tailor started raising his fighting cocks.

I remembered the tailor squatting in the dirt courtyard by the water spigot, holding his precious rooster between his legs, stroking its feathers into a beautiful scarlet sheen, sharpening its claws, fitting it with the bamboo spikes it would drive into its opponent like spurs. My uncle Hyongbu had taken us once to a cockfight, and we had watched as the two birds circled each other and then collided in a chaos of feathers and sound. In an instant, it was over, one cock strutting back and the other listing forlornly before falling on its side, surprising us with the vast amount of blood that suddenly gushed forth. Hyongbu, having lost his bet, never took us again—nor had Yongsu or I ever asked to be taken. It was too awful. The smell of blood and feathers mixed with the acrid sweat and cigarette smoke of the audience had not only settled into our clothes but permeated our very skin.

Now I simply took a few quick steps and got out of the cock's way. I crossed the street and walked toward the train station at the foot of the hill. I planned on paying a visit to the old house in Samnung where we'd once lived, but just as I reached the main road, I saw Kisu's mother leading her ninety-three-year-old mother-in-law out of an acupuncturist's house. Halmoni was oddly dressed from the treatment, in old Japanese-style pantaloons that exposed her emaciated, knobby-jointed legs.

Kisu's mother was having trouble holding Halmoni upright, so I rushed forward to help them back across the street, half carrying the old woman. She was so light I might have lifted her in my arms like an infant, but I hesitated as she mumbled something about the indignity of being outside without her proper white clothes. When we reached the gate of the house, the tailor's rooster gave us only a curious look and let us by without a challenge, merely twisting his neck around with frenetic alertness as we entered the small blue-green door in the gate.

"What's the matter?" I asked Kisu's mother.

"Halmoni was lucid today," she said. "She knew how sick she was, and she wanted a treatment right away."

"I almost died," said Halmoni. "I almost died, and you kept me in that room alone all morning. What kind of daughter-in-law are you now that my son is dead?"

"Quiet, Mother," said Kisu's mother. "This is Kisu's friend who lives across the *maru*. He's the little girl's older brother."

Kisu's grandmother squinted at me as she sat down on the granite stepping-stone and let her daughter-in-law remove her rubber shoes for her. "How old are you?" she said suddenly.

I was about to tell her I was fifteen, though reckoned fourteen in the American way, when she said, "Two thousand and three hundred and forty-four years. That's a long time to be an ancestor. *Yaeya*, how many *hwangap* does that make? How many times does the zodiac turn in that many years, *ungh*?"

"I don't know," I said.

Kisu's mother took Halmoni by the hands now and led her back to their room, while I stood there, trying to do the calculation in my head. Each *hwangap* was sixty years—five turns of the lunar zodiac, which is made of twelve animal signs. Two thousand three hundred and forty-four divided by sixty was . . . thirty-nine, with four years left over. Thirty-nine times five was . . . one hundred and ninety-five. Four years was one-third of a turn, so the zodiac must have turned one hundred ninety-five and a third times in those years. One part of me wanted to deliver the answer to Kisu's grandmother, though I knew she was just lapsing back into her senility.

A FEW DAYS AFTER her lucid spell, Halmoni became very sick. With the steepening medical bills, our rent was a windfall for the Changs—especially after the acupuncture treatments failed, and they talked about taking her to a hospital the following month. Only then, for no apparent reason, she suddenly got well again. She sat out on the wooden floor of the *maru* and watched everyone in the yard as she smoked her long bamboo pipe, smacking her thin lips.

All through the humid heat, she was healthy and lively. She even showed An-na, who had just turned six, the old version of the bellflower-root dance and, miming the picking and putting into the basket, she sang, with great vigor, *Toraji toraji paek toraji.* Though she lisped because she had only two teeth, the song, in her high and scratchy voice, sounded beautiful. It seemed to come from the border of another world. With her few tufts of brittle white hair and her shriveled skin, Halmoni looked as if she had already been dead a thousand years.

After the monsoon rains, Halmoni had a surge of appetite. At mealtimes we all took turns chewing her food for her and spitting it into a bowl. Kisu's mother mixed it before spooning it out, a little at a time. Soon Halmoni started calling Kisu by his dead father's name and treating his mother as if she were the maid. Some days she spoke only Japanese, warning us that we would get into great trouble if we were caught speaking Korean. Her mind seemed to be hastening backward in time.

"It's nothing to worry about," my mother told me one night. "All of us who remember that time have the same fear, and it's just coming out in Halmoni because her mind is getting young again." Mahmi had just put An-na to bed and we were both sitting cross-legged on the floor, under the dangling bulb. Mahmi played solitaire with her small, plastic flower cards while I read a pulp novel I had gotten at the PX in ASCOM, the U.S. Army base in Pupyong.

Mahmi glanced at the cover of the latest installment in the Doc Savage series: the Man of Bronze in his tattered shirt and jodhpurs, his exposed torso gleaming with sweat and blood, his fists clenched, his face as rugged as a rough-hewn god. She took the book from me and turned it over to see the back cover, holding my place open with a finger. "You're reading this because he looks like your father?"

"*Ungh?*" I said. My father was stationed up in Camp Casey, near the DMZ, and he hadn't yet come down to see us since we had arrived in Korea.

My mother handed the book back to me and I examined the photo more carefully. In color, Doc Savage's white-blond skullcap of hair and the creases on his face gave him a passing resemblance to my father, but on the back cover, the small brooding black-and-white portrait of him, with its look of grim wisdom, had an uncanny similarity.

"How could you not notice?" Mahmi said. "You've ruined your eyes from all that reading. Let's get to sleep."

"One more chapter?"

"Let's sleep when I've finished this round, *ungh?*" She slapped another card down on a column. It was the rain card, depicting a man with an umbrella under black jags of what looked like seaweed, and a small toadlike creature running in the lower corner. "That look on the man's face on your book," she said, "it's just like your father when he's angry. Like he could stab you with his eyes."

"He knows hypno—" I hesitated because I didn't quite know the word in Korean.

"Hypnotism," said Mahmi. "Some of the old Taoists could kill you with a look or pull all your life energy out through your eyes. Big Uncle tried to learn things like that—he could tell you all about it. Did I ever tell you the dream I had after you were born?"

"The one about the snake on the palace wall?"

"No," she said. "That was your birth dream. I mean the dream I had when they took me to the hospital."

"I thought I was born at home," I said.

"You were. There were problems after."

"Problems?"

"It was the afterbirth," she said. "I wouldn't stop bleeding. Hyongbu had to run out and find a taxi in the middle of the night, and they took me to the 121st Army Hospital in ASCOM." Mahmi smoothed the hair away from An-na's sleeping face. "They had to give me a transfusion, but they got my blood type wrong, and when the new blood went into me it burned like fire. I started to swell up and they thought I was going to die. I had chills and the most horrible pains. It felt as if my entire body had been asleep and I was getting that terrible pins and needles feeling— but everywhere, inside *and* outside. In my dream I was running away from a ghost. It was the most horrible feeling in all my life, but I got away. If it had caught me, I would have died. It's late," she said. "Now go to sleep."

A GLINT OF LIGHT. Then a shadow across my face. I opened my eyes, still paralyzed by lingering sleep. An old woman was crouched by the door, bent nearly double, shuffling silently forward in her white *poson* socks. For a moment I wondered whether I was still dreaming, but then

I could see that it was Kisu's grandmother. She was holding a kitchen knife, mumbling to herself in a low voice. In her pure white skirt and *chogori*, she looked, in the early-morning light, like a ghost. I tried to sit up to wake my mother, but my body would not move, and when I tried to speak, only a tiny sound caught in my throat.

Kisu's grandmother seemed to be considering something; she turned her head from side to side and shuffled first this way and then that way, as if she was dancing or performing some ritual, and it suddenly occurred to me that she must be deciding whom to kill. Slowly, she moved the blade of the knife up and down as if it were a pestle in a mortar. Then, turning toward me with a suddenly suspicious look, she made a whistling sound.

"Halmoni!" I wanted to shout out, but my throat only twitched again. She raised her knife higher, squinting at me to get a clearer look at my face.

"*Gaijin?*" she said. It was Japanese for "foreigner." Before I could try to speak again, her expression fell, as if she were sorely disappointed, and she turned toward the sliding doors. She looked back at me with a wan smile before she stepped outside, casting her hunched shadow against the latticed panels.

"Mahmi," I whispered when my voice worked, "Kisu's grandmother was just in here with a kitchen knife. I think she was going to kill us."

"What?" my mother said, still confused with sleep. "With a kitchen knife?"

"I think she was going to stab us."

My mother yawned and exhaled a sour breath. "She must have been looking for the man who killed her son."

"I thought her son died of TB."

"The *other* son. He was tortured and murdered by the Japanese for being a subversive. He was in the Language Society."

"But why was she in our room?"

"I guess we'll have to put on a lock, *ungh*? She's getting senile." My mother rolled onto her other side to face An-na and fell back asleep as if nothing had happened.

I got up and went out onto the *maru*, still in my underwear. The cool morning air dried the clammy sweat that covered my body and I shivered before the sun slowly warmed me. The door to the other family room was open, and inside I could see Kisu's mother wagging her finger at Halmoni, who sat hunched on the floor, her legs splayed out in front of her, crying soundlessly. The old woman's head bobbed up and down just like the handle of the kitchen knife she had wielded, while through her sunken cheeks and puckered lips she mouthed words that not even Kisu's mother could have properly heard. As I stepped down into the courtyard to wash, Kisu's mother gave me a tired look.

KOREA WAS STILL A kingdom when Halmoni was a young woman. After the Japanese annexation, she'd witnessed the tragedy of Queen Min's murder, the kidnapping of the royal family, the March First Movement in Pagoda Park, the Liberation, the civil war, the death of the first puppet president, and the coup that put the former warlord General Park Chung Hee in power. During the Second World War, one of Halmoni's daughters had been taken by the Japanese to work in a munitions factory, never to be seen again, and the only news of her whereabouts was delivered by a girlfriend who said she had been murdered in Manchuria in a military recreation camp in the spring of 1945. Halmoni was left with only memories, reminders. A silver hairpin from her missing daughter. A dictionary manuscript from her executed son.

Sometimes, in the early evenings, she would sit and smoke her long bamboo pipe out on the *maru* and lapse into long monologues in Japanese, as if her old family were gathered around her. It was unintelligible to me and Kisu, but to his mother, to Mahmi, and to my aunt Emo—all of them fluent in Japanese from their childhoods under the occupation—what she said often made them weep or cry out for her to stop. But she would go on until it was late, sitting there in the lengthening shadows, everything dark now but for the bright speck of her pipe bowl glowing like the tail of a blood-lit firefly.

"Emo," I said one night, "what's Halmoni talking about in Japanese all the time?"

"She's just remembering," said Emo. "She's old, and she's talking about old things to dead people. She thinks it's still 1939. We weren't allowed to speak Korean then, at least not so anyone outside could hear. There were police everywhere."

"But I want to know what she's saying."

"What for? You don't need to know such things."

"I want to know."

"Well, maybe she'll speak Korean one night, *ungh*?"

"Why won't you translate?"

"Absolutely not."

A few nights later Kisu and I sat with his grandmother as she smoked her pipe, and we took turns whispering to her, "Halmoni, the Japanese are all gone. No one's going to hear you if you talk in Korean." We said this to her again and again, taking turns from each side, until—whether because of our persistence or just some slip of the mind—her cadence suddenly changed.

"*Yaeya*," she said. "Go look by the gate and see if anyone's about."

"Nobody, Halmoni," said Kisu.

Halmoni said a phrase or two in Japanese, as if to make sure, and then in Korean she said, "Wrap him hand and foot, head and body. Put boiled eggs in his palms when you bind them. You don't know if he might get hungry on the journey. Fill his mouth with dry rice to keep the cheeks from sinking. He can cook it in the next world.

"Wrap him tight, really tight, until you can hear his bones and gristle crunch *uddu-duk, uddu-duk*, and lay him snug in the lacquered coffin. Have you washed his hair? Who's making the banners and the funeral clothes? Where are the long bamboo poles? Why can't I smell any incense, *ungh*?" The *maru* was thick with her pipe smoke and Kisu squinted at me in alarm, though he was obviously curious.

"Don't burn the calligraphy. Wrap it with the bedding and hide it well. He knows the life story of each word like it's his own ancestor, and we have to keep those words safe, you know, like our own family register."

She made gestures in the air as if she were writing Chinese characters. "Did you hear what he said? 'It's all one single big word, Mother, but we've forgotten what it sounds like. We have to keep looking until we find it again and then everything will be whole again.' What a scholar! Where did he get so wise when we couldn't even send him to a university? What do you think, Chinju? Do you think he'll ever marry, or will he sneak off to Haeinsa Temple and cut off all his hair like he always jokes to me? Imagine that. 'It's all one single big word, Mother.' One single big word. What do you suppose it could be? And what would it look like in that fancy calligraphy? More complicated than 'dragon' or 'turtle,' *ungh*? Or do you suppose he'll be able to draw it with a few quick sickle shapes in *hangul*? You Christians are always saying it's 'God' or 'love' or some nonsense. One single big word. Imagine that. Don't forget to put the dry rice in his mouth so the cheeks don't sink in. Smooth his palms over the eggs to give his hands a nice shape. You don't want his fingers getting all twisted when they dry. Close his eyelids gently and don't push down so hard on his eyes! He's got to see when he goes to that world!"

Someone knocked at the gate just then, and Halmoni stopped abruptly, her eyes going wide with fright. She began babbling on in Japanese again, her voice shrill and fearful until Kisu's mother ran out of the kitchen to soothe her, telling her it was only the Buddhist monks from Medicine Mountain coming for alms.

We never tried our trick again. Halmoni was calling forth the family ghosts before joining them herself, fading away so that by the time the first July moon waned to a sliver she would no longer sit out on the *maru*. Now they kept her, lying on her bed mat in the dimly lit room, and she became deathly quiet. I never went into that room, afraid of being touched by her death. But from outside on the *maru* I would see how stiffly and silently she lay there, just waiting, patiently, for some spirit to come call her away.

While my mother made arrangements to move, and Kisu's relatives—who would take over our rooms after Halmoni's death—came by periodically, we all waited, too, not so much for her death as for the funeral preparations. She had died decades ago, with only her body lingering on to go through the motions of a life. After a while we stopped even scolding An-na when she cried out, prematurely, "Halmoni's dead," because we knew the charade would be over all too soon.

I HAD BELIEVED, when we left Germany to return to Korea, that it would feel like coming back home. From the moment we'd left Korea and landed at McChord Air Base near Seattle—the first leg of our long trip to Baumholder, Germany—it had seemed to me that we were stepping out under a different sun, into different air, as if we had not simply flown to some distant part of the same world but to an altogether new and alien one where things bore only the uncanny semblance of familiarity. The cast of the Korean light I remembered, that taste of air I craved, the smell of roasting silkworm larvae, the sound of the monsoon rain and the cool of it, the comfort of being cradled in the low jumble of hills—it had all become transformed in my memory into something more vivid than reality, like the lingering power of numinous dreams. The world of the West could do no justice to it. But neither would Korea itself, I now realized. All through those first long weeks back, practically sequestered in Kisu's house, when I discovered that I could no longer see as far as the hills—and not because of mist that hung between us, but because of pollution—or when I felt the summer sweat on my flesh sticking with a different thickness, I felt a profound disappointment.

Once, in Germany, in the middle of February, I had stepped out of a U.S. Army gas station into a gust of icy wind and had become momentarily disoriented. I had almost expected to round the corner of the building and find myself back in Korea, in ASCOM, below the PX hill. So strongly had I felt this sensation that when I did turn the corner and saw not the row of barracks but the Autobahn, I felt a betrayal so profound it caused my throat to catch. Now I was truly back home, in the same house I'd been born in. And yet I felt as distant from this place as I had been in America or in Germany. Sitting on the *maru* and looking across the courtyard through the shadow under the open gate, at the bright glints of sunlight on the metal of passing cars, I felt as if part of me had been forever trapped in the past even as another part hovered in the future.

I had left my friends behind when we'd left for Germany and now purposely stayed away from them, even knowing, through my mother, that they were all back in Korea again, just like us. Paulie, Patsy, Miklos. I told myself I'd see them soon enough, when school began. We had all met because of the bus in the first place, except Patsy, who'd known me since I was a baby. She and her younger cousin Paulie were the ones who had taught me about all the stations we stopped at on the way to school on the army bus, and it was because of them that my mother stopped taking me to school before the end of first grade. She trusted these kids and their mothers, who were long time friends of hers, and she put me in their care, never suspecting that Patsy—who was instructed to be an older sister to me and Paulie—would let us skip entire days of school to play on Yongsan's South and North Posts.

When Miklos moved from Yongsan down to Pupyong, he and Paulie and I had become like brothers—inseparable—getting into trouble and enduring all our punishments together as brothers should. By then Patsy was older and had secretly started skipping school by herself, disappearing all day into Itaewon or downtown Seoul only to show up on the bus, waiting for us with treats and gifts when it was time to go home.

Miklos, with his sandy hair and freckles, looked the most American of the three of us. He had lots of Korean relatives everywhere and had attended Korean school up to the sixth grade, getting off the bus just outside the Yongsan back gate. Then his mother had switched him to the American school and started him in the fifth grade. Paulie and I never knew, really, how old Miklos was, because his mother changed his age to make him younger so he would do better in the American school. All we knew was that he was older than us—maybe only a couple of months younger than Patsy.

I missed those days when we would get off the army bus before we ever reached the school stop, how we might play half the day and then appear in the lunch line with the notes Patsy forged for us on loose-leaf notebook paper in imitation of our mothers' awkward handwriting. The GIs would do anything for Patsy. All she had to do was flirt with them and they would buy all of us a meal at the Snack Bar or the bus depot.

Miklos was a tough guy and seemed to know lots of things he shouldn't, like where to change money at the best rate and the prices of premium black-market items, but Paulie was sensitive, with a sort of introspection about him. Maybe it came from the church his mother forced him to attend, which ironically also made him unpredictably ignorant about the simplest things. Once, he'd insisted the world was only seven thousand years old because someone had calculated it from the Bible.

My friends were near, and yet they felt distant to me. Everything in Pupyong did. But when I remembered my mother's village and the mountain where our ancestors were buried, I could see it as if I were there. Perhaps that is where I would find what it was I longed for. Wandering off the road, down a cart path overgrown with hip-high grass dried to a razor sharpness in the sun, hearing the trickle of water in the distance and through the trees, I would once again see the gray thatched roof of the old mud-walled farmhouse, and beyond that, mirroring the shape of the roof, the green arches of the grave mounds on the hill.

# Five Arrows

## 1974

After Kisu's grandmother died, everything was loaded onto two-wheeled *kuruma* carts and we moved to the other side of Pupyong, near the district police station. The new house was encircled in a plain cinder block wall with barbed wire along the top, and the compound inside was divided in half, into two residences—each with its own kitchen and courtyard—and we lived in the southern half. It was quiet, at the very edge of Pupyong, while the unusually wide streets there were still unpaved, awaiting the developers.

By then I had started ninth grade and, bored by my classes, I began to skip entire days of school. One morning, instead of getting on the school bus, I decided to visit our old house on the hill in Samnung, the place where my cousin Gannan had committed suicide years ago. I walked down to Pupyong Station and found that the old wooden pedestrian overpass was gone. They had built a new one out of concrete and lined it with chain-link fencing. I was tempted to cross where I used to, just going over the tracks, but knew that it would be unwise now. I was already taller than some Korean men; someone was bound to notice me and report me to the police as a North Korean spy.

The new overpass didn't give under my feet the way the old one used to, and there was no longer any danger of splinters. When the wind changed, I detected the lingering dank, powdery smell of fresh concrete. Beneath me, the tracks appeared far more humble than I remembered, the oil-soaked ties between the gleaming steel rails in sore need of replacement, while the rails themselves lay subtly askew, missing an alarming number of spikes. The overpass connected directly to the trail that led up to Samnung, and now the bottom part was wider and covered somewhat haphazardly with hexagonal cement paving stones. As I walked the curving path that soon grew narrower and more eroded as it switchbacked up the incline, I began to feel a sense of foreboding. I knew the old house would not be there.

At the very top of the hill, where the wall began, I stopped and closed my eyes for a moment. I could see it in my mind then: the house of the Japanese Colonel. The orchard, the rock garden where I had seen Gannan's ghost, the layout of the buildings, the clay drainage pipes, the transparent colors of the glass shards protruding from the top of the wall that surrounded the house. For an instant I felt as if I were falling into the past, but then I opened my eyes. A brand-new stretch of cinder block appeared, interrupted now by two green metal gates. My heart felt suddenly heavy.

I jogged the next few dozen paces, in a hurry to keep the disappointment short-lived, but then stopped abruptly at a point in the wall I knew. I instinctively reached up, grabbed hold of the green iron spikes, and lifted myself up. With my cheekbones jammed between the rusty, blue-painted rods, I peeked over the wall into the enclosed yard. There was nothing there now except a row of clay storage pots, a water spigot, and a small patch of vegetables—not even a sapling. I wanted to let go and fall back to the earth, but my arms had frozen and my fingers had cramped like the claws of a bird around a branch.

"*Ya!* What're you doing up there?" said a voice. "You a burglar?"

I relaxed my grip on the metal bars and, as my weight pulled me down, scraped the side of my face on a patch of rust on the way to the ground. Looking up from the crouch in which I landed, I recognized him—it was the old farmer whose pig I used to feed.

"Not a burglar, Grandfather," I said. "I just wanted to look over the wall to see if it's still the house of the Japanese Colonel. Do you remember it, sir?"

"I remember. Burned down two, three years ago, and then they raised up those three new Western-style houses up there."

"There were lots of beautiful old trees," I said. "And a chestnut tree. Did the trees burn down too?"

"The trees? They were alive after the fire. The developer chopped them down. We got to use some of that wood ourselves."

"I used to live here, sir."

"Ah, with the Yankee father, *ungh*? The family with the suicide?"

"Yes, Grandfather."

"Terrible thing. Poor girl hanging herself so young. How is that other girl, the one who was little like you? Haesuni, was it?"

"She's in America," I said. "She got married to a GI."

"Good fortune, or a shame?"

He looked at me expectantly, but I didn't know what to say to that, so I reached into the pocket of my sweatshirt and produced an unopened pack of Marlboros. "Here, Grandfather," I said, "please take them." I presented the cigarettes to him with both hands and had to insist and insist again in the customary way until finally he relented and accepted.

"*Ya*, I haven't had a Yankee cigarette in a long time," he said. "That geomancer fellow with the ruined foot who came here used to share some of these *Mal*boro."

"That was my Big Uncle," I said.

"Tell him I dug the well where he said. The water's pure and tasty, too. I never got to thank him."

"I will, Grandfather."

"That fellow knows a thing or two. You should learn something from him if he's your Big Uncle."

I nodded, said goodbye, and headed back down toward ASCOM.

•  •  •

WHAT THE OLD MAN SAID to me in Samnung made me restless. His question about Haesuni when I was thinking about Gannan, his advice about learning something—it made me want to visit my mother's old village and see Big Uncle, who was her oldest brother. He was the one who had come down to exorcise Gannan's ghost after her suicide. So when my newly unemployed cousin, Yongsu, Haesuni's brother, came to live with us for a while, I asked him to go up to Sambongni with me. He wasn't interested at first, and it wasn't until Mahmi bribed him with the promise of a carton of American cigarettes and a new tailored suit for job-hunting that he seemed almost enthused about the trip. We arranged to take a train to Seoul and then switch there to the one bound for Yangp'yong. From there we could walk to Sambongni.

The next day we took the first train from Pupyong. Hardly anything had changed about the station or the train, but as we approached the outskirts of Seoul, I sensed a new density and, pushing out in all directions, a frenetic energy about everything. The shanties along the track were no different from before, but the better homes beyond them had a suddenness about them, as if they'd gone up so quickly they hadn't had time to become entirely real. Beautiful tile facades were already falling away to reveal the flimsy sand bricks underneath, and brightly painted signs on the new storefronts seemed to be blistering and peeling from their very garishness. On the platform of Seoul Station, the passengers, with their flimsy bags and rope-bound bundles, moved at a pace that reminded me of jittery old movies—short, choppy steps, twitching arms balancing the weight of luggage, heads jerking left and right to find the faces of waiting relatives or to search out poorly placed signs.

Yongsu and I went out into the sweltering station yard to have a snack of fishcake soup and cold Coca-Cola. Then we bought our tickets and waited outside in the breeze until the passengers with tickets for the Yangp'yong train began to rush out of the waiting area, frantic to get aboard coaches that they all knew, perfectly well, would be only half full.

"Everyone's in a hurry these days," I said.

"*Ya*," Yongsu said. "Why are we really going to Sambongni? What is it you need to see so badly?"

"It's just something I have to do. I can't really explain." He wanted to have a smoke, so I shared a cigarette with him. "Where is Haesuni living in America these days?" I asked.

"How would I know? We haven't heard from her since she and that Yankee moved to Fort Soupcan or somewhere after Nokchon Cousin set it all up."

"Soup can? You mean Fort Campbell, Kentucky?"

"Do I look like a geography expert? Come on, then," said Yongsu, mashing out the cigarette. "We don't want to miss the damned train."

WHEN YONGSU AND I arrived at Sambongni, Little Uncle went out into the yard and butchered us a chicken for dinner, singling out a medium-sized white hen he said wasn't laying as much as she used to. He grabbed her so quickly she didn't even have time to flap her wings. I was surprised at how quiet and thoughtful the hen looked, clucking low under her breath, as Little Uncle smoothed down her feathers. She must have thought he was just grooming her. It wasn't until he brought her to the wood stump, where she must have smelled the odor of blood, that she began to squawk and twist her head around, but by that time it was too late. Little Uncle held her with his left hand, and with his right he brought down the hatchet in a single, quick stroke that severed her neck. Blood gushed forth even as the body continued to struggle, and Little Uncle caught it all in a small basin.

"Haven't had a nice chicken soup in a long time," Little Uncle said as he started to pluck the chicken's body, loosening the feathers in a pot of hot water his daughter had brought from the kitchen. He went on then, catching Yongsu up on the family news, and lit a cigarette as he continued plucking. The feathers and fluff began drifting across the wide *madang* in the breeze along with his smoke.

Little Uncle's wife served dinner just before twilight, when the light was a warm reddish gold and everything was so rich and beautiful it seemed projected onto a movie screen. But for all the beauty of the evening, I found it hard to eat the chicken soup, noticing for the first time the ugly, sagging chicken flesh and the pools of floating fat. I thought of how naked and cold the hen's body had been, how its dirty white feathers had been yanked off, one by one, with those awful tearing sounds.

It wasn't until dinner was almost over, when Little Uncle had had enough soju to lean back and belch a few times, that Yongsu told him the purpose of the visit. I told him I also wanted to visit Gannan's grave.

"Well, you must have noticed," said Little Uncle, "that Big Uncle isn't here. And, Insu, why would you want to visit such an inauspicious place anyway? Nobody goes to Gannan's grave."

"When I was little, sir," I tried to explain, "I was close to her."

"Bad luck to visit an untended grave."

"Yes, but I don't believe those things, Little Uncle."

"Christians. Western learning. Well, I suppose if you don't believe, then the superstitions can't hurt you, *ungh*?" Little Uncle wasn't all that interested in talking to me, so when a few of the village men arrived to share what was left of the soju with Little Uncle and Yongsu, now deemed old enough to drink by the grace of Little Uncle's drunkenness, I was free to leave and hear more family news from my aunt.

IN THE MORNING, after a breakfast of leftover chicken, rice, kimchi, and radish stems, Little Uncle told us a few things we should know before going off to find Big Uncle. He took us outside the gate and pointed across the river, toward a slope of thick woods in the distance. "That's where he's gone off to, out that way. Been there for weeks. His foot's rotting again—it's all eaten away now and running with sores."

"But why did he go away?" I asked.

"The whole village was suffering because of him. All that moaning and groaning at night from the pain. And that terrible stench."

"How bad could it be?" Yongsu said, with less respect than he should have shown.

From the look Little Uncle gave, he might just as well have called Yongsu an idiot. "The smell was only bad in the room, fool. It was the *noises* that got on everyone's nerves. People couldn't sleep with that voice of his—it sounded like someone at a *kut* possessed by ghosts. You want to find him so badly, take the boat across the river to the hill on the bend. Hunt around up there and you'll find a cave with two openings. That's where he is. Made himself a little camp."

"But, Little Uncle, if Big Uncle can't walk, how does he manage?"

"Oh, he can hobble around. And he's got that bow of his. Look, if he asks either of you to fetch his arrows, don't do it. He's hunting birds and rats or something. If he didn't have that damned bow, he'd have been back weeks ago, so don't fetch him any arrows, understand?"

"Yes, sir," I said.

Yongsu nodded. "He was famous for his archery when he was younger, Big Uncle. He could shoot a bird right through the eye at a hundred paces."

"*Ungh*, I doubt he could do that now," said Little Uncle. "So just . . . don't go hunting for him, all right? And don't let him talk you into one of his weird schemes, either. He's been mumbling about getting ashes from a cremation to rub on his foot or some skull water to drink. He used to talk to those geomancers and sorcerers all the time."

"Skull water?" I said.

"That's the water that collects inside a skull after someone's been dead for a while. The old people say it will cure any disease."

"How could he get any of that, Little Uncle?"

"How do I know? Dig up a grave?" He chuckled to himself as he led us down past the first field and pointed us toward the river. "Take that

boat, see? Doesn't leak. That hill over there on the other side? That's it.
Now come back before dark, understand?"

YONGSU AND I launched the flat-bottomed boat from a muddy part of
the river I didn't recognize. It seemed that the bank had risen much
closer to the village, though I knew it hadn't rained much that year. As
we took our places and Yongsu pulled the oars, I scanned the far shore
for a good place to land, a spot for Yongsu to aim for to counter the
current.

"*Ya*, I haven't done this in a long time," said Yongsu. "You remember
the last time you were out on this river? Hyongbu gave us a hard time,
didn't he?"

"Yeah," I said.

Yongsu flipped some water into the air with an oar. "Boatride!" he
shouted, imitating his father's voice.

Though the water missed me, I felt suddenly cold, remembering how
Yongsu's father had terrorized us, how Yongsu's sister Haesuni had almost been sucked under the boat when she misread the depth of the
clear water and tried to step out. The water was so clear back then it
seemed only a few palm-widths deep, shallow enough to reach down and
touch the pebbles that rippled under the play of light and the shadow of
the boat. Now when I looked over the side, I couldn't even see the bottom. "What happened to the water?" I said. "It's green and cloudy."

"Remember how my father had to aim for some other point if he
wanted to go straight across?"

"I know. That's what I'm doing."

"You don't have to. There's no current anymore, not since they put up
the hydroelectric dam downstream." He twitched his head in that direction. "They finished it around two years ago. Ever since, the river's been
riding high all year and filling with green algae. Fisheries all over the
place are raising carp now because they like that dirty bottom water."

"It even sounds different, *ungh?*" I said. I looked out across the flat expanse of the river-become-a-lake and recalled the gentle sound of the current, the clear, cold water, more transparent than air, flowing icy cold under the boat's bottom—and the pebbles, white and gray and black, so distant and yet so close as the shadow of the boat slipped over them, rippling the bright blue reflection of the sky.

How could they have given up the old river for this wide, murky plane of green on which even the reflections seemed stagnant? You could almost smell the faint rot as the oars disturbed the surface. This was the kind of still water suited to skipping stones, round and flat like the copper pennies they put over the eyes of the dead to pay the ferryman. "Crossing the River Jordan!" Yongsu sang out in a crude parody of a Christian hymn, and then the creak and the rhythm of the oars suddenly stopped as we butted against the far shore.

Coming out of my reverie, I thought he must have read my thoughts, but he just broke into laughter. "We've arrived, you idiot!" he said. "And now here we are in the other world."

We dragged the boat up a little ways and I uncoiled the rope to tie it to a sapling.

"Think we'll be able to find Big Uncle?" I asked.

"Well, the air's fresh," said Yongsu. "From what Little Uncle said, we can just track the smell."

He started up the slope and I followed. It didn't take long to intersect the small trail that followed the waterline, and we took that toward the west, into shadowy woods lanced by sunlight. Yongsu seemed oblivious to anything but the trail, but I relaxed my eyes the way I had been taught, scanning back and forth through the underbrush, and it wasn't long before I spotted something odd.

"Look," I said to Yongsu. There were rags draped over the lower branches of a tree, still discolored with the yellow and red of what must have been the oozing from Big Uncle's sores.

"Yeah, he must live around here," said Yongsu. "Can't get far with that crippled foot."

I went over to the rags and hesitated. "They're dry. Should I gather them up?"

"Quiet!" said Yongsu. "I hear footsteps. Someone's limping."

Then I heard it too. And a voice. Someone crawling along the path, barely moving. It was still far away, but I could make it out—the sound of an injured man. "He must have fallen," I said. "Sounds like he's hurt."

Yongsu started up the trail, but I ran ahead of him, shouting "Big Uncle! Big Uncle!"

"*Ya!*" Yongsu called after me. "Careful!" I heard his footfalls catching up to me as I made my way up the trail through patches of light and shadow, feeling the texture of the ground change under me as I trod on pine needles, then pebbles, and then dry earth.

In a few moments, Yongsu was at my side, pulling at my shirt to make me stop, but I turned away and continued to run in the direction of the sound. The trail made a sharp turn, and as we came around we squinted into the sun that shone through a gap in the trees. A huge silhouette stood before us, massive and black to our sunblind eyes.

"Stop!" the shape said.

But we didn't. We turned and tried to go back the way we'd come, only to hear a loud *thump* as a quivering arrow shaft seemed to sprout right out of a tree to block our way. The bright feathers—one of them scarlet—trembled in the sunlight, and we heard a wild beating that might have been the wings of an escaping bird or the pounding of our hearts.

As Yongsu and I froze, the dark silhouette shifted, looking momentarily like a giant black crane before bending into a more humble shape to approach us. "Ah, it's Yongsu," he said finally, grumbling under his breath. "What reason do you have to be up here? And who's that?"

"Hello, Big Uncle," Yongsu said. "I've come with Insu."

"Insu? *Ya*, you've grown like a bean sprout! All that good food in America."

"Hello, Big Uncle," I said.

"It's been a long time, *ungh*? Pull that arrow out now and follow me. Brought me anything to eat?"

"No, sir," Yongsu said as I went to pull the arrow out.

*"Aigo*, you unmannered fools."

Big Uncle hobbled back up the trail and Yongsu followed, leaving me to struggle with the arrow. The metal tip was like a blade—for hunting— and it had punctured the bark of the tree and buried itself so far in the trunk that I had to grasp the arrow shaft with both hands—as close to the tip as possible for fear of breaking it—and move it gingerly back and forth until slowly it disengaged. By the time I had it out intact, Yongsu and Big Uncle were out of sight and I had to run to find them.

"WE USED TO CALL this place 'Skullhead Cave,'" said Big Uncle, pointing out the pale rock formation behind his campsite, where he had set up an old U.S. Army cot and small fire pit for cooking. "It looks like the top of a skull, see, with the two openings like half-buried eye sockets. But now no one even knows what it's called anymore. And why do you suppose I live in here, *ungh*?" He stared at us a moment. "Don't you think I'd live in a house if I could?"

"Yes, Big Uncle."

"When I was young, we used to put the old people out in caves like this to die after they started to go senile. After they shat and pissed in their clothes and couldn't remember the names of their children, the family would bring them up into the mountains. They'd seal them up in a cave and roll a big rock in front of the entrance with just a little opening for food. And every day they'd leave some food until it stopped disappearing. When they knew the old person was dead, they'd wait a few more days just to be sure, and then they'd open up the cave and take the body out for a good funeral and burial. Everyone would mourn, crying and sobbing as if the old person had died in some tragic way. But secretly they'd all be relieved.

"Why not save them the trouble, *ungh*? They won't even have to roll the rock aside for me, since I'm already living in there. Of course, maybe the animals will get in and eat my shriveled corpse before anyone even finds me. Wouldn't that be a shame?"

We didn't know what to say to Big Uncle. We had never heard him so bitter before, so crude and angry.

"Now tell me why you came up here, *ungh*? You couldn't have come up all this way just to *visit* me, now, could you?"

"No," I said. "Well . . ."

"Did Little Uncle send you up to get me to come back with you?"

"No, Big Uncle," I said, so uncomfortable now that all I could think of was to take the carton of cigarettes out of my jacket and present it, holding it out politely with both hands. "Here, Big Uncle. Please enjoy these."

"*Ya*," he said. "I haven't had one of these Camel cigarettes in years! Thanks, Insu-ya." He fumbled around looking for matches, and then, giving up, simply pulled a thin stick out of the fire pit and blew on it until its tip glowed and burst into a tiny flame. He held the stick in his mouth as if it were a pipe stem while he unwrapped the carton, putting the cellophane under his U.S. Army cot; then he ripped open a pack of the Camels, tapping a couple expertly out onto his palm. "You two smoke?"

We shook our heads.

"*Ya*, it feels like I'll live a while now," he said, pushing the extra cigarette back into the pack and then slipping the pack into his vest pocket. He lit the cigarette and took a deep first drag, savoring the smoke in his lungs before blowing it in a long plume at his gangrenous foot. "Helps cover the smell, *ungh*?"

How were we to answer? If we said yes, it would be to admit we had smelled his rotting flesh before the cigarette smoke; if we said no, we would be saying that the smell of smoke *wasn't* enough to cover the gangrenous odor of his foot, which he had wrapped in some dry moss with makeshift strands of straw.

"Listen," said Big Uncle. "You two go into the woods and fetch me five of my arrows, and then I'll tell you a story. It's going to take you a while, so I'll have something good for you to eat when you get back. Understood?"

"Yes, Big Uncle," we said.

"What is it?" he said then, reading our expressions. He broke into an embittered chuckle. "Little Uncle told you not to fetch arrows for me, didn't he?"

We nodded dumbly.

"So who do you listen to? Your Big Uncle or your Little Uncle, *ungh*? Who's older? And does it *look* like I've lost my mind, like I've become a child again?"

"No, Big Uncle."

"Then go fetch the arrows. And bring up some water while you're at it. Here's the container. When you get back, I'll have some delicious mountain chicken for you." He tossed Yongsu a clay jar wrapped in straw and shooed us off. We walked a little way down the trail before he called out to us, "*Ya!* Don't look together, either. Go in different directions and be sure to check the lower branches of the trees. That's where you'll find them. They should be easy to spot. I dyed the feathers red, yellow, and blue like the one I shot at you."

"Yes, Big Uncle!" we called back.

When we were out of earshot, Yongsu smacked me on the shoulder. "*Now* what are we going to do, *ungh*?"

"Find the arrows, I guess. What else can we do?"

"Ah, fuck it! We shouldn't have let him talk to us like that. I'm not staying out here in the woods to fetch some damn arrows for the old man." He shoved the water jug into my belly and stalked off down the trail to the river.

"You're going back?" I said.

"That's right."

"But—how will I get back across the river if you take the boat?"

"I'll come get you in the morning. You're going to be out here all night looking for arrows in the trees, stupid."

I watched Yongsu disappear down the trail. In a few moments, the heavy crunch of his footsteps had fallen away, and the woods grew so quiet I thought I could make out the sound of blood rushing through my ears.

I searched for Big Uncle's arrows until the light waned and I could no longer discern colors within the shadows. I had been terribly frustrated at first, impatient and even angry as I waded through patches of high grass, cutting my flesh, or picked my way through tangles of thorny shrubbery, thinking I might have glimpsed a yellow feather on the other side. At one point, the heat of the day seeped into my sweaty body, and I rested under a tree, half dozing in its cool shade, feeling the breeze that came across the river. In a momentary lapse into real sleep, I had the briefest of dreams.

I was sitting with my back against a tree, but it was nighttime and it was raining hard; water sluiced down on me each time the wind shifted, and I tried to huddle against myself, chilled to the bone. I was going to die, and the fear and the cold woke me up into the thick, groggy heat of the waning afternoon. It must have been the heat, I thought, making me dream of the opposite thing, even though I was doing the same thing as in the dream—looking for Big Uncle's arrows. I resumed my search, and over the next two hours, while the light held, I found four of them.

"MY, YOU'VE GOTTEN yourself quite dirty," Big Uncle said when I returned to his camp with the arrows and the water jug. He had a small fire going and had skewered a couple of small birds that were now browning slowly above the flames. It was a good thing I had been upwind all day, because the moment I smelled the cooking my stomach clenched with hunger and my mouth filled with saliva.

Big Uncle took the arrows with a nod. He didn't bother asking about Yongsu, so I didn't mention him either.

"I'm sorry, Big Uncle," I said. "I did my best, but I only found four arrows."

"An inauspicious number," Big Uncle said. "*Sa*. The death number. The snake number, *ungh*?"

I nodded. "It was getting dark under the trees."

"Well, since you plucked that other arrow this morning, let's say you found five. Five, see, that's an interesting number. *O*. It sounds like the sign of the horse, or a mistake, or a word for anguish. *O-da*. You have come. *O-do*. You have awakened." He ran each arrow through his fingers, checking to see if their shafts had split or if their feathers had come undone. "So what do you think, Insu-ya?"

"I don't know," I said. I had no idea what he meant by the numbers and their sounds. All I knew was that Koreans were as superstitious about the number four as Americans were about thirteen. Buildings didn't have a fourth floor, and most Korean locker rooms had sequences that went from thirteen to fifteen and thirty-nine to fifty.

"Let's eat. I'm as hungry as you are. Here." Big Uncle unfolded a small square of paper full of sea salt and poured some onto my palm. "No spice, so this will have to do."

I sat at the edge of the fire and took the spitted bird from Big Uncle. He had cooked only two birds, I realized, and I looked from mine to his.

"What's the matter? That I gave you the small one?"

"No, sir. I was just wondering—"

"Ah," he said, smiling. "If both of you had come back? Well, then, I suppose you'd be fighting over the one, *ungh*?" He laughed and tore a piece of meat from the breast to dab in his salt.

I ate too, and despite my queasiness at the chicken the night before, despite the clump of black crow feathers I could see in the underbrush, the meat tasted wonderful, its gamey tang cut by the salt. My face warmed by the fire and stomach rumbling even as I ate, I tore my bird to shreds and sucked at the bones until they were dry. It was dark when we were done, and we passed the jug of water back and forth to wash down the last dry scraps of crow meat.

"The nights are long if you're the thoughtful sort," said Big Uncle. "So—tell me what you're thinking about."

"I was wondering about your foot," I said.

"The smell bother you?"

"No, sir. Just that I found your wrappings on the trail this morning, and. . . . How did it happen?"

"Well, it's a story. Like some folktale. But then everyone's life is like a story, isn't it? A story from a long, long time ago."

I expected him to smoke while he talked, the way Hyongbu used to, but Big Uncle just closed his eyes, as if to let the firelight warm his eyelids, and sitting there with his legs crossed, his bad foot on top, he told the story into the fire.

"I was coming home after some celebration—the hundred-day party for Old Pak's grandson. It was past sunset and they told me to stay the night there in that village, but I stubbornly decided to come home over the mountain. There were still wild animals in the woods back then, and even rumors of tigers, though no one had seen one since the Japanese came. That's why people said not to go—because of the tigers—but what they were really afraid of were ghosts and goblins.

"I was walking fine. The moon was out. It wasn't full, but there was enough light to see the trail. I was feeling fine because I'd had a good time at the celebration. I wasn't even thinking of ghosts when I first saw the light. It was a little light in the distance. That's what it looked like—a lamp in the woods or a candle in the window of someone's house—something small and bright only because it was so dark in the trees.

"I thought someone was out there, so I called out to him. '*Yobosaeyo!* Who's out there? Is anyone out there?' No answer. Then, I thought maybe it was someone who had gotten injured, so I started into the woods to find him.

"I shouldn't have left the trail. That was a mistake. Before I knew it, I was lost, and the light—it had been just in front of me—suddenly blinked out and everything was pitch-black night. I couldn't see anything. I was grabbing around myself so the tree branches wouldn't scratch out my eyes.

"Then the light blinked on again somewhere to my right. And then out again. Then it reappeared somewhere to my left. And that's when I knew it was a goblin light or a ghost. I started thinking about all those terrible stories about the woodcutters who see the lights at night and then get enticed by fox demons and have their life energy sucked out of them. I started running back toward the trail, or where I thought it should be, but that light kept appearing in front of me and I would change directions and run headlong into a tree or fall into a hole.

"I must have run around like that for hours. I was a mess. All scratched up, my ankle twisted, my clothes torn like floor rags. Bruises all over my forearms and shins. But I kept running, because I could feel it, see? It was some female spirit, and it was determined to get me. I had heard stories about the ghosts of dead virgins and how they hunted unwary men at night. That was what I was afraid of.

"I ran and ran until finally I just didn't have the strength anymore, and I collapsed against a tree. The light came at me then. It grew brighter and brighter until it was a brilliant blue, and then a blinding white, and I lost consciousness.

"When I woke up, it was past dawn. The sun was above the horizon, and a streak of sunlight was shining on my face. I sat there for the longest time because I thought the ghost had tied me up to that tree. But then, when I finally had the strength and the courage to look around, I saw that all that held me were a few dried-up strands of grass around me, not even enough to weave into a flimsy straw rope.

"And there were two little scars on my foot. It didn't look much worse than a couple of mosquito bites, but that's what festered later and spread all up and down my foot. Even with the best Chinese medicine it never really healed. Everyone says it was a snake bite, but that's not true.

"It wasn't until years later that I remembered what had happened to me after I was blinded by that light. And I remembered it in a dream. A beautiful woman came out of that light. She was dressed in a white costume in the old Chinese style. The fabric was like the finest silk, and it was so white it was like silver. She had long black hair and big round eyes. She told me to come with her, and I could understand her, though she didn't seem to speak. I went into that light, and I found myself on a high, Chinese-style bed with no bed mat under me.

"The woman's servants were standing around me, looking down at me. There were shiny silver ornaments and decorations everywhere. Beautiful things that looked like jewelry and weapons and eating utensils. The lamp they shined down on me was brighter than the sun. White light was floating everywhere like flour dust, and the beautiful woman climbed up on the bed, on top of me, and then, right in front of her servants, she took off her clothes and pushed herself down onto me. I thought my penis would burst, only she was slightly cold, not like a Korean woman, and it was almost impossible to feel anything with all those servants watching. But somehow I managed to squirt my seed into her, and then everything grew dark again.

"Now, why do you suppose this was? Why would I remember this part of the night only years and years later? That woman was like a heavenly maiden, but I know she must have been the ghost of a virgin who had died a very long time ago, maybe when the Chinese or the Mongols were in our country. She had to have been a princess, with all that jewelry and all those servants, and she must have been waiting centuries for some man to come along and release her into the next world with the power of his yang.

"Sometimes, when I get a little drunk, I can remember even more about how beautiful everything was, but then when I'm sober, I forget all over again. She was the most beautiful woman I've ever seen, and coupling with her was wonderful. I think I can remember, sometimes, that there was more, and we rutted like animals without all those servants around. And that's why I don't ever regret having this wound on my foot. This is the price I had to pay. I'll have to suffer it until I go into the next world. But when I coupled with that ghost woman, I was like a *kidung* post spouting a waterfall.

"Now Little Uncle didn't tell you that part of the story, did he?"

"No, Big Uncle."

"Throw some more wood into the fire and light me a twig for a cigarette."

I added the wood, then handed him a long splinter burning on the end like a match, and he lit up one of the Camels I had given him. He gazed into the fire, thinking his thoughts as if I wasn't even there, breathing deeply through his nose, exhaling long plumes of smoke after he sucked on the cigarette, his black eyes glinting in the red-and-yellow firelight. Perhaps, had I not been there, he would have spoken to himself or sat in some trance, communing with his spirits and his dreams. Had I not been there, he might have sung himself to sleep with the songs from his childhood, the ones his mother and his aunts had once sung for him on warm summer nights, or wept with sadness or shouted out his anger at the family that had driven him across the river to live like a Taoist hermit.

"Insu-ya, say what's on your mind now," said Big Uncle. "At times like this you should let the thoughts leap off your tongue. You don't want to be regretful."

"I was thinking about your bow, Big Uncle."

"What about my bow?"

"Where did you get it? Where did you learn how to shoot it?"

"Our ancestors were fierce archers," said Big Uncle. "I don't know where we learned it. From way before the Mongols, probably. In the old days, there were men in the Lee clan who galloped on horseback and shot arrows so straight they could hit the hole in a dangling coin."

"It reminds me of a book I read about an outlaw named Robin Hood," I said. "He lived in a secret camp in the woods, and his bow was as tall as a man."

"How did they get a bow that big?" asked Big Uncle. "It must be a fantasy."

"It was a wooden bow, Big Uncle. They called them longbows, and they could shoot arrows that pierced armor."

"And how did they use them on horseback?"

"They didn't ride."

"*Ah*." He moved the half-burned Camel to the other side of his mouth.

"Robin Hood robbed the rich people and gave the money to the peasants. When he knew he was about to die, he shot an arrow out of his window and told his most loyal follower to bury him where it fell."

Big Uncle was silent again. "Now that's a good story," he said after a moment. "This Ro Bing Ho sounds like a good man. Did he come from a family of warriors or farmers?"

"I don't know," I said. "His father was an official in some district, I think, but he was wrongly deposed by an evil advisor to the king. When he died, his son had to hide in the forest with his band of outlaws."

"Like our folk hero Hong Kil-tong, *ungh*?"

"Yes, sir."

Big Uncle tossed another piece of wood into the fire and yawned. He put out the Camel and placed the butt behind his right ear. Beyond the flickering boundary of light the night sounds suddenly grew louder until Big Uncle cleared his throat and spat into the flames, where it made a sizzling noise. "Ro Bing Ho," he said again. I didn't bother to correct him.

"He sounds better than some charlatan doctor of wind and water," he said. "Any fool can take a fancy compass and mumble phrases from *The Book of Changes*. But that Ro Bing Ho, he had the right idea." He rose stiffly to his feet, then picked up his bow and the arrow with the red cock's feather—it must have been a precious one. I knew what he was about to do, and the thought thrilled me, though I immediately sensed its terrible consequence.

Big Uncle stretched and limbered his neck, and then he drew the bow, bending the ox horn against the nocked arrow nearly back on itself. He looked directly up into the night, and I followed his gaze to see a circle of blackness ringed by branches and leaves that quietly rustled in the force of the campfire's heat. How odd, I thought. It was like looking up at a domed wall of foliage with a hole in the center. This must have been what it was like to bend back your neck and stare up at the ceiling of a basilica to see the holy murals of Christ and God and the angels. Out here in the forest, that center was a blackness not even punctuated by a star because the light of the campfire had made us night blind. Now Big Uncle turned four times, once in each direction, and though it seemed impossible to know the cardinal directions at night without the stars as guides, I sensed that Big Uncle knew the points of the compass exactly.

"Insu-ya," he said.

"Yes, Big Uncle."

"Bury me where this arrow falls." And he let the arrow fly into the darkness with a loud whoosh of air torn by string and wood. Had Big Uncle told me then that he'd hit the eye of the moon, I would have believed him. The arrow was gone. He lowered the bow to look at me, his eyes flashing cold and bright—brighter than the fire.

"Swear to me," he said. "My son's mind is tainted by useless stuff and Western learning. He thinks I'm crazy, and he'll never do it. When I'm dead, you'll find the arrow and you'll have them bury me where it lands."

"Yes, sir."

"Do you swear?"

"Yes, Big Uncle, I swear." I was suddenly afraid, but then he gave me a big smile and sat down again in a single motion. He looked tired and old.

I WAS TERRIBLY STIFF in the morning, waking just before dawn. Big Uncle had kept the fire burning low to keep us warm, and he'd let me sleep on the cot with his green U.S. Army blanket while he curled up on the hard ground. Even so, I was cold with an ache that didn't go away until I struggled to my feet and stretched a few times to get my blood moving again. All night long I had awakened at intervals when the wind shifted, carrying the stench of Big Uncle's foot in my direction. Even the strong smell of the smoky wood Big Uncle must have picked for my sake could not mask the odor of decay, and now, in the morning dampness it bore the unmistakable note of sewage mixed with rot.

As I tightened my abdominal muscles and pressed my palms together to do some isometrics, I noticed Big Uncle crouched over a small sooty teapot that was quietly steaming over the fire.

"Let's have some *ch'a* before you go," Big Uncle said without looking at me. "I would offer you coffee, which is what Yankees drink instead of tea, I suppose, but I'm fresh out."

"Did you sleep well, Big Uncle?"

"Yes, I slept. I'm half asleep all the time, anyway. The night doesn't make much difference. Any dreams?"

"I don't remember."

"You should always remember your dreams, Insu-ya. Dreams are your real life. It's a shame if you don't remember it." Big Uncle turned to face me now, wide awake. His face had none of the puffiness of someone who had been asleep; it was drawn tight, the wrinkles fine and shallow until he smiled. He lifted the teapot off the arched stick that kept it well above the fire, and he poured me an old C-ration can full of Japanese green tea swimming with leaf scraps. "The Japs are terrible, but they make a fine tea, *ungh*?"

It was bitter and soothing, Big Uncle's tea, and the steam warmed my face. I sipped a little at a time, holding the can between my palms when it had cooled enough not to burn me. "Why do you say dreams are our real life?"

Big Uncle made a sweeping gesture around us. "This here? *This* is all a dream," he said. "When you die and move on, you forget it, just like you forget your dreams now. And yet this is where you should have learned all your karmic lessons, *ungh*? What a shame to forget."

"I don't know much about religious things," I said.

"We all know." Big Uncle lit one of the cigarettes I had brought him and sucked on it with the same motion he had used to sip his own can of tea. "Now let me tell you how to find Gannan's grave, since you want to visit it so much."

"How did you know that's what I came for?"

"I dreamt it, *ungh*?" He laughed, and then he was quiet until he had finished his cigarette and tossed the filter into the fire.

"Take the path that goes north and east from Sambongni. It's the one that leads past the old village tree. Turn left there and cross the new road, and the mountain should be right in front of you. Be there at noon, when the sun is directly overhead, so the shadows fall straight down, because you don't want to be distracted. Understand?"

"Yes, Big Uncle."

"There will be a pine tree in front of you, and you'll see the slope of the mountain cutting through it, behind. Put your eye on the tree and let your mind relax, and your eye will naturally follow the shape of the slope upward. As your eye does that—though you won't be looking for it—you'll see the trail. Do it a few times until your heart and your mind remember how that trail feels, and then follow the feeling. That will take you all the way up to Gannan's grave."

"But if I'm not looking for it, how will I see it?"

"Have you ever looked at stars at night?"

"Yes."

"Notice how the ones you look straight at are never as bright as the ones at the edges? And then, when you look straight at those, they grow dim and others become bright around them?"

"Yes."

"It's like that. If you look directly for the trail, you'll see nothing. But if you just look up at the mountain, you'll see the trail in the edges of your sight. Understand?"

"How will I know where the trail starts?"

"It starts at the base of that pine tree."

"And how will I know when I find the grave?"

"You'll know. Maybe not now, but when you're ready, you'll know. You'll feel the spot because you have the blood of the Lee clan in you. You'll feel it in the pit of your stomach and in your heart and in your throat, and right here—between your eyes. Thickness, falling, tingling. You'll know. Just keep your mind focused when it's time, understand?"

"Yes, Big Uncle."

"Now go, because you're going to be hungry and I have nothing to feed you. When you come back to see me again, bring me some coffee and something good to eat."

"Yes, Big Uncle."

"Yongsu won't be there with the boat. You're going to have to swim across. Can you do that?"

"Yes, sir."

"Good. Now go." Big Uncle motioned as if to dust me away, and I walked slowly down the trail, trying to remember what he had told me.


I LEAPT INTO the warm water just behind the little raft I had made for my clothes, and slowly rising from the depths of my plunge, opened my eyes to find myself suspended in the very center of a terrible sphere of green nothingness. Below me the greenness grew darker and darker, by imperceptible degrees, into a murky blackness, and above me it grew suddenly lighter into the rippling clarity of the surface. But all around, receding into a darkness that was never quite black—an indeterminate green fog—in every direction, the unknown: things lurking just beyond the threshold of vision, where sense became imagination. There was nothing in that river that could have harmed me; still, that instant of perception so terrified me, I would never again swim in open water without believing that something waited, just beyond the range of my vision, to drag me down until the light above me had turned as black as the green-black nothingness below.

My nose was beginning to fill, and the pressure in my head told me I should kick up. For some reason I felt I had been in that very place before—right there—or would be again. Suddenly I wanted to look around to see if I could watch myself looking back at me, but the feeling that gave me was so strange I shook my head, releasing bubbles that showed me which way was up. I slowly raised my sluggish arms, moving them against the unexpectedly fierce resistance of the water, and then arced them back down again as I gave a violent scissor kick. Green light. Green shadow. Infinite gradations of green, subtle and distinct, numerous as all the names of God. At the surface, a dark, irregular silhouette protruded—it was my raft of clothes—and I raced my own rising bubbles toward it as I thought I glimpsed, just for a second and out of the corner of my eye, a giant green carp beneath me, flicking its broad tail.

# The Milkman

## 1974

The rocks were slippery, and I stumbled a few times when I came out of the water on the Sambongni side of the river, pulling my little raft up after me by my belt. I found a spot on the riverbank where the water was clear, and there I rinsed myself off, squatting down to wash the scum out of my hair. I got goose bumps where the breeze touched me and was quick to shake out my wet hair and squeegee myself off with my hands.

It would be a while yet before noon, and so I laid my clothes out to dry on a patch of grass. People were outside working—I could see them in the distance. Out of a sense of decorum, I put on my wet Fruit of the Loom jockey shorts after I rinsed them and wrung them as dry as I possibly could. Laid flat, my jeans, T-shirt, and shirt looked like a pattern for the clothes of a giant paper-doll man. Then I lay down, with my hands behind my head serving as my pillow. Gazing up at the blank, blue sky and feeling the warmth of the morning sun on my skin, I fell asleep.

I WOKE UP SUDDENLY to the sound of a machine gun, but as the residue of dreams wore off, it became the sound of a cultivator engine stuttering in the distance. For a moment I lay there with my eyes still closed, trying to remember what I had been dreaming.

"How long are you going to roast here?" said a strange voice. There was a flickering of light and a rushing sound, like fluttering fabric, and then a light thud, like someone had leaped and landed on the ground. A quick exhalation.

I tried to sit up, but for some reason I couldn't move. I felt as if I had a large stone on my chest. I answered, "I don't know."

"Who are you?" The voice was strangely high and melodious but also harsh.

By raising my hands and blocking the sun, I could make out the figure standing over me. "I'm Insu," I said. "I came to see Big Uncle."

"You must be Hwasuni's boy then," the voice said, softening. "Here— get up. There's a snake."

Suddenly the weight was gone. I rolled and leaped to my feet, looking back over my shoulder at the ground. "Where?!" I said, but I could hear the raspy sound and saw the dark flash in the grass.

"That snake knows you."

Now, standing, I looked down on a strange old woman with short hair. She wore a traditional Korean black-and-white *ch'ima* and *chogori* appropriate for someone of her age, but her shoes were black leather men's shoes—an old pair shined so often it seemed the shoe polish was thicker than the cracking leather.

"What are you looking at?" she said.

"I—"

"You know the snake too?"

I shook my head no.

"And now you're struck dumb?"

I shook my head again.

"Then say what you need to say."

"How do you know my mother?"

"That's not what you need to say."

"I came to see my Big Uncle and I have to find a grave."

"Say something more necessary for right now. What you need *right now*. Say it."

"You're dressed like a grandmother, but you wear grandfather shoes and white socks. And your hair is short."

"That's not it, either! I dress how I want because I'm a *manshin*. Ten thousand spirits! Ten thousand shoes! A room full of shoes, a *shinbang*! Didn't your mother tell you about me? Didn't your Big Uncle send you to say hello to me and bring me a little something to offer the spirits?"

"N-no."

"*Aah!*"

"What's the matter?" I asked.

"I've looked after your family all these years and not a little gift for the spirits? Didn't your mother tell you I was the one who taught her how to behave properly like a girl?"

"No."

"She had no manners. No culture. Knew nothing. No *nunchi*—didn't know how to read a situation. Or maybe it was all just *nunchi*."

"My mother never said anything about you," I said.

"*Ah*, and yet I know whose grave you're looking for, Insu-ya."

I felt confused and lightheaded, as if my head were spinning. "Are you a grandfather or a grandmother?" I blurted.

"I'm a *shinbang*! A *manshin*! Kubong Manshin of Sambongni! I am your grandfather *and* grandmother. What does *this* matter?"

From the obscene gesture that went with the outburst, I took it to mean that the *manshin* had a penis, so I decided he was a grandfather. I knew that women who were shamans got possessed by the spirit of the Great General and then behaved like angry and powerful men, but I had never seen a male shaman who could be a woman.

"If you know whose grave I'm looking for, could you help me find it?" I asked. "Big Uncle gave me directions, but they're . . . kind of hard to follow."

"You shouldn't be looking for Gannani's grave now," said Kubong Manshin. "You aren't ready to see the path to her grave because she's still in *there!*" He jabbed me in the chest so hard it felt like I'd been hit with the corner of a brick. "Now show me what you have with you that could make a gift to the spirits."

I looked down at the clothes I had spread on the ground, which looked ridiculous now, like a mockery of a scarecrow, and my standing above them in my sagging jockey shorts didn't help. I picked up my pants and put them on, though they now felt steamy inside. I reached toward my back pocket, then realized I had kept my paper money in my front pockets. I pulled out the soggy dollars from one pocket and the Korean won from the other.

Kubong Manshin made little, abrupt gestures, indicating that I should unfold the bills and spread them out to dry. "How much?" he asked. "Is that all you have?"

"Yes, but I can't give it all to you because I need fare to get home and also something to buy offerings for Gannan's grave."

"Didn't I say you shouldn't go to Gannani's grave now? Didn't I tell you the snake knows you?" Suddenly, Kubong Manshin reared up and seemed to grow to twice his size. His eyes widened until they were two full white circles with black dots in the center. "Your father is dying!" he shouted. "Your Big Uncle is dying! Your grandfathers are dead!"

He raised his arms and opened his hands so they looked like claws, and he slowly danced a circle around me as I bent over to lay the money out in the sun. Even with all the won and dollars together, it wasn't enough for much more than train fare and a couple of meals.

"All this death of male ancestors around you and you want to visit the grave of a girl? A suicide? No! Go back to Pupyong! Go back and

prepare medicine for your uncle! Go back and talk to your Yankee father who spawned more children than he knows! Go back and make
yourself quiet, so you can see, and when you see the light that rises like
smoke, *then* breathe it in you! Do you hear what I'm saying?"

I nodded and mumbled "Yes," but I didn't think he could hear me.
He was looking up at the mountains to the west—the ones where my
Korean grandparents and Gannan were buried.

"I see," he said. "I *see*. I see the *ki* rising. I see the back of the dragon
moving. All the things your Big Uncle sees, I see better. Your yang is too
weak to visit a suicide grave. Wait until you've lived another cycle with
her memory in your heart or her ghost will do you harm!"

"But then I'll be almost thirty years old," I said. I didn't understand
what he meant about my yang, but I knew that a cycle of the lunar zodiac
was twelve years.

"Turn to the north and hear the sound of tears all falling. Turn to the
south and hear the sound of mouths all crying. Turn to the east and see
the strands of hair all blowing—they're flying in the wind to the Beautiful Country, but they're forgetting the West Sky West Country, and their
progeny will forget *them. Aaahaa!*"

Now Kubong Manshin seemed to shrink into his former self.
He stopped dancing and looked a bit dizzy. He put a hand across his
chest, as if to feel his heart beating. "Leave the money there," he said.
"All of it."

"But how will—"

"The spirits will give you more than you need to get home. Come
back later when you're ready, and the path to Gannani's grave will call to
you. Now, go away!" He stood there, arms akimbo, looking up at me.

I put on my shirt, gathered up my things, and sat back down on the
ground to put on my socks and sneakers.

"Your family is complicated," he said. "And then your mother made
things even more complicated by marrying your long-nose father."

"I don't understand anything you're telling me," I said.

"Just listen. Be *here*." He gestured to his belly—or maybe his groin—I couldn't tell which. "And you'll know everything I say when it's the right time. Now, get out of here, and the next time you come up to the country, bring an appropriate offering!"

When I was finished tying my sneakers, I quickly bowed and jogged off toward the village. I looked back—Kubong Manshin was twirling around with his arms outstretched, drying the won and the dollars, which dangled from his fingertips.

I had only a few coins left in my pockets. "Shit!" I said to myself.

I HAD PLANNED TO return to Little Uncle's house to ask for *ch'abi*, travel money, to get back home, but when I reached the road I saw a U.S. Army jeep approaching in the distance, headed west. When I stuck out my thumb, the jeep passed me and pulled over, kicking up dust next to a patch of white cosmos.

The driver was a young sandy-haired buck sergeant, named Phillips according to his name tape, and he was grinning under his sunglasses when I reached him, out of breath and already sweating from the heat.

"Didn't your mama tell you it's dangerous to hitchhike?" he said.

"Didn't your CO tell you not to pick up any gooks?"

Phillips snickered and gestured for me to get in. "Whatcha doing out here in the boonies, boy-san? I never seen any locals stickin' out their thumb." He grabbed the strap of the camera he had in the passenger seat and tossed it gently into the back on top of a pile of bulky green canvas sacks. When I climbed in, he shifted gears and pulled onto the empty road. He was driving with the windshield folded down, with the names of various destinations written on the glass in what appeared to be soap.

"I was visiting my uncle," I said.

"Don't you have school?"

"Nah," I said. "I got a three-day hooky pass."

He laughed again. "Live and learn, motherfucker. School of hard knocks. Your old man in the service? You're a half 'n' half, right?"

"My dad used to be up in Panmunjom," I said. "He was the sergeant for the Honor Guard. He's in Casey now."

"Fuck me! Your old man's the Mad Russian?" He beeped the horn for emphasis.

"Yeah," I said. "He said that's what they call him sometimes."

"Your old man and his crew beat the living shit out of a bunch of commie fuckers up in the JSA. Pick handles and aluminum bats. Heard they got to crack some skulls. Angry Alpha, man!"

"How do you know all that? Are you from there?"

"Heard it on the grapevine. I take it you're going to Eighth Army?"

"Can you get me to the bus depot?"

"Roger."

Phillips stopped for a moment to let an old farmer cross the road with his ox cart piled with sacks of cement. In the yard of the tin-roofed house on the right, a young woman with bobbed hair, wearing a black *ch'ima* and a blue-and-white polka dot blouse, was hanging laundry by a little empty doghouse with her baby strapped to her back. The baby looked at us, wide-eyed, a trail of snot dripping from one nostril. Phillips shifted into neutral and put on the hand brake. He grabbed his camera from the back—a Canon F-1—and stood up to snap a few pictures. I could hear the mirror in the SLR flapping open and shut with each shot.

"You go to the Yongsan photo lab?" I asked.

"Yeah. The one in Casey sucks as bad as the *saxis* in the Ville."

"ASCOM has the best darkroom," I said. "Hardly anyone uses it. You can get bulk Plus- and Tri-X if you roll it yourself."

"No shit?" Phillips got a few shots of the ox cart and the old man. He seemed unconcerned about being parked in the middle of the road, but then, we hadn't seen a single other vehicle yet. "You a photographer?" he asked.

"Nah. I just read a bunch of photography magazines while I worked at the school library in Germany. You got a pretty expensive camera."

Phillips smiled as he squinted through the viewfinder and focused on something—probably the woman. He adjusted the shutter speed dial expertly with the thumb and index fingers of his right hand. *Flap-click.* "This here's my baby," he said. "GI Bill's gonna work for me, kid. When I'm out I'm gonna shoot for *National Geographic* or *Life.* You know them magazines, right?"

"Yeah. What do you do in Casey?"

He jerked his head toward the back. "I'm the honcho mail clerk. See them bags? I deliver good news mixed with all the crap mail and Dear Johns. Know what I mean?"

I pantomimed smoking a joint and he nodded. "You know Dupree in ASCOM?" I asked.

"Uh-uh."

"He's a spec 4 in Graves Registration."

"Yeah?"

"He's got body bags full of good shit and he's looking for someone to help him."

Phillips peered at me, lowering the camera for a moment. "*What* did you say you were doing out here? And how the fuck do you know about body bags and shit?"

"I hang out in ASCOM," I said. "I hear stuff. My best friend is friends with Dupree."

"Spec 4. Graves Registration?"

"Yeah."

"You ain't shittin' me, are you? Maybe spyin' for your old man?"

I laughed.

Phillips gave me a high five and skipped out of the jeep on his side onto the road. On the far side of the pavement, a man with two green water buckets made of five-gallon metal paint cans was slowly winding his way down to a vegetable patch. Hanging on ropes from a wooden frame he wore over his shoulders, the cans swayed gently, left and right, as he walked. *Flap-ap click.* The farmer had a light blue bathhouse towel draped over a sleeveless white T-shirt to block the sun, and his straw hat—with its cheap recycled celluloid band—looked like a cow had taken a bite out of the brim. His black rubber boots were folded down at the top under a pair of cut-off army khakis. *Flap-ap click.*

"Hey, *ajoshi*!" Phillips called out to him. When the man looked up, curious and annoyed, Phillips said, "*Mira mira!* I want to take your picture, okay?"

"He says he wants to take your picture, sir," I said in Korean.

The man grimaced, showing a gold-banded front tooth. "Tell him I'm a famous movie star!" he said. "I'm Park No-shik and he has to pay me, that son of a bitch, bothering people who have work to do. Why don't you go patrol the Thirty-Eighth Parallel, you son of a bitch long-nose bastard?" Then he smiled and said in English, "Ten dallah!" and held out a hand.

Phillips gave him a pack of Marlboros and a one-thousand-won bill, a little over a dollar, and the farmer was happy to pose for some portraits. I translated for them both as Phillips made the farmer move from one background to another and then fill up his water cans from a paddy field.

On our way back to the jeep, Phillips got some more shots of the woman with the baby and their house, where swallows were nesting under the eaves. I explained to him that it was good luck. He gave the woman a one-thousand-won bill and a pack of Juicy Fruit gum.

"What do *you* want to do when you grow up?"

I shrugged.

"When do you even get out of school?"

"A few more years. If I finish."

"You gotta stay in school, little man. I joined the Army because that was all there was where I'm from. Or be a rancher. Only I hated that shit. I upped for the old FTA shit for the GI Bill and 'cause they said we wouldn't be in 'Nam anymore. Never finished school. You?—you finish school, man."

By "FTA," he meant the Army's old "Fun, Travel, and Adventure" ad, which all the GIs now knew as "Fuck the Army" and which they scrawled in every bathroom stall. The way Phillips stuck out his right index finger on the steering wheel reminded me of my old yellow-haired GI Joe doll, once my favorite toy, which I associated with my father, who was blond. The doll's right hand was its trigger hand, forever in a sort of pincer pose, its index finger and thumb slightly apart. At some point, I had broken off the trigger finger.

"I was thinking maybe I was just gonna be in the infantry like my father," I said.

"Fuck that!" said Phillips. "Go Navy or Air Force, or at least go OCS and be an officer, man! If *I* did it again, I'd finish high school and go Navy."

As we drew closer to Seoul, we began to hit traffic. Only a few of the blue three-wheeled *surikoda* pickups at first, then buses and taxis and military vehicles, both American and Korean. The buses spewed a terrible brown diesel exhaust, and Phillips would either try to pass them or pull over to wait them out. The road grew thick with small motorbikes loaded with deliveries and the ubiquitous large black bicycles, their racks piled dangerously high with cases of bottled OB beer. The loud rumbling of engines, the bicycle bells and car horns, people shouting, and the noise of music over loudspeakers made it hard to hear each other in the open jeep, so we were quiet.

When we reached the Eighth Army compound in Yongsan, the Korean MPs who guarded the gate waved us through and Phillips parked at the Friendship Arcade just past the bus depot. He said he would have taken me all the way to ASCOM but he had business in Itaewon later in the day—it was one of the destinations he had soaped onto his windshield.

"You take care," he said.

When I thanked him for the ride, he pulled out his fat wallet and gave me a twenty. That was a lot of money. "I should be thankin' *you*," he said. "When I come back here as a big-time photographer for *Life*, you be my translator, awright? Here—you buy yourself some lunch. A *confection*."

I thanked him again.

"Spec 4 Dupree, Graves Registration, ASCOM, right?"

"Yeah."

"If you see him, tell him to get in touch with the Milkman."

"That's you?"

"Phillips Milk of Magnesia—right? Makes deliveries. He'll know who it is." Phillips gave me a mock salute and drove away toward the Main PX.


THAT NIGHT AT home, when I asked my mother about Kubong Manshin, she was surprised that I even knew his name. "I never told you," she said. "How did you find out?"

I lied and told her it was from Big Uncle, a long time ago when he had visited us.

"Big Uncle learned some things from Kubong Manshin too," she said. "But they didn't get along, because Big Uncle is so handsome and Kubong Manshin wanted to be a woman. He said he could cure Big Uncle's foot if he would just fall in love, and that made Big Uncle mad because he said he would never do *that* with a man."

"What's *that*?"

She made her eyes go wide. "*That*. So they wouldn't even look at each other—or Big Uncle would never look at Kubong Manshin, but the *manshin* would make a big deal of pining for Big Uncle whenever anybody saw the two of them. Big Uncle could have learned so much from him, but instead he just kept his head stuck in those old Chinese books. And he couldn't even read half of them!"

"Is Kubong Manshin crazy?" I asked. "Is he just pretending he's a woman?"

"Crazy? All shamans are crazy. The old people said Kubong Manshin was old even back when they were kids. Nobody remembers him not living in that hut with the shrine—maybe going back to before the Japanese came.

"When I was little, he used to have long white hair, and he would dye it so he didn't scare people at night. One time, some Japanese soldiers came to his hut because they pretended to study shaman shrines in those days and then burned them down, but they left him alone and the captain even gave him a big donation."

I remembered how Kubong Manshin had gotten my offering from me. "What did he do?"

"They say he told each one of the soldiers how he was going to die and how he might change his fate. After the Second World War, the Japanese captain came back to visit him. The captain had joined a Zen temple and become a monk. His Korean was really good, and he stayed in one of those little hermitages up in the mountains until the war started in 1950."

My mother laid out the flower cards on the blanket and started methodically flipping them, shifting them from one line to another. I could never figure out the flower card solitaire game, but I liked watching her play. It was as if she were an automaton possessed by some force that made her a part of the math that governed the cards. She would always calm down when she played, and sometimes she could even skip the cigarettes.

Now Mahmi exhaled again, and under the incandescent lamp the shadows from the plumes of Salem smoke wafted back and forth like tangled hair in a breeze. She removed a whole line of the cards, turned another one over, and said, "Guest."

"Who do you suppose?"

"Oh, I wouldn't know. Is it time for anyone to visit?" She mashed out her cigarette, took a fresh one out of the pack, looked regretful for an instant because she could have used the stub as a light, and lit up with a match.

"So how old do you think he is?" I asked.

"Who could know? But when he taught us how to behave like proper girls, it was in the old style. Nobody acts like that these days."

"Old style?"

"You know—like what you see in the old historical dramas and movies." She turned her head to one side, looking at me out of the corners of her eyes. Then she made a subtle gesture with her hands and gave a slight half smile, and she became an entirely different person. "How's that?"

My mouth hung open in surprise.

"How's this one?" Mahmi lowered her head slightly and touched the back of her neck, which now looked extremely pale and long, as she looked upward and subtly opened her mouth so that her lower lip pouted. She looked no older than a teenager. I could imagine the multicolored *chogori* she would have worn back then—even the square headdress of a just-married girl.

"That's the sort of thing he taught us," she said, turning back into her normal self. "But the old people said he could actually transform into anything—a dog, or a cat, or maybe even a fox. When some people became Christians, they said he wasn't even a human being but a nine-tailed fox. They said he would do little backflips at night in the moonlight and then go out and seduce some poor young man and bring him to ruin."

"Why are the people in your village so superstitious?" I asked. "It's the twentieth century and the Christians say all of those things are just old stories."

"Is that so?" My mother made a frown with half her face, the Salem still between her lips. "All those new Western things, those scientific things—germs, molecules, electricity, atoms—those are just stories too, you know. People will believe what they need to believe. The old things are *mishin*, and people make light of it now, but *mishin* isn't going to go away."

"So you think all the things Big Uncle says are true? *Real*, I mean?"

"*Real?* Big Uncle had a hard life in the family, though he deserved a lot of what he got. He's the oldest son, but he didn't do a lot of the things the eldest is supposed to do. He was lazy as a farmer, and he didn't pay enough attention to his studies because he had eyes for women. But he's a smart man and he knows things—a lot of things. That's why he can be a geomancer and see the future with his oracle book. I just can't figure out why he can't cure himself of that foot. It must be a curse."

Talking to me about Big Uncle must have reminded her, because she added—almost as an afterthought—"Go visit your father this Saturday. He's at the 121 Hospital in Yongsan."

"When did he go *there*?"

"I don't know. It must only be a day or two ago. I got the message from the NCO Club manager today. Go talk to him—it will make him feel better to get a visit from his son."

Now I wondered if the shaman was right about my father dying.

## II

# Crows

# Crows

## 1950

They had come for him very early in the morning. It was still dark outside, and he was dreaming about his childhood—catching grasshoppers in the hills, roasting them in the small metal brazier, the red embers turning to gray ash. He could still taste their peppery flavor and feel the light crackle between his teeth as the burnt shells popped. He was hungry when he woke, eager to finish off the previous night's leftover soup of pork and bean paste. But then the men came.

There was no time, they said; the Reds would kill him and probably his whole family if they found a grown man still in the village. He had to rush. Everybody in the village knew about his foot and his ritual of preparing his sock; they couldn't afford to have him slow them down. The artillery in the distance wasn't thunder—or bamboo popping in a fire for that matter—it was the North Korean People's Army advancing toward Seoul, a surprise attack, and there was nothing stopping them.

He couldn't see all the men outside the room, but judging from the voices, there must have been at least a dozen. He heard a sparrow call, then an owl, and a rustling sound from above, which he knew was the black rat snake that lived in the roof thatch. It was only then that he realized he really *was* awake.

"I need to eat something," he said.

"No time, Big Brother." It was Kunsu. "We can eat when we've made it up into the mountains."

"Didn't you hear the owl? It's not a good time to go."

"Please, Big Brother, don't be like this now!" Kunsu stepped up into the room without even removing his dirty boots and started throwing clothes at him. Then others were in the room too, stomping the bedding under their muddy shoes, manhandling him into his clothes while he was still on the *yo*. He couldn't even protest about his foot, which had another day to go under the poultice of Chinese herbs and mugwort. Legs everywhere and feet trampling everything. He didn't have a moment to look up at their faces because his eyes kept jumping to the footprints they left on the bright flower pattern of his new coverlet, and on the newly lacquered and papered surface of the warm floor.

They flung his blanket aside and pulled him to his feet, rudely stealing from him the last warmth of sleep, and he shivered. Only it was a shiver of fear now, and it left a hollow portent in his gut.

There were guffaws and expressions of disgust when they smelled what came from under the blanket, mostly the foul herbs and not his rotting flesh. Kunsu threw him a bundle of wool army socks and told him there would be no time for his foot-cleaning.

"I'll catch up to you," he said, raising his hand in protest.

"No, Big Brother. You can't do that." And they dragged him outside half dressed, before he could pack a thing. Later, all he had was what Kunsu had thrown into a little carry sack.

Outside, in the *madang*, he heard the owl cry again and felt its *ki* pointing at the southwest hills in the direction of the ancestors' graves. "We should take the boats," he said when he had his wits about him. "The river will be safer."

"We don't need a geomancer's nonsense right now," someone snapped. "We know where we're going."

Kunsu tugged at him while he was still trying to tie his boot—an old American combat boot a size larger than the other one. Odd, how he remembered that so vividly after all these years.

THE SUN HAD JUST begun to rise. It would be a while, yet, before it was hot, but already he was wiping sweat from his eyes, already breathing like a woman in labor. Hobbling on the grassy path up the slope, his boot slippery inside from the oozing fluid, he felt dizzy and off-center. He had to stop and fix the socks before there was bleeding.

Already, his foot was chafing, as the delicate new layer of skin coaxed by the Chinese herbs began to peel off in little patches. He could feel the precise spots from the burning. It felt like tiny red ants biting between the wool sock and the layer of tender flesh it rubbed against, tiny pincers chewing him raw.

"Just a moment," he called out to the men.

In the dawn light he saw that they were all wearing extra clothes and carrying large *pojagi* bundles that had been wrapped by their wives or mothers. Some of the *pojagi* cloths were beautiful—perhaps they had been wedding gifts. One man carried his bundle on top of his head as if he were a woman, the black rose-printed cloth oddly delicate and precious-looking in the early sun.

"Wait a moment for me," he called out, but no one stopped. They continued up the path past the chestnut trees and azaleas.

Old Kim called back, "You just sit there and sing 'Arirang,' why don't you?" A couple of the others laughed and Kunsu joined in.

He was sitting now, pulling off the boot. "You all won't get ten *li*, then, before you all go lame!" He spat.

They all just laughed again. "*You're* the one with the foot disease!" said Old Kim. "*Ha ha ha!*"

Some of the men had reached the crest of the hill. Their heads seemed to bob up and down before they disappeared into the ground.

"Damned bastards!" he yelled. "Why didn't you just leave me at my house? *Ungh?*"

But no one replied. He saw Kunsu pause for a moment to look back down at him before disappearing over the ridge himself.

And so he sat there, alone, one boot off, removing the wool sock to look at the mess his foot had already become. From downslope, near the bend in the path where the acacias had been planted the year before, he heard a rustling noise and glanced down, hoping it was someone he could ask for help. But it was only the mangy yellow dog that belonged to the Kims—the one everybody always threatened to eat but never got around to because it was a shit-dog. It paused to look up at him, and their eyes met—his black eyes and the dog's, glinting in the early-morning sun. Then he heard the first shots.

Just crackling noises, really, not even especially loud, from the other side of the ridge. He tried to tell himself that these were not gunshots; but then, remembering why they had taken him out of the village, he was afraid.

He heard shouts now—and more shots—and then a scream. Another shot. He froze, listening for too long, until it occurred to him that he was in danger. Quickly, he jammed his foot back into the boot, tearing some flesh, which made him wince, and then scrambled on hands and knees into a patch of tall grass along the trail by a boulder. His nose was so low to the ground he could smell that someone had pissed on the rock. He closed his eyes, felt the insects crawling up his good leg, the dry grass against his sweaty skin.

IT WASN'T LONG BEFORE he heard the first soldiers come down the trail. They walked hard on the ground, carrying rifles and heavy packs, no doubt, and they stepped carelessly, cursing when they slipped on the loose stones. They hardly spoke to each other, their breathing fast, the breath of men past exhaustion. It seemed to take all morning for them to get down the hillside.

How large a unit would this be, he wondered—a platoon? A company? A battalion? Not that he even knew what any of those military terms meant, really. He was just the son of a farmer, the one meant to become a scholar, who'd failed and become instead a professor of nonsense—an *ongtori paksa*. When he opened his eyes, the sweat from his face trickled in and stung. He blinked, squinted, blinked again. He listened. Surely, they were all gone by now—unless they had cleverly posted someone to watch for stragglers.

The wind was blowing down from the mountain. He heard nothing from the direction of the village. Rising slowly up from the grass, he stretched. There was no sign of anyone, but from the way the grass had been trampled he guessed there must have been at least a hundred soldiers. The open wind dried his sweat. His stomach rumbled. The first thing he wondered was whether Kunsu had packed anything to eat in his little sack.

He felt around inside the sack and found a rice ball and some strips of dried cuttlefish wrapped in a cloth. The sharp smell made his mouth suddenly fill with saliva—so fast he drooled—and he had to spit. Unwrapping the food reminded him that he had to see to his foot, but he was so hungry his hands trembled, and he stuffed half of the salted rice ball into his mouth. He chewed, and he was wondering where he would find water to wash down the cuttlefish when he saw the procession of trucks on the road below. It was far enough that he couldn't hear them, but even from here he could feel the coarse vibrations of their engines, their heavy tread on the land.

It must be a battalion, he thought—or a brigade—and then, realizing its forces must be equipped with binoculars, he hunched back down into the patch of grass, chewing furiously. He watched a flock of crows fly upward from the fields into the clear sky. Where would he get water now? He was suddenly very thirsty.

He closed his eyes. His old teacher, the old geomancer from Yangp'yong, had shown him the *p'ungsu* maps of the local landscape—wind and water maps. "Look at these with your heart," he had said. "Study them until they rise up in your vision when you close your eyes." But he'd always wondered, when he did that, how much of what he saw was memory and how much just imagination. He did it now—saw the faded brush lines on the old, discolored rice paper and followed the *um* lines over the ridge. Over that he superimposed his memory of the trail and followed it as if tracing the line with his fingertip.

And there it was—the spring—only partway down the other side where they'd found the old demon posts that protected the village when he was a kid. It wouldn't even take all that long to get there.

WHEN HE FINALLY removed his boot and peeled back his sock, he winced not from the pain, but from what he saw—the pus and lymph on his foot smeared together into a creamy amber paste. The smell, in the heat, reminded him of the dried residue left on a pot of boiled chicken. He unfolded paper packets of salve and foot powder Kunsu had put in the sack for him. He had to wipe away the ooze first—which was painful and difficult without water, but he managed to get most of it off with the cloth the rice balls had been wrapped in.

He applied the herbal salve and put on a fresh wool sock, carefully rolling it onto his foot the way he had seen the sexy Western starlets roll on their stockings in movies. Over the first sock he applied the Chinese foot powder that always made him feel a little more secure somehow. And then another fresh sock, less delicately this time, since his flesh was now protected. When he was done, he let his foot steep for a few minutes before putting it back into the boot and adjusting the laces so they wouldn't be too tight.

It was time for a cigarette. Odd, how the craving for tobacco came so strongly and suddenly now that he had time to take a breath or two. He found the matches in one vest pocket and the crumpled pack of Shintanjin in the other. He pulled an unbroken smoke and lit it. The scrape of the match on the box and the smell of sulfur seemed especially dull in the heat and silence, and after a few puffs he felt his strength return—or perhaps just a sense of clarity—and he rose to make his way up the slope.

Soon enough, the line of military vehicles below had passed, and no one was outside in the village. He only hoped the women had taken the children across the river to hide out in the cave downstream.

BY THE TIME he crested the ridge he already knew what he would see on the other side. The crows were there, with their intermittent cawing. He counted eleven bodies already bloating in the sun, and when the wind shifted uphill he could smell the blood and the shit. As the crows pecked the bodies, swarms of flies would briefly explode upward like dark bubbles, the gold-backed ones glinting in the sun, and then they would light back down to lay their eggs in the soft places around the eyes, the lips, the nostrils, the gaping gunshot wounds already black with clotted blood.

He recognized old Kim from the mole on his forehead—the rest of his face had been smashed. And there was Suni's father, with a large hole in his chest covered with flies; when the flies stepped across his open eyes, sucking at the space under his puffy lids, he looked almost alive.

But where was Kunsu? He didn't want to touch the bodies, for amid the buzzing of flies and the crow caws there was the unmistakable quivering of lost ghosts still unaware they were dead. The old geomancer had warned him never, under any circumstances, to allow himself to be polluted by the negative *ki* of such ghosts.

What had Kunsu worn that morning? It could only have been those old olive drab field pants patched at both knees. That's what he always wore. And now he remembered—the bastard hadn't bothered to take off his shoes. He'd stepped all over the quilt in those low-cut Korean Army boots of his with the spliced laces.

He didn't see Kunsu's boots, but he did find Kunsu's bloody pants between two of the village men. Why would they kill him and take his body away but leave his pants behind? Or perhaps Kunsu had managed to run off. Maybe he was hiding down here, somewhere, with a terrible injury.

For some reason he was not all that concerned, and he was surprised at how little he felt at this scene of death. He performed the Taoist breathing that would protect his spirit from the lingering ghosts and made his way toward the water, shooing the crows out of his path. Then he saw the other body—a North Korean soldier of the People's Army, shot through the heart, lying with arms and legs spread in the grass. His entire chest and torso were black with blood and flies, and he was naked from the waist down—not even a pair of underpants. A crow, pecking between the dead soldier's legs, looked up thoughtfully, as if to reconsider something, then went back to feeding. There was something under the body, protruding into the grass.

"*Ya!*" He waved his arms and chased the crow away. He stepped carefully up to the spread-eagle figure and pushed at it with his good foot. The body seemed ten times the weight of a living man, like a sack full of sand. He grunted with exertion and, swatting away flies, reached under the body to yank it out—a canteen! He wrestled it off the body, pulling the strap over its shoulders and head, careful not to touch it, all the while enduring the horrendous buzzing of the flies.

With the satisfying weight of the canteen in his hand, he walked downhill, away from the stench, and sat on a rock. He could drink now and refill the canteen at the spring. He wiped sweat from his eyes with the back of his hand, looking briefly up at the clouds that now covered the sun. Suddenly, he couldn't bear his thirst any longer. He took out the stopper of the canteen and started gulping down its contents.

It was not water. At the same instant, he knew that Kunsu must have joined the North Korean People's Army. As what he believed to be water suddenly became a cheap soju burning his throat all the way down to his stomach, he could see Kunsu in the dead soldier's baggy uniform pants and he started to cough and laugh at the same time. Soju went up into his nose, the alcohol burning so fiercely it made him blind, and now he was sobbing, too, crying for the dead men of his village and his little brother become a traitor.

# Front toward Enemy

## 1974

The 121st Army Evacuation Hospital had been in ASCOM since after the Korean War, but it had just recently relocated to the South Post of the Yongsan Garrison in Seoul. The army bus that we rode as a school bus stopped there near the back gate. The 121st had once sprawled out under the helipad hill in ASCOM, through numerous rows of Quonset huts and some permanent brick buildings left over from the Japanese, and my friends Miklos and Paulie and I all used to go to the emergency room there whenever we had cuts or scratches. That was where they had taken Mahmi too, when she'd nearly bled to death after giving birth to me.

Even after the hospital began to shut down in ASCOM, just after a mysterious fire that inexplicably burned down whole rows of unconnected buildings, the 121st had been useful to us. Miklos, Paulie, and I scrounged the clusters of burnt-out Quonset huts for surviving medical supplies and other odds and ends of military equipment that we could sell on the black market in Sinchon. The MPs didn't waste their time guarding or patrolling the damaged buildings, and we found whole boxes of tubing, cases of IVs, and loads of first aid supplies like sterile gauze, surgical tape, and scissors; we'd even stumbled onto a few complete surgical kits. In one of the buildings, we had found a supply closet standing intact in the middle of some charred plywood dividers, and we dressed ourselves up in surgical gowns and masks—even the latex rubber gloves—while we rummaged through the ruins pretending to be the "Pros from Dover." We found so much stuff that day that we had to call Mr. Shin of the ASCOM taxi dispatch and made a deal with him to smuggle the loot out in one of his "special" cabs equipped with fake seats.

These days ASCOM looked bleak in that area. They had never bothered to repair or tear down the burnt buildings, and without the hospital there was hardly any reason for us to go much past the Service Club or the library. The help we used to get from the emergency room at the 121st we now got at the small dispensary that was kept open under the maple trees by the post theater. The dumpsters there had plenty of things we could retrieve and sell on the black market—syringes and needles, mostly; tubing and glassware—but after learning in school about how contagious diseases worked, we did less of that.

With some of the twenty dollars I had left over from Phillips, I bought twenty one-pound bags of M&M'S from the little PX by the ASCOM HQ building, where the impatient clerk never punched ration cards. I got two bottles of Taster's Choice instant coffee and a bottle of Pream— that horrible artificial powdered creamer—and sold it off post to Long Legs, the middleman who controlled Tatagumi. That doubled my money, so I could buy my father some paperback westerns to read while he was in the hospital. His favorites were the Sackett books, and I found him *The Lonely Men, Galloway,* and *Treasure Mountain,* along with a couple of Mickey Spillanes with their lurid covers. One of them was called *The Snake.* I had the *ajoshi* at the Stars & Stripes bookstore wrap them as one present, which ended up looking like a large brick bundled in brown postal paper. I carried this—along with a couple of loose cigars (which they certainly wouldn't let him smoke) and a few apple-shaped glass bottles of Martinelli's Gold Medal apple juice—in a rope-handled shopping bag and got on the bus to Yongsan.

The bus was sparsely occupied at this time of day, and I read one of the books I had bought for myself—*The Land of Long Juju*, a Doc Savage novel set in darkest Africa. The banter between the lawyer, nicknamed Ham, and a character called Monk, who had a pet pig he had sarcastically named Habeas Corpus, reminded me of my father's German humor. Ever since my mother had pointed out the resemblance, the Man of Bronze—as he was shown on the back cover—had reminded me of my father, but it was Doc's superhuman abilities and worldly knowledge I wished I could emulate. I had collected two dozen of those slim Bantam paperbacks in the series so far, though out of order.

My father wasn't in his room when I arrived at the 121st. His roommate, a Black first sergeant named Gaines, made a face when he saw the cover of my book. "Your old man tells me you're a reader of discerning taste," he said. "What kinda shit is *that?*"

"It's just a Doc Savage story," I said, holding the book up to look more closely at the cover. There was a Black African witch doctor in a big Afro with a long, sharpened bone or quill poking through his nose. Behind him stood two strange, doughy shapes with disturbing holes for faces, looking like Klansmen who had melted into their white cone-head robes; and in the foreground stood the Doc, in his usual torn shirt, left fist clenched and the veins of his arm bulging.

"You gonna rot your brain with that shit. Put it away—it's making my ulcer act up." Gaines reached over to his night table and tossed me a paperback. "Now *that*'ll grow hair on your chest." It was called *Manchild in the Promised Land*—nothing but those five words on the cover, flanked in stylized red flames. Norman Mailer had written something there, too. "You read that," he said. "A lot of bad stuff in there," said Gaines. "Good stuff, too, though. Like life. You never know which stuff gonna happen. I end up here—bad. But I get to hang and shoot the shit with a buddy from 'Nam—good."

"You served with my father in 'Nam?"

"Oh, yeah. Your old man ever tell you what we did in 'Nam?"

"He doesn't talk about it much."

Gaines rubbed the stubble on his chin with one hand, as if feeling for a beard there. "Then I got a story for you." He pointed at the chair next to my father's bed, and I sat, lowering the shopping bag to the floor.

"We was together at the same fire base for a while after Tet," said Gaines. "He's a smart motherfucker, and all the Montagnards loved him 'cause he got things done and he wasn't afraid to *kick some ass*. One time we kept getting mortared by Charlie—accurate shit, Soviet 82s. Too accurate, like they already zeroed their tubes. One, two rounds, and they'd hit one of our bunkers dead on. Someone walked the distance and had a map, and we knew no one was gonna be walking through all that wire. So your old man figured out which one of the houseboys was VC and mapping our camp. He started a rumor about some VIP comin' out to the fire base, and we had an old noncom from Da Nang fly in all dressed up like a general with fake press corps and all that shit. Right out of *Patton*, with the shiny helmet and cowboy pistols.

"It was our first lieutenant's Vietnamese houseboy, so your old man made another map and switched it. It had the bunkers labeled different and the VIP bunker marked special. Pretty funny, if you saw it, like some kid with a crayon making a 'TOP SECRET' map, except this one was in grease pencil. The date and time and everything was marked on it, and your old man knew the VC houseboy was always in the camp when we had incoming. That was his *alibi*. Why would he put his own ass in danger?

"That night we made it look like everybody was in the VIP bunker. Then, a few minutes before it was time for the mortar attack—it was always right around 0300 on the button—we had the houseboy take some beer in there. It was empty, and we locked him in. He was shoutin' and bangin' away at the door in there while we hauled the sandbags off the roof. He wouldn't confess. Started cryin' and shit, about his family, but we could hear he was digging in all the while. It was all an act. Or maybe it was true, but we wasn't gonna count on that.

"Right around 0300—*Whump!* First 82mm round hits the northeast corner of the VIP bunker. Next one hits dead center and blows the shit out of it. Then—*Boom! Boom! Boom! Boom!* They knock off four more rounds for good measure 'cause they had that special intel and they thought they was getting them a general. But since we were ready for their asses for a change, we got a bearing on their position and called in an air strike. Lit the canopy with flares, and then their asses got na-palmned all to hell. We went out after first light and there was dead gooks all over the place. Never had no trouble after that."

My father came into the room just then, looking especially pale in his powder-blue hospital pajamas. His face was more wrinkled than I re-membered, and the edges of his cheeks sagged from fatigue. I knew he hated hospitals because he said you could never get any sleep in them. "I see you met Top," he said to me.

I realized he had been eavesdropping from just outside the door. "Yeah, he was telling me about you."

"Oh? Some bullshit war stories?"

"Same ol' same ol'," said Gaines.

"When'd you find out I was here?"

"Mahmi told me yesterday," I said, standing up. "I got these for you." I handed him the shopping bag.

My father made his happy chuckling sound as he took out the bot-tles of Martinelli's apple juice and lined them up on his bed table. He opened one for himself and walked one over to Gaines, who admired the glass leaves for a moment before unscrewing the cap and taking a big sip.

"Well," said Gaines. "I see what you mean, but this shit needs to be refrigerated."

"We'll get an ice bucket," said my father, sipping from his bottle. He looked at me to see if I wanted one, but I shook my head.

"Your sorry taste in reading's rubbing off on your kid, so I set him straight," said Gaines.

My father glanced at the title of the book in my hand. "Don't let Top here ask you for a back rub," he said. "And that's only on the first couple pages!" Both of them laughed loudly.

"Boy's already taller than you, and he obviously takes after his mother," said Gaines. "I told him not to *ever* be a grunt like his old man."

"*Infantry*," said my father. "Anyway, how many sons you got to be giving mine advice?"

Gaines pretended to be thoughtful. "Oh, I don't *know*. I had so many wives in the *buon*s."

"Top had to marry a Montagnard chief's daughter so we could keep our fire base," said my father. "And her sister too, I think. Come on, let's get out of here. I want to get some fresh air and smoke one of these. I have to get the taste of that cottage cheese crap out of my mouth. 'Hospital food' is a contradiction in terms."

Gaines held his hand out and I shook it goodbye.

"Thank you for the book."

He winked and turned to fluff his pillow.

I followed my father down several turns in the hospital corridors. We reached a set of metal doors with wire-reinforced glass windows on them and they opened onto a part of the building that was like a shady courtyard with trees and some flowering bushes. There were benches with standing ashtrays next to them, and we sat down. My father bummed a light from a passing medical orderly and lit up one of the cigars.

"How are you doing, Daddy?" I still called him that.

"Medical expertise—that's also a contradiction in terms," he said, pulling on the cigar. "They don't know *what the hell* they're doing here! I might have to be shipped stateside."

"What's wrong? What should I tell Mahmi?"

"Don't worry her about it. The hospital's not that bad. I find out in a couple days. Next time you come up, bring Sergeant Gaines a bunch of those Slim Jim meat sticks. They won't let him eat them here."

"Why is he here?"

"Bleeding ulcer. His stomach's been kaput since his second tour in 'Nam with me. He tell you about the time he saved my life?"

"No, it was about the VC houseboy. You heard."

"Son of a bitch never came *out* of the bunker is what happened. We just left him buried in there out of spite. A few days later one of the Montagnards killed a rat that was eating part of a hand. We let him have the fucker's wedding ring. No more Vietnamese houseboys at the firebase. They said it was haunted."

"So how did Sergeant Gaines save your life?"

My father grinned, remembering. "Ambush," he said. "We were on a night ambush and Charlie snuck right up to us and turned our claymores around. Then they made noise out in the bush to make us pop them, and I was exposed. Gaines grabbed the clacker away from me just in time, before I could detonate the claymores. We had a bunch of them daisy-chained along a trail, and they woulda chopped half our guys to hamburger, starting with me.

"Then he and I crawled out real quiet and turned them all back the right way. The VC didn't know. Later when the squad of them went down the trail and hit the kill zone, we got *their* asses instead. We used to call him 'Front Toward Enemy' for a while after that. Sounded like an Indian chief name, which fit, because he used to put red war paint on his face. Scared the piss out of the VC. Buckskin Charley, Rain in the Face, Yellow Hand . . .

"You know, sitting out here reminds me of when I was stationed in Germany. Do you remember the time we went *kosari* picking with your mother when we lived in Baumholder?"

"Which time was that? We went a bunch of times."

"That time I cut the bark off that stick for you?"

"Yeah," I said. "You stripped it like a candy cane." We had gone into the woods to pick fiddlehead ferns with my mother and her friends, and he had sat for a while, smoking his pungent cigars to keep the mosquitoes away. Then, with his hunting knife, he had sliced off a green branch from a young tree, cutting the bark in a spiral from end to end to peel off an even strip, revealing the fresh white wood underneath. I had seen him strip the last few centimeters of the long spiral of bark, but when he called me over and presented it to me, I received it as if it were some magical sword handed from King Arthur to one of his knights.

"That was the last time I remember thinking of you as my little boy."

I had run, whooping, into the woods, mowing down patches of the tender fiddlehead ferns for my mother to collect and dry to send to her friends and relatives, to make a woody-tasting side dish to eat with kimchi and rice. I had thought that spiral-barked stick to be invincible as I mowed down patch after patch, getting the white wood stained with the green juice of the broken fern stalks, and then, quite suddenly—so quickly I didn't even have the time to perceive it—the magic stick had snapped in two, leaving me with only a little stub in my hand.

"How do you think of me now?" I asked.

I had looked back toward my father in alarm, hoping he would know what to do, how to somehow make it magically whole again, but he was looking the other way, his crew-cut head obscured by the bluish haze of his cigar smoke, and in that instant I had been full of shame and disappointment. My high spirits had snapped as abruptly as my magical spiral-barked stick, and I had slunk off into the forest until the end of the outing. My mother noticed, and after eating our picnic dinner, she asked my father to cut me another stick, but by then we had to leave—it was getting dark—and the magic was gone, anyway.

"I don't know," my father said after a pause, puffing his cigar.

"A *man?*"

"You have a ways to go before you're a man."

"I don't think of myself as a boy anymore," I said.

"When you talk to your friends. . . ."

"Yeah?"

"I know you must call me your 'old man.' That's what they all call their fathers. Like what Gaines said. Is that what you call me? Your 'old man'?"

"No. I'm not them."

"You don't have to tell me different, you know."

"I know," I said. When I thought of my "old man," I thought of Big Uncle.

# Heaven & Earth

## 1974

A nother cholera epidemic had ended.

In the morning, the sky was a dark blue, anticipating the cold that would come with the autumn. A stretch of wispy clouds moved slowly up from the horizon, and from beneath them patches of gray staggered down, becoming darker and darker until they grew thick and black where they reached the earth below. I suddenly realized that I had followed the haze in the wrong direction—something was burning out in the rice paddies near the new highway. But I was headed in the other direction. And I had to walk quickly because I was meeting Miklos near the butcher shop in Tatagumi and I had lent my bicycle to Yongsu.

At the mouth of the alleyway in front of the police headquarters, the air became warmer, almost foggy, carrying an odd, cloying smell. From the trash heap in the alley I heard a wet scurrying sound and paused to look. There was a sudden *kaaaaaak!* as a crow flew from beyond my vision, down into the garbage, leaping out again just as suddenly to perch on a shattered crate and flutter its wings like an impatient man shuffling his feet.

The crow looked down at something. I could see it now—a patch of matted yellow fur and two legs protruding, stiff as bones. The dog had been dead for several days, its lips shrunk back to reveal a snarl of white teeth. I knew this dog. It belonged to the wholesaler down the street. Its name was Dokku, a Korean approximation of the English "dog." Another crow swooped down from the power line above, and then another.

I turned my back and continued down the street until I got to the main road. It took a while to reach the central rotary. I turned right there, where the share taxis lined up outside the train station, and then walked up the street, past the Taehan Theater, the bank, and the two drugstores until I was facing the butcher shop at the alley that led into Tatagumi.

Gold-flecked flies swarmed in the window of the butcher shop, and Mr. Kim was swatting a slab of pork to clear them away before cutting slices for a customer. Across from the shop a Japanese maple tree stood just beyond the entrance to the alley. This was where I would meet Miklos today, on the platform under the shade of the maple, where, for as long as I could remember, Old Man Heaven and Old Man Earth had parked themselves all day every day. Hyon and Hwang were their surnames, but since they happened to correspond to attributes of the first two Chinese characters in *The Thousand Word Classic*, which every educated Korean had to memorize, everyone called them Ch'on and Chi, Heaven and Earth. Yongshiggi's grandfather, their friend who usually sat with them, hadn't yet made his appearance, so I took his place at the edge of the platform and watched the two old men puffing on their long tobacco pipes as they played their traditional game of *chang'gi*.

*Clack! "Chang-gun!"* said Old Man Earth, and Old Man Heaven slid a pawn sideways to protect his king. The flat wooden piece was dark with the oil from Old Man Heaven's fingers. When the pawn reached its place at the intersection of lines that demarcated the king's court, Old Man Hyon flipped it over and snapped it for emphasis onto the board. *Click!* I had watched many times, but today, for the first time, I examined the Chinese characters carved into the flat chess pieces. Old Man Hwang played with the red, and his characters were carved in a clean, blockish script that looked like the printing in newspapers, but Old Man Hyon's pieces, the blue, were in a strange, tangly style, like plant roots swimming in water. My curiosity got the better of me.

"Grandfather Hyon," I said. "Why is the writing on your stones so strange?"

"*Ungh?*" said Old Man Heaven. He tilted his face toward me, only now noticing that I was there. The rim of his horsehair hat threw a gray shadow across his wrinkled brow, and he slowly scanned my body, examining my Wrangler blue jeans and my white Cannon T-shirt. He paused a moment to pull a strand of beard and squinted, as if he were about to say something disapproving. When I had grown taller than the first knot in the maple tree, he had scolded me for not addressing him in honorifics. He opened his mouth now, revealing, behind the smoke drifting up from his throat, his long yellowed teeth. I felt suddenly guilty, as if he could read an evil secret written on my face.

"The writing on my stones is harder to read because it's harder to write in this style," he said, looking toward Old Man Earth. "It takes more skill to play the blue side. Any dullwit can read the red."

"Why do you lie to this child?" said Old Man Hwang. *Click.* He moved his horse and took Old Man Hyon's pawn.

*CLACK!* Now Old Man Hyon's blue elephant came down on a red intersection. "*Chang-gun!*" he said.

Old Man Hwang started. "And what is this?" he said. Old Man Hyon had already lifted his old paper fan on which he had neatly marked the number of games he had won that year. Each year, they began in the spring with new fans, and this one was already full on one side with the orderly markings of Heaven, each four wins underlined with a thicker line that curved up at the side. Old Man Hyon's fan looked like it had been marked with hundreds of tiny left and right paw prints.

Old Man Hwang's fan, on the other hand, was scrawled haphazardly with tiny slashes. It looked like it had been on the floor of a barbershop and littered with black beard trimmings that had gotten stuck to the rice paper. Each time he tallied his wins, Old Man Hwang would have to count every one of his marks while Old Man Hyon sat and impatiently puffed away, having calculated his total in an instant.

"*Aigo, kurok'un*," muttered Old Man Hwang, admitting defeat.

"See there," said Old Man Hyon. "I've defeated him again. But Heaven always defeats the Earth, because that is the nature of the Tao."

"Grandfather," I said, "please don't argue on my account. I'm just waiting here for my friend."

"Ah, that demon friend of yours," said Old Man Hwang. "Ma-gwi or something."

"It's not *Magwi*," said Old Man Hyon. "Ears rusted? It's Mikkuraji or something, *ungh*? Slippery fish?"

"It's Miklos, grandfather."

Before they could say anything more, Miklos appeared, leading Yong-shiggi's grandfather, and said his hellos. He was respectful to the old men, but he still called me "Fifty-Seven," after the fifty-seven varieties of Heinz products.

Miklos lived in a traditional old-style house north of the rotary near the market, and we would go to the Gold Star Theater together whenever I happened to be in that neighborhood. Lately, he was on the U.S. Army bus I took to school with Patsy and Paulie only about half the time. Our mothers knew each other, and when I asked Mahmi why it seemed like Miklos sometimes lived in two places, she just told me that his family was very big and full of complications.

"Let's go, Fifty-Seven," he said. "I don't wanna be here when they start fighting."

We said goodbye to the old men and walked along the main street to the second ASCOM gate, where the guards knew us and waved us through without looking at our IDs. Just past the gate, we sat down in a patch of clover under the bus sign to wait for the bus from Yongsan, which we could ride the rest of the way up to the Snack Bar.

✦ ✦ ✦

I HAD FINALLY met up with Miklos after my visit to Big Uncle, and I had told him about Big Uncle's foot and all the medicines he had tried. Miklos said he had heard from his mother that there were two things that could cure anything—a hundred-year-old wild ginseng root from the deep mountains or, even better, the water that soaked down into a human skull after the body had been buried for a while.

"I heard that too," I said.

"From who?"

"My Little Uncle talked about skull water. But what kind of water would be inside a skull? That's where your brain is."

"Your body's mostly water," Miklos said. "Or maybe your brain turns to water when you die." He wasn't sure how long the body had to be buried, but since his mother had definitely said "skull," he figured that seven months and seven days was an auspicious amount of time.

"What's so special about seven months and seven days?" I asked.

Miklos knew lots of things because of his Korean relatives, and he explained that 49 was the number of days it took for the soul to prepare itself for its passage into the next world, but since we had to wait until the body decomposed and became a skeleton, that seemed about right. "It's still a forty-nine," he said. "And it's also because we call you 'Seven,' right? This is for you and your Big Uncle—seven days for you, seven months for him."

Together, we calculated that it would be 217 days, counting a month as 30 days. Three times seven plus three. Twenty-one and seven. All combinations of lucky numbers. What more could we have asked for? As far as Miklos was concerned, we didn't even need to go to a shaman or a fortune-teller before making our plans.

And this was how we decided—that fall after I visited Big Uncle in the woods—that we would dig up the skull of a dead man and bring the water to Big Uncle to cure him. If it was a success, we would take some to Miklos's grandfather, who was dying of TB.

"My mother said the water can't be from someone who died of a disease," said Miklos. "That would only make your uncle sick. We have to find someone who dies of old age or a beating or something like that."

I imagined an old, shriveled body, as old as Kisu's grandmother. How could her ancient skull help cure anyone? "What if we find someone who died pretty young?" I said. "You know? Someone who died in an accident."

Miklos nodded. "Plenty of people get run over by taxis. And people get murdered all the time."

Already, I could see how we would do it: Wait for news of a death, follow the funeral procession to the cemetery mountain near Medicine Mountain, memorize the location of the grave mound, and then wait until the following year. It would rain on the grave, it would snow, the snow would melt, and the water would soak into the dark, red earth. Worms and centipedes would eat away at the dead body, and the bullet hole, the knife wound, the scar from the accident would melt away with the rest of the flesh. Waiting for us, under the rotting wood of the coffin lid: the shiny white skull full of the purest, healing medicine water. Big Uncle would be cured, and Miklos's grandfather could start smoking his pipe again—hell, even the bitter Korean cigarettes he liked.

"But how will we get the water out?" I wondered out loud. "And how much of it will we *need*?"

"All of it, Fifty-Seven." Miklos looked over toward the Crafts Shop and scratched his head. "Hey, Paulie's coming."

I squinted and saw him pedaling his green Huffy Spider toward us. "Should we tell him?"

"His mother's a Jesus-monger."

"So? That means he can't help us?"

"I don't know."

"He'll help," I said.

"I guess," said Miklos. "And if he says no, I'll just kick his ass." He got up and waved until Paulie saw us and pedaled in our direction.

"Hey, you bastards! Why didn't you come to my house and get me before you came to post?" Paulie lived in Sinchon, the "ville" just outside the ASCOM gate.

"Cause we had a secret, man!"

Paulie leapt off his bike and let it fall onto the grass. "Yeah? So tell me the big fuckin' secret!"

"If we tell you, it wouldn't be a secret anymore," I said, and then, in Korean, "You can't tell this to anyone. No one."

"Something important, then?" Paulie said seriously in Korean. He was in ninth grade and claimed he was thirteen, but he always sounded older in Korean and, like Miklos, we all knew his American age was a lie.

We nodded. Miklos outlined our plan while I watched Paulie's face carefully for signs of betrayal. I knew Paulie believed in God and wasn't afraid of ghosts because of what he learned at his church, but I also sensed that he would help us. Sure enough, he had a suggestion right away.

"Why don't you just get some skull water from Dupree at the morgue?"

This puzzled us for a little while, but Miklos came up with a good answer after we had all shared a cigarette. "You fuckin' Christian," he said. "They don't let the bodies rot in the morgue, do they? And besides, you really think American skull water would work for a Korean, *ungh*?"

"You guys already thought it out, didn't you?" Paulie looked innocent, but I knew that a great many ideas were spinning through his head from the way his eyes sparkled.

"Why do you want to do this with us, anyway?" I asked. "Isn't this heathen and bad for your soul?"

"Nah. I can repent right before I die."

We laughed. Just then, the flat-faced green army bus came through the gate—we heard the hiss of air brakes—so Paulie quickly locked the back wheel of his bike against the signpost and got on with us. The bus was nearly empty, with only two white GIs in starched khakis sitting near the middle. They had duffel bags in the seats next to them and their garrison caps—which everyone usually called "cunt caps"—neatly angled on their heads. One of them, we could tell from his sunburn and blank eyes, was coming from Vietnam. The other, pasty-looking like dough, was clearly fresh from Stateside. We sat in the empty seats just behind the bus driver.

Paulie had questions about the number of days we had decided upon, but even for him the magical number 217 seemed a good idea. "Have you guys figured out how you're going to bring the skull water *back*?" he asked.

"Sure," said Miklos, but then he was quiet for a moment, as if deciding how to answer. "Fifty-Seven?"

"We'll have canteens," I said. "Since we'll have to camp up at Medicine Mountain. A canteen would work, right?"

I tried to imagine how the water would be pooled in the skull. Would it be clear and cold, pouring like soju out of a white china decanter? Or would it be milky and warm, like *makkolli* at night, with steam rising as it trickled into the canteen?

We got off the bus at the Lower Four Club and crossed the street to walk down to the Snack Bar, where Paulie collected some money from the shoeshine boy. It was a large wad of bills, so we knew it was for his mother and didn't bother asking him to buy us food.

Paulie sat on top of a Patio picnic table, dangling his legs in front of the bench seat. One of his dirty, white canvas shoes had black laces and the other was laced in horizontal lines with white nylon parachute cord. "You know," he said, "you guys should just forget about it until you hear about an accident. I haven't seen any in a long time, so there ought to be one soon. What do you want to do today?"

"The Service Club has a BBQ," said Miklos. He jumped up and grabbed the leftover fries some GI had abandoned at the next table.

"You're such a fuckin' pig," said Paulie.

"I'm hungry."

We were sitting downwind from the Patio grill, where the Korean cook in a white paper hat slapped hamburger patties onto a cooker made from a fifty-five-gallon oil drum cut lengthwise in half. When all the fat from the ground beef dripped onto the charcoal there was a loud sizzle, and then a burst of flame. I could hear my stomach growl and Miklos's even louder. It was torture.

"Let's go up to the Service Club," I said.

"Sure. They don't have the same BBQ sauce," said Miklos through his mouthful of fries. "But, hey, it's free chow, right?"

THE OUTDOOR BARBECUE at the Service Club was run by GIs rather than the usual Koreans who worked for AAFES concession stands. A corporal and a spec 4 were preheating the two sets of grills out on the deck, using lots of Ronson lighter fluid from the little yellow rectangular cans they had lined up. We could smell it even before we got there, and the charcoal too.

"Shit," said Miklos. "They're white guys."

The white GIs usually followed orders and wouldn't let us do anything at the Service Club, which was reserved for active-duty personnel only.

"Come on," I said, "We'll give it a try anyway."

"Hey," Paulie called to the corporal. "What time's the barbecue?"

"You little fuckers get at the end of the line," the spec 4 answered. He pointed to the glass doors that led out to the deck. It looked like the entire inside of the Service Club was packed with GIs waiting for chow. The corporal continued to squirt lighter fluid into the coals and the flames arced up toward the nozzle of the can. Even through the lighter fluid, I could smell mashed potatoes, spaghetti with meat sauce, macaroni salad, cole slaw, and sliced pickles. My empty stomach gurgled.

The corporal, happy with the flames, started peeling the wax paper off the hamburger patties on one of the metal flats. "What the fuck are you lookin' at?" he snapped at us. His name tape said GEROLD; he was still sunburned from Vietnam.

We didn't say anything.

"I said what the *fuck* you lookin' at?"

"We just want some burgers," said Miklos, reasonably enough.

"You mother*fuckers* aren't even supposed to *be* here. So you wanna eat? You wait till everyone got his chow." He pointed to the far end of the deck where a set of steps led down to the lower patio.

There was no point in arguing with this Gerold, and no one else stuck up for us, so we left, Miklos swiping a can of the lighter fluid as he walked past the grill. Down at the other side of the deck we discovered that they had set up one of the small grills there only to abandon it, probably because the spot was too windy. We sat on the brick ledge and did our best to rescue our soured moods by catching tree frogs in the branches that overhung the wall.

"Do you know the story of the green frog?" I said.

"The guy who never listens to his mother and does everything the opposite of what she says?" said Miklos.

"Yeah."

"Like our moms don't tell that story to us all the time," said Paulie.

"You saying these frogs are *those* frogs?" Miklos held one of his up in front of his face and squinted at it.

"No, not really."

"The green frog lived by the river," I said, "and he cried when he thought his mom's grave was gonna be washed away."

Paulie dangled his frog by a hind leg. "Wasn't he supposed to bury her on the mountain?"

Miklos laughed. "That's what his mother said, dumb fuck. He was supposed to bury her by the *river*."

"You got it wrong," I said. "She said bury her by the *river* because what she *really* wanted was to be buried on the *mountain*. What moron would bury his mother by the river?"

"Well, fuck it. There's no mountain *or* river right here, man. Just the fuckin' Service Club." Miklos took his frogs and dangled them over the grill. I could see the waves of heat rising, the moisture on the frogs' backs drying until their skins looked like paper. "I don't see why they couldn't just let us eat, man." Miklos dropped the frogs onto the black metal grill where they stuck and sizzled loudly, their skin bubbling until their bodies suddenly popped from the heat. "Shit," he said.

Paulie tossed his frog on the grill. "Hope they enjoy all the burgers off this fucker," he said. I took my frog and tossed it on the grill too but didn't watch what became of it. I could hear it well enough, though, and the image of Miklos's frogs was fresh enough in my mind to turn my stomach. We all listened for a few moments as the sizzling sounds died down into a sort of whistling, then stopped. The air was thick now with the smell of burnt skin and meat, but the frogs left very little on the grills—just some charred black shapes like lumps of coal.

"They're not even gonna know," I said.

"Yeah, but *we* know, man. We know their fuckin' hamburgers have dead frog meat on them. Serves 'em fuckin' right for kicking us out."

"Yeah," said Paulie.

"Come on. Let's get outta here." Miklos put the can of lighter fluid next to the grill just before we jumped over the side of the stone patio, down onto the sidewalk where the bus to Yongsan stopped.

"Let's go to the Snack Bar, huh?" said Paulie. "This smell's gonna fuckin' make me puke, man."

"You're a pussy, Paulie," said Miklos.

"Fuck you."

"You got any money, Fifty-Seven?"

"Some."

We emptied out what was in our pockets, but all of it combined didn't amount to enough for a single burger. Miklos and I looked at Paulie until he shrugged and pulled open the roll of bills he'd gotten from the shoeshine boy for his mother. Three hundred dollars in twenties.

"You fuckers have to promise to pay me back," he said. He took a twenty and folded up the rest. "One burger and small fries for each of us. That's it."

I reminded him that his mother always gave us money for food when we visited, and he smiled. By the time we reached the Snack Bar, we were in better moods, and we even bought the more expensive flame-grilled burgers. Still, the image of the charred frogs and the story of the green frog lingered in my mind. I knew we had done something very wrong that day.

A FEW DAYS LATER we decided we needed to see a dead body for practice. All of us had seen dead people before, of course—relatives laid out on the *maru*, hastily covered accident victims—but we wanted to rehearse in some way, so we visited Paulie's friend, Spec 4 Dupree, who saw dead bodies all the time. We had been to the ASCOM morgue a few times since Paulie first met Spec 4 Dupree and had an open invitation to visit whenever we wanted.

The weather was perfect that day, but there was always something off about the doubled Quonset huts of Graves Registration. Each of us agreed that it was a bad place, even if it was only because we knew that it was where the unfortunate dead had to await their transfer, in black body bags, back to "The World." Spec 4 Dupree had told Paulie that you got used to the bodies after a while. He said that everyone was afraid or disgusted at first, but, as with anything else, the routine sets in and you hardly mind it, even when they come in mangled and unrecognizable. The only thing that would bother him now, he said, was prepping the body of a child or someone he knew, which hadn't happened yet.

We had determined to get so used to the dead that when we finally dug up the body near Medicine Mountain, it would be no stranger than digging up some inert object like a discarded shell casing. We didn't want to be frightened of a skull or a few bits of hair and rotted flesh. We wanted the act to be as mundane as possible.

"It has to be like we're digging up a kimchi jar after winter and sampling what's inside, right? Even the smell, huh?" Miklos had said.

"Man," said Miklos now to Paulie, "I don't see how you can come here by yourself. Gives me the fuckin' creeps."

"It's just some dead bodies."

"Yeah? Hell, my mother's seen ghosts, and she said one of my uncles sat up and grabbed someone after he was dead."

"That's just bullshit," said Paulie. "Like all that zombie and vampire shit Fifty-Seven's so afraid of."

"I'm not afraid of it," I said. "That's just in the movies. I know there's no such thing."

Miklos changed to Korean, making what he said suddenly more solemn. "*Ya*, you should speak respectfully about the dead. Their spirits might be everywhere listening to us, and we don't want to offend them."

"*Araso*," said Paulie. "Talk in English, man."

"Yeah. You sound like my Big Uncle," I said. "Fuckin' weird, man."

"Well, fuck you guys then."

Miklos didn't say anything else for a while, but with just a simple change of language he had reminded us that the spirits of the dead could be made real. When we talked about vampires and zombies and werewolves in English, it was the world of the Hammer Films and Hollywood B movies. The only horror film that had truly frightened us was *The Night of the Living Dead*, with its utter lack of mystery, its sheer black-and-white deadness that had removed the layers of Hollywood from the story and brought it straight into the world of our daily lives.

Paulie was about to say something, but just then we realized we were standing in front of the GRREG building, the Graves Registration Service, and before we could open the doors—which were doubled to allow gurneys in and out—they mysteriously opened for us, as if we were in one of those horror flicks we had seen the previous week, and out came Spec 4 Dupree.

The last time we had visited, Dupree had dared us to open one of the storage drawers, which he said contained the body of a GI who had been run over and mangled by an armored personnel carrier. None of us had had the courage to open the drawer that time, but today we were determined to see, up close, at least the head of a dead man. Paulie explained to Dupree why we were there at that hour.

"You wanna see a stiff?" said Dupree. "Right now?"

With no further prompting, he took us back to the refrigerated room, where the stink of chemicals made the air seem even colder than it was. The metal gurneys and the stainless steel autopsy table gave off an oddly grayish gleam under the buzzing fluorescent lights. Water dripped in the steel sink in the corner, and something a bit darker and thicker had pooled in the gutters around the steel table. We had been in that room before to cool down when it was hot outside, but today felt entirely different.

"That drawer over there," Dupree said, pointing at a wall of what looked like large filing cabinets. "Open it."

Paulie, Miklos, and I just stood and looked at each other until finally Paulie shrugged and went over and pulled on the handle. "God, it's heavy," he said.

"Ever hear of 'dead weight'?" said Dupree. "Dude might weigh 180, but when he dead it feels like 250. Or maybe he's carryin' some product as extra baggage."

Paulie averted his eyes and slowly pulled out the drawer, which rumbled a little as it coasted over its rollers. I expected to see a pair of stiff feet with toe tags, or smeared plastic bags full of unidentifiable body parts, but the drawer turned out to be filled with cans of beer and soda. Dupree laughed.

"Shit!" I said to Paulie, whose eyes were still closed. "He's only got stumps for legs, man!"

"Look at it, pussy!" Miklos said to Paulie.

We all watched Paulie's already disgusted expression as he slowly turned his head, looking out of the corners of his eyes as if to keep the image as far away as he possibly could. When he saw the cans of Michelob and Coca-Cola, his expression went suddenly flat. "Man, you guys are fucked up," he said.

"Gimme a Mick," said Dupree.

Paulie hesitated before tossing Dupree the beer. "Fuckin' assholes," he muttered.

WE TOOK A STACK of toe tags from the morgue and that night, up at the Main Snack Bar, we labeled them all with made-up names and "DOA," followed by the most obscene causes of death we could imagine. We were still laughing when a GI entered from the patio-side door all bandaged up like the character in *The Unknown Soldier* comic book. He looked like he was H. G. Wells's Invisible Man in his bandage disguise.

"What the fuck happened to him?" Paulie said, not really expecting an answer, but he must have said it a little too loud.

Two Black GIs were sitting at the table next to us. One of them snickered and said, "He's the BBQ man. *Barbecued.*"

"How'd he get so fucked up?" asked Miklos.

"Napalmed his own ass," said the GI. "Just mindin' the burgers, man. Big time barbecue at the Service Club couple weeks back."

"Oh, man," said Paulie under his breath.

"*Zippoed* his ass with lighter fluid," said the other GI. "*Kaboom!*" He made an exploding gesture in front of his face and the two of them laughed and slapped hands. They told us the corporal had leaned down to pick up a can of lighter fluid on one of the grills on the lower patio. It had exploded in his face.

"Don't look at *me*," said Miklos.

III

# The Train to Pusan

# The Train to Pusan

## 1950

By the second day of the invasion, he no longer knew where he was. Perhaps if he had taken the better-known roads or met people who could have told him what village he had just passed . . . but everyone was hiding, or, if they saw him approach—those old men and women who had stayed behind to look after their crops—they would run the other way into the woods or hole up inside their thatched farmhouses.

The only man who talked to him was an old farmer who'd been abandoned by his family two nights earlier, as he'd slept, and was now waiting to drum up the courage to kill himself.

"What's the use in living anymore?" he said. "My wife left me and went off to the next world by herself seven years ago. She made me promise to look after our son and our daughter-in-law, and their two stupid brats who probably won't amount to anything now. How could they, with the world gone to ruin? And look at me!" He gestured to himself, sitting on the wooden *maru* with his legs hanging off the side over the straw sandals he had left on the stepping-stone.

"You look perfectly fine to me," he said.

"I said *look* at me!" The old man raised the side of his undershirt, which was all he wore other than the cut-off green army pants of a farmer. His left side, under the ribs, was mottled with scar tissue, and a raised red line ran from his navel diagonally up to his right kidney. "You see! I'm not all here. Something had to be taken out—a spleen or a bladder, or something of that sort—I don't even know what. But now I can't eat properly. I have no stamina. Everything—sound, smell, taste, touch—it all bothers me to no end, and I haven't had a decent night's sleep since that doctor cut me open. Cost us half our land, that surgery. Now do you see why they left me?"

"Seems to me it must have been because of your attitude."

At this the old man burst out laughing, wagged a finger, put on his sandals, and went into the kitchen to return with a kettle of *makkolli*. "Let's have a drink and eat up all the good stuff that's left. I'll bring out the kimchi that daughter-in-law of mine hid away. Why don't you make us a pot of rice and we'll celebrate my trip to the Westward Land. Can you cook rice?"

He did cook an acceptable pot of rice, though they both understood the danger of smoke being seen by soldiers or refugees. The People's Army had already been through the village, plundering everything they could, and the ox, and the pig, and most of the chickens—even the dog—were already gone. They had ransacked the house, and although the old man had cleaned up the *maru* and one of the rooms, which he had decided to die in, the place looked abandoned, with most of the sliding doors kicked to pieces and rice-paper panels torn.

They took their time eating, chatting aimlessly about this and that, the old man reminiscing about the years under the Japanese and how his life had actually improved, if you thought about it—but who would want to live even a good life under those savage bastards when they made you change your name and mute your own language? "Better to curse each other in Korean than fawn over each other in Japanese," he said. "And yet, look at us now, at each other's throats as usual. What sin do you suppose our ancestors committed to give us such terrible karma?"

After that, they smoked, and the old man gave him the two packs of cigarettes he'd buried in a storage jar by the cow shed. He even took some sturdy cloth from the smashed cabinet and made a traditional carry sack that could be worn over the shoulders like a knapsack, and in it he put whatever he thought might be useful for a traveler.

"Consider yourself a wandering *nagunae*," the old man said. "Take your time and be cautious, because the soldiers from either side will kill you as a spy. Or just for fun—who knows what happens to their minds in war? You take all this. I won't be needing it, and to have distractions like food and cigarettes, well, it's only liable to give me an excuse to live longer."

He gave two of the cigarettes back to the farmer—one from each pack—and that made the old man laugh again. "You're not going to stop me from doing away with myself, but you don't want to be around to see it either? Is that it? Two cigarettes doesn't buy much time. You could hardly get far with that putrid foot of yours.

"I have a small favor to ask of you," said the old man. "Come with me for a moment." He went out to the back field, where a walnut tree grew and a small platform had been rigged around it to offer a seat in the shade. From there he took a couple of steps to the east, facing that way, spreading his arms like wings, as if he would flap them and rise into the overhanging branches. "Stand here, where I'm standing, and when you look straight ahead, you'll see the point where the rounded tops of two hills form a sharp valley in the middle. Think of a plump woman's buttocks. Now if you look where your left arm is pointing, you'll see the central peak of another hill, a breast, and if you look down your right arm, you'll see the same, the other breast. There's only one spot in this valley where you can do this." He pronounced the names of the four hills and repeated them, saying, "Now you have them memorized and you can return to this very spot after the war. Who knows who will win? Maybe some descendant of yours—a communist even—will be the one to come here. Just remember.

"Below my feet, if you dig down five or six hand spans, you'll find a small clay jar. There's some gold in there, enough to buy yourself a good house, and there's a hairpin made of white gold and a set of jade eggs. Keep the gold, but promise to bury the pin and the eggs again in an auspicious place so they'll be together and undisturbed." When he said he could just take everything after the old man killed himself, he got more laughter. "You can't be carrying gold and jewels with you at a time like this in your condition! And I can see you have some learning in you, and some honor, for what that's worth. That's why I'm telling you, though I never told my own son, that unfilial bastard! Now come and stand here and show me you can find this spot, since the tree may be gone, for all we know, with bombs and tanks and the like that the war might bring this way."

He found the spot precisely at his first try, and the old man was happy. "So you have a sense of *p'ung* and *su*. You must know a bit of geomancy then. Now I know you can find those things. I insist you do as I ask or my ghost will torment you."

"What about your body? And your ancestral graves?"

"We came down from Manchuria," said the old man. "My wife is cremated, and what the hell do I care about the disposition of my body when I'll be leaving it? Let the animals have it, for all I care. I can't exactly expect you to linger here and bury it or burn it. If you have the wherewithal, maybe you could burn this old shack down with my body in it?"

"I suppose that's not too hard for a last request," he said to himself under his breath, but the old man heard it.

"Let's go in now and finish the *makkolli* and have a smoke. Then we'll call it a night."

Again, though it was especially dangerous after dark, they lit a fire. They heated up another pot of *makkolli* and drank it, chewing on dried squid the old man produced from somewhere. The old man seemed magical. Perhaps it was his resolve to die that made him so easy with everything, like a comfortable warm breeze in fall. Or perhaps he was just like that, naturally, and what a terrible thing, then, that his own son would abandon him in his sleep.

They stayed up late into the night, drinking, telling each other stories, exchanging bits of wisdom when they learned that they were both inclined toward the lesser-understood paths of Taoist alchemy, though they were ignorant dilettantes at it. The old man even examined his foot and helped wrap it again in fresh herbs, despite the horrid smell, and before they slept he explained that the People's Army had mentioned a push all the way down the peninsula. They anticipated that the bridges across the Han River would be blown up to delay them. "Go across by ferry or make yourself a raft," the old man said. "Just don't go anywhere near Seoul, and when you're across the Han, make your way south to Pusan. Once you cross the Nakdong River, you should be safe for a while."

"How do you know all this when you're just a farmer?"

"I overheard a couple of Red officers talking when they commandeered this shack. I don't even know why they bothered to let me live, but now all this has attached itself to your karma, my friend. I was in the Japanese infantry during the Pacific War—too old to be conscripted, but I had special surveying skills. I was in Nanking during the terror, and it still haunts me. Everything they say is true, all the atrocities, the rape, the murder of children, even worse than you can imagine. Your karma— make the best of it, because I fear all of that will happen here, but with Koreans against Koreans." The old man confessed his sins in Nanking, and he described secrets of ecstasy he had learned from an old Chinese Taoist, which had to do with how the hairpin and jade eggs were used.

By then he was so drunk and tired, he couldn't tell if he was awake or dreaming. He passed out listening to the old man's rambling.

Early in the morning, he woke to the twittering of birds in the walnut tree. He was cold out on the exposed *maru*, and he went into the main room to find the old man dead, wrapped up in a blanket as if he had already put himself in a shroud. He didn't think it was possible for a man simply to lie down and die, and he was right—the old man had strangled himself with a thin piece of rope rigged with a one-way knot that could be tightened but not loosened. On the floor by the bed mat was an assortment of items that could be used for barter: a gold pin, a watch, a broach, two rings. Underneath them, a scrap of rice paper torn from a door panel, and on it a terse note scrawled in pencil: "Do what you promised."

He gathered up what food and other supplies he thought he could carry, including the leftover rice from the night before, which he pressed into several balls and wrapped in cloth. He gathered up some of the broken furniture in the house—a couple of tables, a smashed cabinet, a stool—and stacked them around the old man's body. Then, lighting himself a cigarette, he turned the match to a wad of newspaper, which he used to ignite what was left of a door. It caught slowly, just as the paper exhausted itself into black ash and a few red embers.

Once the wood caught, he left the room with his makeshift rucksack and a cloth bag of additional supplies. At the walnut tree, he found his bearings and located the spot. Smoke curled out of the open door of the main room, and then a side window collapsed with a white billow that obscured the entire side of the mud-walled house. He checked to be sure he had filled his canteen and then headed off southeast across the remnants of the vegetable fields. When he looked back at the farmhouse, the thatched roof was dancing with wild red flames.

HE WANDERED AIMLESSLY for several days, unable to decide whether to go back to Sambongni and join the women or make his way south to Pusan as the old man had instructed. Near Wonju, where the terrain grew too rough for him even with his improvised walking stick, he stopped in a school and found a useful map in one of the empty classrooms. He hid for half the afternoon when he heard military vehicles passing, and when he finally came out into the schoolyard, he found several bodies—two of them in student uniforms—and from the weeping woman who had come to claim her son, he learned that the old man had been right.

The Han River bridge had been blown up in the middle of the night on the twenty-eighth with thousands of people on it, but that had delayed the North Koreans only momentarily. The next day, their Russian tanks took the railroad bridge. He should go southwest, the woman told him, staying away from the roads, and he should be careful at the river. The South Korean Army was useless, and the North Koreans were already bringing down their propaganda and re-education corps. The fall harvests would go on as if there had been no war, they had told the woman. That was a promise from the Great General Kim Il-sung himself, who would arrive shortly and visit each community in person to bring inspiration and motivation. And then they had shot her father and son.

Making his way westward now, he saw ruined villages every few miles, some still smoldering, and, all along the roadside, dead villagers, refugees, and soldiers—mostly South Korean. In order to avoid the bridge, he took a full day to walk farther south and reached the river at Tokun-ri. He crossed the road under the cover of night and followed a young woman with an infant and widowed mother to the place where they said a boat would take them across.

The river shimmered in the moonlight. The bloated bodies floating in it hardly looked human; they were so swollen, the seams on their clothing stretched to bursting. They all floated facedown in the river, looking like so many large waterskins filled to capacity; and because he could not see their faces, he did not even mind having to push them out of the way with his walking stick as the boatman pulled his long creaking oar back and forth.

On the other side, he learned that he would have to go north again if he wanted to get over the hills. Southward was too dangerous at the moment, though the roads would be better. The infection in his foot had flared up from so many days of walking, and he had run out of medicine. The only thing to do now was to keep it clean, give it some air, and rest—hard enough to do under normal circumstances but impossible now.

He had time to think about the old farmer—the man's uncommon resolve. How easy, it seemed, it had been for him to take his own life. Perhaps that was from his training in the Japanese Army, where the code required suicide before surrender and to be taken prisoner was the biggest disgrace of all. He had heard about the Japanese contempt for their European and American prisoners of war, how they abused and humiliated them while they kept them alive to use as slave labor and bargaining chips. But the old man's bravery had been more than just training. It was only part of the journey, he had said, not the ending, and this life—the one you knew only because of memory—was surely not the whole story.

I wish I had the old man's courage, he thought to himself. Why am I so afraid? Is it fear, or is it my attachment to life that makes me this suffering coward when I could simply do what he did? And what if he was wrong? What if this *is* all there is?

At the next village he met a helpful middle-aged woman. He exchanged one of the rings the old man had left for him, and with some herbal medicine, food, and fresh socks, he holed up in an abandoned woodcutter's shack on a hillside in the forest. It was not much of a dwelling, but it had a roof and a stove, just as the woman described, and even a small creek not too far away. He applied a poultice to his foot, made himself some rice, and slept with his belly full and warm.

He awoke in the middle of the night with terrible stomach cramps and staggered out of the shack to empty his bowels in the moonlit woods. He barely had time to get his pants down before the diarrhea started. His body shook, as if he were freezing. Before he was done, he heard voices coming up the path, so he kept quiet, continuing to squat there even while his legs burned with the strain of holding that position.

It was the woman who had sold him the food—and two other voices, both men—speaking just above a whisper. He couldn't judge how far away they were, the trees distorting sound as they did, but they were clearly coming up the hill toward the shack.

Why are they not calling out to me? he thought. Maybe they don't want to wake me because the woman knows I'm sick. Maybe they're coming up to help me. He had to stop himself, then, from laughing out loud at the ridiculous, wishful thought. How likely was it, really, that she'd be bringing help to a stranger? No, they were probably policemen, these men, or soldiers coming to investigate a suspected deserter.

"I'm sure he's dead by now," said the woman.

"I told you not to use too much," said one of the men. "If he's dead, how will he tell us if he hid something?"

"Don't worry—I only gave him a little bit. He was too sick and weak for more than that."

"It should be right here," said the other man. "There's a tree stump at the side of the path."

He saw their silhouettes in the moonlight as they passed, hardly more than an arm's length or two away. The two men were carrying farm tools—a long-handled shovel and a hoe. They intend to bury me, he thought. The woman must have poisoned me.

In a moment they had entered the shack, and he heard them thumping around and arguing. One of the men wanted to track him, but when they found his carry bag and its measly contents, he heard slapping sounds, then the woman crying and recriminating. The second man stopped the beating. "How was she supposed to know this was all he had? They usually have more with them. Let's go."

"Should we find his body, at least? The rice is still here. He wouldn't have left it if he was alive."

"Maybe he knew that was what made him sick. Maybe you dosed him right and he crawled into the woods somewhere and died. What difference does it make now?"

"He may go to the police."

There was only laughter in reply, even from the woman. Leaving the shack, they made a quick circuit around the premises before finding their way back down the path. He hardly knew if he could remain as he was, squatting with his pants around his ankles.

Finally, they were gone, but when he tried to stand, his legs were dead, like logs, and he tipped over. He lay there for several minutes, massaging his legs and moaning as the blood returned and brought with it the searing pain, the pins and needles, about which he could do nothing.

Back inside the shack he squinted and crawled around on the floor trying to determine what they had taken and what they had left, but it was too dark. At dawn, when he awoke early from uneasy sleep, he found that they hadn't even bothered to take the sack, only the money and trinkets they thought worthwhile. He could barely move, and his face seemed swollen to twice its normal size.

The day felt unusually hot. But it was actually his fever—soon he would have the chills. I should write a note to myself in case the fever gets serious, he thought. Who I am and where I should be going. And where *should* I be going, now that once again I have nothing?

Already his mind was clouded by the fever. With a scrap of rice paper and a pencil he had taken from the old man's house, he wrote himself a note. Something a stranger or a simpleton could read and understand. He wrote his name, and under that: "I am going to Pusan." That was all he would need.

"Now I must wash," he said to himself, "before the fever gets any worse," and he knew the fact that he was speaking out loud was a bad sign. "I have to wash," he said again. "If I get any of my shit on my foot, I'm a dead man." He nodded to himself as if to reinforce the seriousness of that observation and then dragged himself out of the shack onto the small path that led to the creek. He was able to walk a couple dozen steps with the help of his walking stick before collapsing to crawl the rest of the way. He felt sleepy and, his mind wandering, he began to suspect he was still at home, lying on his comfortable *yo*, dreaming that the war had begun.

"I am going to the creek to wash," he told himself again. "I am going to wash," he said yet again, only this time he answered, in his mind, "After I rest a moment. Just a moment to close my tired eyes and let my limbs recover. Just a moment. Just five minutes in the sun." And then he closed his eyes.

HE WAS ON a railway platform. He knew, even before opening his eyes, from the distinctive smell of creosote and tar. It felt as if he were just waking up after a long and heavy sleep, but he was already sitting up with his back against a pole.

There were people everywhere—civilians and soldiers alike—and the civilians had piles of belongings stacked around them, as if to form the walls of temporary homes. At first he couldn't seem to hear anything but a dull, loud murmuring, and then the noises resolved into a terrible cacophony that made his head pound. Everyone was yammering and shouting, and above all that was a horrible, unintelligible, mechanical din.

What had jolted him into consciousness, in fact, was a conical green loudspeaker at the top of the pole that emitted a string of crackling, distorted announcements. Half of this was in a foreign language—probably English from the number of American uniforms he saw on the platform—but the other half, surely Korean, was incomprehensible because the voice was too distorted or spoke some rural dialect. Or was it his own ears that had turned the speech to gibberish?

He looked around to get his bearings and saw that he had a fresh hospital dressing on his foot; it felt almost comfortable. But his boot had disappeared. He was sitting on a thick cushion, what seemed to be a small, rolled-up *yo* for bedding, tied with straps to make it easy to carry. His clothing was gone too, and in its place he wore a clean white shirt, far too large for him, and green army pants rolled up to the knees. Looped around his good leg was the carry strap of the knapsack the old man had made for him, and attached to his shirt pocket by a large safety pin was the piece of rice paper on which he had written the note to himself, now neatly folded into quarters.

Hearing a loud explosion behind him, he jerked his head around to look, fearful that the North Koreans were attacking. It was just the steam blast from a black locomotive pulling into the station. It continued to push forward with a thunderous chuffing, followed by the shrill hiss and scream of its brakes, and then the mass of people on the platform surged forward, carrying, pushing, dragging their belongings. There were mountains of huge *pojagi*s everywhere, packed with clothes, bedding, housewares, and even, occasionally, books. A few families had A-frames, and on one of them he saw an expensive black-lacquered wardrobe inlaid with mother-of-pearl. The poor and the rich mingled here like rice and chaff.

Two-wheeled *nikoda* carts piled with possessions had been blocked off at the far end of the station, where the American soldiers maintaining order seemed to give up as the crowd rushed the train cars, already half full of troops. People crammed themselves through the narrow doors of the passenger cars and then opened the windows to receive their baggage and haul their friends and relatives through. Others scrambled up the metal ladders at the ends of the cars and set up on the roofs, lashing themselves to their belongings, even as the American soldiers gestured with horizontal cutting motions, yelling at them to get back down.

Though he still did not know where he was or how he had gotten there, he realized he should probably get on the train. And so he stood up, bracing himself against the pole, only to be knocked down by a fat bundle slung from someone's back. Cursing, he tried getting up again, this time more warily, with his back against the pole, suddenly fearful of getting trampled by the crowd. Having someone step on his injured foot could be a fatal disaster.

"Mr. Lee, you're awake!" called a cheery voice—a woman's—in a peculiar accent he had never heard before. "Please be careful!"

He turned to see a strange form in long black skirts and a black robe, with a white headdress that curved like an awning over her face and a white collar piece that extended to the shoulders, separating her into black and white with the demarcation line across the heart. This was no hallucination, he realized momentarily, but a nun, a Christian woman married to the God whose son was nailed to the cross. A Catholic, too, not one of those overzealous Protestants who said everything Korean was of the devil and tried to convert people through fear. Only, what was she doing here? And the other figures, just like her, at the far end of the platform?

"What happened to me, sister?" he asked, raising his voice to be heard over the din. When she stood in front of him she loomed—a giant of a woman, more than a head taller than he was. The skin of her face was so pale from being sheltered under her coif that he could see the bluish veins at her temples, where strands of damp golden hair peeked out. Her eyes, large and round, looked like transparent holes through which he could see the sky beyond the back of her skull.

"You were bringing from that hospital," she said in her broken Korean. "You say you go to *Puusan*. Yesterday. Today your fever returned this morning. How are you feeling, Mr. Lee?" Her accent was unearthly— the way she made everything round made it seem that something other than a human was speaking, and yet not an animal either. He wondered what her own language must sound like from her tongue, whether her voice was pleasant or melodious, her inflection that of a peasant or an aristocrat.

"Where am I?" he said. "All I remember is that some people tried to kill me and rob me. I was in a woodcutter's shack in the forest."

He must have spoken too quickly, because she did not seem to understand. He spoke in the Seoul dialect, which was what she was trying to speak.

"Mr. Lee goes into the train," she said, pointing. "Into the train. Please go." She pointed now to the roof of the rail car and made an exaggerated shake of her head, causing her white headpiece to extend and contract like the wings of a preening egret. "The top is not possible," she said. "The leg is too short." And then, like the American soldiers, she made a sweeping, cutting motion with her hand. "Do you know, Mr. Lee?"

She had used the word "leg" instead of "foot," a mistake understandable from a foreigner. "I know," he said. "If I injure my foot trying to go up there, it may have to be amputated." At least that was what made the most sense to him. The nun was smiling brightly; her lips were so red they looked like fresh-cut meat. She gestured for him to follow, and as she led him to the train, her black skirts billowing, people cleared the way. All the cacophony seemed to recede now. The American soldiers were gesturing like angry deaf-mutes and shouting in their *shwalla-shwalla* language, and Korean soldiers had taken to hitting people, shoving them, smacking them on the backs with their rifle butts. But the nun had a supernatural calm that touched everything around her, and he knew it must be the power of her God. He had seen plenty of Taoist charlatans, two-bit shamans, Christian preachers, and none of them had power like this.

The far end of the car was full of soldiers, but on this nearer end the civilians, already packed to overflowing, somehow made room for him; they pulled him and his bedroll in through the door and down the aisle into the compartment, where the air was hot and stifling, reeking of sweat and food gone bad. He saw the nun kissing her crucifix out on the platform, and then she waved at him, her bright smile full of beautiful white teeth. Then she was gone into the crowd.

It wasn't long before the people in the compartment had begun to crush against him. Desperate to guard his foot, he tried to get to a corner.

"Who are you?" some woman asked. In her headscarf, which was a thin towel, and from her dark skin, she looked like she might be a local farmer's wife. "Why did that *tokkaebi* woman bring you here to this car?" she asked.

He tried to explain that he himself didn't know, but the woman clearly didn't believe him. "How do we know you're not a spy?" she asked loudly, so others could hear. "He got special treatment! Does anybody recognize him? He's not *from* here."

"Where *are* you from?" someone asked. But nobody recognized Sambongni, and when he described its location, someone shouted that he was making it up. "He's a collaborator!" shouted the woman. "That foreign woman was a Russian, for sure, and she put him in here to inform on us!"

"What could I possibly be spying on?" he asked, incredulous. "Is there something secret going on in here that I don't know about?" His attempt to dismiss her question with sarcasm, however, was exactly the wrong thing to do.

"He's a spy!" the woman yelled. "Let's get him out of our car!" She grabbed at him, and the people around her helped drag him away from the window and shove him into the aisle between an old man and a plump young mother whose infant began to wail. They started pushing, kicking, and pinching, as he clutched his knapsack and bedroll, hopping this way and that, each time closer to the door, until they had managed to shove him out of the car and back onto the platform.

Suddenly, he could breathe again, and he paused to see that people were still scrambling to get their possessions and themselves onto the train.

A Korean military policeman was making his way toward the locomotive engine, poking at people with his billy club. "Mr. MP, sir!" he called out. "They threw me off! Where can I get back on?" He gestured at the note pinned to his shirt, as if that would make a difference, but it was gone. The safety pin had torn off, leaving a rip over his pocket. The MP just gave him a contemptuous look and pointed to the top of the car.

All the cars, and even the engine, were covered in baggage, with people sitting on top and in between bundles. Some of them were lashed to their belongings with rope or strips of cloth. The whole train suddenly reminded him of the time he had seen a large, fat silk moth caterpillar swarming with ants, squirming in vain to get them off even as they bit it to pieces. Quickly, he looked around for help, but the nuns were gone and the American soldiers had probably boarded the passenger cars toward the back of the train. At the far end of the platform, a fresh crowd of civilians was pushing against a locked gate where Korean soldiers stood guard with rifles. The train began puffing steam and let out a sharp whistle, and a black-uniformed rail worker signaled from the rear.

Now the train began to move, almost imperceptibly at first. It hardly seemed possible under all that weight. He gawked for a moment at its awesome strength and then he rushed to the metal ladder at the end of the boxcar and climbed up, his bedroll slung on one shoulder and his knapsack around the other. The motion of the train swung him momentarily to the left, and he saw a young woman with a small *pojagi* bundle sitting on the coupling between the cars. "Come up!" he called, but she remained where she was, and he continued climbing, one rung at a time, pushing with only his good, booted foot. The other foot hurt terribly at the slightest bit of weight put on it.

"Where do you think *you're* going?" said a middle-aged Korean man in a threadbare European suit when he reached the top of the car.

"I'm going to Pusan just like you. I was told to come up here by the MP back there." Already, the station was receding behind them, and he could see the huge mass of people that had been left behind. Some of the more able-bodied were running after the train, trying to scramble on, but the people on board pushed them off.

"Go back down," said the man. "This place is ours."

"Where?" he protested. "There's nowhere to go."

"Go!" Now the man drew a large kitchen knife and scooted forward from where he'd been sitting on top of a bundle of clothes.

"You have space up here. I can sit over there."

The man came closer and tapped the handhold of the metal ladder with the knife blade—*ting!*

"I'll fall off! How can you do this?"

The man rummaged in a *pojagi* and produced a long cloth belt—it was yellow, probably from one of the martial arts *kwan*s that had become popular in those days. "Tie yourself with this, then," he said. "But if you try to come up again, I'll cut your throat."

In no condition to fight the man, he took the belt and began to climb back down, wondering how he would tie himself to the ladder. The wind was fresh as the train sped up and it felt cool against his skin. He understood why people would prefer to ride on top, certainly in this kind of weather. His hair slapped against his face, stinging, and he squinted to protect his eyes.

The train rattled and creaked horribly, and at certain points on rough track it leaned one way and then the other, nearly shaking him off the ladder. He tied himself to it, but it wasn't long before he realized there was simply no way to get comfortable. Whether he stood or sat with his knees hooked over the rung, whether he faced the wall of the car or away, every position was painful after only a few minutes. His injured foot throbbed, and the wind from the train, he discovered, was chilling him. He began to shiver and realized he would have to find some way to cover himself with the bedroll.

When he tried to climb back up and plead for a space, the man nearly cut off his finger, and he quickly scrambled back down. The only solution would be to make his way to the next car and try there—though that maneuver would be dangerous. The ground, when he looked down, was a dizzying blur, so he focused on the rivets on the railcar as he made his way to the bottom of the ladder, the yellow belt streaming beside him in the wind. The only way to make the traverse to the ladder of the next car was to walk along the tiny ledge, around the corner, and over the coupling, where the woman still sat, hunched and shivering now from the wind chill in the shadowed space between the cars.

Now that he could see the gravel and the rail ties blurring by underneath him between the cars, he was even more afraid of falling. With the yellow belt he rigged a kind of harness that he could untie when he had more secure footing at the coupling, and he inched forward. The woman watched him, her chin tucked into her chest like a bird in the cold. She had put on all her spare clothes since leaving the station. He thought of the bloated bodies he had seen in the river.

It was only a few feet to the coupling—hardly anything when the train was stationary, but with everything shaking like this, and the wind howling, it took what seemed hours before he was able to step past the hose hookup and reach the rusted metal knuckles, far more massive than he'd anticipated. They looked like two giant turtle heads, one protruding from each car, biting each other by the mouth and refusing to let go.

The woman sat just past the middle, toward the other car, and he could not tell how she managed to hunch over like that, bent nearly double, and yet keep her perch. He untied himself, then cinched the belt around his waist. He tied the other end to the strap on his bedroll, which he placed on the grimy metal knuckle. He straddled it, feeling foolish as he scooted along the coupling toward the woman. He remembered how he had sat on a log like this once when he was a boy, how the other children had made fun of him because they could all easily walk across the log to the other side of the creek.

The way the woman looked at him—with her chin lowered and the whites of her eyes showing at the bottom—seemed wary, almost sinister. She was trying to hug herself to preserve her warmth, but because she had to keep her legs apart and her feet on either side of the metal knuckles, the wind blew up under her skirt, up to her chin, flapping her headscarf and her hair. Even in the roar of the wind, he thought he could hear her chattering teeth.

"Why don't you go up?" he shouted at her, pointing to the top of her car. She just shook her head.

He scooted forward and asked again, his face now practically touching hers.

"It's too dangerous," she said. He understood that her experience at the top of the other car had been similar to his.

"Why aren't you inside a passenger car?"

"They threw me out."

"Why would they throw *you* out?"

She didn't answer but moved her eyes as if to say, "Look at me."

He looked at her, curious now, with fresh eyes, and saw that her headscarf, though soiled with grease and dirt, was made of a fine, patterned cloth, and her hairstyle was one the country folk would criticize for requiring a beauty parlor. Her clothes might also have been fashionable Western clothes, for all he knew, though they were hardly attractive all worn at the same time. Her shoes were certainly impractical. With his nose barely an inch from her face, he could also smell her faint perfume in the wind, a pleasant floral scent, probably overpowering in normal circumstances but here just the subtlest reminder of rose and hibiscus. Suddenly he realized she must be a GI prostitute. That was why they had thrown her out of the passenger car. But then why wasn't she riding with the American soldiers?

"I'm going to try to go up," he said after a while. "Will you move so I can get past you?"

Grabbing hold of a metal bracket, the woman braced herself so she could move to the side. He scooted forward again and reached past her, leaning into her body as if they were embracing. Now, on the same side of the huge metal knuckles, they had to twist and contort, practically wrestling each other, until he was safely across. Covered in sweat now and breathing heavily from the effort, he suddenly felt the intense cold.

"Thank you!" he shouted. But even as he was stepping onto the ledge of the car, the woman grabbed him by the yellow belt, nearly yanking him off balance. He was about to kick her with a well-spent curse when she said, "Don't go. You'll die."

"What?" he responded. "And how would *you* know?"

"Stay here with me," she said. "Just until the train stops at the next station. Then you can go. I'm freezing to death, see? Please."

He looked up at the top of the car and at the metal ladder, which on this side seemed dangerously rusted. He was shivering now, and so he made his way back to the woman and they unrolled his bedroll, which had a thin blanket inside. They made a seat with a back, lashed themselves together with the belt and the bedroll straps, and hugged each other, covering themselves with the blanket. After a while he was warm. The woman stopped shivering, and although they were hardly in comfort on top of the steel knuckles, he began to feel drowsy.

"You saved my life," said the woman.

He made a dismissive noise, which she probably couldn't hear in the wind. He could look down now at the blur of gravel and wood without being afraid. He felt like a kid sitting out a cloudburst inside a hay rick. "If only there was something good to eat," he said.

"I have some chocolate," said the woman.

"Cho-co-late," he repeated.

Just then the train lurched, as if struck by a giant hand. And again, and again—there was a rhythm to it—and at the ninth or tenth strike, which was the strongest, they heard screams, even above the noise of the train, and suddenly the air was full of bundles and people, raining down from the sky: An old man in glasses, wearing a blue business suit; a woman with her infant strapped to her back, still lashed to a bundle of bedding; *pojagi*s of every size and color; a little girl with her eyes and mouth wide open, missing her two front teeth; an old grandmother in traditional white, her eyes clenched shut.

Beneath them they saw that the tracks were suddenly gone, with no ground, only water below, and the sound of their motion suddenly opened up, like a vast sigh. They were hurtling over a steel-framed bridge, and its low crossbeams were sweeping everything on top down into the river far below. It happened so fast he might have missed it if he had closed his eyes even for a moment.

Years later when he closed his eyes, he would still see it.

# The Fort

## 1974

Every Korean kid—even those who don't know a single Chinese character—knows the opening verse of *The Thousand Word Classic: Hanul ch'on tta chi, komul hyon nurul hwang.* *Ch'on* and *chi* are "Heaven" and "Earth," and *hyon* and *hwang* are their colors, but more than just visible colors, they refer to their cosmological qualities. *Hyon* and *hwang* could be translated simply as "dark" and "yellow," but they are more accurately "darkling" and "dunning," the old Chinese characters being noun, verb, and adjective all at the same time.

This is one of the things Housebound Uncle had taught me when he discovered how ignorant I was about language. He had been a schoolteacher down near Pusan, but since he had dodged his required years of service in the Korean National Guard, he'd had to stay out of public places until the statute of limitations expired. Otherwise, he risked being arrested by any curious policeman. Housebound Uncle stayed in the back room of the house with his wife, Nokchon Cousin, usually playing solitaire *paduk* all day, or working out the strategy puzzles that appeared in the newspaper. We all knew when he had solved one because he would let out a loud "That's it!" and snap the black and white stones so loudly on the wooden board it sounded like shots from a cap gun.

Sometimes when Little Uncle came down from Sambongni, he and Housebound Uncle would sit out in the courtyard and insult each other as they played on the special *paduk* table that Housebound Uncle saved for guests—an unusually heavy one with the grid lines burnt into the wood. *Paduk* was supposed to be much harder than *chang'gi*, everyone seemed to agree, though no one could explain to me how such an apparently simple game could be more sophisticated than one that had more complicated rules and playing pieces. I had thought *chang'gi* was like Western chess while *paduk* was like an extra-large game of checkers in which you couldn't move or jump pieces once they were on the board. Housebound Uncle and Yongsu both laughed at that, and that is when I found out that Old Man Heaven had died.

Old Man Earth and Yongshiggi's grandfather had come out to the maple tree late that day because they had run into each other down the alley in Tatagumi and got into an argument about *chang'gi* and *paduk*. Old Man Earth told Yongshiggi's grandfather that he was a master *paduk* player—as good as the Japanese *go* masters who had played the *toketsu no ikkyoku*, the legendary "blood-spitting game" with the three ghost moves. He excused himself for having spoken some Japanese and said he only played *chang'gi* to humor Old Man Heaven and to let him win. Yongshiggi's grandfather didn't believe that story, of course, because he himself was a real *paduk* master of the fifth *dan*, and he challenged Old Man Earth on the spot. They had stopped at the rice seller's store to borrow his board and stones but couldn't leave politely without a cup of coffee and some chitchat with the rice seller's father. When they finally got to the tree after lunchtime, they were shocked to see Money Changer Grandfather sitting on the platform. In over twenty years of acquaintance, they had never seen him sitting before.

Money Changer Grandfather wore traditional white, just like they did, along with a horsehair hat and black leather shoes. That day he had taken his shoes off to sit on the platform, and they could see the bottoms of his white socks as he sat there with his legs sticking straight out, smoking his bamboo tobacco pipe. Old Man Earth was about to yell something and give the money changer a piece of his mind. But when he rushed forward, his finger already wagging, he realized why Money Changer Grandfather was sitting in that strange pose: Old Man Heaven's head was in his lap. No horsehair hat—just his head, wearing the traditional headband—and when Old Man Earth was close enough, he saw that Old Man Heaven was dead and that the money changer was chanting sutras under his breath as he smoked.

The three old men sat there with the body under the Japanese maple, silent, then sobbing, by turns, and the neighborhood people went about their business for more than two hours not paying any attention, until Old Man Heaven's granddaughter came with snacks and discovered what had happened.

That morning, while waiting with his usual impatience for Old Man Earth to arrive, Old Man Heaven must have dropped his hat as he fidgeted with it. He would have leaned forward to pick it up, and his heart stopped. Just like that. Old Money Changer Grandfather had found him bent over as if he were examining something fascinating, perhaps a bug, on the crown of his horsehair hat. It took him a while to realize that Old Man Heaven had stopped breathing. And then there was nothing to be done save comfort the passing spirit. The *chang'gi* board was still laid out with the last position from the previous day's game, and Money Changer Grandfather was sitting there, smoking his pipe, working out the near-infinite possibilities for both the red and the blue sides when Old Man Earth and Yongshiggi's grandfather showed up.

Since then, Old Man Earth had taken to his bed from grief, and preparations were underway for Old Man Heaven's funeral. Many of the younger people in the neighborhood didn't want a traditional funeral that would put a stop to everything else for days, but the old people insisted, and so Tatagumi was preparing for the long procession with the bier and the hempen-clad mourners all the way to Medicine Mountain.

◆ ◆ ◆

THE NIGHT BEFORE the funeral procession, Miklos, Paulie, and I met up at the ASCOM bowling alley and bowled a few games until closing time. Afterward, we went to the "Fort," our secret hideout in the rafters of the GIs' latrine and shower house.

There were also showers at the post gym, with lockers that made them safer, and we usually showered there after our Tae Kwon Do class, but the Fort was special. Miklos had discovered it by accident during the summer while he was sitting in one of the toilet stalls in the back part of the building, the common bathroom facility for the group of barracks near the baseball field and the obstacle course. The middle part of the building was lined with four rows of sinks, with a door leading to the communal shower room and another door leading to the toilet stalls and urinals.

Every stall had its requisite KILROY WAS HERE tag with the little cartoon of the bald guy sticking his penis nose over the wall. The stalls also had at least one FTA (Fuck the Army) and a few SHORT! declarations, the word "Short" followed by the number of days the GI had left in Korea— SHORT 22 DAYS—or sometimes an ETS with a date for the GI's Expiration of Term of Service in the Army—ETS 02/09. Sometimes there were mysterious messages with rendezvous times: FRIDAYS 2130 HRS. SHOW IN 3RD PISSER. SHAKE 3 TIMES, or, more simply: SHOW FOR BLOW. Two of the corner stalls had large holes drilled into the dividing walls near the toilet paper dispensers. Paulie and I thought these were for sharing paper in case you ran out and had to borrow from a neighbor, but Miklos explained they were called "glory holes" and you stuck your dick through them for a blow job. We didn't believe him until he demonstrated that the holes were at the right height by sticking his own flaccid penis through one, and we laughed at him from the other side.

Miklos happened to be looking at an obscene drawing of a vagina on the stall door when he looked up and saw the hatch in the ceiling.

Climbing up the partition between the toilet stalls, he found that the hatch was just a square sheet of plywood placed over the opening. He moved it aside and climbed up into the rafters, thinking he was the first to have discovered the space, only to find evidence that it had already been a hangout.

The first time Miklos took us up to the Fort, we figured out why GIs would bother to climb up there at all. It was terribly hot in the summer, but not as dirty as we expected. On the east side, someone had laid out sheets of cardboard from C-ration boxes to make a floor between the exposed two-by-fours. There was another hatch, which we discovered was in the ceiling of the single room on the southeast corner of the building—the women's bathroom. That room was usually locked, and it had no shower as far as we knew, but when we opened the hatch from above, we saw that in addition to a sink and toilet, there was a built-in drain in the floor, making it a place where Koreans could bathe.

When we asked one of the *ajoshi*s at the bowling alley about the women's bathroom, he told us it used to be for women GIs when they were TDY—on temporary duty—in ASCOM, but they had gotten a new building and now it was for the Korean women who worked on post. "Sometimes *we* use it as a bath house, too," he said. When we pointed out that there was no shower or bath in there, he said, "Korean style," which meant they would fill up the sink and use a little plastic bucket to scoop the water over themselves while they crouched on the cement floor.

All around the opening in the rafters, on the cardboard floor, was the detritus left by the people who'd been sitting or lying around up there, peeking down at what was happening in the women's room. The cigarette butts and gum wrappers looked pretty old, and the stack of *Playboy*s and *Penthouse*s were a couple years out of date.

There was a week when Paulie and I didn't see much of Miklos. We assumed he had gone up to Seoul for a few days to spend some time with his Korean relatives, but when he reappeared, he proudly took us up to the Fort to show us how he had made improvements up there to turn it into what he called our "home away from home." "Just like the Service Club or the fuckin' USO," he said. But it would be all ours. That's when we named it the Fort.

It was dark up there when the hatches were closed. The only light came through the two louvered window vents, one on either end of the building. Miklos had brought up a box of candles and a couple of army flashlights fitted with red filters. On one of the two-by-fours just above the hatch to the women's room, he had tacked a schedule.

"I watched who was using the bathroom," he said. "That list is when the pretty chicks from the bakery and barracks cleaning come up to take a bath. Man, one of them looks just like that actress Kim Jihmi! Don't you wanna see her naked?"

We had all seen plenty of women naked when we were little, in the public bathhouses, where our mothers took us because we had no showers or bathtubs in our houses, let alone hot running water. But there was a big difference between seeing naked women in a bathhouse as a kid and being older, like this, doing something so obviously illicit. I could imagine Patsy punching Miklos for what he had in mind for us, calling him a sick motherfucker.

"You're going to hell," said Paulie. "Fuckin' pervert."

"We didn't come up here for that," I said. "You're on your own, man."

Miklos was pissed off. "You little pussies don't appreciate anything," he said. "Come over here then." He had brought up more sheets of cardboard and laid them out on the western end of the rafters by the vent window. When we crawled all the way across, keeping our feet on the joists, being careful not to step accidentally through the ceiling, we discovered the big surprise. He had gathered up hundreds of feet of discarded parachute cord from the jump tower and laced it criss-cross over the diagonal two-by-fours to make rope beds, which were surprisingly comfortable, though we had to lie on them at an odd angle. He had shored up the floor on that end and even made a flap to cover the vent window, explaining it was to keep the light from showing outside.

"We can spend the night up here now," he said. "I'm fucking tired of always going home before curfew when we're having fun. Just tell your moms you're staying with me and I'll tell my mom I'm staying with one of you guys. They'll never find out."

"What if they all see each other at the same time?" Paulie asked, but then he thought a moment and answered his own question. "Not that they'd care enough to even want to figure it out," he said.

After that, we spent many nights in the Fort during weekends or when we played hooky. The Army kept the shower house so hot it was warm up in the rafters even in winter.

WHEN THE THREE OF US met at the Fort before Old Man Heaven's funeral, I expected we would discuss whether to get the skull water from his grave. On the one hand, it was the perfect opportunity to mark a grave and know, to the day, when we would have to dig it up for our numerological formula to work. On the other hand, Old Man Heaven was someone we knew and respected despite his cantankerousness. When I voiced my misgivings, Paulie pointed out that Old Man Heaven was intelligent—we knew that from his *chang'gi* playing and his knowledge of the classics. If we wanted skull water, his would be ideal for curing a Korean man.

"I read about it somewhere," Paulie said. "There's a headhunter tribe where they eat the brain of their enemy, and they get the dead warrior's power and even the stuff he knows."

"If that's true," said Miklos, "Old Man Hyun was such a bastard he would want his brain to get eaten just so the stuff in there could live longer."

"His soul will be gone, anyway," said Paulie.

Miklos considered this. "We only have to wait forty-nine days for that," he said. "If you believe in bullshit like souls in the first place. So what do you say, Fifty-Seven?"

"Do you think if we had asked him when he was alive, he would have said it was okay?"

"Are you some kind of moron, or what?" said Miklos. "Of course not! You ever hear of a Korean donating his organs? Leaving his body to science? His family would never let some part of his body go missing. They want the whole damn body in one piece, for whatever reason."

"What would your Jesus-mongers say, Polly?" Miklos often called Paulie that to annoy him.

"His soul's gone, man. What happens to his body don't matter because he'll be brought back for the final judgment, regardless."

"See," said Miklos. "*Regardless.* So what're you being such a pussy about?"

"I don't know," I said. "It's just the idea—"

"It's his *ghost*, isn't it? You're afraid of his ghost! Woooo! Woo hoo!" said Miklos. "I'm coming to *get* you, Insu-ya!"

"Shut up!" I said.

"It's only a body," said Paulie. "And besides, you're doing it for a good reason—to help someone. Remember those rugby players who crashed in the Andes and had to eat their teammates to stay alive? Even the Pope said it was okay, like eating the body of Jesus."

I remembered the book about that plane crash, *Alive.* I had flipped through it and seen the pictures of the fuselage half buried in snow and the survivors huddled together, gaunt and scraggly. But I had never actually read it, nor had I ever seen Paulie or Miklos with it. So how did they know all this? Paulie wasn't even a Catholic. I had only noticed the epigraph at the beginning of the book, which I remembered because I thought it was so heroic: "Greater love hath no man than this, that a man lay down his life for his friends." I even remembered the verse number: John 15:13. Thinking of the verse made me think of Catholics, and the way communion was all about eating the body of Christ and drinking his blood and how that wasn't symbolic but actually true, that the wine and the wafer magically turned into the real thing once they were inside you.

Now I was no longer concerned about the savagery or the barbarism of getting the skull water for Big Uncle. Even the Catholics had a ghost— the Holy Ghost, which, according to my father, was the same as God the Father and Christ the Son. My father said I was required to believe that, no matter how illogical it was, if I was going to be a good Catholic. There was no argument allowed—this was church *dogma*, the *real* truth—and I had to take it on faith. "I'll have you talk to a Jesuit sometime. But now you just go ahead and go to confession and get your first communion," he'd told me. He had never brought up the issue again, and I had never gone to confession or communion.

"I'm not afraid of ghosts," I said to Miklos and Paulie.

We left it at that, and before it got any later, we went to the Main Snack Bar and bought a bunch of hamburgers, fries, doughnuts, chocolate bars, and cans of Coke to go. We also got a large Styrofoam cup of percolated to-go coffee for each of us to help us stay awake. The nights always seemed longer in the Fort because we stayed up late to bullshit and play cards by candlelight. We packed everything into paper shopping bags and hauled them up through the hatch, using the parachute cord left over from the woven beds. It was 2230 hours, 10:30 p.m. civilian time, when we closed up the window vent with the black plastic flap and lit our candles for the long night.

We talked about all the people we knew who had died. How they had died. Disease. Old age. Accidents. War. Murder. Suicide. There were plenty of people dying each year, and between the three of us we had seen our share of dead bodies with their limbs protruding from under the straw mats that always covered the evidence of tragedy in public places. Each of us had relatives or friends of the family who had died in the cholera epidemics, were KIA in Vietnam, or just worn out from life. I talked about my cousin Gannan, who had hanged herself when she was pregnant with a GI's baby, and Miklos told us about his aunt who had

been shot at night by a sentry while she was going through the back
fence of an army base near Camp Casey. Paulie had a cousin who had
died after eating a bad batch of pig slop stew, the army mess hall food
scraps cooked in fifty-five-gallon drums and sold in the villages.

"Man," said Paulie. "They scooped that shit up with helmets."

One helmet liner full of pig slop stew was enough to feed a whole
family. I remembered it used to be one of my favorite foods—sometimes
you would find a big hunk of steak or hamburger in it.

"What're you thinking about, Seven?" Paulie asked. He had short-
ened my name.

"I dunno. All this talk about dead people. You know what happened
to Kallah?"

"Kallah? Oh, man," said Miklos, who at that very moment was wearing one of Kallah's shirts.

Kallah was what we called Yongsu's friend; his nickname was "Collar" for the shirts he designed with the fancy swallowtail *chebi* collars.
Yongsu and he had met while they were in juvenile detention together
after getting picked up by the police for *changbal*, having long hair.
Kallah's family was well-off—his father worked for a drug company connected to Hoechst, and they lived in one of the old estate-sized Japanese
houses that had been modernized with hot running water and flush toilets. They even had a personal car and driver. The police didn't usually
detain kids like him for long, but Kallah refused to study for his college
entrance exams and threatened to run away before it was time for his
military service. His father deemed leaving him in detention an appropriate punishment.

As a designer, Kallah was a failure—his trademark collar was just a
sharper, larger version of one that had already gone out of fashion in the
late '60s. He spent two years living in the back room of the big Japanese
house, playing guitar and drawing sketches of shirts, which his mother's
tailor would make as samples. The result was that his friends got the
most unusual shirts. Yongsu, Miklos, Paulie, and I each had several in

cotton, silk, or polyester, all paisley and polka-dot patterns with bright pastel colors. We were meant to be walking advertisements for Kallah, but it was the tailor who got all the business.

Kallah's mother spoiled him, but after he was released from his second round of police detention for long hair, his father stopped giving him money and forbade the production of any more shirts. Then Kallah decided to be a musician, which by his father's reckoning was about the same as being a prostitute, and everything spiraled tragically downhill.

"When's the last time you saw Kallah?" asked Paulie.

"It was with you guys before I left for Germany," I said. "He's dead, man."

WE HAD ALL SEEN Kallah after his failed suicide attempt, when his father had put him in a second-rate Western hospital in Pupyong to avoid scandal. When we visited him there, all wearing his tailored shirts to cheer him up, he was in a dingy room on soiled sheets. With only one staff nurse in the hospital, families had to make their own arrangements to feed and clean the patients. Yongsu had come for several days to change Kallah's diapers, and then, when he had recovered some more, to empty his bedpans. Kallah could barely speak—he just sat against his pillows with one side of his face contorted into a smile and his eyes looking the other way—and he cried when he saw us. Yongsu could make out some of what he was trying to say. "He's happy," Yongsu told us. "He says he never knew his shirts were so beautiful until he saw them on you. He says he's sorry he fucked up and didn't kill himself properly and now you have to see him like this."

The boys who grew up in Pupyong—in every neighborhood, whether it was Tatagumi or Samnung—had a strict code: Any threat, no matter how small, had to be serious. If you picked up a rock in a rock fight and made a threatening gesture, then you had to throw it or use it like a club to smash into someone's head. Otherwise, you were a coward and no one respected you. We challenged each other all the time on those little gestures until hardly anyone made an empty threat. After his father had insulted him and threatened to kick him out and remove his name from the family register, Kallah had threatened to kill himself. He'd just failed to eat enough rat poison to make good on it.

A few weeks later, he told Yongsu, in a note, that he had finally found a purpose in life—revenge. He had resolved to stay alive and devote himself to punishing his father by bringing his entire family to ruin. Kallah knew his mother could never keep a secret, and so he concocted a false confession about why he had really tried to kill himself. He told her that his anger at his father was just the excuse, and that the real reason was his guilt over having raped his brother's fiancée. He told his mother, in strictest confidence, that this was why he always wore women's silk panties instead of men's underwear—to remember the rape.

Kallah's mother was devastated, and it wasn't long until she had told Kallah's brother. In the ensuing fight with his fiancée, Kallah's brother cut her with a scalpel and was arrested by the Seoul police, who beat him so badly he lost the use of an eye. The marriage was off, Kallah's brother was expelled from Seoul National, and shortly thereafter, his father had a stroke from the stress and then lost his job. His mother, who bore the blame for all this misfortune, hanged herself at the front gate of the fiancée's house. Kallah's revenge had succeeded beyond his dreams. He didn't even have to commit suicide afterward because his brother smothered him with a pillow. And now Kallah's brother was in prison.

"EVERYTHING IS ALWAYS fucked up," Miklos said when I finished telling the story. "That's the only thing you can count on with people like us."

"Like us?" said Paulie. "I'm not like Kallah, man!"

"You know what I mean."

"No, I don't," said Paulie.

"That's because you're just a big pussy," said Miklos.

"No. It's because I try to be good." Paulie's statement had a kind of resolve to it. I didn't contradict him by bringing up any of the dozens of things that immediately came to mind, like the very fact that we were spending the night here in the Fort, or that we all helped our mothers with their black marketeering, which could potentially get our fathers court-marshaled and sent to Leavenworth.

"When did you hear all this?" Paulie asked.

"It was when I asked Yongsu why he was wearing silk panties."

"That cousin of yours is so fucked up," Miklos said.

We were silent for a moment and we could hear the patrol jeep driving by outside past the baseball field and the jump tower.

"What would you have done if you were Kallah?" Miklos asked. He put his hands behind his head and leaned back into the ropes.

"I would never try to kill myself," said Paulie. "Suicide sends you right to hell. Maybe I'd run away somewhere. Get away from that family."

"Yeah? Where would you go, man? This is Korea."

"I would be too afraid to kill myself," I said. "What about you?"

"I would've eaten enough of that rat poison in the first place. Couldn't bear it if my friends had to wipe my ass and feed me like a baby. If I ever get like that, one of you promise to shoot my ass, okay?"

Paulie and I didn't answer.

"Okay?" Miklos said again, moving his face back into the candlelight.

"All right," we said.

"Fuckin' A."

"Hey, Seven," said Paulie. "Why does Yongsu wear women's panties?"

"He says it's because they're more comfortable. He learned it from Kallah."

"You should try it sometime," Miklos said.

"Fuck, no."

We didn't actually get to sleep until the siren announced the end of curfew. It was already getting light outside—we could see a line of pale light leaking in under the black plastic curtain. Wrapped in the green wool army blanket and suspended at an angle in the crisscrossed ropes, I felt like a sailor in the hull of an old wooden boat. It took a while for the smell of the candle to dissipate once Miklos blew it out, but eventually I didn't notice the smoke any longer, and I drifted off.

IT WAS THE HEAT that eventually woke me, and when I checked my Timex, I bolted up, nearly launching myself out of the rope bed. I pulled the plastic aside and squinted as the late-morning sun blasted into the rafters, illuminating every speck of suspended dust.

"We'll be late!" I said, looking into the shadows for Miklos and Paulie.

"What's the rush?" said Paulie. "Miklos said it will take them all day to haul the coffin to Medicine Mountain. He went down to get us breakfast."

"Why didn't we all just go for pancakes or something?"

"Beats me."

We quietly crawled to the other side and scouted the room below us to be sure it was empty before we climbed down through the hatch onto the partition of the toilet stall and then dropped to the cement floor. Miklos had just come in the north entrance with bags of food, and we all went out through the south door to the baseball field, where we sat in the bleachers to eat our bacon and egg sandwiches on rye toast. Afterward, we headed out to the gate to catch up to Old Man Heaven's funeral procession. It had gotten only as far as Shipjong-dong, a couple hundred yards past the railroad tracks to Inchon. At this rate it would take them hours to get to the cemetery.

We walked behind the procession of hempen-clad mourners, behind the bier, a fancy box decorated in red, blue, and yellow banners and carved to resemble a rooster or a dragon—we couldn't decide which. It was carried on poles, like a palanquin, by twelve men. At the very head of the procession was Old Man Heaven's eldest son, with his hemp robes over a black suit and tie, a hemp hat that looked like a brown paper bag, and a black-banded portrait of his father, a rather elegant black-and-white photo from what must have been thirty years earlier. Behind him walked another dozen men carrying long poles from which hung banners with Chinese calligraphy on them. And then family members, both men and women, all the men in hemp hats and the women with straw rope wrapped around their heads. Everyone was wailing and weeping and the traffic was backed up in both directions. With drivers honking their horns and yelling for the parade to hurry up, all the racket reminded me of the time I had been in the crowd on this same road a decade earlier, watching the Ethiopian runner Abebe Bikila run the marathon barefoot to Seoul.

After twenty minutes or so we went back to ASCOM to have lunch. It would be late afternoon before the funeral procession reached the cemetery hill, so we decided to take a taxi and catch up to it later, before they finished tamping down the dirt on the grave. At the ASCOM Snack Bar, we ate and played the old pinball machine, winning game after game until 3:30 p.m., when we left all the free games on the board for a GI and walked down the hill toward the NCO Club. The question was whether we would just take an Arirang taxi from there or go outside the post wall and take one of the tiny Korean Corona taxis, which would be much cheaper. But Miklos didn't like sitting in the back of the little Coronas and neither did Paulie. While they argued about whose turn it was to sit in front, one of the "special" Arirang cabs pulled up beside us and the driver motioned us over.

"You boys going off post?" he asked.

We said we were.

"Could you do me a favor and let me take you?"

"How much will you pay us for letting you take us off post?" asked Miklos.

The driver laughed. He knew he wasn't fooling us. "You must be Mikuraji," he said.

All the drivers knew our mothers, and we all knew what his request meant. With us in the cab, the gate guards wouldn't search it and confiscate whatever black market goods he was carrying in his "special" compartment. Sometimes, if the gate guards were in a bad mood, they would detain the Arirang drivers and even call the Korean police, who would usually demand a huge bribe that cut into profits.

"Come on, *ajoshi*," said Paulie. "Give us each five thousand won and bring us back from Medicine Mountain later. We'll do it."

The driver tapped his steering wheel for a moment, considering the offer. He nodded. "You clever little bastards," he said. "Already acting like gangsters!"

We reached Medicine Mountain in plenty of time to climb up the hill and memorize the location of Old Man Heaven's grave before the men had finished burying the coffin. The day was beautiful but hot, and when we came down the hill all sweaty, the taxi driver was waiting; he treated us all to ice-cold bottles of 7-Star Cola before taking us back to ASCOM.

The next day we returned to Medicine Mountain to make sure we'd remember the exact grave site. We spent a few minutes walking around Yaksa Temple to see the golden Buddhas in the main shrine room and the standing Buddha, which was about twenty feet tall and made of white stone. Its right hand was raised and its left hand pointed downward, with palms showing, and I was reminded of statues I had seen of Jesus and Mary in similar poses. But this wasn't like any other Buddha I had seen—it had a thin Fu Manchu mustache and a curled, single strand of beard on the very bottom and center of its chin, and it wore an elaborate head piece that looked like a fancy Mexican sombrero or maybe a chandelier.

Paulie asked an old woman why the Buddha was wearing the strange hat and had the beard and moustache. She laughed. "You kids need to learn more about our Lord Buddha," she said. "This is the Mireuk Buddha, the Buddha who will come in the future. He may even have been born to this world already. The Buddha you're thinking of, who sits in his meditation, is the Sokkamun Buddha, the Prince who once lived in India." We thanked her for the explanation but still didn't understand the hat and facial hair.

"That's the second-coming Buddha, huh?" said Miklos. "Except I don't think Buddhists think the world is gonna end the way the Christians do."

"The world is definitely coming to an end," said Paulie. "All the signs are here. At least that's what my mom says, but I wouldn't know. I'm not a preacher, man."

"It's all bullshit," said Miklos. "Come on, let's get some of that *yaksu* they got here and go up and find the grave."

We went down to the medicinal spring and each had a couple of scoops of the *yaksu* water from a gourd. Miklos excused himself to go take a piss, and then came back with a little package wrapped in newspaper and tied with string.

"What did you get?" I asked.

"Just some stuff. Let's go."

We hiked up the hillside on the trail, and then left the trail and went over the ridge to the public cemetery on the other side. Old Man Heaven's grave site was away from the other grave mounds and about a quarter of the way down the hill, just under a little ridge and outside the shade of the plum trees that grew there. It must not have been picked by a geomancer according to the traditional practice, or maybe it had been but was limited to a place on that particular hill. The gravediggers or the family had piled a fair-sized mound on top of the grave and left it partially swarded—there were a few patches of live grass, and it would take until after the rains for it to spread and make an even covering. The headstone was small, and I couldn't read the Chinese characters on it.

"This will be easy to find," I said.

"At night? You think?" Miklos pointed up the ridge to the peak of the highest hill to the right. "We can camp up there when it's time and come down."

"All right."

"Let's get back then," said Paulie. "Gives me the heebie-jeebies standing here right after the grandfather's buried."

.

"Wait," said Miklos. He unwrapped the little paper package he had brought up. Three apples and a bottle of soju. "We can't go without paying our respects, right?"

It hadn't even occurred to me, given what we were planning to do. And to have Miklos be the one to do the proper thing made me especially embarrassed. "Thanks, Miklos," I said.

"I thought you didn't believe any of this stuff," said Paulie.

"What does *my* believing it matter?" said Miklos. "It's the right thing to do." He snapped open his switchblade and started peeling the top of one of the apples. I unfolded the newspaper wrapping and spread it out, and we made a small offering in front of the grave. Miklos took a shot glass from his pocket, wiped it with his sleeve, and lifted the soju bottle. "Shit," he said. "I don't have an opener. I'm gonna have to break it."

Paulie reached into his pocket and took out his Swiss Army knife. He unfolded the bottle opener and handed it to Miklos, who opened the soju, and then we each poured an offering and made our bows to Old Man Heaven. Paulie was supposed to condemn heathen Korean rituals like this one according to his church, but he went along with no objection. Afterward, when Miklos and I looked at him for an explanation, he said, "It's for you, Insu. I don't want Grandfather Heaven's spirit to be offended if we're coming back for his skull water. Shouldn't you be saying something to him?"

"I don't know what to say."

"Aw, come on," said Miklos. "You don't need to say anything. If his ghost's hanging around, he'll know what you're *thinking.*"

That was fine with me. We picked up our offerings. Miklos and I each ate one of the apples, but Paulie refused to go that far with what his church considered a heathen ritual, so we left the third apple on top of Old Man Heaven's grave mound along with the bottle of soju with the shot glass as a top, and then we headed back over the hill to Yaksa Temple to catch a cab back to Sinchon.

◆ ◆ ◆

IT MUST HAVE BEEN the fifth day after we visited Old Man Heaven's
grave. We were at Miklos's house, the larger new place they had moved
to. It was a modern house, low and flat, stacked like three rectangular
slabs at different angles. The gate was rivet-studded iron with rebar
spikes, and it swung open in two pieces, on metal wheels on a track, to
let a car through even though Miklos's family didn't have one; they used
the parking area and the garden like a traditional *madang*, where they
did all the housework and sat around in the evenings smoking.

We had stolen a few OB beers from their new refrigerator and we
were drinking, busy with our knives, practicing how to throw them so
they would actually stick. We had seen lots of knife throwing in movies,
but it turned out to be much harder than it looked. Paulie ended up with
a hole in his shoe, having almost cut his toe with a bayonet Dupree had
gotten for us, and he griped about having to buy a new pair of expensive
Converse high-tops. The tip of the blade had gone all the way through
the white rubber above the toes and into the ground. Each time Paulie
took a step now, the slit on the white rubber would open, like a little
frog's mouth, and Miklos and I would say "Ribbit."

We sat under the young plum tree, under a decorative curtain made
of aluminum pull tabs, listening to out-of-tune piano music from the
next-door neighbor's house. We had realized that we knew nothing,
really, about how a human body decomposed, let alone how long it
would take until a brain would become skull water. We needed someone
who was an expert in the subject. I was wondering out loud how we
would approach one of the Korean gravediggers when Paulie suddenly
raised his hand to interrupt.

"It's Dupree!" he exclaimed, unable to hide the excitement in his voice.

"*What's* Dupree?" I asked, looking at the bayonet, which Miklos had
jammed into the tree trunk.

"He's the morgue honcho!"

"Fuck, you're right for a change," said Miklos.

"Let's go," said Paulie. "He's working today. He owes me ten bucks, anyway."

We finished our beers, hid the empty bottles in the garden, and took the dry laundry down from the line for Miklos before we walked out to the road to the place where the army bus from Yongsan stopped. After a ten-minute wait, we caught a bus, and a few minutes after that we got off at the clover field and walked in silence along the wall to Graves Registration.

A green army sedan—the kind used by officers—drove by, forcing us nearly against the wall, and Miklos identified it as a CID car. "Oh, man," he said. "What do you suppose they're onto?"

Everybody—GIs and Koreans, and even the American MPs—hated the CID, the Criminal Investigation Department. They were all either corrupt or power hungry, driving around in sedans in their sunglasses, and they could do pretty much what they wanted as long as they didn't attract too much attention and get caught themselves.

Was Dupree in some kind of trouble?

Paulie went in by himself, leaving Miklos and me out in the parking area. I felt cold and hot at the same time, the pit of my stomach tightening into a queasy knot. Miklos lit up a cigarette and offered it to me.

I took a drag of the cheap Korean cigarette and coughed.

"It's my cousin's pack," he said, shrugging. "It'll keep your mind off things."

Miklos lit another cigarette for himself, and now I could see that he had a pack of Pagodas, and it reminded me of the temple at Medicine Mountain.

"Don't be a pussy, Fifty-Seven. We all got other stuff to worry about, so don't make a problem if there isn't gonna be one."

The double doors opened a crack, and Paulie's arm poked out, a Budweiser in his hand—a good sign—and when we went in, we found Dupree, eyes glazed, smoking a joint and having a laugh. "Come gimme

some skin!" he said, holding out his hand for us to slap. When Miklos
and I had both dapped him the way he had taught us, he took out his
wallet and gave Miklos a twenty. "Go to the bowling alley and get us all
some hot dogs and Cokes," he said. "I mean like five each, 'cause I got
serious munchies coming."

"Did you get busted?" said Miklos. "That was the *CID*, man."

"Oh, man, you only *wish*! Just some more white meat on ice down
here. And no sweat on the CIDs. That's just their SOP—standard oper-
ating procedure to get a piece of action."

"All right," said Miklos. "Back in a skosh. But I'm getting a burger
for me."

"Me, too," I said.

When Miklos had gone, Dupree said there was something he had to
tell me—something serious—and it had to do with my mother. The CID
who had left just before we arrived was a Captain Taylor, who investi-
gated ration card fraud and black marketing, and he had mentioned that
he was going after a couple of Korean wives who had recently bought
appliances.

"Last time you was here, didn't you say your mom sold a fridge?"

"Yeah," I said, feeling a sudden and irrational sense of guilt.

"Well, she's in deep shit if Taylor's the one who comes after her," said
Paulie.

"Yeah, Taylor's a mean motherfucker," Dupree said. "He got it in for
Koreans 'cause he got his ass burned by his moose. Dumped him and
married a major. Can you believe that shit?"

"That she married a major?"

"Any of that shit. It's like fucking *General Hospital*."

"You *watch* that?"

"I'm just sayin' . . . Look—since you told the Milkman about me and
we got a *skoshi* thing goin', I'll put in a word for you, scratch yours, dig?
The least I could do for an honorary brother."

"Thanks," I said.

Dupree hugged me and pounded my back a couple of times. "I'm short, Seven. I'm gonna be outta here soon. I told Paulie. You guys gotta come see me sometime when I'm back in The World, away from all this rinky-dink bullshit. I'm gonna be big-time someday."

"Taylor was here picking up his cut," said Paulie.

"A change in product," said Dupree. "We ain't got any shit comin' from the usual, so we got to move some local stuff. You all know how that is."

We *did* know. We also knew that Dupree really did care about us and would do whatever he could to help. Dupree made a pot of coffee and told us how Captain Taylor's girlfriend—who was a college girl from a well-to-do family and not just a prostitute—had actually written out her game plan for how she would move up the ladder of American boy-friends, using one to meet another, and then marrying the one at the top and emigrating to the States, where she could then sponsor members of her Korean family until she got the whole clan to America. Taylor had found this out after she had already hooked up with the major and then had a friend of hers seduce him so she would have an excuse for the breakup. Her friend had felt betrayed, too, and had given Taylor a little ledger book she had taken from his girlfriend's dresser. He had a KA-TUSA intelligence officer translate it for him, including the captions on the diagrams, and now he was out to get her *and* the major, though both of them were now in Fort Benning, Georgia.

"These smart moose bitches must do this shit all the time," he said. When he saw our expressions, he added, "No offense to you all's mommas, right?"

We usually avoided talking—or thinking—too much about our mothers' histories, about what they did. It was enough to have to be involved in their day-to-day schemes without wondering why all of their friends and acquaintances were technically criminals. But then, what could we expect, living in a military dictatorship in Korea under the umbrella of the U.S. Eighth Army, where everything was a SNAFU and every other GI was out to make a buck at Uncle Sam's expense, where the war was mostly over but the casualties kept mounting and usually turned out to be people like us?

We entirely forgot to ask Dupree what we had come for.

# Skull Water

## 1975

We had brought four shelter halves, ponchos, sleeping bags, and other assorted army bivouac gear: tent poles, metal pegs, rope, and entrenching tools. Our parents expected us to be gone for three nights, but we had also brought a couple of cases of C-rations we had scrounged from GIs in ASCOM and were prepared to stay longer if we had to. It was a lot of gear for the three of us to carry. We didn't have military rucks, so we had stuffed everything into old duffel bags and roped it all together to hump up the mountain along with some empty plastic water jugs.

Near the top of Medicine Mountain, there was a spot we had eyed on our last trip, where two ridges converged and a triangular patch of grassy dirt stretched between some large, jagged boulders. It was flat there, and we wouldn't have to clear many stones before we snapped the shelter halves together and set up two pup tents. My father had given me a fancy E-tool he'd brought back from Vietnam—a compact triple-folding all-metal shovel with a saw-tooth edge. It was what I planned to use to dig up Old Man Heaven's coffin. Miklos used it to hack some branches into a waist-high tripod, and he put a black plastic bag at the intersection, rigging a standing wash basin while Paulie and I gathered wood and rocks and built a campfire near a burnt patch of ground.

We were just below the summit of the hill, and from the ridge above our campsite I could look west all the way to Inchon. To the northeast, a couple of ridges over, was the valley with the vast public cemetery dotted with grave mounds and, somewhere between the hills, the place where lepers were said to live. A plume of smoke was rising in that direction from the crematorium, and closer to us, from just outside the Buddhist temple grounds, a haze of cooking smoke dissipated among the trees.

The temple was called Yaksasa, and the ridge we were camped on was probably Manweol Mountain, though everyone called it Yaksan. We took this to mean Medicine Mountain, since there was the *yaksu*, the medicinal spring, down by the temple, though *yak* could also mean "weak" and *sa* could mean "snake" or "death." The second *sa* was for "temple." The weather was clear, but just in case it rained, we dug shallow drainage trenches around the tent. Miklos said his uncle had told him that tobacco kept bugs out, so we ripped open packs of unsmoked Lucky Strikes and mashed the cigarettes between our hands to sprinkle the tobacco into the dirt.

"Ham and motherfuckers," Miklos said as he opened his M-2 pack from the C-rations. "I always get ham and motherfuckers. Wanna trade?"

I opened my box and took out the accessory pack to see what was underneath. "Beef slices with potato and gravy chunks," I said.

"Fuck," said Miklos. "Paulie, you got beenies and weenies?"

Paulie shook his head. "Spaghetti and meatballs."

"Now we're talkin'. Trade?"

"Fuck you. Open another pack."

Miklos just grunted and flicked open his P-38 to open another green can. "Your loss, man. I mean, the taste I don't mind, but I'll get gassy as all hell."

I opened my can of Beef Slices with Potatoes and Gravy and handed my P-38 tool to Paulie, who quickly twitched it around the top of his can of Peaches in Syrup. He opened it only part of the way, bending the jagged lid back into a makeshift cup handle, and he slurped the syrup before poking at the mushy fruit pieces with his white plastic fork.

We sat looking at each other's expressions until the warmth on our faces from the fire turned to tiredness. But we didn't want to crawl into the pup tent yet to sleep, so we sat some more in silence, listening to the sounds from the temple below.

"Aren't you afraid of the ghost?" Paulie said finally.

"What?" I said, surprised.

Miklos scoffed. "I lived in a house that was haunted and it was nothing," he said. "The old people in the neighborhood said there was a *tokkaebi* too, and that was nothing but a cat that got stuck in the sewage pipe. You ever actually *seen* a ghost or a goblin?"

"I used to see ghosts," I said.

"Bullshit." Miklos spat into the fire.

"I *did.*"

"Who were they?" Paulie asked.

"There was a Japanese colonel in the house in Samnung where we used to live. They spread his ashes in the garden, so his ghost used to come out there. He was just sad. And there was Gannan's ghost."

"Wasn't that your aunt who was a whore?" said Miklos. "I know all about that from Patsy."

I smacked his shoulder with the back of my hand. "Fuck you."

"I wanna hear about it," said Paulie. "I thought she got pregnant from some GI and then she killed herself. Isn't that what you told me, too?"

"She ate rat poison," said Miklos. "Patsy heard about it from Yongsu's sister Haesuni that time she was on the bus."

"Man!" Paulie said. "Rat poison!"

"She didn't eat rat poison," I said. "And Gannan was my *cousin*, not my aunt. She hanged herself."

"Fuck, I don't know which is worse," said Miklos.

"I don't want to talk about Gannan now," I said. "And I don't see ghosts anymore."

"Yeah?" said Miklos. "That's 'cause you never saw them to begin with."

I didn't tell him that I didn't *want* to see ghosts anymore, that it was enough that I still woke up sometimes with the memory of Gannan in the moonlight, hanging from the chestnut tree. I was glad not to see ghosts. "You remember the fluoride treatments we got in school?" I said.

"Man, that was fun," said Paulie.

"Man, you scared the shit out of your mother!" Miklos gave him a high five. "Ghosts!"

Paulie spat into the fire and laughed. In fifth grade, the DOD school had given us all fluoride treatments one class at a time. The Army Medical Corps came with tiny tubes of gritty toothpaste, indicator tablets, and toothbrushes. They demonstrated proper dental hygiene, and then they had us chew the cherry-flavored red pills. When we spat out our mouthfuls of red saliva, we all looked at each other, amazed by how much plaque must be on our teeth, since they were all rimmed in purplish-red stains. After that we all brushed twice and then used the indicator tablets again to prove how the plaque had all magically disappeared. Then they told us we could keep the toothbrushes and the little string of plastic-wrapped pills. Paulie had chewed one at home to show his mother, and when he opened his mouth she had screamed, thinking it was blood.

"Why was your mother so scared, anyway?" I said. "Didn't you tell her?"

"Yeah, I told her. But my grandfather died of TB. He spat up a lot of blood."

Miklos tapped his big, white front teeth. "What about the fluoride, man?"

"I couldn't see ghosts after that."

Miklos laughed. "What the fuck does clean teeth got to do with seeing ghosts?"

"I don't know. I was just telling you bastards," I said in Korean.

"Hey, Patsy's coming tomorrow," said Paulie.

"So's I can pop her cherry," said Miklos.

I looked down at my feet at my entrenching tool, and for a moment, I felt like using it on Miklos. I thought of Gannan, how I missed her, the years Kubong Manshin said I would have to wait to visit her grave. I thought of Haesuni far away in America somewhere, and Patsy coming all the way up the mountain to visit us. When I glared up at Miklos, he turned away.

ON THE SECOND DAY of our campout, Miklos's older brother Danny arrived with Paulie's cousin Patsy and her Korean girlfriend, who carried a small *pojagi* full of lunch boxes and rice cakes. Patsy had an old Boy Scout knapsack full of stuff she wouldn't show us, and Danny carried two rolled-up sleeping bags and a green laundry sack lumpy with clothing and C-ration cans.

Danny was seventeen, and Patsy, in her "American" age, was too. Her girlfriend must have been a dropout or a club girl—she looked like she could be eighteen or nineteen. She never told us her real name, but Patsy called her "Natalie" because she thought she looked like Natalie Wood, while Natalie jokingly called Patsy "Holly," after Audrey Hepburn from *Breakfast at Tiffany's,* Patsy's favorite movie.

I hadn't seen Danny in a while because he usually lived up in Yongsan. He had freckles like Miklos and sandy hair that seemed to have gotten darker over the past year. When he rode the bus back from school when he lived in Pupyong he would sit near the back by himself and masturbate, squirting spit through the gap in his front teeth onto the tip of his strangely pale penis. We could always tell what he was doing because he would slump down in the seat, only the top of his head visible, bobbing up and down while he panted like a dog.

Patsy went to school with us only occasionally these days and spent the rest of her time at the Itaewon clubs—the ones for the white GIs—just outside the Yongsan Army Post. She treated us all like family, and she always had money—more than most of the adults I knew. She could make the bus driver stop anywhere she wanted, and when the bus wasn't too full she would often send us out to buy snacks for everyone. Patsy was nearly as tall as me and skinny; she had been a long jumper for the school until she missed too many practices and was kicked off track-and-field. She dreamed of becoming a movie star and claimed she was saving money to have plastic surgery when she moved to America.

Natalie was a mystery to us. When I asked Patsy who she was, she just punched me lightly on the shoulder and pointed to Danny.

"What does that mean?" I said.

"He can't exactly go home with her, right?"

I didn't understand.

"He came up here to *fuck* her," said Patsy.

I felt suddenly polluted, as if I were doing something morally repugnant, though this hardly made sense given why we had come up to the mountain in the first place. "Did you come with him, too?" I asked.

"Me? I just came to keep an eye on Paulie," she said. "Come on, Seven, let's open up some of the cigarettes."

"*You* do that," I said, handing her one of the packs of Lucky Strikes no one else would smoke. She was one of the only people I knew who wasn't afraid of the bad luck from the bull's-eye logo. "I gotta help set up another tent."

No one could sleep that night because Danny and Natalie were so loud in the pup tent. When Miklos complained, Danny told him to shut up if he wanted to have his turn. Paulie went out into the night to gather more firewood while Patsy and I sat at the fire under the lean-to I had rigged out of some branches and a poncho. She smoked one of the Lucky Strikes and I smoked a Pall Mall. Some of the lumps in Danny's laundry sack had turned out to be beer cans, and Patsy had one open—a Falstaff, my father's brand—though she had already had two.

"Is it true?" she asked.

"What?"

"You really gonna rob a grave?"

I exhaled through my nose and took another drag. From the temple below us, we could hear the monks chanting sutras—an oddly harmonious descant to the sounds Natalie and Danny were making in the tent.

"I mean, do you really think it will work, Seven?"

"I don't know," I said. "It's what I *heard*. You can't know anything one hundred percent, right?"

"You just have to pretend?"

"I'm not pretending," I said.

"I meant like religion." Patsy pointed up at the sky. The night was so clear we could see the pale blur of the Milky Way if we looked away from the fire for a while. "Sometimes you have to pretend to believe in God to make God exist, you know? That's what *I* do."

"I don't think pretending makes anything really exist."

"You're so young," said Patsy, taking a sip of her beer. She said that to us a lot, and I wondered if it really meant she felt so much older and more experienced or if it was just a true statement of our age.

"You know," I said, "Danny used to tell us he wanted to pop your cherry."

She laughed until some beer came out of her nose, and then she had a coughing fit. "You guys are all such idiots," she said.

"Is that why you brought Natalie? Because you don't want to sleep with any of us?"

"I'll sleep with *all* of you tonight. You mean why won't I *fuck* you?"

"I don't like that word."

"You want to do it but you won't say it? That's fucked up. I hear you say it all the time to Miklos and Paulie. *Hypocrite.*"

"You sleep with other men." I paused to gather some courage, my heart pounding as I said, "You fuck them."

"Yeah. So what? Guy sticks his dick inside you and grunts a few times. He gets all tiny and pathetic again. Then he pays you fifty bucks. Japanese business guy'll pay a hundred. Not like you'd know, *ungh?*" The last part she said in Korean.

"I wouldn't, no. I mean, how can you do it?"

"Pay me fifty bucks and I'll show you."

"Why do you have to talk about it like that?"

"Just shut up, Seven. I'll sleep with you. But I'm not about to fuck any of you guys. You're all my little brothers."

I COULDN'T SLEEP for the longest time, and when I did I dreamed about Patsy. She and I were standing on the mountain waiting for the temple bell to ring. I felt her soft hair under my hand as I stroked her to be quiet, and we both listened as the temple bell sounded and made us shiver. My arm was around Patsy's waist and I could feel her trembling, all of the night's tensions gone.

We didn't hear the monk, and I didn't see him, until Patsy turned her head and seemed to lean into me. Then the monk's shadow covered us and he moved past, making no noise at all. We could smell the temple incense on him in the light breeze that came down from the mountain, and when he was past I saw that his flute was so long it seemed to touch the ground.

We waited, but no other monks came by, and then Patsy and I started running through the morning fog. She kept close behind me, and when I stopped, she pushed her hands against the hollow of my back. I wanted to see the monk again, and we came up on him at the edge of the woods. He was walking toward the temple, disappearing into the heavy mist. I came close enough to see him cut off the moon, and to smell the pungent incense once more, but I could no longer make out his bamboo flute.

I felt Patsy's warm hand against the side of my neck, and the two of us followed the monk until he came to an opening in the trees. His body was in the mist, but the moon reflected on his bald head. Patsy and I backtracked out of the woods into the clearing near where we were camped. She was ahead of me now. The moon was high, and I wondered why there was no chanting from the temple. Something was strange if the monks were there and there was no chanting.

IN THE FALSE DAWN, the early morning when the sky was still a neutral shade of gray and the others were still tangled asleep in their sleeping bags, I got up and crawled out of the tent into the cold air. I shivered as the heat of sleep flew from my body like a bird and the cold touched me all at once like water, but lighter, and almost like ice. I blew into the embers of the campfire, which were still smoldering from the night, and I added a few dry twigs until the fire burst alive again. The wind shifted, sending the smoke into my eyes, and then again, taking it away along with the heat on my face. Savoring those sensations that took me from the world of sleep and once more into the world of the living, I boiled water in the stainless steel canteen cup and ripped open two packets of C-ration creamer along with four packets of sugar.

I drank the warm, sweet milk, feeling its temperature flow down into the heat of my belly, enjoying the quiet morning, muffled by mist, waiting for the world to wake. The breathing of the wind, like the mountain's breath, the soft rustle of leaves, the distant sizzling of a passing car, a bird calling from over the ridge, small crackles and an occasional flapping from the fire; the coarse sound of my sipping, the sigh of my breath.

In a while I imagined I could hear each particle of mist touch the earth or a twig, or the surface of my own flesh. I closed my eyes. In the distance, from the far end of the ridge, I could hear the crunch of footsteps, the sound of straw-sandaled feet, which I recognized now, from my dream, as the tread of a monk. For the longest time I could not see him, even after I opened my eyes, and I thought for a moment that I was dreaming again. But then I saw him. He was wearing a gray robe in the fog, and his bald head glowed paler than the rest of him. When he paused at the top of the ridge I stood up and waved. He waved back and then he was gone. I saw him again in the late afternoon when I had made my way up the other side of the ridge looking for firewood. He was sitting on a rock, one leg outstretched, the other folded in, his arms raised as if he were stretching after a nap. When he saw me, he motioned for me to come over, and I went to him and sat beside him on the rock.

"What are you all doing up here?" he asked.

"We're just having fun, *sunim*. Camping."

"Your face is familiar," he said. "Did you used to live in Tatagumi when you were little? In the house by the tailor, with the three-colored *t'aeguk* on the gate?"

"Yes!" I said, surprised.

"All monks look alike to you, *ungh*?"

"I'm sorry, *sunim*. I don't recognize you." He was right. I couldn't tell how old he was, and in his gray robes and gleaming, shaved head, he could have been any monk in his thirties or forties.

"You once put spoiled rice and a cigarette butt in my begging bowl, and you and your friend thought it was so funny when I ate it."

My face suddenly grew hot. I awkwardly bowed to him from my seated position and said, "I'm very sorry, *sunim*. Please forgive me!"

"You know, I didn't *have* to eat the food you put in my bowl that day."

"You didn't? Isn't it a rule? That you have to eat everything people put in your bowl?"

He laughed. "Not sour rice and garbage!" he said.

"Then why did you eat it, *sunim*?"

"I ate it for you," he said. "I ate it so that you would learn a lesson from it."

My embarrassment turned into a terrible feeling of disappointment in myself. I was just a kid then, I thought. I didn't know any better. I was about to say as much when the monk pointed at me and said, "You were just a little boy. You didn't know any better." He saw my eyes go wide. "But now," he said. "Now you can look back and understand that a little thing you did for your innocent amusement could have made someone very sick. There was a lot of sickness that year. Someone eating bad food

could have died. I might have choked on the cigarette butt and suffo-
cated. Or maybe I would have spat out what was in my mouth because of
my surprise, and my fellow monk might have slipped on that patch of
sour rice and stumbled into the street and been hit by a bus right where
that poor waitress was run over in front of the restaurant." Then he
chanted the traditional Buddhist invocation everyone knew: "*Kwanseum
Posal, Nami Amitabul.*"

"It was so long ago," I said in a small voice. A strange feeling of
helplessness and horror was coming over me, and I wondered if he had
put me under some sort of spell. Big Uncle had once told me that some
monks practiced a thing called *kiapsul* and could hypnotize people or
incapacitate them from a distance. But this monk was speaking calmly,
without a hint of anger or resentment in his voice—what I imagined a
tranquil monk's tone should be—though he seemed to be enjoying
himself.

"I'm sorry, *sunim,*" I said again.

"There's no need to apologize. What if, instead of what I told you, I
said my fellow monk had been carelessly about to step in front of that
speeding bus, but then he slipped on the sour rice I spat from my mouth,
and that saved his life? What if that thing you did for your amusement—a
mean thing—had had an unexpectedly good result instead?"

I was confused now. I thought he had been chastising me for the
prank. "Well, I guess that would be good," I said.

"That makes you feel better, then, to know that?"

"Yes."

"Good. And what if that monk, whose life was saved thanks to your
mean act, turned evil and ended up assassinating the president? How is
your good feeling?"

I didn't know what to say, but my face must have shown my sudden
change of mood.

"Don't get carried away," said the monk. "It's all imaginary—an
illusion—these things I said to you. What is true is that you did a mean

thing for your enjoyment and now here we are—what is it, ten years later?—sitting on this rock together like two lizards in the sun.

"The human mind cannot know all the outcomes of causes and conditions. We are only people. But by looking at the trails of causality we leave that are visible to us in memory, which is also an illusion, we may learn a little about a thing called karma." He looked at me with a smile. "Did you follow what I said?"

"I'm sorry, *sunim*. What you said is too hard for me. I guess you're saying we can't know what will happen from our actions except when they happen?"

"Not even that." He stood up in one motion, without using his hands to raise himself. "I'm practicing on you, as you can see. But remember this: We cannot know all causes and conditions with our limited minds, so we must be especially pure with our intention, even when the outcome of our action may have nothing to do with that intention.

"And look—all this has happened because you once gave me some bad food when I begged at your house. *Ya*, whatever happened to that beautiful red rooster the tailor had?"

"It got hurt in a fight and died," I said. "The tailor's wife wanted to eat it, but he wouldn't let her, and he buried it somewhere secret."

"That was a beautiful cock, the colors in his feathers." He spread the fingers of both hands and looked at them, admiring the rooster in memory. "You know, you're not allowed to camp up here," he said. "Everybody in our country is scared of North Korean spies and infiltrators since the president's wife was killed. The police have been watching you and they know you're just a bunch of kids with American GI fathers. I told them your dads probably told you that you could camp anywhere, because that's how it is in America."

"We didn't know."

"Of course. Causes and conditions. I was in America for a few years. In California state. What a vast, beautiful, empty country! Giant red pine trees wider than a house, reaching all the way up to Heaven. Rocks as big as whole Korean mountains! So much empty space. Have you ever been to America?"

"Only a year or so," I said.

"I'm going back there in a couple of years. To teach the Dharma to Yankees." He laughed.

"What is the Dharma, *sunim*?"

"The Dharma—" He motioned all around him. "The world is the Dharma, but it is also the teachings of the Buddha. Come down to Yaksasa Temple and learn."

"Our family isn't Buddhist," I said.

"That's what so many people think these days now that Jesus has come to the East. Looking at you—what you're doing up here—I take it you're following the Tao at the moment."

"I don't think I'm a Taoist, *sunim*."

He chuckled. "All young men are Taoists first. Then they become responsible Confucians when they have children and wives, and property, and money, and then when they realize it's all going to be gone, they become Buddhists. What do you think of that?"

"I don't understand," I said. "But I'm not married and I don't have money or property. I'll learn as I go, I guess."

"You'll learn as you go on with life. You'll forget. You'll succeed. You'll fail. You'll get sick. Finally, you'll die, and then, still, it won't be done. For now, you should have your fun and do what you came up here to do."

"We will, *sunim*."

The monk looked in the direction of the public cemetery, and I knew that he knew we were there for more than camping. I also realized, just then, that he knew all this—even the fact that I knew. Suddenly I felt as if I were trying to think too many moves ahead in a high-stakes game of *chang'gi*, in the middlegame where consequences of a wrong move could be tragic. There was a terrible unease, a tension in my whole body, and I wanted to be rid of it, and I wondered if this was why Catholics, of my father's religion, went to confession. But I didn't want or need to confess. "*Sunim*," I said. "I have a question."

When he turned to look at me, he did it so slowly it scared me for a moment. "What is it you want to know?" he asked.

"Someone said to me that if you drink the water that's inside a human skull, it will cure any disease. Is that true?"

"You have water inside your human skull right now. Why would you need to drink more?"

"No, I mean someone who's sick, drinking the water from the skull of a dead person."

"I wouldn't know much about that. That seems to be the business of Taoist wizards and shamans. I'm just the monk Mumyong Sunim, not a dealer of Chinese medicine or an acupuncturist or a qigong master. Why would you ask me such a thing?"

"I don't know," I said. "I just thought someone like you might know about skull water."

I thought the monk had gotten up to leave, but now he sat down again on the rock, moving his robes aside and crossing his legs not in the Buddhist way but in the old Korean way that made it look like one leg was twisted over the other. "Well, now that I think about it, I suppose even a monk like me should know about the skull water, since that is what illuminated the great monk Wonhyo!"

"A great monk?"

"It was more than a thousand years ago. That would be the time of Shilla, when Buddhism was still pretty new in Korea. Wonhyo and his closest friend, Uisang, were on their way to China to learn more about Buddhism. They were walking thousands of *li* through all kinds of mountains and wilderness, and one night they took shelter in a cave because of a terrible storm. Wonhyo was exhausted, hungry, and thirsty, and in the dark cave he found a gourd full of fresh, pure water. He drank it and he was refreshed. The hunger and exhaustion left him, and he had a good sleep.

"The next morning, when they woke up and it was light enough to see inside the cave, Wonhyo was shocked. They had stumbled into a burial cave! There were corpses and skeletons everywhere, and what he'd thought was a gourd full of fresh water was a moldering human skull!

"But then he realized something. The previous night, he'd had no doubt that he'd drunk pure water from a gourd. That had been *reality*. It was his *mind* that created that reality. The world he lived in, he realized, was created by the mind. That was his insight, and he decided he no longer needed to go all the way to China to study Buddhism." Now the monk stood up again and stepped down from the rock to head back down to the temple.

I quickly leaped up and followed. "*Sunim!* What did he do then?"

"He came back to Korea, of course. He took off his robes and he became one of the greatest teachers of the Dharma, though he was a womanizer and a drunk."

"And what about his friend?"

"Uisang?" The monk paused and turned around for a moment. "Uisang didn't have an illumination. He continued on to China and learned a lot from the Chinese and from books."

"So skull water is good, then? It illuminated a great monk?"

"Who knows if it was really the skull water? It's just a story about Wonhyo Taesa. Don't follow me unless you plan to sit three hours with me on a meditation cushion." He strode down the hillside in his white sneakers as sure-footed as a goat.

"Was Wonhyo Taesa sick before he drank the skull water?" I called after him.

Mumyong Sunim's answer echoed—he was facing away from me. "If ignorance is a disease, then maybe the skull water cured him of it." In a moment, he made a turn around some stunted pine trees and disappeared.

IT WAS THE 217th day since Old Man Heaven's death and the sky had split into two halves, the bright sun beating down in the south and an uneasy drabness in the northeast that could have been pollution from the city of Seoul or the edge of an approaching storm front. A warm wind blew from that direction, and we felt a sense of relief, but also an uneasiness, as we stood on the ridge in late morning and waved goodbye to Danny and Natalie. Patsy had decided to stay with us to see our task through, although she made it clear that she was only an observer and her presence was for moral support. She had no intention of using a shovel, or touching the body, or even watching more than just the beginning of the procedure.

Our plan was to wait until the moon came up early in the evening—it was over three-quarters full, and bright—and we would use its light to avoid being seen with our flashlights. We had watched Old Man Heaven's coffin being interred, so we knew which side his head would be on. I had said we could assume the position from the placement of the headstone, but Miklos had reminded me that burials were sometimes careless, just like how surgeons sometimes amputated the wrong limb, and we had to be sure or risk wasting a great deal of energy. The gravediggers and the family had tamped the earth down around the coffin, but the mound on top was likely to be looser because of the grass planted on it. If we dug starting at the bottom of the mound opposite the headstone, we could reach the head of the coffin without having to remove much dirt. The Koreans didn't bury their coffins six feet down. If everything went as planned, we would be done before midnight.

Miklos and I made two quick trips down to Old Man Heaven's grave to place tent pegs as markers since it would be dark when we came down to dig. It made us sad to see that the grave had been neglected over the past months. His children must have been less than filial, or perhaps they were too poor to observe all the rituals and pay for the daily upkeep of the grassy mound. Part of it had already eroded in the early spring rain, exposing a patch of pebbly earth, and the water that flowed down from the little ridge of plum trees had made a small channel that cut the hillside only a few feet to the left of the headstone.

"He must be lonely," said Miklos. "Look how they put him here all by himself when all those other graves are close to each other. They should bury Old Man Earth right next to him." He tapped a wooden peg into the dirt about two feet from mine at the base of the mound to mark where we would dig. "Look," he said, pointing with his hatchet to the base of the headstone.

At first I thought it must be a fragment of bone, but I brushed the dirt away to reveal a *chang'gi* piece—the blue *sa*, the blue general's guard piece. I handed it to Miklos. "There should be another one," he said, and we found it on the other flank of the headstone, also partially buried in the dirt.

A sparrow flew from one of the plum trees and made a frantic circuit around us before flying away into the valley toward the crematorium. We looked on the back side of the headstone and found the blue general piece in the grass. In *chang'gi*, the general sits in a space called the palace, in the center of a combined + and × formed by intersecting lines, and his two guards sit below him to the left and right. None of them can leave the nine positions of the palace square.

"Old Man Earth must have been up here," I said. "I heard he was sick and his family moved to Kwangju. Maybe they brought him for a visit before they moved."

Miklos put the blue general on top of the headstone, in the middle, and then the two smaller guard pieces at its sides, where they belonged. "These are the ones they used when they played," he said. "See how this one is chipped here? That's from when Old Man Heaven got mad and knocked all the pieces off the board. He was such an asshole sometimes."

"I feel so bad about this, Miklos. I guess Old Man Earth is never playing again."

"Yeah. What's Earth without Heaven? Look, you can't back down now. You already put all this in motion, man. We planned this for a year. We're here. It's a done deal, and digging up the skull water is just the paperwork. That's what my old man would say."

"It just doesn't seem right to do it like this, but how else can we do it, right? I'm going down and getting a bottle of soju for Old Man Heaven."

"Be my guest. If I was him, I'd think all this was a gas, man. Who knows if that shit's gonna do anything for anybody? But he's still getting our attention, isn't he?"

"I guess," I said.

"You got your canteen all set?"

"Yeah."

"I got a funnel, so don't forget it." He looked up at the sky, to the northeast. "It looks like rain, man. Keep your fingers crossed."

"I'll pour the soju myself, okay?"

"You're the boss."

Miklos headed back to the campsite, to Paulie and Patsy, to finish the preliminary packing and cleanup. I went over the ridge and down to the store at the entrance to the temple and bought a bottle of soju and three apples. I also bought some sweet bean buns to take to everyone for later, though the buns would be cold by then.

Back at Old Man Heaven's grave mound, I performed the ritual the way Miklos and I had done it a year earlier. I felt I had to say something after peeling the apples with my switchblade and making the three pours of soju, and not just in my head this time. I borrowed words from the monk: *Kwanseum Posal Nami Amitabul*, invoking the Bodhisattva of Mercy and the Celestial Buddha, and I left everything there on top of the sheet of newspaper I had spread out like a small picnic blanket. It was an old newspaper from 1973, a page of the *Hanguk Ilbo* that said something about the White Horse Division returning from Vietnam, and already, bees and flies were buzzing around the peeled apples.

◆  ◆  ◆

"You guys are filthy pigs," Patsy said when I got back to the campsite. "You left shit and toilet paper all over. Couldn't you just do your business in one place?"

"We didn't want to step in each other's shit," said Miklos. "Who made you the Boy Scout leader?"

"I had Paulie dig a hole and bury all of it. Did you ever wonder if other people come up here?"

"Well, they can't be camping," I said, remembering what the monk had told me. "Koreans would get arrested."

Patsy just glowered and pointed to the mound of our trash she had gathered from the perimeter. She had exaggerated about the mess, but I was surprised by how many C-ration, beer, and soda cans we had thrown away in just those few days. Before she said anything about it, I told Miklos we would burn the paper and flatten and bury the cans.

"Here," I said to Patsy, handing her the sweet bean buns. "We can have them for dessert."

"Thanks, Seven. I guess we're all kind of antsy because of tonight. Paulie's so nervous he had to go throw up. How about you?"

"I'm scared." I couldn't describe to her how much.

"You don't really have to do this, you know."

"I have to, Patsy. This has gotten bigger than just me."

"Okay." She said it with an odd tone of resignation before she perked up again. "Let's make something to eat." She had decided to cook us something by using various C-rations as ingredients, and while she busied herself with the improvised kitchenware and the fire, Miklos, Paulie, and I finished clearing and burying our garbage. We pretended that had been our plan from the beginning, but Patsy was right—we had made a terrible mess around our campsite, the same kind of mess for which we criticized Koreans who went hiking or visited some mountain hermitage and left the trails strewn with their garbage.

"Patsy would make a great sergeant," said Paulie. "She can be such a bitch when she wants to."

"Our dads are all sergeants," I said.

"So she takes after your old man or your old man's a bitch," said Miklos. We had a laugh about that before we went back to the campsite and walked another circuit.

By the time we had finished eating, the weather had come down from the northeast with a slight drizzle—hardly a rain—but it grew dark early and the wind blew colder. We put everything into the tents and sat around the fire for a while drinking the hot cocoa from the C-rations, which Patsy had mixed with the powdered creamer and one of the hockey-puck-shaped chocolates. Like the dinner she had improvised, her hot chocolate was far better than what came straight out of the C-ration packages. I wondered how she had learned to cook like that, and she reminded us that all our families had had times when they got by on whatever they could scrounge.

I decided we would go down to the grave as soon as it was dark enough, even if it was raining. If we dug the grave quickly, we could break camp and get off the mountain before curfew. If it took longer, then we would break camp at 0400 so we could be gone just as curfew lifted, before morning brought people up the mountain.

"No one's coming up if it rains," said Miklos. "Even those hard-ass Confucians don't want to get their nice clothes all muddy."

"It's the caretaker we've got to worry about," I said. "We don't know when he might come up. Maybe he checks the graves when it rains so they don't wash away. I don't want to end up getting caught because we didn't think of that."

"You saw all that runoff," said Miklos. "How likely is it, man? That caretaker sucks."

Paulie and Patsy agreed with me, and Paulie was now concerned about the possible legal consequences of grave robbing. "I thought you were gonna ask about that, Seven?"

"Stop fucking obsessing," said Miklos. "We're not gonna get caught and you're not going to hell for this, so chill out, man!"

"You guys, stop arguing," said Patsy. "You don't want to be on each other's cases when you have to do this together. Okay?"

"Yeah," said Miklos.

I realized, now, why Patsy had decided to stay, and for some reason it made me suddenly nostalgic and sad, even through the jangle of anxiety I felt. I went to the tent and dug out my windbreaker and put it on over the two shirts I was already wearing. I wished I had brought gloves; my fingers felt like ice. I rubbed my hands together, blew on them, and I remembered the time I had held Patsy's hand at the Paekma theater, where she had made me take her so she could watch *Breakfast at Tiffany's* again. Her hand had been so warm as she looked up at the flashing screen with tears in her eyes. I wondered why she loved that movie so much, following it from theater to theater until she had all the lines practically memorized, down to the inflections. She could probably perform the whole thing on her own now.

It was dark enough now that no one would be able to see who we were or what we were doing, even from a short distance. I checked my Timex—7:09—1909 hours in military time. The year 1909 was when the freedom fighter An Jung-geun had assassinated Ito Hirobumi, the Japanese resident-general who ruled Korea. Three shots to the chest. I supposed this was an auspicious time, if there was one.

"Let's go," I said.

Paulie and Patsy looked startled, but Miklos slowly got up from his crouch by the fire and started kicking dirt into the flames. "As good a time as any for this shit," he said.

As we made our way down past the large patch of mugwort to the two plum trees, the drizzle became a light rain. We wore old green army ponchos, under which we carried the E-tools and filtered flashlights. In the murky overcast, with our hoods up, we looked like large bushes ourselves—or four members of a strange monastic order.

"Those trees must have been beautiful when they were blooming," said Patsy, her voice muffled and amplified at the same time by the poncho hood. "We should come back again before Ch'usok to take care of the grave for them."

"We haven't even dug it yet," said Miklos. "And if we do the *polcho* for them before Ch'usok, the family will be suspicious. We just put it back the way it was."

"I'm not coming back," said Paulie.

I told him Miklos and I would take care of it in a few days. Ch'usok was the Korean version of Thanksgiving, celebrated on *hangawi,* the lunar mid-autumn. Families visited their ancestral graves then and laid out a table of offerings. I imagined the grieving family all gathered on a warm day in fall, the sky a clear blue without pollution. Thinking of the contradiction of that scene with what we were about to do, I had a feeling of regret, in advance, for something I could choose, at any moment, not to do.

We walked between the plum trees and followed a little rivulet down to Old Man Heaven's grave, which looked like a dark lump in the earth.

"Why is the headstone at the side?" Patsy whispered. The rain was harder, and I could barely hear her through my poncho hood.

"The geomancer probably said to put it there," said Miklos. "My cousin said there's no rule about how it should go. Poor families don't even have a grave marker." He flipped his poncho aside and took out his entrenching tool. "You ready, Seven? You do the honors."

"Let's take a moment to pray," said Paulie.

"What?" said Miklos. "Old Man Heaven wasn't a Christian, man. You want his ghost to be pissed off at us? How would you like it if a Buddhist prayed over *your* grave, man? Seven already made an offering. See the apples and the bottle?"

"It's okay, Miklos," I said. "I want to take a moment to apologize."

"You're the boss, Seven." Miklos lowered his E-tool.

We stood for a minute, not speaking, and I listened to the rain pounding on the hood of my poncho as I tried to make my mind go blank. I could feel every rain drop hitting the rubberized fabric, and every rustle of my own clothing sounded so terribly loud I thought anyone nearby could surely hear it. Inside the hood, even my breath was loud. I found it impossible to quiet my mind. Old Man Heaven's grave felt like an annoyance now, and I had no thought about honoring his spirit or his memory, only a sudden and fierce impatience.

"All right," I said, and I stabbed the tip of my pentagonal black E-tool into the edge of the grave mound.

Miklos followed, and then Paulie, making room for each other to work. The top layer of dirt was soft, and each jab of an entrenching tool made a raspy, chuffing noise as it cut into the soil; then we would hear a dull, wet thud as we threw the shovelful away from us into one consolidated pile. It wasn't going to take long to reach the coffin. But just after we began, the rain fell harder, turning the exposed dirt of the grave mound to mud, which began sliding down into the hole we were digging, thick as oatmeal. We were now digging watery gruel instead of dirt. We dug faster, widenening the hole as it collapsed again and again. Soon, I was breathing hard and sweating heavily under the poncho. The hood became such an annoyance that I pushed it back so I could see, and the rain came pouring down the back of my neck into my clothes, drenching me until the poncho was useless and I threw it off into the mud. Miklos took his off as well, and Patsy picked them up so we wouldn't throw the mud from the grave onto them. Paulie kept his on, and with his face hidden inside the hood he looked like a giant insect, the tip of the entrenching tool poking out from the shadowy green mass like a proboscis, again and again, to bite into the earth.

Soon all three of us were panting, and my arms and back burned with strain and exertion. I knew that if we stopped then, even for a moment, we would not be able to continue until the rain ended. At a certain point

I thought my vision had gone red with blood, but it was Patsy turning on the two red-filtered flashlights so we could see. Paulie dropped his E-tool and sat down, his poncho seeming to collapse as if there was no one inside. Miklos moved even more fiercely, huffing and puffing like a train, keeping the rhythm of his shovel tip cutting into the mud steady, and finally, when I could hardly see from the rain in my face, when I was deciding to give up and go back to camp, I heard the dull thump of Miklos's E-tool hitting the coffin.

"Come on!" he shouted.

Paulie got up again, and tearing off his poncho, he joined us with fresh strength until the top of the coffin was visible under a thin layer of muddy water. Now, while Paulie held back the mud that slid down the side of the grave mound, Miklos and I dug around the narrow rectangle of wood until enough was exposed for me to pry at the lid. But the wood hadn't rotted away as we had expected—it was still firm. I started hacking at the corner of the coffin until pieces began to break off and float away.

"Help me!" I said, and Miklos began hitting the top of the coffin too, until a large triangular piece broke off. I stuck the tip of my E-tool into the hole. The whole lid was much narrower than I'd imagined; it couldn't have been much wider than Old Man Heaven's head, which meant his shoulders must have been crushed together into a strange shrug or he had been put into the box on his side. "I got it!" I cried, and just as I bore down on the handle, and the wood let out a weird creaking noise, the rain suddenly stopped—from solid sheets of water to nothing. In the odd silence, we all heard the loud crackle, and then the sharp *crack!* like a gunshot, as a big piece of the lid snapped off, and we saw the hemp-wrapped head of Old Man Heaven in the trembling, red-filtered light.

I bit my tongue, and because my hands were shaking, I jabbed my E-tool into the mud at the edge of the coffin.

"Here." Miklos held out his machete now, which had a flat tip that could cut straight down. I took it. I looked across the coffin at his red eyes, and down at the shrouded head. I had somehow not thought this through. I couldn't tell where the neck was. I didn't want to hack at Old Man Heaven's chin and destroy his face. I would have to cut the shroud off first. I would need a smaller knife. Why was the cloth still so solid? I would have to hold the decapitated head to split open the skull. Would there still be blood? And what if rainwater and blood mixed with the skull water? I looked up again at Miklos. Patsy and Paulie were just shadows. A cold wind began to blow from the north. I felt a few fresh raindrops. I leaned forward, closer, to use my knife, and something struck me in the face between the upper lip and my nose and went up into my brain. It was like a blast of steam from a punctured pipe, but indescribably putrid, a violent mix of fertile earth and rot and excrement. It hit me so hard I fell backward into the mud, where I immediately rolled to the side and threw up, my stomach clenching. I could hear the others exclaiming now, and the red light went out as Patsy dropped the flashlights and doubled over, sick. I heard muddy squelching sounds—Paulie running—and Miklos's groan.

It was the smell coming from the coffin. When I got back to my feet, still dribbling sick, and covered my nose and mouth in the fold of my left elbow, I thought I could see it wafting like a cloud of blacker darkness from the hole in the coffin lid. Miklos was retching onto the side of the grave mound. When Patsy retrieved the flashlights she had dropped, the narrow red cones of light illuminated a patch of mugwort, making it look hellish and hot.

I pulled my E-tool out of the mud, but when I lifted it to hack down at Old Man Heaven's neck—where I thought it should be in that black, triangular hole—another wave of odor engulfed me, and I turned my head aside to throw up again. Now the stench was everywhere. It seemed to dissolve in the rainwater and soak into my skin. I felt as if my very flesh could smell it. My gut and stomach cramped into a painful knot even after there was nothing left to come up, and I was afraid my throat would somehow break and close up like a bent pipe.

"I can't—!" I gasped to Miklos, waving my free hand at him.

"Fuck!" he said in Korean, stumbling back to his feet. He had a hand covering his face—I could make him out, now that Patsy had picked up the flashlights again. We all looked at each other. I shook my head, and Miklos and I started shoveling mud back onto the broken coffin lid until we doubled over again, vomiting bile from our empty guts. Dragging our ponchos and E-tools behind us, we staggered up the hill to where Paulie was sobbing between the two plum trees.

In the morning, with the sky still overcast but not raining, Miklos, Paulie, and I sat in the tiled central tub of the Samhwa bath house, soaking in scalding water up to our necks. Patsy was next door in the women's bath, also trying to purify herself of the terrible stench that had seemed to follow us all the way down the mountain as we broke camp and trudged to the main road to flag down an early taxi. Miklos and I had returned to the grave at first light to cover up what we had done, but we only had to go as far as the plum trees to see that the rain had cut a small gully all the way down to the side of the grave and washed away more than half the mound. The headstone stood askew, leaning toward the damaged grave, which was partially covered now by the new soil the water had carried down from the ridge. There was no trace of us having dug there—the family, the caretaker, everyone would assume it had been the rain.

We stayed at the bath a long time, coming out of the hot soak to sit on the little black plastic buckets, turned upsidedown, to have our skin professionally "peeled" by the old attendant with his rough green Italy cloth, then rinsing with the hose and shower head at the row of steamy mirrors, and then soaping up, showering off, soaking yet again in the hot tub and showering once more. That early in the morning there were no other customers at the Samhwa, and yet we still worried that the attendant would smell the rot that exuded from our skin and wafted from our breath. We had brought a change of clothes from Paulie's house while the taxi driver idled impatiently by the gate. When we finally left the bath and met up with Patsy—who looked like a little boy in Paulie's old clothes, with her wet hair tucked under a baseball cap—we thought we could still smell the grave on each other. Even days later, I would suddenly pause and wonder if I smelled it—a faint scent of mortality, decay, and sin.

☰
IV

# Three Days That Summer

# Three Days That Summer

## 1950

He never reached Pusan on that train. What made it impossible for him was having witnessed the people swept into the river. The images—the open mouths, the wide eyes, all glimpsed in an instant—left his brain after a while but would not leave his sight, and every time he saw something move suddenly in his periphery, or if he shifted his head too quickly, he would see them again, as if their ghosts had haunted his eyes.

At the train's next stop, he made an excuse about the coupling being uncomfortable, though he and the woman had been quite cozy at times and had even endured the intimate embarrassment of each having to urinate while in the other's arms. He climbed off, untying himself, and made his way stiffly to the platform, where, much to his surprise, soldiers were disembarking. There were civilians at the station too, but the panic of evacuation had not yet reached this far south.

The woman, who had followed him onto the platform, told him that the People's Army had overwhelmed the South Korean and American soldiers to the west, where the roads and terrain suited their Russian-made tanks, but in the middle of the peninsula and to the east, their progress had been slow. He wondered how she had learned all this, and she laughed. "Do you think I don't have ears to hear with," she said, practically shouting to be heard over the activity on the platform. "Do you think I'm deaf, Mr. Lee?"

He was blank for a moment.

"Mr. Lee?" She was holding her bundle at her belly.

"Ah," he said, embarrassed for some reason. "It looks like there will be room in the cars now. You can ride without being cold."

"And where will you be, Mr. Lee?"

"Oh, you go on ahead. I'll take the next train."

"I'm getting off here too," she said. "It may sound strange, but I think that train is bad luck. Perhaps we could . . ."

His first reaction was to feel terribly offended. How rude and presumptuous of her, he thought. A whore who serviced Yankees propositioning him to be her travel companion? What did she think? That he had money? He'd be her pimp? It surprised him how quickly these thoughts rushed through his head—a flurry, a flock of starlings wheeling to avoid a hawk. She doesn't know who I am, he thought. I could be anybody right now. She knows nothing about me. She calls me *Misutah Lee* because that's how she heard the nun address me. Then he thought, I could become anybody, and that made him giddy, and then it frightened him to realize that he was also nobody, just a refugee with a bum foot wearing charity clothes. A nobody with nothing but a bedroll and a mostly empty knapsack. He suddenly realized he was terribly hungry. He felt as famished as the Buddha must have been when, as a mendicant, he had reached to touch his belly and felt the knobs of his spine. It was his hunger that made him look at the woman and give a subtle nod.

She had been patient but clearly also nervous during his long silence, because now she smiled, and her face lit up like the face of a young bride who has discovered a kind mother-in-law.

"Yes, I suppose we could travel together for a little while," he said.

"You must be hungry."

For an instant he thought she must have read his mind, but that was just his imagination getting the better of him. "How can you tell?" he asked.

"Because I've been terribly hungry for hours." She put her bundle down on the platform. "Wait for me here," she said. "I won't be long, and I'll bring us some food."

"Where—" he began, but then he realized she must know something he did not, to be so confident. He sat down on his bedroll and resigned himself to waiting.

The woman untied her *pojagi* and removed a small bag and a small bundle wrapped in a scarf. She headed to the station house, taking small staccato steps like a Japanese woman in a kimono. How habits stick with us, he thought. They seep into our bodies until we don't even recognize them as having come from outside ourselves. Everything inside at one time outside.

He sat idly for a while, watching the people on the platform—troops embarking and disembarking, perhaps making a transfer to another unit; civilians frantically loading their possessions on board; and people both on the platform and in the passenger cars weeping, probably for those who had fallen to their deaths and those they'd had to leave behind. As the station began to empty out, a Korean MP came up to him and asked if he was planning to get on the train. "We're leaving in a minute," he said. "You can ride in one of the cargo cars. There'll be plenty of room until we get to the next station."

"I just got off," he said.

"Don't you want to go to Pusan?" asked the MP. "The Reds will kill you if they get you. If they don't, the people here might take you for a sympathizer for staying, and your life will be in danger."

"I guess it's like a dog's testicles," he said. "One side or the other— either way, you lose."

The MP laughed. "*Ajoshi*, you wouldn't happen to have a cigarette among all those worldly possessions?"

He rummaged in his knapsack and found a crushed pack; he removed two broken butts and the MP lit them with a cheap lighter. They smoked together as the train puffed steam and blasted its whistle twice. The MP thoughtfully regarded the train for another few moments as it started moving, then he said a quick thank-you and jogged toward the last passenger car and hopped onto the steps.

When the train was gone, the station seemed strangely deserted, even as people still went about their business. In the quiet he could hear a woman sobbing, sitting between two bundles with her legs splayed out on the cement. He wondered who she had lost—a child? a husband?—but found that his heart had gone numb and he was incapable of feeling sympathy for her. It shocked him, this new kind of emptiness. The sympathy he felt was only an understanding—an idea—and there was no emotion to it. He felt as if he were looking at a photograph or a film and not a real woman of flesh, bone, and blood in front of him, suffering. Something terrible has happened inside me, he thought. Something inside has broken.

He felt suddenly dizzy; the cigarette dropped from his lips onto the cement, scattering sparks. He reached out to steady himself and tipped over. It felt to him that the platform itself had heaved like an ocean wave, so he lay there, resting his head on the woman's open bundle of possessions, and in the next moment, he was asleep.

"Mr. Lee? Mr. Lee, wake up. I brought us some food."

He opened his eyes. The light had not changed much, so he must not have slept very long, and yet he felt rested, as if he'd had a full night's sleep for once. The crying woman was gone, and the woman from the train was there, though he would not have recognized her if not for her voice. She had fixed her hair into a Western style, applied makeup, changed her clothes. Only her shoes were the same.

"Ah," he said. "I must have nodded off."

"Did you have a good sleep?"

"Yes. I feel much better." He looked around the station, which was truly quiet now. A group of American soldiers and a few Koreans stood at the south end with their eyes shaded, looking up at the sky, apparently waiting for something.

"Here," said the woman. She had already laid out a blanket and placed in the middle of it an open *pojagi* with an assortment of cans on top. She sat down, smoothing her skirt, and handed him a small metal device, which he recognized as a GI can opener. "Do you know how to use it?" she asked.

He nodded.

"My English isn't very good, so I did my best with these canned foods. I'm sorry, but the Americans don't eat rice. I never feel like I've eaten properly without rice, but these will fill you up. Here." She handed him one of the green cans.

It was remarkably heavy. Like a chunk of granite, he thought. What could be in it that was edible? "What is it?" he asked.

"That one is beef slices and sauce."

After a couple of false starts with the can opener, he punctured the lid, and the smell of potatoes and beef shot out through the long hole with a small hiss. His mouth filled with saliva, and he could hardly keep his composure as he rushed to open the can halfway. When he finally folded over the dangerously jagged lid, a snaggle-toothed goblin's mouth, he was shaking so much he had to put it down.

The woman smiled at him like a mother watching her child, and she gave him a small metal spoon. "I think the other can is pork and eggs," she said. "I'll be back in a moment."

He didn't bother to watch where she went because he was already preoccupied with the task of cutting into the white blobs of coagulated grease and the solid mass of meat. It made a sucking sound when he spooned some out; the grayish liquid, with dark brown masses floating in it, spilled over the side of the can onto his fingers, and he shoved the spoonful of meat into his mouth, then another, and another, before he was even finished chewing. He even caught himself suspiciously looking over his shoulder, as if he were indulging in some immoral act or someone was lurking over him waiting to snatch the food away. I'm behaving like a dog, he thought, and that brought back the feeling of something broken inside.

After he finished the first can, scraping out its remnants loudly with his spoon, licking the residue smeared on his fingers, he let out a loud belch and regarded the other can. Pork and eggs, he remembered, and his impulse was immediately to open it and eat. He'd had this much meat all at once only a couple of times in his life—once just before his father died, when he had slaughtered a cow—and he had eaten hardly anything in the past several days. The way the mass of food distended his belly made him feel satiated and sick at the same time—like a rich glutton, he thought. Like a dog.

He sat back against one of the bundles, holding his belly with both hands. "I'll have a cigarette now," he declared out loud, looking away from the station toward a line of hills in the southwest. "I shall take my time and digest my food." Ah, that was the sort of thing a rich glutton would say.

The woman returned while he was fumbling for his cigarettes. She handed him a steaming green can whose lid had been bent over to make a handle, and as he reached for it, he smelled the rich aroma of coffee.

"There's only a little bit of sugar in it. I hope it's sweet enough," she said. "The cream packets are always rancid."

He took the makeshift mug in both hands. It was so hot he held it by the bent lid and took a sip, closing his eyes to savor the taste. "Ah, now I can die in peace," he said. "I haven't eaten this well since my father died, and that was so long ago I can hardly remember."

"You shouldn't say such things, Mr. Lee. It's bad luck."

"Bad luck?" he said. "Look at us . . . woman whose name I don't know. We're refugees in a civil war. Relatives are murdering each other, and these foreigner *tokkaebi* have become our protectors. Now, how could luck get any worse than this?"

"My name is Hwang Ch'unhwa," said the woman. It surprised him.

"Ch'unhwa—as in the Chinese characters for 'spring' and 'flower'?" he asked. It was actually a name suited for a courtesan, especially since the surname, Hwang, meant "yellow."

"Yes."

"Yellow Spring Flower. Then you must've had a nickname?"

"Yes." She covered her mouth with her hand. "It's Forsythia."

"Forsythia. Ah." He sang her the forsythia song that all children sang in early spring when the blossoms first came out, and she sat down at his side, smiling. "That's what I'll call you," he said. "Kaenari. But the *kae* part sounds like 'dog,' so I'll call you 'Nari,' which sounds like 'Your Honor' but also means 'Lily.' So now you have three flowers in your name." He didn't tell her that he had learned, from an herbalist, that forsythia was good for fever, inflammation, and infections, and that he often dried it and kept it to use in poultices for his foot.

"You must be a scholar or a poet, Mr. Lee."

"I failed at both," he said, pointing at his wrapped foot. "And you— you must have some education to speak English the way you do."

"I used to be the secretary for an American officer," she said. "I went to a Catholic college, and after my studies I couldn't find a husband, so I went to work on an American Army base. My priest made the introduction . . ." When he looked at her expectantly, she continued, "I made the mistake of getting involved with the American major I worked for. He was married, with a family in America. When he left, I lost my job, and this . . ."

"I see," he said, not wanting to make her give more details. "Thank you for looking after me like this. It's a great debt I'm going to owe you."

"You don't need to say such things, Mr. Lee. Those GIs down there are on their way to Taejon. From there they'll go to Taegu and then on to Pusan. Everybody is going to Pusan. They're planning to make the Nakdong River the last line of defense against the People's Army. I guess all the American soldiers in Japan are coming into Pusan, but someone has to keep the North Koreans back, so the GIs here are scrambling everywhere."

"What about *our* army? Is it as bad as they say?"

"I don't know if it's true, but the Americans are saying it's bad because the officers all ran away and there's no leadership. The only thing delaying the People's Army is that they're moving too fast. They have to wait for their supplies to catch up."

"I feel like I'm talking to a man."

Nari laughed, showing her bright teeth. "I've been around soldiers so long I guess I'm beginning to sound like one."

"Oh, no," he said. "You aren't using enough foul language for that!"

"Well, fuck," she said. Then she quickly raised her hand to cover her mouth again; this time the gesture made her seem suddenly younger, and he found himself thinking of his little sisters and what they must be doing. The youngest of them, Hwasuni, was only seventeen. He couldn't imagine her holed up in the cave across the river from the village or hiding in the woods on the mountain.

The hot coffee and cigarette had left him feeling fortified. Nari, it seemed, was from a decent family—not *yangban*, but one that had done well during the Japanese era. Both her brothers had died in the Pacific War, and she herself had narrowly escaped being recruited to work in a munitions factory because she had been sickly. After the war, one of the women who made it back to the village had told a story about how there was no munitions factory and how all the girls were taken to Manchuria and China to be sex slaves for the Japanese army. No one believed her. No one had heard of such a thing or could imagine what she described, and in a couple of years she had become the village crazy woman.

"How could we know it was true?" said Nari. "Even when we heard the same thing from the men who came back, we didn't want to believe there was such a thing like the spirit girls. My family still insists that my older sister died when her factory was bombed by the Americans. Isn't that ironic? Now the Americans are saving us from our own countrymen and I'm a Yankee princess."

"I didn't have to serve in the Japanese army because of my foot," he said. "I can't speak from experience, never having been a soldier, but from what I hear and what I see now, war seems to be a far more terrible thing when you're a woman."

"Do you feel sorry for me, Mr. Lee?" Nari asked, looking suddenly vulnerable and yet ready to be angry.

"I do," he said. "That's the truth, but I don't quite know if I should."

"Please don't feel sorry for me."

NARI TOLD THE AMERICANS that he was her older brother, and they did not mind taking him along to Taejon with them. Two other Koreans—an orderly, who was a sergeant, and an interpreter, a lieutenant, both named Kim—were attached to the group, and when Nari was busy, he spent time with them chatting and smoking for the first couple of days. He tried to explain himself to the Koreans, telling them a story of how he had found Nari again after they had been separated during the evacuation, but they were both preoccupied with their own troubles, and it became clear to him that regardless of what story he told, he was Nari's pimp as far as they were concerned. Whether he really was her older brother or her husband posing that way to avoid an even greater shame would have made no difference to the Koreans. This was a time of chaos, when Heaven and Earth had changed places, and at such times anything was possible and everything was a kind of charade.

And being with the Americans had immediate benefits that went beyond the good food and relatively comfortable transportation. They quickly found him a pair of boots that fit both feet, and they had a medic with them who cleaned his foot, replaced the dressing, and gave him extra socks and antibacterial sulfa powder. They even gave him an army shirt labeled SMITH with the warning that he wear it at his own risk. He folded it away in his knapsack to wear at night so he wouldn't be taken for a deserter.

Their third day in Taejon, they learned that the Kum River just north of the city was what the Americans had picked as the first line of defense against the approaching People's Army. As Nari had said, the North Koreans seemed to have paused, perhaps to amass more forces and wait for supplies. An American general named Dean had been dispatched from Japan to defend Taejon. His nickname was "The Walking General"—though there was already a general named Walker in Korea—because of his daily walks around town. Sergeant Kim said that Walker wasn't much of a general, but a decent man from what he had heard. It was a shame that he would be responsible for an impossible military task.

"Why is it impossible?" he asked the sergeant.

Kim scratched a map of the peninsula in the dirt and indicated the location of Taejon, halfway between the Thirty-Eighth Parallel and the bottom of the country. The town was a rail center with lines running in all directions, and as far as the terrain was concerned, it might as well have been the middle of South Korea, though it was southwest of the geographic center.

"This is how all the tanks are coming," said Sergeant Kim, drawing a straight line between Seoul and Taejon. "The roads are all clear and there's nothing stopping the Reds since they crossed the Han River. The Americans don't even have bazookas big enough to stop the Russian tanks. They're T-34s—the best tanks of World War Two. Even the great German Panzer generals said so."

"But don't the Americans have tanks of their own?"

"They have a few light tanks, but those might as well be taxi cabs to a T-34. The Americans are getting Pershings and Shermans, but they're not here yet. My guess is that the Americans are just sacrificing the Twenty-Fourth Division. Hardly any of them have any combat experience because they've been here and in Japan sitting on their fat asses in the occupation force. They're not much better than our own army full of fat-assed officers who sit around whoring and drinking all day with our military pay."

"I'm sorry to hear it's so bad," he said to Kim. "But if this is all true, then why do the GIs not seem to be scared? I see them playing cards and having a good time. Shouldn't they be digging ditches or foxholes or something like that?"

"So you've never been a soldier?"

He pointed at his foot, which was outside the boot at the moment, airing out while the wrappings dried in the sun.

The sergeant winced. "You're a lucky bastard. I'd gladly give up *both* feet not to be in this damned army of ours. Generals getting rich off all the American support that's supposed to come down to us and *we* don't get shit." He spat onto the pebble that represented Seoul.

"Are you scared?"

"No," said the sergeant. "It doesn't make one whit of difference whether or not I'm scared, so I choose not to be until it's inevitable. Look at what a fine life I have in the meantime."

"You're quite the philosopher," he said.

"I'm an even better philosopher with a few drinks," said Kim. "Come on. They took the jeep today and won't be back for another few hours. Let's go down to the village and have a couple. Can you walk?"

While he was bent over wrapping his foot and securing his boots, the sergeant rummaged through his own rucksack looking for cigarettes. As he pushed something out of the way, there was a momentary flash of faded cloth—the color of a North Korean uniform. He looked up and their eyes met for an instant. The sergeant smiled—an uneasy smile charged with possibilities. "It's just my insurance," he said. "In case I'm trapped behind enemy lines."

"I have a GI shirt myself," he confessed to the sergeant, though he must have known already. "Let's get going."

Taejon wasn't so much a city as a town with clusters of villages all around. They walked down a well-worn path to the village at the northern edge of the town. As they walked, he could not help thinking of the North Korean uniform in the sergeant's rucksack, and the look in the sergeant's eyes when he realized it had been seen. It made sense, of course, that he might have it as insurance given how the People's Army was routing the resistance, but it also meant he could be accused of being a spy. If it were discovered by anyone other than his friends, he could be shot, regardless of his explanation. Perhaps the Americans would not shoot him, but if they detained him, the Koreans would probably kill him—the South Koreans for being a spy, a traitor, or just a sympathizer, and the North Koreans for being a spy or a deserter. He knew the sergeant was probably none of those things, and yet the possibility of accusation now hung in the air between them, and he knew the sergeant would be wise not to trust him now—he was a stranger, after all. And this meant he could no longer risk being alone with the sergeant, especially when he had his rifle with him. But he could not make any of this known. He had to keep a naïve and friendly facade. He had to perform a dangerous mask dance.

They headed toward a cluster of thatched houses where some farmers were gathered under a large sycamore. One of the houses there had a wooden placard with the Chinese character for wine painted on it in a schoolboy's calligraphy.

"Do you think the place is still open?" he asked. "I can't imagine they could have any customers during a war."

"They have something or other," said the sergeant. "Otherwise those men would be hanging around elsewhere. How much money do you have?"

"Money? I'm afraid not much."

"Don't worry about it," said the sergeant, waving as the villagers noticed his uniform. "Let's be their guests for today."

The place did have something to drink—remarkably good *makkolli*, which the owner of the house shared with great generosity, since he was planning to evacuate and didn't want the Reds getting what he couldn't take on his cart. Up close, they saw that the local men were already red-faced and soused—useless for anything but contention, complaint, and gossip.

By the time his own face was flushed with the heat of the liquor, the farmers were comfortable enough that they no longer suspected him of being a spy for the People's Army. It was clear that Sergeant Kim was an authentic South Korean, since he knew the area. The oldest of the men, who wore a sleeveless vest shirt over his baggy pants, had the innkeeper bring out some noodles, and while they slurped them, he said, "Why did they do it?"

"Do what?" the sergeant asked, not looking up from his bowl.

"You heard the gunshots this morning, didn't you?"

"We hear shots all the time."

In fact, the sound of gunfire had become so common it didn't frighten him any longer. It was just a signal to be cautious, to keep his wits about him, to prepare an escape. In the presence of the GIs, the gunfire didn't even concern him much, though he knew it was irrational of him to feel so secure with them. Even hearing about their defeat at the hands of the People's Army didn't change that feeling. They were somehow different— charmed, protected by some alien God that regarded them with a favor not bestowed upon Koreans.

"There were five truckloads of them," said the old man. He grimaced, as if he were feeling a sudden pain, and his gold-banded front tooth glinted in the sun. "Prisoners, from the look of their clothes."

"What are you talking about?" said the sergeant.

One of the other men slapped the floor of the wooden platform; the shock rattled the metal chopsticks on the table. "What did they do that was so evil, *ungh*?! They're our own flesh and blood! The Reds are already all over the place—why did you have to go and kill your own country-men? Why?!"

With everyone looking at him expectantly, the sergeant put down his chopsticks with his mouth still full of noodles. He looked from one face to the other.

One of the farmers began to weep, and his friend comforted him, tapping on his thigh, saying, "It's all right. It's all right."

"What are you talking about?" the sergeant asked again. "What truckloads of prisoners?"

"It was an execution," said one of the farmers. "There's no mistaking it. They didn't even finish burying the bodies."

"You witnessed this?" said the sergeant.

"Why do you think we're sitting here?" said the old man. "Do you think we have the time to loaf around all day in times like these? We have work to do, but we're afraid."

"Where was this?"

"Just north of here. You two came down from Kubong Mountain over there. Couldn't you see the trucks from up there?"

"We saw trucks. We couldn't see what was in them." How funny, he thought, that there was another Kubong Mountain down here. He'd felt, for a moment, that he was near home, even with the farmers speaking a different dialect.

"Can you show us?" said the sergeant.

The old man didn't answer, and the other farmer looked frightened by the question. It was the weeping man who answered, finally: "Why don't you just kill everybody and get it over with? Every day we strug-gle. We bleed and we cry and now most of us are going to leave our homes. Will we ever come back? How can we know with the likes of you snatching our lives away even while we're doing our damnedest to keep living?"

"Why are you saying all this to me?" said the sergeant. "I didn't kill anybody. Can't you see I'm just trying to stay alive like you?"

"We're not showing you," said the old man, pointing at the sergeant's uniform. "But if you go north on the main road and then right when you get to the long buildings, you can get a look for yourself. The graves are behind a wall. It's a long wall—you can't miss it. They haven't even finished burying everyone. It will stink. There will be crows everywhere."

"You have to report it to someone," said another farmer. "Surely it's a crime. It's murder!"

"Who's he going to tell?" said the crying man. "The Yankees? A couple of them were following the trucks! How about our honorable President Rhee? How about him, *ungh*? Why not report it to *him*!" He slammed his palm against the floor for emphasis, sending another shock through the table.

Just then, when it seemed a fight was imminent, they all heard a dull roar in the sky to the south. Three American bombers came into view and lumbered through the clouds, and while they craned their necks to watch the planes pass, they heard the revving of a jeep engine, then the rattle and clatter of the vehicle drawing near.

"It's Lieutenant Kim and the Americans," the sergeant said, quickly getting to his feet. "It looks like they're back."

"You Yankees here to take our picture before they kill us?" said one of the farmers, waving his empty cup.

The jeep stopped. The lieutenant, who was sitting in the back, looked closely at everyone, and when he was satisfied he said something to the two GIs in English—something having to do with "Reds." The GI in the passenger seat nodded and the sergeant climbed into the back.

"Hurry, Mr. Lee," said the GI who was driving. "*Bali-bali*, okay?"

He nodded a quick goodbye to the farmers and grabbed his boots before scrambling onto the jeep.

"You know this area?" the lieutenant asked the sergeant.

"Yes, sir."

"Go ahead—shoot us now!" said the crying man.

"Sir, they're all senseless drunk," said the sergeant.

"I can see that." The lieutenant drew his sidearm, and that immediately silenced the farmers. The old man *tsk-tsk*ed and sat, impassively, with his arms folded. The lieutenant said, "You're going to direct us north of here on the main road, Sergeant. We're looking for a place where some two-and-a-half-ton army trucks went earlier today."

The jeep lurched forward. The GI wasn't very good at shifting the gears, and everyone winced when he missed and the transmission let out a growl.

He noticed that the GI sitting in the back with them had a Thompson submachine gun. When the GI lifted it, the farmers, who were already receding behind them, all ducked involuntarily at the same time. They started gesticulating and yelling, but they couldn't be heard over the noise of the jeep. The driver took them to where they were billeted, where he would be dropped off to stay with Nari, whose work for the day was in afternoon intermission.

THE ABANDONED HOUSE the GIs had commandeered earlier in the week obviously belonged to someone wealthy—a land owner or a merchant already evacuated to Pusan. From outside it was still impeccable except for some charring on the wood of the traditional gate, which someone had tried, unsuccessfully, to burn down. The tiled roofs shone blue under the summer sun and the *madang* courtyard, where all the everyday work was done, had a smooth surface of packed earth, rich with clay. The water came from a well at one corner of the *madang*. The sergeant had hauled up a couple of bucketsful, and it was cold and refreshing.

On the inside, there had been some vandalism and looting by the locals—smashed door panels with ragged holes in the expensive rice paper, rain shutters torn from their hinges, some communist graffiti (which was odd, but also somehow predictable), and some burning of the Confucian sayings that had been carved into the wooden columns. The name plate by the gate had been torn down, and someone had scrawled *chinilpa* there—Japanese sympathizer.

Hardly any damage had been done to the *sarang*—the outbuilding usually used as the husband's room—from which most of the furniture had already been removed, and that was where Nari had set up. Or, rather, that is where the GIs had set her up so there would be privacy for her and her various visitors.

It wasn't clear to him who was getting the money for this arrangement—whether the senior GI or the Korean lieutenant got a cut, or whether there was any pimping going on at all, but even with the North Korean army only a day or two away, the Taejon GIs seemed to know where to come, and Nari was occupied much of the day and night. She moved like a woman twenty years her senior, he thought, when he saw her that afternoon.

But she tried to be cheerful, and somehow she'd even had time to supervise the local girl they had found to serve as the cook and maid.

"*Oppa*," she said, "how was your little trip? Your face is all red." She remembered to call him "older brother" with the others in earshot.

"Oh, we had great fun," he said. "Sergeant Kim and I went down into a village." He watched the sergeant out of the corner of his eye and said nothing more.

"It looks like you need to eat, *Oppa*. Come, Suni cooked, and the rice is still hot."

While he ate on the *maru* at the little food table, the soldiers made some sort of preparation in the courtyard. The two Kims went into the main room to confer for a few minutes and came out smoking and looking grim. The lieutenant and the GIs discussed something, and the GIs looked shocked, shaking their heads in denial. Nari looked on curiously and asked him if he knew what was going on. "I wouldn't know," he lied. "Probably something about the North Koreans approaching."

In fact, he had never heard the GIs' voices so angry and loud. They were clearly disagreeing with the Koreans, and it looked to him like they were blaming them for something that the Koreans, in turn, were denying.

"Let's go inside for a little while," said Nari. She seemed to realize it was wiser not to witness the altercation. "Suni," she called, "take the table inside and boil some water for coffee."

The girl bowed and stepped down into the kitchen.

As they went into the main room and slid the *chabudon*s over to sit on them, Nari asked if he had any cigarettes left. It was an odd question, since she clearly had some. But he found his knapsack in the corner by the bedding chest, and when he leaned down and opened it to look inside, he saw the North Korean uniform shirt—the same one he had seen earlier that day in the sergeant's rucksack. The shirt the GIs had given him was gone. He felt his bowels turn cold; his legs nearly gave out, and he sat as quickly as he could, pulling another item of clothing over the uniform to hide it from Nari's view.

"I don't seem to have any cigarettes left," he said. His voice sounded odd even to himself.

"Is something the matter, Mr. Lee?"

"Oh, no," he said. "It just looks like someone stole them from my knapsack."

"It was probably Sergeant Kim," she said. "Never mind. You can always steal some back when the Americans give him his share."

"I'll remember to do that," he replied with a dull laugh. But he was terrified. He had been looking forward to staying with Nari and the Americans on the road to Pusan, and then living with Nari when the war ended. On their second day in Taejon he had told her all about the old man's buried treasure and how they could retrieve it after the war. He planned with her how they would sell the valuables, then pick an auspicious spot together and rebury the eggs and the hairpin, as he'd promised. He had imagined how they might set up their household in a similarly wealthy house, the Parker fountain pen with which he would scribble some essays, the chrome-plated Zippo lighter he would use, the Chivas Regal he would drink, the cartons of American cigarettes he would hide in the wall closet and ration out to himself as he studied the classics. He had imagined so much—the stylish clothes she would buy him, how she would take off her Western clothes, though he would make her keep her nylons on when they made love. And now all this washed over him like a wave of disgust, a repulsion he felt for his own weak and lazy imagination.

The sergeant could expose him at any moment. He might, in fact, have already told the Americans and they were preparing to interrogate him or simply shoot him for being a spy. He knew that no amount of protesting or telling the truth would make any difference. And now he began to wonder if the sergeant had told the truth—or if he *was* actually a spy or an informer for the communists. He was a driver, after all, with access to a jeep, traveling with an interpreter and Americans who seemed to know something about the South Korean defense strategy. He had known about how the Americans were routed at Osan on the eve of their Independence Day and how it had demoralized the GIs of the Twenty-Fourth Division. That was precisely the kind of intelligence the North Koreans would find useful.

While Nari busied herself with her makeup, waiting for the maid to come with hot water for their coffee, he stepped out to the *maru* to watch what the men were doing. Sergeant Kim stood at the side of the jeep filling the gas tank from one of the metal jerry cans usually strapped to the back next to the spare tire. The lieutenant had a map unfolded, and he was pointing at a place north of what looked like Taejon, speaking English. The two Americans regarded the map suspiciously and one of them mentioned General Dean. No one looked in his direction, and he went back into the room, momentarily relieved, to have his cup of coffee and a last cigarette Nari had found for him.

Wherever they were going, it was important—important enough that the sergeant would wait to turn him in. He wondered if it would work if he simply got rid of the North Korean uniform. That would make the sergeant's accusation ring false. But it would make no difference now. It was too dangerous—for the both of them—if he stayed with Nari. His life with her had come to an end.

"Mr. Lee, you seem melancholy today."

Nari had managed to find a coffee service from the American mess hall in Taejon—blue-banded white cups, saucers, and stainless steel teaspoons. She had emptied dozens of C-ration packets of powered coffee and sugar into small celadon containers she had found in the house, and somehow the clash of old Korean celadon and the cheap china—probably from Japan—looked elegant.

"Oh, no," he said. "I'm just feeling nostalgic for some reason. Here we are on the slope of Kubong Mountain in an elegant house in the middle of a war, and I'm happy. There's a Kubong Mountain near my home—it's the place where our village shaman came from. And I realize I'm happier right now than I was before the war began. Strange, isn't it?" He allowed her to pour the steaming water from the kettle into the cup full of powdered coffee and sugar, and when she stirred it, making that tinkling sound, already so familiar now, he was thinking of the Tao and the elements, the *um* of black coffee, the yang of white sugar, metal spoon, earthen cup, wood table, fire and water making steam. And now it was time to move with the Tao of the moment—be happy, be content, things are as they are and will be what they will be, an extension of now, flowing as unstoppably as the water of the Han, the Kum, the Nakdong. It was time to leave.

"Yes, it is strange," said Nari. "I worry about my family, but despite everything I feel happy too. I think we must be strange people, Mr. Lee." She covered her mouth as she laughed, and his heart felt sore.

"I suppose a war would make anyone strange," he said. "Here I am in a house where I would never even be invited at any other time, and I'm living here as if I own it. It's apt, that saying about when Heaven and Earth change places."

"If only things could stay the same for a while," she said wistfully.

"Are you having visitors today?"

She nodded without answering and took a tentative sip of her coffee.

"They're leaving in the jeep," he said—he could hear the engine revving. "I think I'll step out for a little while to exercise my foot and get some air. I drank too much down there."

"Only two," Nari said, her face still lowered. "I won't be busy all night."

They sat in silence for a while communicating something to each other. Later, he would imagine that they had exchanged a secret message in those moments, but in reality he knew nothing of what she might be thinking. They took their leave of each other then, and he retrieved his knapsack, under the pretense of having to sort his remaining socks, and left the house.

He had seen the lieutenant's map enough times over the past few days to know that the Kum River stretched west and east, west to its mouth at the coast and east to the hills, where it widened and expanded into what looked like the body of a contorted dragon made of long lakes. To the east of the city was Kyeryong Mountain, where the terrain would make it safe for him to hide but might be too difficult with his foot. Water dragon or Earth dragon—which way? He could not decide, so he did what a child would do—he took off a boot and tossed it into the air, and when it landed, he resolved to go in the direction it pointed—north.

Damn it, he thought. North was the direction from which the People's Army was approaching, the direction from which the refugees were pouring southward. If there was any doubt that his life was in danger, it was gone now. The very fact that he had run away would confirm his guilt, and if they found him now he was surely dead. He could imagine it quite clearly—the sergeant shooting him, claiming it was in self-defense.

They would be looking for him in the south, knowing he couldn't get far because of his foot, and that would also make him easy to remember and identify. The childish game was right in the same way the *I Ching* oracle was right, even when you could rationalize its advice away. They would look for him in every direction but north, and so that was the direction he would go.

When he was far enough from the house, he followed the buzzing of flies, knowing they would lead him to something—an animal's den, a fertilized field, even a dead body that he might pilfer from—and found a badger's hole in an acacia grove. He buried the North Korean uniform there. That night he would have to eat one of the C-rations he had hidden in his knapsack, and he would have to sleep in the open unless he found an abandoned house.

It was a while before sunset, and he was still uncertain about the advice of his boot, so he gathered small, flat pebbles until he had three of approximately the same size. On one side of each, the yang side, he chipped a small white spot with a sharper, harder stone. He cupped the three prepared stones in his hands, shook them up and down, rattling them like dice in a cup, and tossed them onto the ground. He did this six times, producing the forty-first hexagram: *son*, mountain over marsh, representing restraint, diminishment, disadvantage.

It was a reading of his current condition, his location near Kubong Mountain, which rose over a winding river and a marsh. In Korean, *son* also sounded like the word for monkey—those GIs, and also the Monkey King, who would journey to the west, as did the Kum River. *Son* was also the fragrant iris, humbleness, and simply to sit down and eat supper. He chuckled at the oracle's wisdom, and in the dirt he scratched out the pictogram for *son*. It looked to him like a plant waving in the wind next to a fox standing under the sun or moon. The pictogram was supposed to symbolize a human palm and an empty sacrificial urn, if one followed the official dictionaries, but the pictograms of the *I Ching* always spoke to a particular moment in a particular place, and now the oracle was telling him to hide among the trees and reeds, day and night, like a fox. The Monkey King's journey to the west began in the north, so he would go in that direction until the signs said otherwise; and like a fox, he would use cleverness to disappear by leaving his clothes and his rucksack to be discovered on a roadside corpse.

He put the three make-do pebbles in his pocket and searched for a cluster of trees in which to spend the night. He heard gunfire as he ate his supper of cold C-ration, and now that he was no longer under the Americans' protection, he was afraid.

HE AWOKE EARLY in the morning before sunrise, feeling stiff and achy like an old man, his face puffy from mosquito bites though he had covered himself with his extra undershirt. When the sun came up over the long line of trees, he realized he had camped too close to a road with a footpath only a few meters away. Quickly, he gathered his things together, buried the C-ration can, and made his way north through the fields, trying to move from one patch of trees to another until he found one suitable for biding his time. There were people still about their daily business, much to his surprise, and later in the day when he glimpsed the main road in the distance, he saw lines of refugees carrying their belongings on A-frames, leading oxcarts, pulling overladen two-wheeled *niko-das*. He pitied those who had to bear all of their worldly possessions wrapped in huge *pojagi*s on their heads.

By late morning he had found an abandoned farm where he searched for food. People had already been there before him—he could tell from the condition of the place—and they had poked around in all the likely hiding places. There were holes in the *madang* and in the back where they had dug, looking for buried valuables, and it made him laugh bitterly— *as if a poor farmer would have anything to bury!* But they had somehow missed a brown hen, which he followed as she made her way back to her nest. He ate the eggs immediately, sucking them loudly through holes he poked in their shells with a fingertip, and even knowing he might have to eat her raw, he snapped the chicken's neck to keep her quiet. When she hung dead and limp from his fist, he felt a pang of guilt and a strange sense of longing that nearly brought tears to his eyes. He put the hen in an empty sack he found in the kitchen, and he continued northward.

It was already late afternoon and overcast when he heard the crows and saw them wheeling in the sky above a row of trees. He did not want to go there at first, but it was the direction that offered the most cover, so he trudged his way through a small grove between two freshly manured fields until he reached a dirt road that led to several long buildings. They looked like they might have been a factory complex at one time. Many of the Japanese-run businesses had shut down after the Pacific War, and the country was still littered with empty buildings for which the Koreans had found no use.

He should have known better than to cross the road there. On the other side, he saw the long wall and remembered what the drunk farmers had described, and by then the faint and unmistakable smell of death was wafting toward him in the breeze. He felt his mouth fill with the sick saliva that precedes a fit of vomiting. He bent over for just a moment to gather his wits, and then he heard the sharp, irregular reports of gunfire coming from beyond the wall. A volley of rifle fire. There were fainter sounds—voices shouting and crying out—more gunshots, and then the rumble of a large engine, larger than a jeep's.

Quickly, he scrambled down into the ditch that paralleled the road and climbed up the other side through a patch of cosmos, where thick foliage abutted a crumbling cinder block wall. He crawled under one of the leafy bushes to hide himself from the road, pressing his back against the wall, sweating and panting so much he thought anyone nearby must surely hear him. He waited what seemed to be an interminably long time until his breath settled and his heart stopped pounding.

Other engines started now on the far side of the wall—trucks, jeeps. He heard some shouted commands, phrases in English, which sounded angry. The sun broke through the clouds just then, and a bar of light shone through a gap in the wall. He couldn't help but look through it.

What he saw were two or three long, parallel ditches, with long mounds of dirt on top. On the far side, the mostly empty trucks and a couple of jeeps were idling, ready to leave, waiting for the signal. Crows had already begun to alight on the walls and on top of the empty buildings, and two Korean MPs—one with a rifle and the other with a sidearm—were walking along the mounds, looking down into the ditches, occasionally firing their weapons at what was below. Not all the bodies had fallen in—there were dozens of them in soiled and bloody white prison uniforms still stretched across the mounds, facedown in the dirt with arms and legs contorted. Some had their wrists or arms bound together behind their backs and others were reaching, as if they had been interrupted while pulling themselves forward by their fingertips.

One of the MPs stopped, apparently out of bullets, and went toward one of the idling trucks. The other continued, slapping another magazine into his pistol, and when he reached a body that hadn't fallen into the ditch he would kick it in the ribs—a sharp jab with the toe of his boot. If he suspected any remaining life, he fired his pistol into the back of the head. There was a little jolt, sometimes a puff of dirt, and then he walked on.

# The Dog Market

## 1975

What happened at Yaksan put me in a foul mood. I stayed home for a few days, contributing to some of the chores around the house, playing *paduk* with Housebound Uncle, and enjoying the quiet of the little yard we had inside our half of the brick-walled compound.

Yongsu had set up a small bench press with weights made of cement-filled coffee cans, and I tried it along with his cast-iron dumbbells. But I didn't understand the purpose of weightlifting—it only made me tired and sweaty, with thick and heavy-feeling limbs. Yongsu had also gotten a guitar from one of his friends, and when he was home he tried to teach me a few chords, but it all seemed too complicated, with too many configurations to memorize. Instead, I installed training wheels on the little pink Huffy bicycle my mother had bought for An-na, added some colorful streamers to the handlebars, and taught her how to ride.

Since school was out for the summer, I slept late and listened to American music on the request shows that played on the Korean pop stations. The DJs usually read the request postcards out loud, making me wonder if those Koreans actually spoke the way they wrote or were just trying extra hard to sound poetic and sentimental. By the third day I was crouching in the yard by the garden patch, watching ants carry dead flies into one of their big holes at the foot of the wall. The ants were diligent and relentless. I admired their patience and great strength, which I tested with offerings of grasshoppers, beetles, and caterpillars, and then I would watch them pull the larger bugs apart with their tiny pincers or gang up on the carcasses and carry them whole to their entrance.

Late the next morning I was sipping a cup of Maxwell House instant coffee when I heard Paulie calling me from outside. I opened the inset door of our blue metal gate and let him in.

"Are you sick?" he asked.

"Nah."

"Where have you been?"

"I was just staying home."

"Why?"

Paulie and I both knew why, but neither of us could really say the truth, so I said what we both expected. "I don't know—just felt like it."

"Miklos said you were gonna kill yourself."

I was genuinely surprised. "What?" I said. "Are you crazy?"

"He said your Big Uncle is dying and you feel so bad you decided to die with him."

"I haven't even seen Miklos since we came back!"

"He said he came to see you."

"Fucking liar! He's always lying about everything."

"Then why didn't you come to ASCOM for so long?"

"Three days! Can't I just be alone sometime?"

"Well, if you're okay, why don't you come to Inchon with us today?"

"Who?"

"Me and Miklos. His cousin has a dog in a dogfight and he wants to go watch."

"A dog fight?"

"Yeah. His cousin is a dog trainer. It's in a boxing ring this time."

It was probably all just a ploy to get me out of the house. "I'll go," I said. "How do we get there? Where's Miklos?"

"We'll go eat at the Chinese restaurant first. We can catch the Korean bus from Sinchon after."

WE ORDERED *TCHAJANGMYON*, noodles with black bean sauce. While we waited for our food to come, Miklos ate half a raw onion dipped in salty black bean paste, and his breath stank the rest of the day. This was going to be a special dog fight, Miklos said, with some of the best dogs, and the event had been quietly publicized only by word of mouth for people in the dog-fighting circuit. Miklos's cousin Jongbae trained dogs on the side while he worked for a meat packer who contracted with the Army and Navy mess halls in ASCOM and Inchon. He could read and write English passably, but whenever he had to do anything important he would have his mother ask Miklos's mother to send Miklos to translate.

"I hate that shit," said Miklos. "But John Wayin pays me and I get free meat when I want it."

"It's *John Wayne*—and what do you mean he pays you?" I said.

"No—*John Wayin*. That's what Jongbae calls himself so the GIs will think he's cool. Sometimes he sells them dog meat so they can see what it tastes like."

"Why the fuck would a GI want to eat dog meat?" said Paulie.

"John Wayin says they rank on Koreans for eating dog, but lots of them are curious. You ever have dog?"

Paulie shook his head. "Man, how can anyone eat a dog?"

"I had it once with you," I said to Miklos. "You remember that time we saw those dudes on the rice paddy by the road to Sosa?"

"Motherfuckers tricked us!"

"They tricked you into eating it?" Paulie asked me.

"Yeah. I hated it."

"You're both pussies," said Miklos, slurping on his noodles. "If you didn't know, you would just think it was goat meat." He paid for our meal and we finished our cups of tepid barley water before heading for the bus stop at the entrance to Sinchon. "I'll pay for the bus, but one of you has to buy dinner. And if you make bets, it's with your own money."

"Bets?" I said.

"Why the fuck do you think they *have* dog fights?"

IT WAS AN OLD BUS, and we had to stand for half of the trip because it was crowded at that hour. I listened to the two bus maids—one at the front and the other at the middle of the bus—calling out their ritual "*Sutop! Oraiii!*" and their loud raps against the metal wall to signal the driver. After a few stops in Inchon, the passengers thinned out. I helped an old woman with a metal basin full of rice cakes take the seat in front of me. Inchon was on the coast, but there was no wind that afternoon, and the city was covered in a pall of brown-gray exhaust. Every other passenger coughed and wheezed, and I couldn't help imagining the bus full of barking dogs on their way to the stadium with us.

"He's named King," said Miklos. "My cousin's dog. This will be his first big fight. If I had money, I'd bet it on him."

"What kind of dog?" asked Paulie.

"Shepherd. He's a big one, too. Looks like he might be part wolf. I saw him rip a cat right in half one time."

"He fights cats?"

"No, man! That's just for practice. They give the dogs little animals and smaller dogs to kill for practice. You know, shit dogs and dogs for *poshint'ang* restaurants."

Paulie looked disturbed by the thought of dogs killing each other for practice, but for Miklos it all seemed very matter of fact. I put those images out of my mind and looked around the bus instead.

The old woman with the rice cakes reminded me of one of my country aunts as she sat drowsing with the basin at her feet. A man in a cheap blue business suit with white socks and worn-out shoes was reading a newspaper as he compulsively smoothed his oily hair. For a moment I thought it was Housebound Uncle sneaking down to Inchon, but when he looked up I saw that he was much too old.

We got off a block from the stadium entrance and had to go around the complex, past piles of garbage and pieces of broken equipment, to one of the back entrances. Inside, the dog handlers had taken up the far corners of the athletic field with their dogs. We could hear the men yelling, dogs barking and growling, sometimes a loud yelp as one must have gotten kicked or hit with a stick. The ring had been set up all the way to one side of the stadium. The audience all sat in one section closest to the ring—only a couple hundred people milling about, with some wandering in from various entrances like ants coming back to the nest. The rest of the stadium was ominously empty.

"Jongbae is over there," Miklos said, pointing. "That's King's barking."

"You gonna go say hello to him?"

Miklos shook his head and put a hand up by his face in a theatrical aside. "Sometimes the police come and bust these fights, you know. Jongbae said it's better not to be connected to the dog trainers."

We made our way up toward the stands across the athletic field to get a closer view of the ring setup: three sets of stairs on the sides not facing the audience and everything, even the ropes it seemed, covered in layers of old newspaper. A man wandered through the audience either checking or selling tickets. When he reached us, Miklos said something to him and he waved us toward the front. We sat in the third row behind two men who were smoking and playing flower cards on the seat between them while they waited.

We felt a breeze, and then the wind shifted. Paulie and I turned our heads at the same time, then looked at each other, a little afraid. We could smell it now—the dogs: sweat, saliva, blood, and shit. Not the warm and comforting dog smell I remembered from my childhood, but acrid and thick.

After a while, as the shadows stretched farther across the field, two teams of handlers approached the ring from the sides, and the announcer, who looked like a trainer himself, though he wore a suit jacket for the occasion, came up the middle steps. He didn't have a microphone, and so he spoke loudly, in a strangely shrill voice, as if he were imitating a woman, and though I could hear everything he said, between his strange tone and his rapid use of words that were alien to me, I understood hardly anything. Was he using some special language of dog fighters? Or maybe I was just distracted by the smells and my mind was confused. He went on for a while with what I heard as gibberish punctuated here and there with some phrase I could make out: "Pomwang, undefeated champion of three thousand *li* with us tonight! Magwi! Who need say anything more about Mawgi!" and then, after some more gibberish: "King!"—though he pronounced it more like "*kkeeng!*"—"The magnificent *hwarang* of the dog species!"

The men in the audience cheered, yelled, and shouted insults at the appropriate moments, though there was a smaller group of them, closest to the ring, who were more reserved and businesslike. Probably the dog owners or the big betters. Pomwang meant "Tiger King" and Magwi was "Demon." I imagined they must be especially fierce dogs to be mentioned by the announcer. King must have been at least as good as the others to have his name shouted out like that.

People in the audience around us were pulling wads of money from their pockets and counting it, rifling through the paper bills at an incredible speed. They gestured at each other, arguing heatedly until the first dog came up into the ring—a huge thing that looked like a Doberman crossed with a Great Dane. I felt sorry for the other dog and hoped it wouldn't be King, but instead of a dog they brought a leashed cat from the other side and tied it to the ropes so it couldn't escape. The cat shrieked and clawed at the handlers—it knew it was going to die, I suppose—and when they left, it crouched there. The huge dog's handler unmuzzled him, and the dog instantly snapped at the air, letting out a deep, stomach-churning growl.

"Yong!" shouted the announcer.

That meant Dragon, and as soon as his handler unchained him, he leapt at the cat, took one swipe of its claws across a cheek, and snapped its neck in one bite. We could hear the sudden silence of the cat's shrieking and the dull crunch simultaneously from where we sat. Yong shook the cat's body so violently we could all see that its head was about to come off, and now I realized why everything was covered in newspaper. Blood splattered in every direction.

When the announcer stepped back into the ring, wiping the droplets from his face with a white handkerchief, everyone was cheering and shouting, "Yong! Yong!" He waited while the handlers leashed and muzzled Yong once again and an attendant tossed the cat's carcass down to the back side of the ring, where we could no longer see it. This time, in an even shriller voice, the announcer said a bunch of things I was able make out:

"*Yong*, everyone! That awesome strength! That speed! That *demonic* violence! People of Inchon, we have a special tournament for you today! Next up is *Inchon Lion* in the red corner versus *Haetae* in the blue corner!" The crowd cheered loudly, drowning out some of what he said before he ducked out of the ring again.

"Haetae?" said Paulie. "Who would name a fighting dog after an ice cream brand?"

Haetae were mythical dragon dogs you found as guardian statues at temples. They looked like bug-eyed frilly bulldogs to me—not the sort of thing to use as an ice cream or cookie brand.

"Haetae is truly scary," said one of the men who had been playing flower cards. "Inchon Lion won't be much of a match for him."

"Yeah, but Inchon Lion is a Tosa," said the other man, as if that was some important detail.

"Will Yong fight another dog?" Miklos asked.

"That was just a demo to get everyone's spirits up. He'll be fighting the big match tonight, probably."

I still felt a bit sick from what had happened to the cat, so I didn't say anything.

Haetae actually looked sort of like his namesake, and Inchon Lion looked a bit like Elsa the lioness from the *Born Free* movie, at least in his coloration. Their match was hard to follow because they tumbled so much and flipped around, this way and that, snarling, spit flying, as each tried to get at the other's throat. But after a few minutes we saw that Haetae, who stood lower to the ground in a more stable stance, was going to win. At one point he jerked his head and grabbed Inchon Lion's throat from the side, and a moment later the handlers were pulling them apart, prying Haetae's jaws open with a little wooden knife. Inchon Lion's tawny coat was half black with blood.

"*Haetae!*" the announcer screamed. "Now for our next match, Magwi versus the undefeated *Togsuri*, who has *just* arrived! Traffic!"

A big cheer erupted from one side of the crowd as the handlers brought Togsuri up into the ring, straining at his leash. Togsuri meant "Eagle," and even from where we sat we could see the dog's narrow snout and talon-like teeth.

"Demon versus Eagle," said the man with the flower cards to us. "Who would *you* bet on?" He gestured at the ring, where Magwi's handler had just come up with their hideous dog. It looked like part of his face had been bitten off—he wore a permanent snarl, his teeth exposed by the missing portion of his lips.

"I would bet on Togsuri," said Miklos. "He's undefeated."

"That's why the odds wouldn't be very good," said the man. "See, that would be a safe and unexciting bet."

"And what would you know about betting, anyway?" said the other man. "You just play go-stop all the time."

"I would bet on Togsuri, too," said Paulie.

"*Ah ha ha*," said the flower card man. "You too. No fun." He looked toward me.

I didn't like the idea of betting, and I was feeling even more nause-
ated now as the breeze brought the smell of blood up into the stands. I
wanted to leave.

"What about you?" said the flower card man.

Clearly, I was meant to disagree. "I would bet on Magwi," I said.

The flower card man and his partner both looked at me attentively.
"Why?" they both asked.

"Look at him!" I practically shouted. "*Look* at him—Magwi's been
beaten up and his face is ruined and he's ugly. He's full of hate and he
wants to kill something. *He's* not afraid to die! How's Togsuri going to
win against that?"

The two men slapped each other's hands. "Good reason!" said the
flower card man, and he called out to someone below just as the handlers
unchained the dogs.

Magwi and Togsuri leaped at each other instantly, and we heard the
hollow thump as they collided. They twisted and turned, snarling and
biting, tumbling over each other to get the advantage. Magwi favored
one side—maybe he was blind in one eye—and Togsuri concentrated his
attack there. Minutes into the fight, they were grappling on the mat,
their growls diminished to a low and continuous rumble. When the
crowd began to shout insults, the handlers pulled the dogs apart, using
their knife-shaped pry sticks, and took the dogs back to their corners.
There was a quick once-over, and then the dogs leaped at each other
once again, meeting in mid-air with a strangely soggy-sounding thump.
In the slant light of the setting sun we could see the blood and sweat
droplets exploding into the air before falling to the ground or dissipating into mist.

The two dogs seemed evenly matched, but we could see very soon,
from their agitation, that Togsuri's handlers were concerned. Half an
hour of round after round, and still there was no clear winner as both
dogs tired.

"How long does it go?" I asked. "Do they fight until one dies?"

"Only sometimes," said Miklos. "This one I think they might end soon. Togsuri's owner isn't going to want him too badly injured."

In the next round, Togsuri hesitated to come out of his corner, as if he had lost his enthusiasm. Magwi was so soaked in blood and his fur so matted he looked like a giant otter. He hadn't lost his fight, but he was limping now and dragging one of his hind legs, and this time, when they disengaged, the announcer stepped in and called a draw.

There were shouts of disappointment and insults from the crowd, but the two men below us looked happy.

"*Ajoshi*," Miklos said, "didn't you lose money?"

"Certainly not," said the flower card man. "It was obvious that Magwi wasn't going to win, but your friend here gave us the idea to put money on a tie." He gestured with his cigarette to the other man, who pulled a roll of bills out of his pocket, peeled off a few one-thousand-won notes, and handed them up to me.

"You boys buy yourselves something delicious to eat," he said.

I looked dumbly at the face of the thin, bearded Confucian scholar printed on the money, then at Paulie and Miklos. Everyone laughed as I folded it up and put it in my shirt pocket.

"This must be your first commission," said the flower card man.

I didn't understand the Korean word he used, so Miklos said, in English, "That's your cut of the take, man." Now he bummed a Pall Mall from the flower card man and thoughtfully puffed on it while they cleaned up the ring for the next match, the one we had come to see.

IT TOOK A long time before the evening could proceed—the blood had soaked through layers and layers of the newspaper, which had to be wadded up and thrown out over the back side. The fresh newspaper they spread made everything brighter in the waning light. Finally the announcer stepped up.

"King! Pomwang!" he called out. "The match you've all been waiting for! Thank you for your patience and consideration and don't forget to ask about our next tournament!"

This elicited only a few cheers at first, but then, as the dogs approached their corners, the supporters of each side tried to outdo the other, standing up, gesticulating and shouting, until it seemed a riot would break out and the announcer asked for quiet. When King was brought up to the red corner, we could see he was a beautiful dog. He looked like a shepherd, but there was obviously some other blood in him because he was larger and thicker, more square-cut. Jongbae had kept him impeccably groomed—his gray-and-white fur gleamed in the last of the sunlight. If he'd fought lots of matches before this, he must have won them all easily, because every dog we had seen thus far had had scars on its ears, while his were sharp and perfect. King stood tall and confident, and I understood why the announcer had referred to him earlier as a *hwarang*, the ancient order of youth groomed to become the military-intellectual elite of the nation.

Miklos beamed, his eyes sparkling, and now they switched on a set of the nighttime stadium lights and King's fur took on an almost golden glow. "That's King," he said, as if it wasn't already clear. "Amazing, isn't he? I've known him since he was just a puppy. I helped raise him."

Paulie and I nodded. The men sitting below us both whistled. All we could see now were their shadow-puppet silhouettes against the lights, as they gestured to the men on either side of them, probably confirming their bets, given the numbers of fingers they waggled.

Now King's support died down and it was Pomwang's turn to make his entrance in the blue corner. "*Pomwang!*" shrieked the announcer, and when the dog appeared between two bandaged men, a roar went up in the audience. When Pomwang waddled into the light, I felt a sudden lump low in my stomach, as if my body were instinctively prepared to take a punch.

He stood low to the ground, bow-legged and wide, so muscular that he looked like an overstuffed sausage whose skin might split at any moment. His wide-set eyes were strangely flat—not evil or menacing, but entirely indifferent until he caught sight of King, and then there was a tiny glint, a thought. Clearly he was called Tiger King for the dark stripes on his light brown fur, but the stripes were not markings, just the remnants of terrible burns or perhaps scars from previous fights. Both his ears bore scars from having been sewn up many times.

Unlike the other dogs, King and Pomwang were quiet, with hardly a growl, until their handlers unchained them and they leapt at each other—so quickly there seemed no interval between their being on opposite sides of the ring and then suddenly linked together like two people dancing. Their collision sounded like two sandbags smacking into each other—dull, flat, and fast, with no echo. And then, as quickly as that, they became a snarling, twirling mass of fur as they flipped and twisted over each other to find their opponent's throat. It looked like two creatures trying, by sheer force, to merge into one trembling, eight-limbed monster.

The handlers shouted, urging the dogs on, shaking and jabbing their pry sticks. Then, when the dogs slowed down, stretching out on the floor of the ring, the handlers pulled them back to their respective corners to end the first round.

King was bleeding heavily, a long gleaming trail stretching to his corner, while Pomwang's left ear dangled, nearly torn from his head. We could see his handlers debating whether to cut it off or leave it hanging as they looked him over and stroked him to comfort and encourage him. King's handlers, gesturing at Pomwang's side, yelled something we couldn't make out in the overwhelming noise of the crowd.

The flower card man made some more shadow-puppet gestures with his hands while, down in the ring, Miklos's cousin John Wayin stomped over to the announcer, pointing angrily at Pomwang, and the announcer lifted up his arms and clapped his hands together, signaling the beginning of round two.

"They're cheating!" cried Miklos.

This time the dogs hit each other sideways with a loud *smack*! King was closer to the audience. We saw him angle his snout and grab Pomwang by the throat, then smartly jerk his head until the other dog turned underneath him, droplets of blood flying and sparkling under the lights. A big cheer had just begun to go up when Pomwang abruptly yanked himself from King's jaws—we could hear the sickening tearing sound—dove under him, and ripped King's belly open. There was no blood at first—it was odd—just coils of glistening pink and gray intestine bulging out and then spilling onto the newspaper, steaming even in the warm air. We all heard the dull wet splashing sound before King's high-pitched whimper, and then everybody was screaming and shouting all at once, jumping up from their seats in excitement or anger—I couldn't tell which—and two of the handlers in the ring were fighting, beating at each other with their pry sticks while the other two jumped in to pull the dogs apart.

After that, it was hard to remember what happened. Miklos screamed and ran down to the ring, leaping over the stadium seats and probably trampling some of the crowd. Paulie and I looked at each other open-mouthed. The flower card man calmly lit another cigarette with his Zippo lighter. Two men sprinted across the stadium field toward a gate at the far end—one of them may have been the announcer. "Police!" someone near the top of the stands shouted, and people started looking all around them, hiding their wads of cash. *Thunk!* Then the stadium lights went out and we were all blind in the dark under a black sky.

AND THEN WE WERE riding in the back of a blue three-wheeled pickup, headed down a dim back street in Inchon. John Wayin squatted behind King, tugging on the blood-soaked blanket he had wrapped around the dog's torso to keep it tight, and Miklos sat with King's head in his lap, sobbing. Paulie and I had never seen him cry before.

John Wayin and the other handler, who was sitting up front in the cab with the driver now, had dragged King halfway across the stadium and met the truck there after someone had opened up the back gate. Somehow, in the chaos, as our eyes adjusted to the dark, we had managed to catch up to Miklos and climb into the bed of the truck before it drove off without us this late at night in a dangerous part of Inchon. Neither Paulie nor I even knew what neighborhood the stadium was in, and without Miklos we would have been lost.

We didn't know where the truck was headed, and Miklos wouldn't say anything except to the dog. He didn't want King to die, though it was pretty obvious to all of us that there wasn't much to be done for him. John Wayin, when he could manage to say something through the cigarette clenched in his teeth, told us we were going to see a "specialist."

"You mean like at an animal hospital?" asked Paulie.

"Animal hospital? Don't be funny. We're going to the Inchon dog market."

I had heard of dog markets before, and to distance myself from what was happening in front of me, I tried to imagine a different sort of dog market, a market full of dogs, with dogs as merchants and dogs as customers, all different breeds of them—and it was almost funny for a moment, the vision of dogs walking upright with their bundles of purchases and dogs squatting over their goods—until the clinking sounds of the chains dangling from the cargo door flap of the truck and the roar of the engine reminded me where I was. King had stopped whimpering—or maybe I just couldn't hear him through all the noise. But I could see him breathing each time we passed from a dark patch of road to one illuminated by a yellow streetlamp.

We must have been close to the ocean because the air grew cooler and fresher from the coastal breeze. The continuous rattling and rumbling, even the grinding of the gears, blended into an unexpectedly comforting rhythm and I found myself suddenly exhausted, drowsy. Paulie sat hunched with his back against the cab, his head propped on a rolled-up sack, and he nodded there, occasionally glancing up at me. I stood up a few times, bracing myself against the cab to try and make out where we were going. The stores along the streets had begun to close up their wooden shutters, their lit windows swarming with moths and other bugs, and people headed down the narrow black alleyways returning to their homes.

I no longer had any idea how long we'd been riding down those dark streets. Finally, the pickup slowed and turned onto a narrow alley barely wide enough to get through and so dark the headlights hardly illuminated anything. I thought we had pulled into a dead end until the driver honked the horn, and then what looked like one of those common corrugated metal storefronts slid aside to reveal yet another alley, this one lit up with a string of bare lightbulbs dangling from phone pole to phone pole. The truck turned left now and came to a stop in front of a building that looked like a garage.

As our eyes adjusted to the lights, we could see that we were in a semi-enclosed neighborhood of storefronts, each lit from inside by hanging fluorescent lights, some of them blinking erratically. The air was terribly thick after the coastal breeze and the wind from the moving truck, and so foul that Paulie and I both started coughing. It was a combination of shit and meat—raw, roasting, boiling—and animal sweat. I didn't smoke much, but now I gestured to Paulie as I gagged, and we both lit up with Salems, dulling our noses with menthol.

John Wayin told us to get out while he and Miklos lifted King, still wrapped in the blankets, and carried him into the place that looked like a garage. The driver came over to us after we jumped out of the truck bed and explained that we should wait there. I didn't say anything, but Paulie stopped John Wayin's partner before he left.

"We want to see King," Paulie said.

"There's nothing to see."

"We have to go back to Pupyong. Miklos has to take us back," Paulie said.

"Go back on your own!"

"We don't know which bus to take," I protested.

John Wayin's partner spat and cursed under his breath. He walked over to where the driver was smoking and they exchanged a few words. There was more cursing, and then he came back to us, lighting another cigarette.

"You two can go get Mikuraji in a little while," he told us. "Don't go into the front of the store where they went in. You two go around the back"—he pointed out another alleyway—"over there. There's a pool hall sign on the ground and the door is next to it. It's open. You go in that way and Mikuraji will be there. Understand?"

"Yes," we said.

Paulie was about to ask why we couldn't just go in the front way, but then he sort of shook his head to himself. "How long should we wait?" he asked instead.

"Use your judgment, little bastard," John Wayin's partner said as he stalked off, wiping at his blood-stained clothes. I couldn't tell whether we had done something to make him mad or if he was angry about what had happened to King.

I turned to ask the driver for help but he was gone, too. "Do you even have any idea where we *are* in Inchon?" I asked Paulie.

"No, man. Without Miklos, we're fucked. And I get a bad vibe from this place." He hardly needed to say it. The lump in my gut had moved up into my stomach and I was shivering. Paulie glanced left and right, looking past me, and I quickly turned around.

"What?" I said. "What is it?"

"Nothing," said Paulie. "It was just . . . some dude carrying a bucket and a pipe."

"Let's go get Miklos now," I said. "Come on."

"You're the boss," said Paulie.

That irritated me for some reason. "Why did you say that?" I said. "You *never* say that."

"Look, I'm about to shit my pants, okay? Let's get out of here."

I took one last drag on my cigarette, tossed it on the ground, and smashed it under my foot. Paulie did the same with his, and we made off in the direction John Wayin's partner had indicated.

WE MUST HAVE BEEN in the back part of the dog market now. I had expected storefronts with billboards and signs, display windows, and maybe menus of dog dishes, but the only signs we saw were broken or old discarded ones, all in garish-colored paints that had faded or were peeling. I could make out the word "dog" on some of them, but most of the words I didn't know. We walked past another flat building that looked like it might have been a garage at one time. It had two long pits built into the floor—the kind you saw in auto repair shops—but covered in a metal grill that was caked in rust. We could hear a hose spraying in the back, and under the harsh buzzing fluorescent tubes, the floor and walls glistened as if they were coated with mucus. And even among the terrible smells, there was an especially sickening odor, like pus, that wafted from one of the back rooms.

Paulie and I walked past the shop as quickly as we could without appearing to be in a hurry. That seemed important for some reason—not to attract attention. As we turned the corner into the alleyway, something on the floor at the entrance to the garage-like place caught my eye and I paused for a second. Paulie bumped into me and we grabbed each other for balance before immediately stepping into the alleyway, but we'd already gotten enough of a look. It was a bucket full of what I thought, at first, were boiled pig feet. But then I realized the toes were all wrong. It was a bucket of cooked dog paws with something moving inside.

The alley was narrow and dark, but mostly empty, so we jogged toward the other end, where we could see more lightbulbs strung between poles. We splashed through small puddles of oily water and nearly trampled a rat, then another. The creatures hardly seemed to care enough to run away. At the other end of the alley we looked right and then left for the pool hall sign. Why would there be a pool hall here, I wondered, and for a moment, in a panic, I couldn't even remember what a sign for a Korean pool hall was supposed to look like.

"There," said Paulie, pointing toward a couple of the doorways just past a phone pole. "It says *tangujang*. Pool Hall."

The sign was bent, but it was still possible to make out the crossed red sticks and the four solid primary-colored balls on the white background. It was strangely comforting until we reached it and realized there was an open door on either side, each leading into a dim hallway cluttered with containers, tools, and junk.

"Which one?" I asked, pointing left and right.

"We're *not* splitting up," Paulie said.

"All right, man. It must be this one." I figured that we had made a half circle around the building that Miklos and John Wayin had entered. They had gone into the left side of the building, so my best guess was that we were in the back and should go right. That was somewhat reassuring, because the door on the left led into a darker hallway than the one on the right, and I had lost whatever courage I'd had.

Paulie must have sensed my fear, because he hesitated, and that made me pause momentarily at the threshold. "Come on," I said.

"You're the boss."

This time, I felt an intense anger shoot through me. I punched Paulie hard on the shoulder, and when he cried out "*Ow!*" a little too slowly for it to have been a spontaneous expression of pain, I pushed him in through the door on the right.

In the hallway we could hear things that had only been barely audible out in the alley. Some of the noises were the typical background busyness of a night market, I supposed, but there were other sounds, too, mysterious ones I couldn't place: a regular dull thud followed by a short, high-pitched squeak; a wet smacking, like a pile of soaking laundry thrown on a countertop; irregular thumps followed by a gristly ripping noise. We couldn't tell how close or far away the source of the sounds might be—their volume shifted as we crept down the hallway looking for the room where Miklos must be with John Wayin and King.

We came out of the hall into a large storage room, where we saw our first dogs—just five or six of them, all the dun-colored *nuraengi* breed—in metal cages on the floor along one wall. They wagged their tails when they noticed us, thumping at their cages. I kept my distance, and Paulie stayed to my left, as far from the dogs as he possibly could. One of the aluminum basins full of food had tipped over near the door, and we stepped carefully around the mess of spoiled rice and restaurant scraps, more pig slop than proper food for a dog.

The next room had a long, shallow trench down the center in the cement floor and a water fixture on each end where black hoses were attached, and bisecting the central part of the floor were two long racks, made of heavy metal pipe, from which dangled some steel hooks and various lengths of chain. At one end a pale dog hung by a thick wire noosed around its neck. As the tension in the wire made it slowly spin, a mixture of pale drool and yellowish piss dripped from its bared mouth and the fur on its lower legs, down into the channel along the floor. The dog's eyes were wide open, and its snout angled up, as if it were watching us fearfully, as if we might try to kill it again.

Paulie slipped on the wet floor and caught himself by grabbing onto the metal pipe. That made a violent clattering noise as all the meat hooks shook in unison, and the shock went all the way through the body of the hanging dog, making its hind legs give one last kick in the air.

We entered the next room through a side door, just behind a man who had his back to us. He spun around so fast the long ash on his cigarette flew off and landed, with a strange ease, in the wet channel on the floor. He looked at us for a moment, puzzled, as if he had been expecting someone else. His hair was slicked back with oil and he wore dirty glasses with grimy white tape holding the frame together at the bridge of the nose. In his fashionable red polka-dot shirt, which he wore unbuttoned, and his American Levi's, he looked like he could be one of my cousin's dropout musician friends, but in his hands was a Louisville Slugger—a short one, from what I could tell—covered in dry blood.

"Who are you looking for?" he asked, shifting the baseball bat to his other hand. "Who are you two?"

Behind him, a dog that looked like it might be a German shepherd was letting out a low squeaking sound, like steam escaping from a radiator pipe. It hung from the rack upside down from its hind legs, which had been roped together and strung from a metal hook on a chain. Stretched out that way, the dog appeared surprisingly long and lean, its belly, from its rib cage to its hips, so thin it looked more like a greyhound or an Afghan than a shepherd. Its tongue lolled out, nearly touching the floor.

"I *said* who *are* you?" The man tapped his left hand with the bat.

I had no idea how to identify myself. I pointed toward the open wall that led to the main alley and mumbled, "We came to see John Wayin," realizing immediately how ridiculous that must sound.

"Are you crazy?"

"It's all right, *ajoshi*," said Paulie. "We're friends of Jongbae's cousin. We just came from the dog fight."

"Oh, really?" The man lowered his bat. I noticed he wore a black-handled knife in a large leather sheath on his belt. "Who won, then?"

"Pomwang," said Paulie. "And Haetae."

"Really?" said the bat man. "And?"

Paulie glanced toward me. He must not have remembered.

"The other match was a tie," I said, still looking at the dog.

"And Togsuri?"

"That was a tie with Inchon Lion," said Paulie.

"Fuck!" the man said, and he turned and slammed the bat into the hanging dog's ribs. We heard a horrible dull thud and the dog let out a shrill squeak as it swung to the left and then back, dripping blood-laced mucus from its mouth.

"*Ajoshi!*" Paulie stepped toward the man to interrupt the next blow, but he hit the dog again in a backhand and it seemed to burp a huge wad of blood onto the floor. "*Ajoshi!*" Paulie cried again, and this time the man turned toward him, wielding the bat in both hands.

"What?" he said.

"Why are you beating him?"

"Get lost, you little bastard."

Paulie started edging forward to get between the man and the dog, seeming not to notice as the man lowered his bat and reached with his other hand for his knife. Would he really use it on us? I wondered. The dog was probably dead anyway by now; its eyes were glazed over and it made no more noise. Why would he beat the poor animal to death when he could kill it quickly? He must have hated the dog to torture it like that. I grabbed Paulie by the back of his belt and pulled him toward me just as the man drew the long blade and said, under his breath, "Little bastards, want to die . . ." I knew he would probably just threaten us, but then again, this seemed to be a place where there was blood and viscera everywhere, and who would miss a couple of *t'wigi* kids whose where-abouts were unknown to begin with?

"Come on, man," I said to Paulie. "There's no point."

"Fuck him," said Paulie. "Look what he's doing."

The man now held the bat in one hand and the knife in the other. He was facing us, but he glanced over his shoulder at the dog and said, "Fuck. He's dead." Cigarette smoke leaked from the corner of his mouth. "You fucking bastards!" he said. "Look what happened! Are *you* two gonna buy this?!" He moved toward us, jerking the knife to indicate the dog, raising his bat in his other hand. "*Ungh?* You *buy* it!"

I saw Paulie reach into his front pocket for his switchblade, but before he could pull it out, John Wayin appeared at the front of the room and said, "Over here! Don't meddle!" I couldn't tell if he meant us or the bat man, but Paulie pulled his hand back out of his pocket.

"Who *are* these bastards?" the man said, gesturing angrily toward us with his bat.

"Nobody." John Wayin walked up to the hanging dog, made a quick assessment, and slapped the side of the bat man's head, knocking his glasses askew. "You idiot," he said. Then, while the man sheepishly straightened his glasses, his head lowered in shame, John Wayin motioned for us to follow him. As we left the room I saw the bat man stab his knife into the hanging dog's rib cage. We heard him cursing behind us.

"Why did he kill that dog like that?" Paulie asked. "Why did he have to beat it with a baseball bat?"

"Stupid bastard," John Wayin said. "He was supposed to just beat it for a few days for the taste."

I had no idea what he meant but Paulie made an odd snorting sound.

"How is King?" I asked.

John Wayin didn't answer. He walked so quickly we had to jog to keep up.

We passed the open front of another shop where they had laid out a couple of tables covered in greasy newspaper, and on top of that several roasted animal carcasses that I didn't even recognize at first as dogs. Maybe it was something about their size, or the way they were stretched out, with their paws cut off and head missing; or maybe it was the gleaming, golden-brown color of their cooked skin crawling with flies; or maybe it was just a mental block and I didn't want to see them as dogs. At the end of the table lay half a carcass chopped lengthwise precisely down the middle, like an anatomical cross section. On another table in the shadows near the back they had stacked a cluster of three heads, their fangs bared.

We reached a sliding door, and John Wayin opened it with a grating sound. When we tried to follow him inside, he held out his palm, flat, motioning for us to stop right there.

"Do what I say and wait here this time," he said. "Understand?" Then he went inside and banged the door shut behind him.

"I feel sick," I said to Paulie. "What the fuck was Miklos thinking, bringing us here? Did you know he was doing all this shit with dogs?"

"I don't—" Paulie began, cutting himself off when we heard John Wayin's voice through the door.

"You take those two back to Pupyong or wherever the hell they came from," he was saying. Miklos replied, but his voice was so low we couldn't make out what he said. "For what?!" said John Wayin. "What?" We heard a *smack*, which must have been Miklos getting face-slapped. "Whose money?" *Smack!* "What? *How* much? Do you know what your mother will do, you stupid little bastard? You tell her! I don't know anything about this, you ignorant son of a bitch!" *Smack!* "You don't know a damn thing, *do* you, you stupid fucker?!" *Smack!* "*Ungh?* Now get lost!"

The door suddenly slid open with a loud crash and Miklos came out sniffling in a grimy sweatshirt he must have changed into, head bowed, his hand covering one side of his face. "Let's go," he said, and he walked quickly down the alley without even looking at us. Paulie and I ran to catch up to him before he could turn a corner and disappear again.

Miklos must have spent a lot of time at the dog market. He walked quickly down the narrow streets without even bothering to look where he was going, sometimes making a turn through narrow, pitch-black alleyways where we had to run our fingers along the walls to keep from losing our balance. After so many turns, when Paulie and I had absolutely no idea where we were going—Miklos could have been wandering aimlessly or lost, for all we knew—we emerged onto a main street lit by normal streetlamps. Miklos stopped at a bus stop sign and looked down at his Timex.

"We can still make it to ASCOM before they close the gate for curfew," he said. In the light I noticed that his jeans were dark with patches of blood.

Paulie walked partway down the block to a little kiosk and returned with three open bottles of cold Pepsi, and we stood there silently under the streetlight, waiting for the bus. Miklos's face was swollen, and we could see that he would have a black eye.

I took a large swig of Pepsi and let it foam up in my mouth, then spat it out onto the ground. The next mouthful was sweet and delicious.

THE BUS BACK to Pupyong was practically empty at this hour. One of the bus maids slept in her tiny fold-down seat and the other hugged the metal pole, her eyes half closed, face slack. We sat in the back with our empty Pepsi bottles and, for a while, watched the tired passengers' faces go from light to dark as the streetlamps flashed by.

Miklos sat between me and Paulie, brooding, nursing his face, until I finally broke the silence and asked him if King was still alive.

"What do you *think*?" he replied bitterly.

Why had I even bothered asking, I thought, when the answer was perfectly obvious. "I'm sorry," I said.

"What the *fuck* do you have to be sorry about except coming to the fight? Huh? Why should *you* be sorry when I'm the one who fucked up? I fuck everything up."

"It's okay, Miklos," Paulie said.

"It's *not* okay! Pomwang's guys sharpened his damn teeth, man. They fucking cheated, and King . . ." He hunched over to stop from crying, but I saw the tears splash onto the muddy floor of the bus.

Paulie patted Miklos on the back, then held on to him as he sobbed. "I'm okay now," Miklos said after a minute. He wiped his face with the back of his sleeve. He must have resolved something at that moment, because he gave us a crooked smile and got off the bus at the next stop. "I'm going back," he called. "See you guys at the Fort."

We never saw Miklos again.

# Looking for Miklos

## 1975

When we didn't see him for the next four days, Paulie and I assumed that Miklos wanted to be alone for a while, and the two of us hung out together up in Yongsan at the new Teen Club, where they had Foosball tables and a large color TV for watching American sports via satellite. On the fifth day we grew concerned, so we asked Danny, Miklos's big brother, who we knew sometimes hung out at the Teen Club to shoot pool. He told us he didn't know what was going on. "Am I my brother's keeper?" he said. Danny told us he didn't even live with his mother anymore. We didn't know that because we hadn't seen him since we were camping on Yaksan. Next, we went to Miklos's house, and the maid told us that he and his mother were both out. It was the same the next day and the day after that. On the ninth day the house was empty, and an *ajoshi*, who seemed to be doing repair work, told us the family had moved. He didn't know where to, but he had heard the mother had gone up to Seoul. He told us to have our mothers get in touch with the house's owner who lived in Samnung if we wanted to know more.

It baffled us that they could all vanish like that—even the Korean relatives who lived with them. Paulie wondered whether we should try going back to the dog market to find John Wayin, but I said no. I never wanted to go to that place again. Anyway, we could probably track John

Wayin down by asking someone who worked with the meat suppliers in Inchon. My mother could ask the manager of the ASCOM NCO Club, who knew everyone with any sort of business dealings with the U.S. military.

When I asked my mother, she was puzzled herself because she hadn't seen Miklos's mother in a while, and a few days later she said she'd heard from the NCO Club manager: even John Wayin didn't know. All he could say was that Miklos and his mom had moved out of the house to get the down payment deposit money back. My mother had also heard some gossip among the black marketeers that Miklos had stolen a lot of money from his mother. It was money she had borrowed at a high interest rate from a loan shark to buy large appliances to sell, and when it disappeared she had to pay off a massive debt or risk being turned over to the Korean police and the CID for dealing Yankee goods.

"Miklos wouldn't steal his mother's money," I said. "Where did he go?"

"I heard he ran away. Who knows where."

"He wouldn't do that. He never runs away from anything."

"You can never know with people," she said. "The longer you live, the more surprising things you learn. People will do anything for money. Remember that."

I didn't believe her, or maybe I didn't want to believe her. In any case, I wasn't going to let it rest until I found Miklos and asked him myself. I went to Paulie's house the next day to plan how we would track Miklos down, and we decided the easiest thing would be to find his mother, since he hardly ever had contact with his father. Miklos also had a couple of friends who ran shops in Itaewon outside the Yongsan Garrison—we could try asking them, as well as the money changer at the market just outside Kimpo Air Base. He seemed to have connections everywhere.

WE TOOK A late-morning bus from the ASCOM Service Club to Kimpo. It had been more than a year ago that we had last been there, all dressed in our fancy *chebi* Kallah shirts to say goodbye to Paulie's favorite teacher when she left for the States. The town outside the air base had changed so much we had trouble finding the market. The international airport had also grown, and there were so many planes—both military and civilian—that we winced every few minutes at the deafening roar of yet another low-flying jet, though the locals hardly noticed.

We found the money changer's place inside a store that sold cheap clothing and swim gear. His booth was like a little ticket window with the current exchange rate written in code, in blue ballpoint pen, on a small piece of cardboard Scotch-taped to the frosted glass. We could see a figure inside through the mouse hole slot, and we knew it was him from the plume of cigarette smoke billowing out.

"Monoporri Ajoshi!" Paulie called. He was named that because he liked playing Monopoly and had Monopoly money taped to his walls as decoration. We had lost the game to him many times—we'd thought he would play as the cannon, since he had been an officer in the artillery corps during the War, but he always chose the mini thimble because his mother had been a seamstress.

He tilted his head to the side to peer at us through the slot. The smoke stopped for a moment. "*Waah!* I haven't seen you kids in a long time," he said. "I hardly recognized you!"

"It was really hard to find you," I said.

"Well, it's a good thing you're here now," said Monoporri Ajoshi. "This is all going to be gone soon. Torn down. They're widening the road from Kimpo Airport again, all the way to Seoul, and making it a highway. We're all moving a ways in toward where the movie theater used to be. Tell your mothers."

"Yes, sir."

"Why did you come looking for me? You have some money to change? And where's that friend of yours—Mikuraji?"

"Well, that's what we came to ask you," said Paulie. "Have you seen him or his mother? They disappeared from Pupyong, and they moved out of their new house."

"I wouldn't know much about that," said Monoporri Ajoshi. We heard a couple of thumps, then his face disappeared and an ice cream pop came out of the slot, then another. "These are new," he said. "From Haetae. Just as good as the PX brand. Give them a try."

They turned out to be a mediocre imitation of a chocolate-covered ice cream bar, but we thanked him.

"I need some Similac," he said. "As much as possible. In the green cans. Do you think you could get it for me? I have a grandson now and I want him to be as tall as you."

"My mother could get it," said Paulie. "I'll tell her."

"Not the powdered stuff. I can get powered stuff at a Korean store. And sliced *cheeju*. They say each slice is like ten glasses of milk. I can't just favor the grandson these days like we used to. That's for his older sister. If we feed her that, she's bound to be tall and smart."

"Then shouldn't your grandson have his mother's breast milk?" Paulie asked. "I heard that's the best for having a smart kid."

Monoporri Ajoshi made a *tut tut* noise. "You think I want her to be pumping her tits like a cow? She may want to leave that no-good son-in-law of mine someday, and she can't very well do that with saggy dugs now, can she?"

"That cheese isn't rationed," Paulie said to me in English. "We could get some right now at the little PX in Kimpo."

"*Ajoshi*," I said, "if you give us the money, we'll get you some cheese today. But the formula has to be later."

"Good!" he said. "You get me that *cheeju*. As much as you can. And I'll tell you what I know about Mikuraji's mother. How's that?"

"Man," Paulie said in English, "didn't he just tell us he didn't know shit?"

"*Boshwet?*" said Monoporri Ajoshi. "*What's* boshwet?" "Boshwet" was how some Koreans pronounced "bullshit."

"That's not it," I said in Korean. "We're just saying 'no shit.' That means it will be easy to get."

"That Yankee talk," said Monoporri Ajoshi. He rubbed his fingers together at the opening so we could see. "How much do you need?"

We didn't know the price of sliced cheese offhand the way our mothers would, so we took thirty dollars with the understanding that he was paying double the marked PX price. If we couldn't buy fifteen dollars' worth of cheese, we would return the money that was left over.

AT THE KIMPO PX, which had a small Food Land attached, we bought up every package of Kraft individually wrapped American cheese slices and then had a big lunch at the airport cafeteria before we went out to catch an Arirang taxi back to the money changer's store.

Standing outside the terminal building with the brown, twine-handled shopping bags full of cheese at our feet, it felt like we could have been waiting for the bus for school. A cool breeze came in little gusts from the direction of the runway, and Paulie stood with his hands in the pockets of his plaid bell-bottoms, shifting from one foot to the other as if he were cold.

"What do you think happened to Miklos, really?" he said. "You know, he's been gone longer. Remember the time they moved to P'yeongtaek when his old man was first stationed there? He just disappeared for a while. His mom did too."

"If he took the money, he'll probably turn up when he brings it back," I said. "My relatives steal from each other, but they always show up. You know, I don't know why he would have to steal from his mom anyway when he could just ask her for money. And what would he do with it? He doesn't play cards or the slot machines."

"He's always doing stuff we don't know about. Maybe . . . I don't know."

"His mom will know when we see her." I looked around for a trash can to throw away my empty paper cup of Coke, now just water and ice. The only receptacle nearby was a strange mailbox-like thing covered in sandbags. It had a long snout on it, sort of like the book drop box at the library. I shoved my cup into the slot.

"We're leaving soon," said Paulie.

"What?" I said, confused. "We're waiting for a taxi, man."

"No, I mean me and my mom and my old man. He got orders for someplace in Kansas. Fort Riley, I think. I was gonna tell you and Miklos together."

"Oh, man." My heart sank. It was inevitable with us—at some point, always beyond our control, our fathers would get a change of assignment; their commanding officers would cut them a new set of orders, and we would have to move. I had lived in Fort Lewis, Washington, near Tacoma, for a year, and in Baumholder, Germany. Paulie had lived in Fort Sill, Oklahoma, and Fort Ord, California, near Monterey. Miklos had lived in Fort Campbell, Kentucky, and Patsy had lived in Fort Leonard Wood, Missouri, and Fort Benning, Georgia. We could never anticipate where we might end up, and our mothers always hoped there would be other Koreans there, but sometimes they would be the only Korean—or the only Asian, for that matter—and they would be terribly unhappy. Maybe that was why so many interracial military marriages ended in divorce and broken families. We had all been lucky during the times our fathers served in Vietnam, because they had parked our families here in Korea.

"You can't tell anyone," said Paulie. "My mom said to keep it quiet because she doesn't want any of the black market people to know."

"When are you going?"

"Whenever my old man gets his final orders cut. He says Kansas isn't much better than Oklahoma."

"Man," I said. "Am I gonna be the only one left? I thought I'd be moving first because my father's sick."

"Come on, a taxi's here," said Paulie.

A black Arirang cab had just pulled up. We didn't recognize the driver, but when we said we were going to the money changer at the swim shop, he took us there straight away after a little pause at the gate, where we had to explain why we had so much cheese. If the MP had been a KATUSA, we would have been expected to give him some money or some of the cheese, but it was a young blond GI who was just curious.

"Cheeseburgers," I said, when he gave back my ID.

"That's a lot of cheeseburgers, chief."

"We got two big Korean families for a big-time party," said Paulie. "Everybody wants to know what real McCoy American cheeseburgers taste like. Korean cheese sucks, man."

"I didn't know Koreans *had* cheese," said the GI. "Doesn't milk make them sick or something? My girlfriend says I always smell like sour milk."

"That's just American PX food BO, man," said Paulie.

"*She* smells like kimchi. Every fucking thing in the fridge smells like kimchi," said the MP.

"Kimchi smell number one," said the driver, giving a thumbs-up. The MP waved us out with a dismissive salute.

"So why do Americans smell like that?" the driver asked us in Korean. "Do they really eat meat and drink milk with every meal? I can still smell the two who were in here before you even with that cologne they had on."

"I don't know," I said. "But that other smell is aftershave, *ajoshi*. I think it's Mennen Skin Bracer." It was the one my father used, and I did notice it, lingering faintly.

"You know a lot about merchandise. Can you boys get me a set of socket wrenches and a metal toolbox?"

We had never had a request like that before. "Are those rationed?" Paulie asked.

"I don't know," said the driver. "I asked some *ajuma*s, but they can't tell a socket wrench from a sickle. I'm at the Kimpo dispatch. Ask for Specialist Ajoshi."

"What sort of specialist are you?"

"Why, I'm an automotive specialist!" he said, laughing. He was curious about the cheese, so we gave him a package when he dropped us off. Paulie volunteered to procure the socket wrenches and the toolbox later that week.

Monoporri Ajoshi let us keep the extra money as a tip after he had each of us sample a slice of the cheese to confirm that it hadn't spoiled. He said he wouldn't have known the difference. Then he finally told us what he knew about Miklos's mother. "I don't know where he might have gone, but if you go to Itaewon and look in the alley just before you get to the 007 Club, you'll find an *ajuma* there who sells umbrellas. Tell her the Kimpo money changer *ajoshi* sent you, and be sure to tell her my grandson is doing fine. Then she'll know you know me, and you can ask her how to find Miklos's mother. But don't expect much."

"You mean she might not know?" I said.

"No. She'll know where you can find Miklos's mother. Just don't expect much when you see her, that's all. I'm doing you a big favor."

I didn't quite understand, but I didn't press the issue. We thanked Monoporri Ajoshi. As we were leaving, he waggled his fingers through the little mouse hole. "Be careful!" he called after us. "Don't go seeing what you shouldn't be seeing."

In the Korean taxi we took to Yongsan, I asked Paulie what he thought that meant. "I don't know," he said. "But this all gives me a bad feeling, man. It's like one of those bad years the Koreans talk about, where everything goes to shit. The world really must be ending, right? Pretty soon people's tongues are gonna start rotting in their mouth and everyone will have leprosy or something."

"You don't really believe all that crap from your mother's church, right? You should learn some science and history. Didn't you study the same stuff as everyone else in school?"

"Didn't you notice I started reading, man? And not that Savage Doctor shit you read."

"Those books up in the Fort are *yours*?"

"Dupree made me a list of stuff. I used to go up to the Fort by myself sometimes and read, 'cause then you guys won't give me a bunch of crap about how dumb I am."

"We never said you're dumb, Paulie."

"My favorite now is astronomy."

"Is it that planets book?"

"Yeah."

"The post library has more like that," I said. "Why didn't you tell me? I have lots of books. How come you listen to Dupree and not us?"

"I talked to Patsy, too. She and Dupree told me I should try to go to college and stay out of the Army."

"No shit," I said.

"I'm sick of the fucking Army, Seven. Look at us, man. It's like we're brothers or something, and now we have to be split up. And where the fuck is Miklos, running out on us like this? And what's gonna happen to Patsy, man? Dupree said he saw her in a club at Itaewon."

"I'm not so worried about her," I said. "I think she might be tougher than all of us."

"Sometimes I wonder what it would be like if my mom had put me in Korean school—like Miklos's mom did when he was little."

"You'd probably be a lot tougher," I said. "But your English would suck. We lose both ways, man. That's why we have each other, right?" We gave each other some half-hearted skin.

"Hey," I said, "what was Dupree doing with Patsy at an Itaewon club? They're not, you know. . . ."

"What?! Dupree would *never* do that, man! He just saw her there."

"Was he just saying that, maybe? How would you know?"

"I would *know*," Paulie said vehemently. "Why would he lie to me? He'd never lie to me."

"Okay, okay," I said. "You can chill. I worry about her sometimes. Dupree's our friend, so maybe he'd be good to her."

"He's not interested in Patsy," said Paulie, as if he were stating a simple fact. They had obviously talked about this sometime when I wasn't around. Maybe Paulie had stuck up for Patsy or warned Dupree to keep his hands off her because she was like a sister to us. I had never seen Dupree with a girlfriend in town and he never talked shit about Korean women the way most other GIs did. He would probably have made a good boyfriend for a woman who wasn't afraid of being called a dung-whore by the Koreans, and since Patsy was a half-and-half like us, she didn't have to worry as much about *that* stigma. Being a mixed-blood *t'wigi* was stigma enough in Korea.

We had to sit in traffic for a while on the river road as we approached Seoul. Even with the windows open and the breeze from the Han River, the heat grew oppressive and the diesel fumes from the trucks and buses made us cough. It impressed me how the driver could sit there in his beaded seat and calmly smoke a cigarette listening to Lee Mija songs on the cassette deck he had mounted under the meter. She was singing my mother's favorite, a sentimental ballad about a nineteen-year-old girl on a rural island in love with a bachelor. I remembered how Mahmi would sing that song sometimes, over and over, all afternoon as she fed quarters into the slot machines at the NCO Club in ASCOM.

Once the traffic began to move, it didn't take long to reach the rotary at Samgakji, then spin around it up past the Yongsan Garison main gate, then up the hill to Itaewon. The alley just below the 007 Club, where we got off, didn't seem to be the kind of place to find an umbrella seller. Most of the busy clothing and accessory stores were farther downhill toward the entrance to Itaewon, and the other side of the hill turned Korean, which meant there wasn't much there of interest to tourists or GIs. The alley below the 007 Club led eventually to a Korean outdoor market if you followed it to the end, but up toward the main street it was the quarter for the clubs that catered to Black GIs: the Soul Club and the Motown Club. The names changed every couple of years, but the neighborhood didn't. Once the nightlife began, it was an unwritten rule that white GIs were not welcome here, just as Black GIs were expected to stay away from the Nashville Club and the Blue Grass Club. And, of course, everyone knew that absolutely no Korean men—other than those who happened to work there—were welcome at any of the GI clubs. The neutral clubs like the 007 Club tended to be nearer to the center of Itaewon because they catered to foreigners in general, not just the U.S. military. That's the sort of place Patsy would have gone—sometimes we even went into them ourselves, though we would need to dress more fashionably to look older.

Paulie and I walked down the nearly empty alleyway and paused in front of the Soul Club, whose sign we realized had a lowercase *E* inside the *O*. A couple of years earlier it had been the Malcolm X club for all of two days before someone threw a Molotov cocktail into it. The owner had changed the name to the Player Club, but it hadn't done well until a shaman performed a good luck ceremony and prescribed yet another name change. The door to the club was wide open, revealing some of the dim interior that exuded the smell of stale beer and cigarette smoke even now, a smell that never quite dissipated—even the premium clubs had it.

A middle-aged *ajuma* in flower-print Japanese-style work pants was splashing water out of a small washbasin onto the walkway to keep the dust down. She had a towel draped over the back of her neck and wore a kerchief as a headscarf, just like someone working out in the rice paddies.

"*Ajuma,*" said Paulie, "would you know where the *ajuma* who sells umbrellas in this alley might be?"

"Why? You want to buy an umbrella?" She stood up to her full height, just over five feet, supporting the small of her back with one hand. "*I'll* sell you an umbrella."

"We don't need an umbrella," I said. "We just have something to ask her."

"What kind of umbrella do you want to buy? How much money could boys like you have, anyway? Or would you like to rent one and try it out? Surely, you're not here to *sell* an umbrella, are you?"

We were baffled, but it seemed she must know the umbrella seller. "We're not buying or selling an umbrella," said Paulie. "Could you tell us where the Umbrella Seller Ajuma is? The money changer in Kimpo said we could find her here."

"Well, why didn't you say so in the first place, then?" said the woman. "People are busy, you know. We have lives to lead and business to attend to."

As the angle of the sun changed, a strip of light fell into the dark interior of the club, and I could see there was a man inside, sitting on a chair turned around with his elbows resting on the back. He was very muscular for a Korean—he even had an unusual Fu Manchu–style mustache—and he was smoking a traditional bamboo-stemmed pipe.

"*Ajuma*, do you know where she is?" I asked. "We need to tell her that the Money Changer Ajoshi's grandson is doing well."

"Wait right here," said the woman, pointing at the spot by the opaque club window. "I'll go get her for you." As she walked into the club she made a motion to the man and he nodded and got up from the chair. Both of them disappeared into the darkness.

"This place gives me the creeps," I said.

"It's not so bad. I've been here before with Dupree."

"What? I never knew that."

"Patsy knew. It's not like I don't have my own life, man."

That was news to me, a surprise, though it shouldn't have been. Miklos, Paulie, and I spent a lot of time together, but there were often stretches of days when we didn't see each other. To me, it often seemed like I had parallel lives with Paulie and Miklos. When the three of us were together, that life was the most exciting and eventful. Then there was the life I had with each of them separately, and then the other life, with neither of them, and all of these wove together into the memory of who I was and had been. I knew that Miklos's and Paulie's lives must be like this too, whether or not they thought of it in the same way, but it was a shock to be reminded that Paulie or Miklos had a life in which I was absent, and I wondered, for the first time, which of those lives was most important—or real—to Paulie.

"I told Patsy about it—about Dupree," Paulie said. "I told her first, Seven, 'cause Miklos is always calling me a pussy and making fun of me. She was okay with it after a while, and I was gonna tell you and Miklos together, when he was here, but now where the fuck did he go, *huh*? And I'm telling you by yourself."

I felt like he was confessing some terrible crime, and I was turning to stone as I listened. I wanted to tell him just to get to the point, since it was going to be bad, but just then the woman came out of the club to-gether with the man, except he was much taller and larger, and more muscular, than I expected, and she was in makeup that made her look like an entirely different person. She wore elegant clothes with hand-made shoes, and instead of a headscarf she wore an ornate white-gold barrette. She also carried a black umbrella now, with a dark wooden handle carved to look like an alligator. Paulie and I both gaped at her.

"Come with me," said the Umbrella Seller, and she walked down the alley without even bothering to see if we would follow. The man with the pipe waited until we moved and then came a few steps behind. The Um-brella Seller walked very quickly, her heels clacking sharply, but not like someone in a hurry.

"I'm getting a bad feeling about this," said Paulie. "We're back at the dog market, man. Where is this old lady taking us, anyway? Why did she put on that whole *ajuma* act back there?"

He was right—it did feel like we were back at the dog market, but that might just have been the meaty cooking smell that wafted from one of the houses along the way. By now we were in some anonymous back alley that probably didn't have an address, but it was where people lived, and I wasn't as uneasy as Paulie. I was still wondering what he had been about to tell me. What sort of secret could it be that he would have to tell Patsy before me and Miklos?

In another minute we stood in front of a very old traditional-style gate. It must have been one of the original houses that Itaewon had grown around over the years, with tiled roofs, a courtyard *madang*, and even what looked like a small natural spring whose outlet came through a large semicircular stone with a hole in the middle. When we went in, the man with the Fu Manchu mustache stood at the gate, and he lit his pipe again, preparing to wait for a while. The house was laid out in the traditional square U-shape around the central *madang*, and where the *sarang*—the separate room meant only for men—would have been, there was a more modern structure.

"I don't think we're supposed to be here," Paulie said.

We turned to the Umbrella Seller, but before we could say anything, she spoke in perfect British-accented English. "That's right. You boys aren't supposed to be here. You are foolish boys, and I only brought you here because of the message." Her English was so unexpected that I didn't even register what she had said at first.

"We're sorry," said Paulie. His eyes had gone wide, and he looked toward the gate. I prepared to run.

"Don't worry," said the Umbrella Seller. "You're perfectly safe here with me. I'm not going to turn you into an umbrella or anything of the sort." She smiled, as if it was actually in her power to do so. "Now talk to your friend's mother. I think she's awake by now." She gestured to the door of the *sarang*.

"How did you know why we're here?" asked Paulie.

"I have a telephone."

"You're not gonna lock us up or anything, are you?"

"I told you, you're safe with me. Now hurry and have your visit. We don't have all day." She turned toward the *sarang* and called out in Korean, "Jinju-ya! You have visitors. Friends of your son."

Jinju was Miklos's mother's name. We wouldn't normally have known it, but Miklos had once made fun of it meaning "pearl" and how his mother loved pearl necklaces because of that name. When I mentioned it to my mother, she told me it wasn't a very auspicious name for a girl—pearls were beautiful and precious, but they brought sadness for some reason. Black pearls were especially rare and also brought tragedy.

We went into the *sarang*, leaving our shoes on the stepping-stone by three pairs of expensive women's high heels and a pair of plastic slippers. My socks were damp with sweat and my feet felt momentarily cold as I walked up onto the small *maru*, leaving moist footprints on the polished wood. The traditional sliding doors were sturdier than usual and were paneled with frosted glass instead of rice paper. A dim light revealed shelves made of mahogany or teak built along the wall at the back of the *maru*, and we could make out stacks of neatly coiled rope—red, white, black, and rough hemp—in separate compartments. Along the top of the shelf were other compartments with polished metal bracelets, chains, and what looked like manacles—all stainless steel—and in other compartments were long white and red cylindrical tubes of various thicknesses, which I realized were candles. There were other things, too, but I couldn't take them in at a glance, and some of the compartments were closed, fitted with drawers and doors with brass fixtures.

Through the glass panels, we could hear the familiar tinkling of a spoon stirring coffee. In a moment Miklos's mother's voice, thicker than what I recalled, said, "Come in."

When she said "Come in" for the second time, Paulie slid the door open. The room was much larger than I expected, with a Japanese tatami floor, divided into two parts. A small window, barred from the outside, let in the bright late-afternoon light through a tangle of leafy branches, imbuing everything with a pleasant green hue. It wasn't the kind of room I would have imagined from what I had seen outside on the dim *maru*.

Miklos's mother, looking somewhat puffy, and much younger than I remembered, was still in her pajamas, sitting on a *chabudon* behind a lacquered food table set for the usual coffee service, but with the Pream, sugar, and coffee in elegant white china containers. There were four sets of cups and saucers, also whiteware, and long-handled silver stirring spoons. She had just poured hot water into her cup from a large stainless steel electric kettle. If I hadn't known better, I would have thought she was a rich woman getting up from an afternoon nap.

She took a drink of coffee, making a tiny sipping sound, holding the cup in both hands, but she didn't look up at us. She kept her eyes on the surface of the black coffee, as if to watch us in the reflection there.

Paulie and I glanced at each other in the long silence before he asked, "Miklos's mother, how are you?"

"Sit down," she said, still not looking at us. "Thank you for coming to find me." There were tears in her eyes.

We sat cross-legged on two of the other *chabudong* around the table, and without us having to ask, Miklos's mother carefully prepared us our cups of coffee the way we liked them. All her motions seemed measured and deliberate, as if she were performing a ritual.

Of our mothers, Miklos's mother was the prettiest by Korean standards. She must have been about forty, but with her hair slightly disheveled and her face still swollen from sleep, she could have passed for twenty-five to most Americans, who couldn't judge a Korean's age anyway. I could see why there were rumors that she'd had the chance to be a movie star before she married Miklos's father.

After we had taken a couple of sips of our coffee, she asked, "Did Miklos send you?"

I was full of questions about where we were and what she was doing here and who the strange Umbrella Seller might be, but her question surprised me because, all this time, Paulie and I had simply assumed she would know where Miklos was. We had thought that maybe they were hiding out together from a debt collector.

"No," I said. "We came because we thought you could tell us where he is."

She let out a long sigh.

"Everyone says he stole money from you and ran away," said Paulie. "But we couldn't believe that."

"Why couldn't you believe it?"

"Because he's our friend and we know him," I answered. "He would never do those things."

"I can see you boys are really good friends," she said. "You shouldn't have come here, but I'm glad you did."

"Can you tell us where he is?" Paulie asked. "We can keep a secret if we have to."

"He took the money," said Miklos's mother. "A lot. He gambled with it and lost all of it. He was sure he was going to win, but that's the way with gambling. In the end, you always lose. I told him so, but it didn't help. He was terribly upset because King was dead, and then, on top of that, he thought I hated him because of the money. I told him I didn't hate him, but he didn't believe me." She continued, "I don't care about the money. It's just money. See?" She gestured at the room with her palm up, as if we should place something in it. "Here I am earning the money to repay it. When you see Miklos, tell him he doesn't have to be off someplace all by himself. His father's a bastard, but his older brother can help too. Tell him we're still a family, all right?" She sniffed and wiped her eyes and nose with a white paper napkin.

"Yes, *ajuma*, we'll tell him," I said.

"Miklos sent you, didn't he?" she asked again, her voice brightening as she looked at me, then Paulie.

I didn't have the heart to answer, but Paulie said, "No. We haven't seen him in a long time, *ajuma*."


ON THE WAY BACK to the S☉UL Club, the Umbrella Seller turned down a different alley, and we emerged farther down the hill, near the fancy tailor shops. Itaewon was bustling by then, and the man with the Fu Manchu mustache had disappeared.

"Now you know where to bring a message, if she's still here," said the Umbrella Seller. "I can see that you boys are loyal, but you should try to be less foolish."

"How is your English so good?" Paulie asked.

"I lived in London after the war." I must have given her a questioning look, because she added, "Selling umbrellas is better than being a wife when you're someone like me."

"Ajuma," I said, "how much money does Miklos's mother owe?"

"You don't need to know that, but it's not so much that she can't pay it off." The Umbrella Seller pulled a roll of greenbacks from a pocket I hadn't noticed. "Here. Some *ch'abi*. Let's hope she hears from her boy directly and you don't have to come looking for me again." She gave us each a twenty-dollar bill and we thanked her and said goodbye.

V

Twilight

# Twilight

## 1975

He is lying with his cheek pressed against the cool white plaster of the wall. The spot where the oil of his flesh has so often touched the surface has discolored into a gray patch shaped like a heart. They have kept him in this room for so long, enveloped in his own stink; he is meant to die in this room, meant to waste away or go mad—expire in some convenient way so the family can stop squandering their time on him.

He remembered how, in the old days, the family would send a devoted son or daughter up to the mountain each morning with a bowl of rice for the senile grandparent in the cave—not enough, really, to sustain a life—until that morning when the previous day's offering would remain there, untouched, and then the son or daughter would come back down to the village keening for the old one's death. There would be a funeral. A burial at an auspicious spot picked by a geomancer. And then, on all the ritual days, offerings of food to the spirit of the departed ancestor.

Tonight he had asked his daughter to leave the door open a crack; after the first week they hadn't bothered to lock him in. The wind was blowing from the north, and the air was cool and sweet. They never believed that he had gotten used to the smell of his own rot and pus, that he could smell the food they ate—enough to know that he was getting leftovers. Without even looking outside he knew that the moon would be exactly half full tonight, like a scallion pancake cut precisely down the middle. He knew the night smells that would waft down from the northward hills where there were chestnuts and gingko groves past the thicket of new acacias.

He had been thinking about the distant past, when he was a youth with smooth skin and a quick smile, when he had studied the classics and recited Tang poems by Li Po and Tu Fu while his brothers labored in the fields. He remembered the moon-faced beauty of the girls from Seoul who had come up with their families one spring to visit a local temple. His leg was still strong then, and his sweat was tinged with a musk that would make a maiden's nostrils flare without her knowing. In those days he could have run a hundred *li* without pausing for breath, and when he slept he felt the silky warmth of clean blankets against his naked flesh.

It is dark now. He has been in the twilight of this room so long he has forgotten the joy of light. Lately he's been dreaming of bright summer days, the air thick with powdery light, only to wake to this fever and this dingy dark room where, instead of azaleas or rose of Sharon, he smells the cloying stink of his own decay.

He wants to see some brightness tonight. Not the dim, jaundiced yellow of the twenty-watt bulb over his head, but the cold blue light of the half-moon. He pulls his cheek away from the wall, leaving it slick with his heat. He squints to make out the thick trunk of his gangrenous leg and decides he should wrap it before going out. But where is the cloth? They have taken even that from him—or perhaps simply stopped bothering with it, knowing they would only have to wash it yet again and hang it out to dry in shame like a woman's menstrual rags.

# Holly Golightly at the Bando Hotel

## 1975

I never got to ask Paulie what he wanted to tell me because I only saw him once more, hastily, before he left for the States. With him gone, and his departure a secret I had to keep for the sake of his mother—who was likely to be running from creditors—I felt terribly alone.

It was more than a month since Paulie and I had visited the Umbrella Seller. I had just come up from the underground Hollywood Market in Seoul, where I'd delivered an Omega watch to one of the black market stalls. My mother owed a lot of money to Busy-Busy, the wife of the merchant, and was paying it off in controlled goods. It had been a while since my last visit there, when Nokchon Cousin had impersonated my mother, using her American passport, and hauled me and An-na to the foreigners' stores to buy our full quotas of coffee and other rationed items. We would have to walk with that merchandise all the way to the Hollywood Market because Nokchon Cousin wasn't like my mother and didn't want to waste money on a taxi. Those shopping bags were so heavy that my face would twitch involuntarily when I had to carry two of them, and I would have to stop every half a block to let my hands recover from the biting rope handles. An-na was little, so she never had to carry much, and she didn't understand why people were calling Nokchon Cousin "Insu's Mother."

I don't know why I had decided to walk through Insadong and down toward Uljiro and City Hall. Maybe it was just the beautiful day, the clear blue sky full of gentle, puffy clouds, or maybe it was the stiff, cool breeze that had cleared the air of auto exhaust and the smell of boiling pig carcasses in the alley by the Hollywood Market. I felt like I could breathe freely for a change.

With the U.S. Embassy nearby, you could see lots of foreigners in Insadong—mostly U.S. military and diplomatic corps—out shopping for antiques and celadon, or eating at the restaurants that served traditional foods for a foreign palate. One of the little tofu restaurants was a long-time hangout, every other Thursday night, for spies, bankers, and members of the intelligence corps. The embassy workers and the foreign pedestrians in Insadong dressed in the latest fashions unless they were in uniform. The locals usually didn't make a big deal of the foreigners unless they happened to be blond women. I was wearing green-and-black-striped velvet bell-bottoms and a white Nehru shirt, appropriate for Seoul. Dressed that way, with my long hair, I would have attracted attention in Pupyong, but here the police had to be more tolerant and I was just part of the background. So when I heard shopkeepers exclaiming and pointing down the street, talking about the movie star named Oduri, I was curious.

I couldn't figure out the name at first—"Oduri" sounded Japanese to me—but then, when a silk merchant said *"Breakfast at Tiffany's,"* I realized they meant Audrey Hepburn. Only what would she be doing in Insadong?

I could see the crowd gathered a couple of blocks south now, and there she was, walking from the Chosun Hotel toward the Bando. Audrey Hepburn or, more precisely, Holly Golightly, in her black dress and long black gloves, cat-eye sunglasses, and black kitten heels. She even had the earrings, pearl necklace, and tiara and carried a long-stemmed cigarette holder from which she puffed every few steps as she adjusted her white scarf over her black handbag. I half expected to see George

Peppard in his tweed jacket walking alongside her, and maybe a white paper bag and a cup of to-go coffee in her other hand. Cars were pausing to rubberneck, and everyone was pointing and looking left and right to see if there might be a film crew down the block.

I had to push past a small crowd of middle-school girls in their uniforms to get a closer look, excited, to my own surprise, that I might actually get to see a real American movie star. I had seen the Korean star Pak No-shik once at Pupyong Station, where they were filming a gangster movie. Why am I remembering Pak No-shik? I thought. This was Audrey Hepburn, but the movie she was in must have been over a decade old, and what would she be doing in Seoul, near the embassy, dressed as Holly Golightly?

There was no camera crew on the street, though some people with cameras were snapping pictures of her, and when I got close enough into that strange empty zone where no one seemed bold enough to approach, I saw that it wasn't Audrey Hepburn at all. She wore only three strands of pearls, her black dress was cut shorter, and the highlights in her hair, above the tiara, were entirely the wrong color—it was Patsy McCabe.

And then I felt strange—thrilled in a different way than to see a movie star, but also physically sick, as if I had witnessed a terrible car accident.

"Audrey! Audrey!" everyone was saying, so when I called out to her by her real name, she stumbled and turned to look. She tried to cover up by pretending she was only ashing her cigarette.

"Patsy!" I called again.

This time she saw me, and she made a curt gesture with her head toward the entrance of the Bando Hotel. The doorman held the door open for her, and she quickly slipped inside. I followed in a moment, past the doorman's disapproving once-over.

Patsy stood by the couches near the concierge, and in the muted light of the hotel lobby she looked like Audrey Hepburn again. A Korean man in an expensive navy suit approached her, and they exchanged a few words I couldn't make out. Patsy pointed in my direction and the man looked at me, nodded, and gave a small bow before walking away to attend to other patrons. I heard him call her "Miss Audrey."

"Patsy?" I said again. I hardly knew what to add after that. I couldn't see her eyes, but even behind those Manhattan sunglasses I could imagine her expression—a mixture of defiance and embarrassment—and so what she did was all the more surprising.

Patsy lowered her sunglasses and, looking over the rims at me, took a puff of her cigarette. "My *darling* Fred!" she said. "What brings you to the Bando?" She pronounced "Bando" the way an American would.

I couldn't tell if she was putting me on or simply trying to stay in character. Or maybe she had gone insane since I had seen her last. Fred was Holly Golightly's brother from back home in the boonies of Tulip, Texas.

"What are you doing?" I said.

She walked up to me now and took my hand, leading me toward the elevators. "What the fuck are *you* doing?" she said out of the side of her mouth.

It was Patsy now—she even walked like Patsy in a way that seemed strangely inappropriate for her dress. We took the elevator up to the top floor and I followed her down the slightly musty hallway to what I guessed was her room. Patsy put the cigarette holder in her mouth so she could open her handbag for the room key, and when she bent over to insert it into the lock, the cigarette broke against the door. The tip burned a little black circle into the wood before it fell onto the carpet. I stepped on it.

"Fuck," said Patsy. She opened the door and we went inside.

I had never been in a hotel suite before. It was larger than the whole interior of my house. Patsy had left the tall curtains open all the way, along with two of the windows. I saw the bright blue sky over the tops of the downtown buildings, the white clouds, the distant line of mountains.

The steady rumble and murmuring sounds of Seoul were muffled but loud enough that the sporadic car horns echoed even inside.

Patsy tossed the cigarette holder onto a coffee table and kicked off her black high heels. "God, I hate these fucking shoes," she said. "I'm hungry. You want something to eat?"

"Sure."

She gestured at the bar as she went into the bedroom, pulling off her tiara and tossing her head to release her streaked hair. "Menu's there. Order whatever you want. I'm having a ham sandwich and a pot of coffee. If you want cream and sugar, tell them because I have mine black."

I must have been in some sort of shock as I sat down on the metal-framed leather couch in front of the coffee table, absently looking around the bright interior of the suite. There were magazines on one of the chairs, a tall, messy stack of them—*Cosmopolitan, Redbook, Mademoiselle, Newsweek*. I leaned forward and pulled a *Newsweek* from the middle of the pile, and a *Scientific American* came out with it. For some reason I found this surprising, and I didn't bother opening either magazine, focusing instead on the model on the *Cosmo* cover on top, thinking she looked distorted, as if her body had been stretched on the rack. All the *Cosmo* models looked that way to me—elongated and hungry.

From the other room I heard the water running, the sounds of Patsy washing her face, rummaging about, and then the unmistakable sound of her peeing into the toilet.

"Did you order yet?" she called out from the bathroom. "There's a phone on the end table."

I realized I had forgotten all about the food. I went to the bar and found the menu, which was printed in three languages in a leather-bound booklet. I was used to eating at the ASCOM Snack Bar or at cheap Chinese restaurants in Sinchon where everything was posted on the wall. The thick, off-white textured paper of the menu looked strange to me, and I kept glancing from the English entries to the Japanese, thinking something was imminent, that the film would snap, that everything would go black, and I would find myself alone inside an empty second-run movie theater in Paekmajang. I closed the menu and looked for the phone but couldn't see one.

Over the wide doorway that separated the living room from the bedroom hung a beautiful piece of calligraphy on mulberry paper in bold black Chinese characters connected by willowy lines, all four words a single, beautiful brush stroke. I had only seen calligraphy like that in a museum, and I wondered how much it had cost, or if it had been written specifically for the hotel.

Patsy had left the bathroom door open. We could see each other in the full-length mirror as she leaned over the sink examining her reflection. She was wearing only a sheer bra and black panties, and I couldn't help noticing that her breasts were larger than I remembered from—when was it?—the time at the Yongsan swimming pool when she'd lost her bikini top. But that was years ago. She was still a kid then. Even if she was two years older than me, we were both still kids.

She was doing something with a makeup pencil, maybe touching up her eyebrows, which she had plucked to look like Audrey Hepburn's, although with her hair down over her neck Patsy didn't look quite as much like Holly; it was her neck that made all the difference. As she took off her bra, our eyes met in the mirror. She smiled brightly and covered her breasts, but with only the tips of her fingers.

I blushed but didn't look away. "I can't find the phone," I said. "I'm sorry."

She came out into the living room, still undressed, and stood by the window for a moment, arms akimbo, frowning thoughtfully, and then she snatched a black hat from a side table, revealing the telephone. She sat down in the chair across from me, folding her skinny legs under her, and held the phone in her lap. "What do you want, Seven? You can have anything you want."

"I don't know," I said.

"Do you still eat those horrible egg burgers?"

"Yeah."

Patsy picked up the receiver and dialed a single digit, letting her finger ride the stuttering rotor all the way back—*clickclickclickclickclick*. She ordered in English: a ham sandwich, a pot of coffee, a hamburger deluxe with extra tomato, French fries, a Coke, and a chocolate sundae with two cherries on top. "On that hamburger," she said, "fry an egg and put it on top of the tomatoes. Yes, like a *cheeseburger*, except it's an *egg*. No. No cheese. And cream and sugar this time. Two cups." She hung up the black phone and looked at me, then down at herself, and laughed.

"I'm sorry," she said. "I forgot myself for a moment, like old times. I didn't embarrass you too much, did I? Oh, I *did!*" She went into the bedroom and came back in a white bathrobe. "Isn't this great?" she said, spreading her arms as if to embrace the whole suite.

"What do you mean about old times?" I asked.

"Don't you remember that picture of us standing out in the sun? When we were little kids? My mom has it in her photo album."

It came back to me then, how as children Patsy and I would play together in the garden wearing only baggy underpants in the heat of summer. The picture must have been the one of us at the big old house in Samnung. In my mother's photo album, she had another faded black-and-white of Patsy and me sitting on a coffee table with the washed-out rock garden visible outside through the sliding wood-and-paper doors.

She pointed to a room key on the table. "You can keep that one if you want, Seven. I told the manager downstairs you were my brother and might be staying with me for a while. Do you want to camp out here?"

"What's going on, Patsy? What are you doing here dressed up like Audrey Hepburn? Who's paying for all this?"

"What are *you* doing here, Seven? Why are you all dressed up like George Harrison without the mustache? Do you see my cigarettes anywhere?"

"Come on, Patsy!"

She found her cigarettes in her handbag and lit one, standing by one of the open windows. "My Mr. Yunioshi is paying for all this," she said after a moment.

"That was Mickey Rooney," I said. "He wasn't even Japanese."

"You remember!"

"Yeah, I remember." The theater in Paekmajang, where we had watched *Breakfast at Tiffany's* together, ran old films until they literally fell to pieces. It was in a bad neighborhood where Patsy couldn't go by herself, so she had bribed me to take her, though she must have seen that movie a dozen times already by then. I remembered being annoyed—though the theater was practically empty—when Patsy couldn't stop crying at the end, as Audrey Hepburn and George Peppard, drenched in the rain, go looking for Holly's cat.

"See," I'd told her, "it's a happy ending. Why are you crying?" and Patsy had looked at me, her hazel eyes gleaming with tears, smiling and crying at the same time, wiping her nose with the back of one hand and squeezing my arm with the other. "It's because it makes me so happy," she said. "Even after all that, she couldn't leave Cat behind."

"You don't even *have* a cat," I said, as if that should make a difference.

Patsy ignored me. "Do you think they'll live happily ever after, Seven?" she had asked.

"I don't know. It's not a fairy tale, Patsy."

"I'm going to marry someone who looks just like him," she'd said, pointing up at George Peppard's ten-foot-wide face on the painted billboard outside the Paekma Theater. "Do you think our kids would be blond then? Do you have a handkerchief?"

I gave her the one I had wadded in the back pocket of my Levi's, and she blew her nose on it. "If I was a movie star or a fashion model, I could have a husband like that," she said, folding up my handkerchief, giving it back. "Don't you think Audrey is the most beautiful woman in the whole wide world?"

"She looks kinda skinny to me," I said. My own idea of beauty happened to be Sharon Tate from *The Fearless Vampire Killers* and the Matt Helm film, but she had been murdered by the Manson gang, and I never told Patsy.

She'd taken me out to the Chinese restaurant in Sinchon after that and I ordered a simple omelette-covered fried rice, much to her disappointment. She had wanted to buy me something expensive. So when the Bando room service waiter arrived now with the fancy wheeled cart, and made a big show of laying out the table and unveiling the sandwich and burger under the stainless steel food covers, I wondered if Patsy remembered that part too.

She tipped the waiter a thousand won after he poured our coffees. When he left, we looked at each other over the table, and I felt like I should be saying grace or something. There was an expectation in the air, but also a sense of relief, as if we had just pulled off a big scam together or had gotten away from the police. At least that's how I felt—I couldn't quite read Patsy anymore. She seemed to take it all so matter-of-factly.

"Thanks," I said.

"Oh, it's all on Kenji," she said.

"Kenji?"

"Suzuki Kenji," she said, putting his surname first in the Japanese style. "He's the one paying for all of this. He must be one of *those* Suzukis, since he's going back and forth between Hong Kong and New York and L.A. and Seoul and God knows *where* else all the time. You know, the motorcycle Suzukis." She paused to wolf down half of her ham sandwich, which had been cut into neat crustless triangles.

I put ketchup on my egg burger and tapped out more onto the plate
for the fries. "Why would this Suzuki guy—" I began, but then seeing
Patsy's wide eyes, I stopped.

"As if you even need to ask," she mumbled through her sandwich.

I took my time. "Okay, so—how did you meet him then?"

"At a disco. Look, Seven, he's gone for a month at a time, and this is
his apartment in Seoul. I get to stay here and do whatever the fuck I
want. As long as I'm discreet. That's his word—'discreet.' And when he's
back in Seoul, I'm his *girlfriend*. He buys all my clothes and everything."
She gestured around the suite. "He calls me his Barbie-ji. Isn't that cute?
Kenji and Barbie-ji, the perfect couple by Mattel. Isn't this great?"

"Oh, you get used to anything," I said—and then she slapped me so
hard the food flew from my mouth and splattered, all red, yellow, and
brown, on the couch.

She glared at me. "How dare you!" she said. "How the *fuck* can you
say that? *I* read the book too! I know it doesn't have a happy ending!
And so what if I *was* used to it, bastard!"

I had quoted Paul's line from the movie. Holly's reply was, *I'll never
get used to anything. Anybody that does, they might as well be dead.*

"I'm sorry," I said, touching the side of my face. Inside, my cheek was
bleeding, sweet and metallic. "I didn't mean it that way, Patsy."

"Then what the fuck *did* you mean by it?"

"I don't know. I was just trying to be clever."

"You're an idiot," she said. "Such a fucking *idiot.* You know? You're
always thinking so much, you seem like a dopehead, and you never know
*what* the hell is going on."

The cut in my cheek wasn't bad. "Nobody saw you at school for a long
time," I said after a while. "When I saw your mom she just cried and
wouldn't tell me anything. My mom said your old man was in some kind
of trouble."

"Yeah. My old man McCabe's in the monkey house."

"What?! The place the women go to for VD?"

"Not that one. The stockade. You know how my mom could buy all that big stuff because my dad had a friend who was CID? Well, they got into a fight over something playing poker one night and the fucker backstabbed him. My old man got busted big time for two refrigerators and a washer-dryer set. Isn't that just *perfect*? He'd be in the old ASCOM stockade, but I think they moved the Army prison to Camp Humphreys or somewhere."

"What about your mom? She was the one selling all that stuff."

"It's the Army, Seven. They don't charge the wife most of the time. They just take away benefits. I guess they could have turned her over to the Korean police, but the CID dude wasn't mad at her in the first place."

"Who was it?"

"The CID? Taylor, the sweaty orangutan."

"Fuck. He's the one who let my mother slide with a second refrigerator. He made her file a burglary report to cover for the new one."

"Anyway, it all went to shit," said Patsy. "So I ran away from home."

"Not really, right? I mean, you're in Korea."

"I'm over eighteen now. I have my passport. And I still have my dependent ID card too. So . . . I can do whatever I want."

"So you just dropped out?"

"I can always get my GED later. Fuck SAHS. Seoul American High School, shit. I could've had my diploma there for a blow job."

"So *this* is your plan for the future?" I said, motioning at the room.

"*What* future, Seven? People like us don't really *have* a future. The present just keeps . . . changing, is all. Why? What did you ever want to be when *you* grew up? I seem to remember you never had any plans either, except maybe to bury your face in a book. You're almost all grown up now. Like me. So . . . what do *you* want to be?"

"I don't know," I said. It was the truth. I had never really given serious thought to the future. Was it that the present was complicated enough all by itself, and the past—if we didn't manage to ditch it—was too much of a burden to bear? "I just assumed I was gonna be in the Army and go to Vietnam. But now we lost the war." I had said as much before.

"Paulie decided he wants to go to college."

"How do you know? He writes to you?"

"I got a letter last week. Didn't you know his old man got posted to Fort Riley?"

"How would I know?" I said, annoyed. "That fucker never wrote me even once. Not even a postcard."

"That's not like him, Seven. You're like his only brother since Miklos went missing. I'm sure he wrote you. Maybe he just got your address wrong?"

"How? It's just the Dependent Mail Section 96220. How could he fuck that up?"

"Yongsan is 96301," Patsy said. "That's where he sends my letters. I bet that's the only APO he knows. Why don't you check?"

Paulie wasn't really one to remember a lot of technical information, and the mistake made sense to me. I finished my burger, less angry, while Patsy dipped my fries in the ketchup and ate them one by one.

"How is An-na doing?" she asked. "Does she still play with the Barbie I got for her?"

"Yeah," I said. "She makes clothes for her. She found some of my old GI Joe clothes, and so my mother got her a Ken doll. Did you know Ken is taller than GI Joe? And now Barbie is married."

Patsy laughed.

"Are you going to marry the Japanese guy?" I asked. I couldn't get myself to say his name.

"Are you kidding? His family would never allow it. They'd hire a detective. And he's *Japanese*! How could I marry a Japanese? I'm going to marry a nice white boy from Gainesville, Georgia." She had switched to a Southern accent for the last part.

"The Japanese dude is letting you date another man?"

"Oh, Fred, *dahling*," she said. "It's all in the discretion! Kenji doesn't care about other men as long as I don't bring them here."

"You brought *me* here."

"You're my *brother,* Seven! You're *family*, and Kenji wouldn't mind you staying as long as you like while he's away in Johannesburg or whatever."

"Who's the white boy? Did you meet him at the same disco?"

"Oh, now you're sounding *so* like my Daddy," Patsy said with an exaggerated wave of her hand. "We met at the Officers' Pool on South Post."

"What were you doing at the Officers' Pool? Your old man's a sergeant." I had my answer in Patsy's incredulous look.

"What better place to model my new bikini?" she said. "I'm not ending up like Haesuni—married to some enlisted hillbilly and stuck in a trailer park in Nowheresville, Kentucky." Patsy finished the last of the fries, licked the ketchup and grease off her fingers, and got up. "Want to know what he looks like? I have a picture of him."

"All right," I said without much enthusiasm.

Patsy walked over to the table by the stereo console and flipped through a stack of record albums. I wondered if she kept her private pictures hidden there, tucked away inside some obscure album cover of a record Kenji Suzuki would never play, but she just held out one of the albums for me to see. *Angel Clare.* I thought she must be joking.

"That's Art Garfunkel," I said.

"And there's only one decent song on this whole stinkin' album," Patsy said with some contempt. "But look at his face, Seven. He looks just like Bobby. Bobby Longstreet. A bit older, and wrinkled here and here," she said, indicating parts of Garfunkel's face, "but this is a spittin' image of him."

"He has an Afro?"

"You're such an idiot! He's a second lieutenant fresh out of West Point. 'The Long Gray Line,' he says, and his name is really Robert E.

Lee Longstreet, descended from the greatest Confederate general, second only to Robert E. Lee himself. General Lee called him his 'Old War Horse.' Did you know that?"

"I didn't know," I said. I wondered if Patsy was just deluded about Bobby Longstreet the way Holly was a "real phony" who believed her own fantasies. Patsy had always tended to be either too enthusiastic or too critical.

"I'm going out with Bobby tonight," she said. "Want to meet him?"

"As your brother Fred? Nah. Besides, I fuckin' hate discos."

"Then why don't you stay in Seoul tonight and we can have dinner when I get back?"

"Aren't you gonna be out all night? Or, you know, stay over at his BOQ?"

"What? You mean to to fuck him? Oh, Seven, you're just so stupid sometimes. Bobby doesn't go to discos, first of all, and he'd never let me stay overnight at his lovely Bachelor Officers' Quarters. He's a picnic-and-hiking kind of boy from a good Southern family."

"I think I should get back home, anyway," I said. "My aunt might worry. I haven't been out all night since Paulie left."

"Don't you have friends in Yongsan?"

"Yeah, but not close."

"Does your mom still go to the NCO Club in ASCOM to play those new slot machines every day?"

"Probably. Or whatever's there now that they're closing part of the post."

Patsy picked up the phone again and made a call to the manager of the Officers' Club in Yongsan. In a couple of minutes she had arranged for a message to be delivered to three different NCO Clubs so my mother would be sure to get it. The story was that I would be staying up in Seoul for a day or two with a friend who lived in UN Village.

"How was that?" Patsy said when it was done. "You're all set now. Your poor aunt won't be worried about you."

"I don't know you at all," I said. "Do I? You have all those numbers memorized?"

She was changing now, back in the bedroom. "A girl's gotta know her stuff," she called as she rustled about. "Runs in the family. You'll stay, then, Seven, won't you?"

"All right," I said. "Just tonight. But what do you expect me to do while you're out on your date?"

"Why don't you go to the Main Post Office and see if they have mail for you?"

Patsy dressed in a long-sleeved striped top, black capris, and Mary Janes with white socks. With her hair up, she looked like a young girl from a black-and-white European film or maybe the young helper of the French Resistance on an episode of *Combat!* She transferred a bunch of stuff from her handbag to a larger, more casual shoulder bag, including what looked to me like a wad of cash. Then she called the concierge to have a taxi from post come for her, and we left the chocolate sundae melting on the coffee table.

It was one of the newer Arirang taxis and Patsy knew the driver. She told him she was going to the USOM Club, which I remembered was on the hill overlooking the high school on South Post. I wondered if she expected me to walk all the way from the South Post gate, but then she told the driver to take the back gate of North Post instead of going around the Samgakji Rotary to the main entrance. She introduced me as her little brother Insu, and the driver asked, "Aren't you the son of Insu's mother?"

"Yes?" I said uncertainly.

"You're staying in Seoul a few days at a friend's house in UN Village?"

I was confused for a moment. "How did you hear that, *ajoshi*?"

He pointed to his radio. "Came down from dispatch a little while ago. A message for your mother."

I looked at Patsy, and she shrugged. We exchanged some pleasantries with the driver in Korean and then switched to English.

"I have a question for you," I said to Patsy. "If Bobby Longstreet comes from such a proper Southern family and all, why would *they* let him marry you? Wouldn't they check up on you like the Japanese dude's family?"

She brushed it away with a gesture. "They won't *let* him. You think I'm an *idiot*? He's in love with me, Seven. He doesn't care what his family thinks because he's proving himself to *himself*. Now that Vietnam is over, he can't be a man by going out and killing gooks, can he? So he can prove himself by marrying one."

"You're not that kind of gook," I said.

She laughed. "We're the Real McCoy of gooks, Seven. The Vietnamese are more properly *dinks*, but the white boys can't tell the difference."

"When will you be back?"

She gazed out the window at the crowd of people waiting for a bus by a kiosk. "Before curfew," she said, distantly. "Or never. Wouldn't that be better?"

"Don't joke like that," I said.

She turned toward me. "Do you think I'm evil?" she asked suddenly.

"Evil? What are you talking about?"

"You wouldn't even know, would you, Seven? Not even after all you've seen and all you've been through. Don't you have any evil in you so you could understand?"

"I really don't know what you're talking about."

"Don't worry, I'll be back before midnight—I don't want to be stuck somewhere till four in the morning, and Bobby's not about to let me stay with him to sit out curfew. What would people say?"

"In the BOQ? Why would *they* be saying anything?" I imagined Bobby would be the one talking about it anyway, bragging to his friends.

"I'm just being dramatic," said Patsy. "Never mind."

The taxi had stopped at the back gate, and we had to show our IDs to the KATUSA guard. The driver let me off a moment later by the crowd of Korean women waiting to have parcels packed for them by the outdoor concession behind the Friendship Arcade.

"Do you love him?" I asked as I scooted out of the cab.

Patsy just shut the door and waved through the window.

I WALKED PAST the crowd up to the Main Post Office. Maybe Patsy had already thought it through for me. I would pick up the letters from Paulie waiting for me at the PO, then I would spend the rest of the afternoon at the library reading them—maybe even writing a reply on some paper from the pile of free army stationery they had there. She'd no doubt seen the Pilot fountain pen I always carried in my shirt pocket.

But instead of stopping at the PO, I walked over to the Main Snack Bar behind the Garrison HQ and bought two large cups of Coke with lots of ice. In the theater next door, the poster for the current film said, THE YEAR IS 2024 . . . A FUTURE YOU'LL PROBABLY LIVE TO SEE. I'll be sixty-four, I thought, making a quick calculation. I would most likely still be alive. The top half of the poster was a riveted metal bunker door and the bottom half looked like a stylized ladder going down a manhole, and under that was a barely dressed girl, asleep or unconscious, and beneath that, A BOY AND HIS DOG and, smaller: AN R-RATED, RATHER KINKY TALE OF SURVIVAL. I checked my Timex, though it wasn't necessary. I could watch either showing, and there was plenty of time before the first one.

I went back toward the PO, cutting through the parking lot of the bus depot, where Bus Ajoshi, whom I'd known since I was little, was blowing his shrill whistle to help the green army buses back out of their stalls. I gave him the Coke I had bought for him and he gave me a mock salute. "Have you seen my mother?" I asked. I had to yell to be heard above the diesel engines.

"No!" he yelled back.

"If you see her, please tell her I'm staying in Seoul with a friend for a few days!" I had expected a long wait in the line at the PO behind all the Korean wives who were sending packages to the States, but it took only a couple of minutes before the clerk at a little window called for anyone just there to pick up mail.

I went up to the counter at the far end of the mail room and showed the clerk my military dependent's ID card. "Oh, yeah," he said. "Where you been, buddy? I'll be back in a skosh." He disappeared into the back and returned a minute later with some envelopes tied together with postal twine. "These were about to get forwarded to your old man, but Phillips said to hang on to them. The top one's from him."

I was puzzled. "Phillips?" I said.

"The main man. The Black Horse, right?"

"The Black Horse?"

"Man, why you playin' dumb, kid? No need. He was down this way picking up his new tripod or some shit and he told us to look out for you, awright?"

It was the photographer in the jeep—I remembered now. He had known who my father was. "Okay," I said. "I got it."

"You hang loose now," said the clerk. He winked, pointing a finger at me and making a clicking sound.

Outside the PO, I untied the twine and opened Phillips's envelope first. It had my last name on the front and a black ink stamp, probably made at the Friendship Arcade, that showed a heart, a horse head, and a snake in the shape of an *S* with its forked tongue protruding. There was a rounded rectangular box around the three symbols, making them look sort of like an Egyptian cartouche for the name of a pharaoh. Inside the envelope was a small sheet of white paper folded in half, and when I opened it, a postal money order fell out. One hundred dollars, made out to me, and on the paper a cryptic note: "For the ConneXion—Get a ConfeXion." It was signed with the same black stamp.

The rest of the envelopes—three of them—were from Paulie at his father's new post in Fort Riley, Kansas, 66442. Patsy had been right about him addressing everything to the Yongsan zip code. Paulie's father must have been transferred to the First Infantry Division at Fort Riley—the first envelope had a Big Red 1, their unit logo, drawn on it in magic marker. I opened the most recent letter first, just a single sheet that said, "I'm not writing again, you fucker! Fuck you! Fuck Korea!" It was signed with a big *P* made to look like a penis, and below that a small "PS" with "Miklos?" It made me smile involuntarily, a wide smile that caused my eyes to tear up as I realized suddenly how much I missed the two of them.

Now the only one left in Korea who really knew me was Patsy, and she was dreaming of marrying a West Pointer, one of those guys in a gray monkey suit, and leaving with him for The World. It was like we were all running across a bridge that was collapsing behind us, I thought, this whole world and all the people we cared about in it, falling into an abyss—not an abyss, but a horrific chaos of things changing, the country growing into a modern nation with tall buildings and luxury hotels, but everything a facade of fancy, gleaming tile, stuck on top of crumbling, cheap concrete. That's what was happening everywhere, and it was eating up our lives.

I decided to cash the money order and give it to Miklos's mother when I saw her again. She needed it more than I did, and she wouldn't be changing it into quarters and losing it all in slot machines.

It was nearly time for the movie to begin, and I couldn't read the letters then, so I made my way over to the Quonset hut that was Post Theater #2. A couple of GIs were walking that way, smoking cigarettes they got from the packs rolled up in the sleeves of their ODs, lighting them with their souvenir Zippos. Both of them wore black bracelets woven out of boot laces, and I wondered if it was one of those secret symbols of brotherhood or something special to their unit.

The first showing wasn't very crowded. I sat near the front because I liked the movies to fill my field of vision, and I had time to get comfortable before having to stand up for the national anthem and sit again for the coming attractions. It was funny—one of the previews was for a movie called *Robin and Marian*, with an old Audrey Hepburn playing opposite a scruffy, balding Sean Connery who was Robin Hood back from the Crusades. Audrey Hepburn, who must have been older than my mother, had a different, quiet, and sad beauty now. I wondered if I should tell Patsy.

*A Boy and His Dog* began abruptly with a bunch of nuclear explosions, and many of the soldiers in the audience jumped involuntarily. Then some white text rolled up the center of a black screen: WORLD WAR IV LASTED FIVE DAYS, then, in smaller type along the right, as if it was the punch line to a joke: POLITICIANS HAD FINALLY SOLVED THE PROBLEMS OF URBAN BLIGHT, and then the year: 2024. The boy and his dog are wandering around a bleak landscape, scavenging to survive until the dog finds a girl who is disguised as a boy. The boy follows her underground to the ruins of a locker room, where she strips off her clothes. Some GI called out, "You're prettier than the girl, man!" Someone else shouted, "Bitch in heat!" and a bunch of GIs howled in the back. The boy abandons his dog for the girl, and they go to the weird and frenetic underground world of Topeka. It turns out the girl was sent to entice him down there so he could be used like a stud for breeding. But the girl has fallen in love with him, and they run away together, back up to the blighted surface world, where they find the loyal dog still waiting, sick and starving, on the verge of death. The girl wants to leave and let the dog die. She tells the boy that's what the dog would have wanted too, not realizing that the boy and his dog have a special telepathic connection she can't hear.

In the end the boy makes a hard decision, and the final scene is him walking off with his dog, a cooking fire smoldering in the foreground. The whole theater cheered in approval when they figured out that the boy had fed the girl to his dog. I suppose that was meant to be some dramatic shock ending like the end of *Planet of the Apes*, but I disliked all the characters—the stupid boy, the condescending dog, the conniving girl—so I didn't care. What struck me, instead, was something the boy said to his dog at the end: "Well, it wasn't my fault she picked me to get all wet-brained over." I had never heard that figure of speech. What did that really mean, anyway, coming from that stupid kid?

The movie left me in a bad mood, so I walked out the gate to Itaewon to catch a cab back to the Bando Hotel. It was still light outside, the sun just below the horizon lighting the clouds from below into an uneasy orange-red glow that reminded me of the colors at the beginning of the movie. I slouched in the back seat of the cab, flipping through Paulie's letters, only looking at the postmark dates, reexamining the Phillips cartouche stamp, the one-hundred-dollar money order. Why a money order? I thought. He could have just folded a bill and put it in that envelope. And why a hundred dollars? How much had he made from my telling him about Dupree and the body bags? The movie had made it hard not to think of Miklos and King, probably eaten by a balding, middle-aged Korean in some *poshint'ang* restaurant.

Outside the window of the cab the streets were busy with the close of day, and the air had grown foul again with auto exhaust. Colored neon lights were blinking on in the fancier storefronts, but most were illuminated by cold blue-white fluorescents. I didn't want to have to tip a doorman, so I got off at the U.S. Embassy and walked across the street to the Bando, where all the service staff seemed to recognize me already. I made my way past a couple of blond European businessmen and their wives and took the elevator up to Patsy's room.

When I opened the door and switched on the light, I thought at first that it must be the wrong room, then that Patsy must have checked out. Everything had been picked up, cleaned up, straightened—not a thing out of place—in a way that made the suite feel entirely empty. The windows had been shut and the curtains drawn halfway. The remnants of our meal had been removed, the couch cleaned, and even the Garfunkel album, which Patsy had propped up on the console to look like a portrait, had been put back in its place.

I left the letters on the coffee table and went back to the door to take off my shoes there. My feet felt suddenly cold when they touched the thin carpeting on the floor, but only for a moment. I opened the windows again, letting in some warm summer air, and pulled the curtains all the way back to get the last light glowing on the bottoms of the clouds. I took off my Nehru shirt and thought of neatly folding it, but I reconsidered and just draped it over the back of the couch by the coffee table. Though there was no door between the bedroom and the living room, the opening between them had a feeling to it, a sort of force field, and when I walked through it, because I had to pee and the bathroom was there, I felt as if I had intruded into a secret space.

I closed the door of the bathroom once I was inside, startled momentarily by my own reflection in the full-length mirror on the door, reflected again in the wide mirror above the sink. Patsy's black stockings hung from a towel rack, and on the tray on the counter, she had laid out a razor, bottles of Excedrin, NyQuil, One A Day with iron, and a package of birth control pills. There was also a perfume I didn't recognize, a jar of Ponds cold cream, a bottle of Oil of Olay, and a blow dryer, unplugged, next to a hair brush from which a sharp-handled styling comb protruded. Her soap was plain Ivory.

I flipped up the toilet seat and pissed into the gleaming white bowl. My bladder emptied and the water turned a pale shade of amber, and now, looking around, I felt more an intruder than an explorer. I quickly flushed the toilet and went back out into the bedroom.

I was in no frame of mind to read the letters, and my mood, though not exactly foul now, was strangely agitated. I hardly ever drank alcohol by myself, but tonight I examined the offerings at the bar in the living room and poured myself a glass of Johnnie Walker Black. I hated the smoky medicinal taste of the whiskey, but drank it all anyway, quickly, so I could feel the heat shoot up from my gut into my face. I stood by the window, looking outside at the city of Seoul growing brighter as twilight turned to night.

What would Patsy be doing about now, I wondered, if she planned to get back before the midnight-to-four curfew that kept the whole country battened down in the dark, with only criminals and North Korean spies out in the streets?

After a few sips, the next glass of whiskey wasn't all that bad, and I could even taste something like faint licorice and toffee in the smoke. In a few minutes my eyes were hot and everything felt thick. I took off my pants, stumbling over a chair. It would probably be a good idea to take a shower, I thought, so I took everything off and grabbed the whiskey bottle to drink some more under the water.

In the bedroom I was startled again by my reflection—this time a naked stranger on the back of the bathroom door. What an idiot, I thought, embarrassed at myself for being so skinny. I sat down on the corner of the huge bed for a moment to get my bearings, and it felt so soft I had a desperate need to feel the inside of the coverlet. I was supposed to be Patsy's brother, after all. Who the hell would care if I was asleep in her bed—it was big enough for a family of four.

I woke up terribly parched, and painfully in need of a piss. I rolled out of the bed onto the floor. The bathroom light was on, and I stumbled over, with a sick feeling in my stomach that only grew worse with each step. At the bathroom door I had to kneel, then crawl on my hands and knees to throw up into the toilet, and what came gushing out of my mouth and nostrils was vile and acidic. I held the rim of the toilet for a while until I heaved again, and then I felt well enough to stand up and piss into the bowl. I flushed it and watched the swirl of bile-laced hot dog chunks and liquefied white bread disappear gurgling down the pipes. I went to the sink and washed my hands and face. I grimaced at myself in the mirror, washed out my mouth, sipped a few palmfuls of water, and went back to the bed. It was soft and warm under the sheets, and I shivered once, hugging myself, before I lost consciousness.

WHEN I WOKE AGAIN it was deathly quiet except for the sound of the shower going in the bathroom. I heard the metallic clatter of the curtain rings as I drifted off again and woke up to my mother bending over me, telling me she had received the message, and when I opened my eyes it was Patsy in the white bathrobe leaning over me with her ear to my chest. Her hair was wet and fragrant with a conditioner that smelled faintly of rosemary and flowers. "So you're alive," she whispered, as if she didn't want to wake me. I smiled.

"They're out of hot water again," she said, and she took off the robe and crawled in, naked, next to me in the bed. She felt icy for a moment as her skin touched mine, and I gasped. "You're burning up," she whispered. "Did you drink that whole bottle of Black Label?"

"It wasn't full, I don't think."

"When did you start drinking?"

"I don't, Patsy. What time is it?"

"Go back to sleep, Seven."

She curled up on me, pressing herself against my side and lifting one knee on top of my belly. I imagined I could feel the parallel ridges on her thigh—*one, two, three*—where she had cut herself years ago with the straight razor she used to sharpen her pencil. She had one arm across my chest, and she breathed into the hollow of my neck like a child. "You're so warm," she whispered, and before long we were both asleep.

IN THE MORNING the light was so bright I had to put on a pair of Kenji Suzuki's sunglasses. Patsy had ordered breakfast and was already eating her bacon and eggs when I came out of the bedroom. She had ordered me pancakes and two eggs, sunny-side up, and I ate as much as I could without getting queasy again.

I told her about the movie and she told me about her date with Lieutenant Longstreet as we drank black coffee. I had the strange feeling that we were in a movie and that I was also watching the movie because the matter-of-factness of what we were doing couldn't possibly have been real. With Patsy in her white bathrobe and me in one of Kenji Suzuki's flower-patterned blue-and-white yukatas, which was a little short for me, we looked like decadent jet-setters—or maybe that's how I secretly wanted it to be, knowing it couldn't last.

"Who's paying you in money orders?" asked Patsy.

I explained about Phillips, and how I planned to give the money to Miklos's mother when I saw her again.

"Why is it so complicated? Is she hiding from someone?"

"She owes a lot of money and she lost her PX privileges," I said. "Didn't you know Miklos's old man just dumped her? I don't know if they even got a divorce. It was all of a sudden." I noticed Patsy glancing at Paulie's letters.

"When are you gonna read the rest?" she asked.

"Today. Maybe." I looked up at Patsy, who was casually nibbling a corner of her burnt, buttered toast. "When are you leaving, Patsy?"

"Bobby applied for leave," she said. "Soon as it's approved we're going to Las Vegas. We're *eloping*. I've always wanted to use that word— 'eloping.'"

"Do you love him?" I asked. "You didn't answer me yesterday."

"You know, *I* was drunk too, last night. You could have taken advantage of a girl in that condition. Wouldn't even have been held responsible."

"Don't change the subject, Patsy. I asked if you love him."

"Oh, fuck you, Seven." She made a gesture as if to shoo me away.

"Why can't you answer?"

"Because you wouldn't understand."

She lit up a cigarette and smoked it, without the holder, pinched between her thumb and middle finger. She pointed her index finger at the calligraphy above us on the room divider. "You know what that says?"

"I can't read Chinese."

"I asked the *ajuma* who cleans the room, and she had to ask someone who could read it. It says, '*Sae ong ji ma.*' Something like 'a horse that belongs to an old man who lives on the frontier.' When I asked Kenji, he laughed and said it meant you never can tell what's going to happen, so just go with it. You know? Go with the flow. He said it was probably some kind of sex joke, since it's over the entrance to the bedroom. Even an old geezer can fuck like a horse. I think that's how he thought of it, but the *ajuma* told me this whole story about how the old man's son got his leg broken because he fell off of that fine horse, and everyone said how horrible it was, but then he didn't have to go to war because of his broken leg, and it saved his life."

I looked up at the calligraphy, wondering how so much could be contained in only four words. "That reminds me of my Big Uncle," I said.

"It made me think of him too. And what happened at Yaksan."

"I'm sorry about all that now."

"Don't be sorry, Seven."

"You still haven't answered the question, Patsy."

"Fuck," she sighed, as if she had just resigned herself to confessing a crime, and exhaled a large cloud of smoke. "So last night we were on a double date at the USOM Club," she said. "Bobby brought one of his buddies, a first lieutenant with a German name like yours, 'Fritz' or something, and he had a girl with him—some little blond bitch from Nebraska or somewhere who works at the embassy. You should have heard what she said about Korean women. I could have ripped her fucking eyes out. I mean, she was talking about my *mother*! *Your* mother!

"Bobby's friend was sort of egging her on and talking about the club girls and two-dollar blow jobs in Itaewon and all that shit, probably to shock her, and Bobby just sat there listening for a long time. I was getting ready to throw my drink in Fritz's face and walk out, you know? And I was hating Bobby too, pretty much. But then I noticed he was all red, like he was embarrassed, but it turned out he was furious. He stood up and told his friend and his little bitch to get the fuck out. He actually used the word 'fuck' at them.

"I was expecting to be let down by some kind of coward, and I got a white knight instead. I told Bobby later he should be wearing shining armor."

I didn't quite know what to say because I had been hoping, secretly—even to myself—that the story would turn out badly, that Bobby would prove himself to be a typical sleazy GI, and the turn of events both disappointed and surprised me. I was strangely jealous of him. "Does he know about your mother?" I asked.

Patsy was standing at the window now, looking down at the street. "Sure, I confessed everything. Twice."

"Twice?"

"You know how these things come out. You can never tell the whole truth all at once. You say what you need to when the time is right."

This Bobby Longstreet was either terribly naïve, I thought, or an unusually good person, but another year in Korea would probably change all that. "You told him *everything* and he's okay with all of it?" I must have sounded incredulous.

"I couldn't tell him *everything*! Do you think I'm crazy?"

"Well, does he know what you're doing now with Kenji? Or what you've *been* doing?"

"What the fuck would *you* know about it? What I'm doing. What I've *been* doing?"

"You're dressing up like Audrey Hepburn, Patsy! You're living in a fucking luxury hotel, for God's sake, when your house doesn't even have a flush toilet!"

"Oh, yeah, poor Lula Mae Patsy, who's gonna be your Paul? Is that what you're thinking?"

"I don't even know *what* the fuck to think!"

Patsy sat down again. Under the white bathrobe, her flesh-colored slip looked strangely dark. I was surprised by how pale her skin had become. She must have been avoiding the sun, but in the morning light her hazel eyes, which were usually brownish, had become a bright green.

"Look, Seven," she said. "Our moms have known each other since before we were even born. They're practically real sisters, not like all those women who go around calling each other *on'ni*. We're like family.

And if you look at how our Korean relatives treat our moms, and how everyone treats us, we're about the only family we'll ever have that matters. But what a family, right?"

I nodded.

"Sometimes I think our moms are doing the best they can for us, and sometimes I think they just stopped giving a fuck at a certain point, like they realized their half-and-half kids could never amount to anything and just gave up. When's the last time your mom ever talked to you about your future?"

I realized I had never thought about things in this way. My mother had never talked to me about what I would do after high school, what I might do with my life—nothing about a career or an aspiration or about who I might marry or where I might live. Oh, she might make a comment from time to time: "You'll never make any money with your face stuck in a book." But nothing more than that.

"Maybe it's because she couldn't imagine a future for me. I'm not interested in the things I'm supposed to be interested in. She doesn't understand why anyone would read a book."

"Look," said Patsy, nodding her head sideways to indicate what was outside the window. "You may want to get away from all this by going into your own little world, but me, I want to stay in it, you know, and make it better for myself. You and Paulie and Miklos were about the only ones who didn't judge me, you know that? That's why you were like my real family. Even my girlfriends, all those *on-ni*s, judged me for what I did or what I am. Fuck them."

"Do you think they might have been jealous? I don't see any of them being called 'Miss Audrey.'"

When I looked up from my empty plate I saw there were tears in Patsy's eyes. She wiped them away without even a sniffle. "I'm sorry, Seven. I guess I go off into my own world too. I guess we all have our reasons and our little tricks for making things hurt less. Do you remember I told you a long time ago that my old man would get drunk and beat me because he thought I was my mom? And how I was pissed at her because she'd let it happen?"

"Yeah. I remember." That had been years ago, one day on the bus on our way home from school. We were all going to summer school even when we didn't need to, because it gave us a reason to be away from home. The bus was practically empty, and Patsy had made the driver stop so we could buy ice cream and sodas. We had exchanged stories about what our fathers did when they got drunk. We all had our stories, lots of them, more than we should have had among the four of us.

"He didn't just beat me," said Patsy.

We were both silent a moment. "I'm so sorry," I whispered. My throat had closed up and what came out was barely audible.

"One time, when Paulie was over at our house, he did it to Paulie too."

It felt as if someone had gone back into my memory of that time on the bus—when we were telling each other those stories and laughing—and punched my younger self in the gut. How could I have laughed back then? How could Paulie? Patsy? We had all laughed together when I had tried to sing one of the German marching songs my father sang when he was drunk.

I started to get up, impulsively, to give Patsy a comforting hug, but she held a hand out to stop me. "I don't want to be touched right now," she said, and went into the bedroom. I heard her open and close one of the wardrobes, and for a moment I was worried. I followed her in to see what she was doing, but then she turned around and handed me a stiff white envelope. "It's for your Big Uncle," she said.

The flap wasn't sealed. I pulled it open and found eleven bills. I counted them—ten one hundreds and one single. One thousand and one dollars. I sat hard on the edge of the bed.

"Don't say you can't take it, Seven. I know that's what you're going to say. And don't thank me, either. When you were coming down the mountain that night feeling so bad, Miklos and I swore we would do something to help. We figured the thing to do was raise money. Paulie did something too, but he said it was a secret and we would find out when it was time. Well, he's in the States, and Miklos went missing. That just left me.

"I know your mom's in debt, okay? And your uncle is really sick, and you're doing all that black market shit to help them out. I don't want your mom getting backstabbed or your father getting court-marshaled like mine. I worry about your little sister. What would happen to her if they get arrested? You can't count on anyone anymore, and we're about the only family we have left."

I wanted to say something, but Patsy placed her finger over my lips and looked into my eyes, slowly shaking her head. Now I started to cry. I thought of what Patsy must have done for that money, and for the longest time, I couldn't stop crying.

I LEFT THE Bando Hotel that afternoon to cash the money order for Miklos's mother. Patsy told me she had to give me the extra dollar because in the *Breakfast at Tiffany's* movie, Mrs. Failenson, Paul's "interior decorator," had given him a check for $1,000 at the end of their arrangement. Patsy didn't want me thinking she would compare me to a gold digger who was really a gigolo, and the extra dollar made her think of *The 1,001 Nights*.

Before we parted ways, Patsy said she would send me a message or leave a note at the PO to let me know when she'd be leaving. When I told her I was worried I might still miss her before she left, she smiled.

"Remember how I got the message to your mom," she said.

We laughed about that. We hugged each other, and I waved goodbye as she left for Sinchon-dong in the black Arirang taxi, without ever having told me if she loved Bobby Longstreet.

# Cherry, Cherry, Bar

## 1975

They're going to send me stateside," said my father. "It wasn't what they thought last time, and now both docs want me to get more of my guts cut out. It's a fucking joke, isn't it? I live through all that shit in 'Nam with hardly a scratch, and now I have my own doctors cutting out pieces of me." He puffed the cigar he wasn't supposed to be smoking, and when a passing nurse gave him a look of disapproval, he just grinned and waved at her.

We were in the courtyard of the 121st Hospital again, taking a break from the same room he'd been assigned to before. They had discharged my father after his condition improved, and then he'd had a relapse of what they had initially taken to be malaria, which he'd had in Vietnam.

I was sitting on the bench next to him with a can of Coke between my knees, feeling a sense of impending loss. It was not doom. I knew that, ultimately, we were all doomed. Instead, it was a curious kind of helplessness—not so much a fear of my father dying, or even the realization that our time in Korea was about to come to an end. It was something bigger and also more philosophical. I could not name it, but if I followed the feeling in my mind, it led to particular things: a goodbye to all the people and places I knew, a powerless endurance of unwanted events, one after the other, endless packing and unpacking, sorting and abandoning, dressing and undressing, embarking, disembarking, from one vehicle then another, a cab, a bus, a plane, another bus, another cab, again and again, into a smeared infinity. Sitting there hunched over my-self, I felt like a still point at the edge of a chaos, and I wished I could simply close my eyes and not open them ever again.

"The Seventh Infantry garrison is going to be in Fort Ord, and they have a big hospital there. What do you say we go to California, Booby?" He usually called me that when he was making some sarcastic fun of me, but this time I knew he said it to hide his own fear. On my last visit, when I'd brought him more detective novels, he had talked about his childhood the way old people do before they die.

"Where is Fort Ord?" I asked. "Is it near Hollywood?"

He laughed. "Closer to San Francisco. It would be a six-hour drive from Fort Ord to Hollywood—at least. Maybe longer."

"That must be more than the whole length of Korea."

"You could fit four or five Koreas into California. Maybe a hundred Koreas into the whole U.S. It's a big fucking country if you remember how long it took to drive across."

It had taken five days to get from Tacoma to Fort Dix and McGuire Air Force Base to catch the MAC flight to Germany. Instead of buying plane tickets to fly the family across the States, my father had used the travel allowance to buy a car that he could then ship to Germany. It was an old cream-colored Ford Fury station wagon so big we could all sleep in it. I still remembered the litany of states: Washington, Idaho, Mon-tana, Wyoming, Nebraska, Iowa, Illinois, Indiana, Ohio, Pennsylvania, New York, New Jersey.

"Will they be able to fix you up in Fort Ord? Is the hospital better than here?"

"That's what they tell me, Booby. But who the hell knows?" He put his sunburnt arm around my shoulder. "I'm not planning to die anytime soon, if that's what you're worried about. You ever see how many meters of guts are in a belly? Fuck them. Let them take half of them—I'll still be fine." He mussed my long hair—"hippie hair" he called it.

"Daddy," I began, but nothing else came out, and he leaned back again to take a leisurely pull on his cigar, blowing the thick smoke over to the left, into the glossy leaves of a flowering bush. He looked relaxed and content at that moment, with a smile that reminded me of Burt Lancaster in a western.

"My father went MIA on the Eastern Front," he said. "He was Wermacht. Hated Hitler with a passion. But he put me in the Hitler Youth because he thought that would prepare me for the military. I was a NAPOLA when I was younger than you are now. I lived in a castle—a real *castle*—in Czechoslovakia, and I got the kind of training that makes the U.S. Army look like it's just a bunch of pussies.

"You know, I was remembering—when I got the news he was MIA, which meant he was probably dead, or maybe worse—a POW with the Russians—I wasn't even sad. I was proud of his sacrifice for the Fatherland. That's what Germans were like back then. Everybody else has a motherland, but ours was a *Father*land." He laughed at that, as if it was a secret joke. "It wasn't my father or mother but *me* who dreamed of being in the SS, so I was sad when my school wasn't mobilized to help defend Berlin against the Russians. It was all too late by then, but I was only thirteen, younger than you are now—what the hell did I know about anything? And it wasn't until after the war, when I was working for the Labor Service, that I learned about what really happened. We were in the Sudetenland. When they expelled us and sent us to Germany, they put us in the same concentration camps we used for the Jews. They kicked us out of our house in Czechoslovakia with only two days' notice, and your great-grandmother refused to go. She said she was going to die at home. She went upstairs, got in bed, and the next morning she was dead."

"She had a heart attack because she was so upset?"

"No. She was just a stubborn woman. She just decided to die and did it."

I didn't know what to say to that, so I changed the subject. "Why did you join the American army?" I asked.

"I always wanted to see the world." He sounded half sarcastic. "I had the wanderlust when I was younger, and I couldn't exactly be in the German army after the war. That was a time when everybody was out to punish Germans. Really, it was better to be out of the country where everything had gone to shit and people were turning on each other. Suddenly, nobody had ever been a Nazi, just like after the war every fucking Frenchman said he was in the Resistance.

"I was lucky. My mother knew someone in the Church, and they got me a job in Washington state working on a dairy farm for the Maryknoll Fathers. That's why I send them money every month, if you're wondering about those cards I get. After that I was a tough guy bill collector before I joined the Army."

"But how could you join the U.S. Army when you were the enemy?"

"You don't know nothing," he said. "The American military *loves* Germans. If Patton had his way, the Americans and Germans would have joined while the war was still going on and fought the Russians together. Then there would never have been a fucking Korean War or the Vietnam War! But then again, I wouldn't have ended up here and married your mother. And I wouldn't have you, would I?"

"I guess not," I said.

"I used to wonder what kind of soldier you'd be when you grew up," my father said. "I figured you could never be a grunt like me. You don't have it in you to be humping in the boonies. I always figured you for an officer or some MI type—one of those smartasses who knows everything about Russian vehicle silhouettes and that kind of shit. It takes all kinds, you know, and you're lucky 'Nam is over and there's no hot war for boys of your generation. You're lucky you don't have to go through what I did."

I think it was that afternoon on the bench that made it clear to me that my father would die soon. I had not wanted to think about his mortality. As a child I had worried that he would die in battle in Vietnam and we would only know about it when the letters and the little reels of Scotch recording tape stopped coming, and when the guy in the dress uniform came knocking at our gate with a folded-up American flag. I had never imagined my father dying of a disease or in the hospital. He was a warrior, after all, a kind of Viking with bleached hair on his sunburnt arms and a haggard face that looked to me like Sgt. Rock of EZ Company. But that afternoon he seemed to be canvassing the terrain of his life—seeing where it began and ended. I remembered him explaining to me how to set up overlapping fields of fire, the difference between enfilade and defilade, where to anticipate the dead spots to find cover in a landscape. I wanted to ask him how much longer he thought he could live—or planned to live—but I didn't want to hear an answer that would make the time real.

"You'll have to be the man in the family when I'm gone," he said. "You'll have to take care of the insurance and make sure all the money doesn't disappear. Be a good big brother and look after Anna."

I nodded.

"It never works out the way you think," he said. "Remember that. When I was thirteen I was a gung-ho Hitler Youth. I thought Rommel should be shot for being a traitor. But by the time I was your age, my hero was General Wenck, who disobeyed Hitler and used what was left of his Panzer division to help people escape from Berlin and go to the American zone. The truth is never what you thought it was, but when you learn it, it changes everything forever."

MY FATHER DIDN'T know yet when his orders would come through or where he would be sent, but we would probably have to move back to the States by September in just a few weeks. The Army was accommodating, sometimes, to the needs of children and the timing of the school year. An-na was in second grade now. I would be graduating in a couple of years, and the timing of the move was probably not the best thing for my education, but then again, since I wasn't planning to go to college, it wouldn't make any real difference.

What did make a difference was all the unfinished business I had to attend to, all the things dangling like the knotted ropes on the obstacle course routine I used to do in ASCOM. Miklos, Paulie, and I used to swing from one to another as if we were Tarzan. We had run that whole course so many times we could do it faster than any GI we knew. We would make bets with them to win ourselves some snack money, and the GIs were always good sports about losing, especially when it was payday and they couldn't claim they had no money.

When I returned home from the 121st Hospital, I started assembling the package I would take up to Big Uncle along with the money Patsy had given me. If he was still across the river in the cave, there were things he could use to make his life easier, and so I spent a couple of days shopping for him at the Main PX in Yongsan, the Air Force PX at Kimpo, and the PX in ASCOM. Some of the items I had to barter for, and a couple I got through DuPree: a first-aid kit, two green wool blankets, cigarettes, whiskey, extra matches, a few bars of C-4 to be used like Sterno for cooking, a mosquito net, two flashlights and an electric lantern, an army watch with a radium dial and nylon band, a transistor radio with an extra battery pack, a case of C-rations, and, finally, a Camillus 1760 pocket knife, the U.S. Army's cheaper stainless steel counterpart to the Swiss Army knife. It was three suitcases full of stuff, and I planned to take it up to Sambongni with the money and ferry it over to Big Uncle.

I had found the three suitcases—cheap Japanese models that seemed to be made of heavy cardboard—at the Lucky Tailor Shop in Sinchon. Mr. Lucky Kim, the owner, had even rigged one of them so I could wear it like a backpack if I had to carry all three at the same time. But when I had them all packed, they were so heavy I could barely walk with the load. I would have to get someone to go up to Big Uncle with me—or maybe just hire a taxi from Pupyong for the day, though that would be expensive.

With the three suitcases full and stacked by Yongsu's old bench press under the corrugated blue plastic roof of the patio, I was sitting on the cool cement step watching the cosmos sway in the breeze that blew into the walled *madang*. I heard an Arirang taxi stop outside our gate—its engine was unmistakable, a deeper and richer throbbing than the tiny Korean economy cabs, which were mostly Coronas.

The small inset door in the gate opened, and my mother stooped through carrying her purse and a brown PX bag. "You're home," she said. "Go out and bring the other bags in."

When I put on my shoes and went out, the driver had already unloaded the trunk and the grocery bags were on the ground. He brought two of them into the house while the cab idled, the exhaust pipe throbbing and shuddering and spewing smoke. The bags were all heavy— filled with Similac cans, coffee (both bottled and canned) Pream, and Charms and M&M's. There was no way my mother could have bought so many rationed items in one day, even if she had been to the Yongsan Commissary and a few different PXes on different posts. And these were all items that seemed a bit out of date, as if they were meant to cater to the tastes of someone old, or someone still thinking of the black market from several years ago.

Inside, Nokchon Cousin was already busy repacking everything into *pojagi*s. She stacked the items, pulled the *pojagi* cloths tight, and yanked roughly on the corners to tie them together. She moved like she was angry, and I could see that something wasn't right. If my mother had bought the things at a PX or the Commissary, there would have been price tags to remove. These things must have been bought from another black marketer, which meant there would be no profit—or probably even a loss—in selling them again. But someone was clearly coming for the things. The small table in the room was set for coffee and there were a few fresh apples and tangerines laid out on a plate with a paring knife.

Before the taxi left, I asked the driver how much it would cost to hire him to drive me to Sambongni and back. "That's most of a day," he said. "You don't want an Arirang cab for that. Ask one of the regular *ajoshi*s to take you on their day off and they'll do it cheap. People who go on vacation do it all the time."

"Do you know anybody who drives a Korean cab?"

"Go to the dispatch in ASCOM and tell Eyeball Ajoshi what day. He'll find someone for you."

"Eyeball Ajoshi?"

He closed one eye and opened the other wide. "Glass eyeball," he said. "It's the one that doesn't move when he looks at you."

When I went back inside, Nokchon Cousin was asking Mahmi why she had bought all those things on the black market—couldn't she wait?

"I borrowed some of it," said Mahmi. "If Busy-Busy doesn't want it all today, I can take it back."

"Why didn't you just buy it yourself earlier and save it up?"

"Do you know how much it is?"

"And how much is it now? Did she want to be repaid in merchandise? Why don't you just pay her with money?"

"It's more expensive that way," Mahmi said. "I told her I'd get her these things and we agreed. That's why I had to borrow it."

Nokchon Cousin wasn't fooled. "You *bought* it all, didn't you?" But before my mother could answer, Nokchon Cousin realized something, and she said, "You *did* borrow it! You borrowed it like money, with interest!"

My mother didn't answer.

"You said you had a thousand dollars to repay her. Is that what she's coming for today?"

"I don't have that money."

"You showed it to me just the other morning. Where did it all go?"

When Mahmi was quiet again, Nokchon Cousin said, *"Aiguuu!* How could you do that again?! In one day! A thousand dollars in *one day!"* She came stomping out of our room, then across the *maru,* which had been set up as a kind of living room, to the kitchen door. She paused there, and when she saw me she said, "Ask your mother what she did with all that money!"

I didn't have to ask, because I already knew.

While my father was in Vietnam, my mother had become addicted to slot machines. There had been times when, after getting the monthly allotment check—which was most of my father's pay—she'd spend the whole day at the Lower Four Club or the NCO Club feeding coins into the slots. She usually started in the morning with nickels, then moved on to dimes around lunchtime, and then, after pausing for coffee, she would play the quarter slots, each four pulls a dollar disappearing under the spinning blur of cherries, oranges, watermelons, lucky 7s, bells, and bars. The occasional jackpot, with its stuttering payout of coins—a machine gun shooting metal disks instead of bullets—seemed like a win to her even when she always lost in the end.

When I was little, I had often spent time with her in the slot rooms, watching her feed coins into the tiny slit and then yank the bent chrome arm tipped with the black plastic ball. The grinding sound of the gear at the base of the arm reminded me of a transmission on a military vehicle, and when the colorful wheels spun, I thought of jeep and truck tires. It would usually end with the clatter of the lost coins somewhere in the belly of the machine, but when she won, there would be a burst of loud chimes—frenetic and exciting—and coins would come spewing out of the chrome-plated mouth at the bottom like silver candy.

I played the nickel and even the dime slots with her a few times. But with the quarter slots it occurred to me that each pull was more than the price of a hot dog. Four pulls could feed me for a day, and I remembered how much food we could buy at a Korean market for a dollar. Sometimes my mother would come home in a good mood with whole dinners for me and An-na, cheeseburgers and French fries, or fried chicken gone cold and greasy, after winning a fifty-dollar or a one-hundred-dollar jackpot on the slots, but even those times always reminded me of how much she had actually lost to earn the illusion of winning.

A car pulled up outside the gate—a Korean cab from the sound of the engine. A door opened and thumped shut, and there was some muffled conversation before a voice called, "Insu's Mother! I'm here. Are you home?"

Nokchon Cousin came out to the *maru*. "Please come in!" she called. "It's not locked."

The little blue door in the gate opened. It was Busy-Busy in her visiting outfit—a strange combination of tailored clothes that reminded me of fashions from the 1960s. She even had a beehive hairdo and wore big rose-tinted sunglasses and a yellow silk scarf. At the market, she would usually wear the universal mid-calf pants and the many-pocketed flower-patterned quilted vest and grimy apron of a vendor.

I greeted her when she noticed me, her eyes instantly going to the stacked suitcases.

"Oh, it's Insu," she said. "How have you been? It's been a long time since *ajuma* saw you."

"I'm okay," I said.

"Is your mother home?"

"She's inside."

Busy-Busy had no interest in me. She quickly took off her white sandals and went inside, with one more curious look at the suitcases. "Are they going somewhere?" she asked Nokchon Cousin.

"He's taking some stuff up to his uncle and he doesn't know how to wrap a *pojagi*," said Nokchon Cousin.

Busy-Busy laughed, but it was obviously a fake laugh—she wanted us to know she didn't believe the explanation: she was onto the fact that my mother might be getting ready to flee without paying off her debt. Nokchon Cousin went into the room with her, and then I heard them making small talk, the tinkling of coffee cups and the sound of packages being unwrapped, then wrapped again. There was no talk of money for a while, but I could tell from the tone of their conversation and the rhythm of the silences—which were always just a bit too long—that things were not going well.

Usually, if my mother had the money she owed, she would pay it quickly, and then the rest of the visit would be pleasant and friendly, everyone chatting, exchanging gossip, drinking coffee, sometimes even playing flower cards. When she didn't have the money, the person who came to collect would have to be polite and find an appropriate way to while away the time until it was acceptable to bring up the issue. Busy-Busy wasn't very good at it, and the amount my mother apparently owed her didn't make things any easier. Busy-Busy always claimed she was just the go-between, and that late payments got her in trouble, but hardly anyone believed her. The stall she ran at the Hollywood Market was often occupied by a middle-aged man who had an ugly scar across his forehead. She told everyone he was her boss, but anyone watching them together could figure out that she was really the one in charge.

I had just picked up a Mickey Spillane novel when I heard Busy-Busy beginning to yell. I had tuned out most of the conversation until then, but now she had worked herself into the fit of ranting she was known for, and she started narrating the long history of how many times she had lent my mother money, and how much, and how patient she had always been about the late payments; how she charged less interest when she could easily be lending at higher rates to other people, how her husband scolded her and even beat her for being so generous, how she endured humiliation and long train and taxi trips again and again for nothing, and how could my mother think—even for a moment—that getting her those Yankee goods, which she was due anyway, would make up for the money that she was actually owed.

I knew it would go on for a while. Busy-Busy would repeat herself, each time more intensely, until she reached the kind of ecstatic frenzy a shaman would achieve when she was possessed by a spirit. People even joked that Busy-Busy would be a *mudang* if she wasn't a black marketeer and money lender. I was ready to go out for a while to ASCOM to get something to eat at the Snack Bar when Busy-Busy said something that made me stop. I had just stood up with my shoes on, and I collapsed back onto the cement stair.

"You made a big deal about how you *had* the money this time," she said to my mother. "A thousand and one dollars! Was that extra dollar a bonus for my time? Did you plan to give me a measly *tip* after all these years? Was it a joke? Were you making fun of me?" She went on and on while my mother remained silent and Nokchon Cousin tried to make some appropriate noises that would calm her down.

But Busy-Busy's mention of the extra dollar made me go immediately to my secret hiding place, which was actually not so secret. It was the small army safe my father had brought home from Camp Casey one week, a black cube—the size of an ice chest—that must have weighed two hundred pounds. We didn't have anything to keep in it, so I had been using the small space to store my Doc Savage novels, twenty-eight at my last count, and I had put the envelope from Patsy under them. I kept it locked with a cheap combination lock like the ones used at the gym, but the one I had was rusted and would sometimes open if you just yanked on it.

The safe was behind the couch on the *maru*. I knew immediately that someone had opened it—the lock was unlatched, dangling open so the bent bar looked like a fishhook. Kneeling on the couch, I removed the lock and pulled up on the heavy door. My Doc Savage books were all there, but some of them had been turned the wrong way, and I knew without even looking that the envelope would be gone. I lifted the books out, tossing them on the couch so that some of them bounced and hit the floor. The envelope was still there but it was empty, and I felt a chill in my heart.

In the room, Busy-Busy was still ranting, this time about how my mother could put an entire month's paycheck into a slot machine in an afternoon. "How long did you play with my thousand and *one* dollars?" she said. "I hope you had at least until dinnertime. I hope you had fun throwing *my* money away into those Yankee-made robbery machines!"

"Please stop," said Nokchon Cousin. "You know she'll pay you what she owes. She always does, doesn't she? Give her some time."

"Give her some *time*? What's time? Time is my *life*! Why don't you just take some of my *life* then, *ungh*?!" I had seen all this before: Now was the moment Busy-Busy would reach for the paring knife. It was part of her money-collecting ritual, and her clients had to have one on hand or she would complain and ask for one to peel the fruit she always brought with her.

I heard the gasps then. Busy-Busy must have picked up the knife. She would be holding the blade against her left wrist now, glaring at my mother and Nokchon Cousin, pausing just long enough to let them leap forward and stop her. I got off the couch and went out to the veranda, where I could look into the barred window and see Busy-Busy at the table, the yellow-handled paring knife flat against her wrist, covering some of the scars there. She was yelling something, but I couldn't quite hear her because my mother suddenly said, after all that silent listening, "Go ahead and cut it then! I can't stand this anymore! *Cut!*"

I don't think Busy-Busy had had anyone call her bluff like that. All her scars were shallow—just deep enough for some blood to ooze out so she could make her point about the money being her life. Nokchon Cousin was sitting open-mouthed, her eyes wide, as Busy-Busy looked to her, then to my mother, then gritted her teeth and sliced her wrist. I couldn't quite see it from where I stood, but I thought I could hear the sound of the blade cutting through the meat of her wrist, and when she pulled it away, dark blood—almost black—was dribbling onto the newly peeled Fuji apples.

Everything seemed to stop for a moment, until Nokchon Cousin grabbed what looked like a scarf and lunged forward, knocking the ashtray off the table. My mother's eyes were closed, as if she wanted to deny what had just happened, and Busy-Busy let out a loud wail.

I picked up my light jacket and two of the suitcases and, while all the excitement was going on, I went out to the taxi Busy-Busy had left waiting and loaded them into the back seat.

"What's all that racket?" the driver asked.

"Busy-Busy *ajuma* and my mother are fighting," I said. "She said it would be a while and she would get another taxi. Could you take me, instead?"

He started the engine. "Where are you going?"

"Could you take me to Sambongni?"

"*Sambongni?* Where is that?"

"It's up just past the Paldang Dam. Busy-Busy *ajuma* said you'd take me for twenty dollars."

"That's a long way."

"I'll give you twenty-five dollars, *Ajoshi*. And you don't have to bring me back. You could spend some time up in Seoul or get some share passengers from Yongsan on the way back."

"All right," he said, turning off the meter. "I know how to get to Paldang, but you tell me from there."

I went in and got the other suitcase and loaded it in the trunk. Busy-Busy was throwing things and Nokchon Cousin had run to her room to get the first aid kit. I couldn't see what my mother was doing.

"I hate driving that woman," the taxi driver said as we started off for the main road. "Every place she goes, there's some sort of racket."

"Just like a *kut*?" I said.

"That's right. Just like those ceremonies with the crazy *mudang* jumping up and down on knife blades."

✦ ✦ ✦

THE DRIVE TO Sambongni didn't take as long as I expected. We reached the Paldang Dam around lunchtime and stopped to have some noodles at a roadside eatery before continuing north. There was only one road leading that way—I hardly needed to give directions, and the driver dropped me at the new storage building in my mother's village, a long rectangle of cinder block with a corrugated tin roof. They had built it as a public toilet with money from the government-sponsored New Community Movement, a presidential initiative to modernize rural areas. Little Uncle had told me that President Park had been hosting a foreign dignitary, the president of a Western country. They were in Park's limousine, driving toward Seoul, and they were looking outside the window at the countryside, passing a village. President Park was fond of that rural community, and when the foreign dignitary pointed out a thatched house, admiring it, the President was pleased. But when the dignitary said, "You Koreans have such beautiful barns," the President felt terrible shame, and he resolved to replace all the thatched roofs of Korean houses with Western roofs. That's what the New Community funding was for, according to Little Uncle. If a village set up and maintained a tin-roofed bathroom with Western-style flush toilets, they were given regular allotments of cement and other building materials.

Nobody in Sambongni used the public toilet building—the whole thing, excepting one working toilet, was used as a storage facility, and as long as the government inspectors saw that the one toilet was working, the New Community support kept coming. Little Uncle was proud of his storage building, and he liked to remind me that the working toilet was not to be used—it wasn't connected to anything, and whatever was flushed through it would simply soak into the ground in the foundation of the building.

One of the government's stipulations for receiving the New Community money was that villages also had to participate in the Destroy

Superstition Movement, which meant getting rid of local shamans and
the old village holy trees. In Sambongni they had complied by sending
Kubong Manshin away for more than a year but managed to keep the
village tree, claiming it was just a shade tree for the old people. Some of
them were sitting out there under it now.

I didn't want to have to say hello. Out past the tree, in the fields, I saw
Little Uncle working near the red pepper plants. He had just wiped his
forehead with a small white towel and was leaning down to get something out of his pants pocket. A lighter. He lit a cigarette and blew out a
plume of blue-white smoke, looking off toward the south and west.

I paused. No one had seen me, even with the noise the taxi had made
coming down the unpaved track to the new bathroom building. Most of
the men were probably still out in the fields, working, like Little Uncle.
Some of the women would be home cooking by now—I could hear
sounds of daily business coming from Little Uncle's house—and the distorted dialogue that came out of a television turned too loud. I had
brought lots of things for Big Uncle, but if Little Uncle or anyone else
knew, they would expect something for themselves. Coming up to Sambongni always required the bearing of gifts, even if it was just a bag of
fruit and some cigarettes, and I didn't have anything to spare. Before
Little Uncle noticed me, I made my way quietly down the path toward
the river to see if any boats were moored on this side. As I walked between the row of young acacias, smelling the human excrement used to
fertilize the vegetable patches, I realized I had decided to go across the
river in secret.

There was only one boat on this side of the river, an old waterlogged
one. The wood was patched with tar at the bottom and parts looked
fuzzy with mold or dried algae. The single long oar had been spliced and
the oarlock at the stern looked tenuous after a shoddy repair job. But the
bottom looked relatively dry, so I made my way quietly back to the storage building and retrieved the three suitcases, carrying two with one

strapped on like a knapsack. I hurried down to the boat, panting and covered in sweat, to find a woman standing there, with her back to me. She turned around and became Kubong Manshin.

"I see everything," he said. "Last night I saw you arriving with a truckload of supplies. It was still wartime and all the people in the village were waiting for you. They were starving. They knew you had come with food, because you had somehow grown up all at once and become a blond GI. Isn't it a curious dream to have about you?"

"That sounds more like my father than me," I said. To my surprise, I felt at ease with Kubong Manshin, as if his being there was just a matter-of-fact thing, like the presence of the village tree. "Did they all get the food they needed?"

"The truck didn't have any food in it. There were refrigerators, TVs, cameras, and even motorcycles and sets of dishes and silverware from the Yankee soldiers' dining halls. But there were also people inside. Strangers. And the Sambongni people ate those people. They tasted very good, come to think of it."

"That's terrible."

"As they were eating, they realized all those strangers were themselves."

I took the suitcases to the boat. "Are you just making up a story?" I asked. "Someone told me that shamans just say anything when they have a spirit inside them."

"I have no spirit in me now," said Kubong Manshin, spreading his arms. "The spirit is everywhere. My whole life—and yours—is a story that's made up as we go along. Do you remember that?"

"I don't know," I said. "I don't remember being taught that by you, Manshin."

"I taught you that in your blood. In your dreams," he said. "Your Big Uncle is sicker. He won't be needing all of that stuff."

"I have to take it to him," I said.

"Then go across the river and find out for yourself. You'll know soon enough." He spun around, turning away from me, and looked across the river. "Sad," he said. "Very sad." He didn't turn back around, so I opened one of the suitcases and left him a carton of cigarettes.

I stood in the back of the boat and, using the oar, pushed off. It rode low, and I floated for a few minutes, rearranging the suitcases so they wouldn't get wet when the boat took on water. There was nothing to bail with except my cupped hands, but I also had to row the boat across and I didn't have the time to do both. The solution was to get to the other side as quickly as possible.

The oarlock creaked as I used my whole body to push and pull. A wake began to appear behind the boat, little ridges of water piling one upon the other, spreading and dissipating until the green surface was flat again, almost oily. When I finally found my rhythm, the oar made a steady *lap-lapping* sound.

I wondered why Kubong Manshin had come. I didn't want to think it was just to get something from me, but that was possible. I had felt ripped off the last time, but what he'd told me had come true, too. I hadn't needed the money he took from me, and I'd even come out ahead in the end.

The boat slowed as it filled with water, riding even lower, but by then it had the momentum to coast smoothly, cutting the river with its sharp, triangular prow, and I was on the other side more quickly than I had thought possible. The weight of the boat brought it to a grating halt against the lip of the eastern bank, and I picked up the suitcases and tossed each one onto a grassy spot before I jumped out, pulling the rope behind me.

The shoreline wasn't what I recalled from my last visit to Big Uncle. I couldn't tell whether I had landed somewhere else or if the foliage had changed or if the level of the river was different. I would have to find the path up to Skullhead Cave before I tried to carry all three suitcases—I couldn't afford to be wandering around in the woods burdened with them, walking in circles.

The wind blew through a patch of pines, carrying the scent of needles and sap. I remembered how Yongsu and I had found Big Uncle's rags hung out to dry, and how we could smell him when we got close. I followed the bank south for a distance and then doubled back when I didn't see any familiar landmarks. There was garbage here and there— empty bottles and plastic wrappers, an aluminum can or two—but nothing that seemed like it was from Big Uncle. When I came back north, I found the path only a few dozen yards from the boat, and so I returned once again to load myself down with the suitcases.

I walked up the trail, and this time I recognized the spot where we had found the bandages, where Big Uncle had stood, blocking the light and frightening us with his silhouette. I could almost feel his presence as I drew closer to his camp at Skullhead Cave.

Somewhere, there was an arrow I had yet to find. That's what I was thinking when I saw the cave. Now, in the glare, the stone looked all that much more like bleached bone, and the two arched openings like half-buried eye sockets. Big Uncle had moved things from across the river to make it more comfortable for himself—or maybe the family had brought them. A table and three chairs, and even a little box that had been made into a cabinet, were arranged around the mouth of one of the caves near the fire pit, which had also been enlarged and equipped with a bent metal rod for hanging a kettle or a pot.

Big Uncle had kept his site neat and piled all his garbage in one place behind a big rock. I had expected him to sneak up on me, for some reason, so when he wasn't there, the site felt more empty than it was. Not abandoned, but somehow desolate.

"Big Uncle!" I called, putting down the two suitcases in my hands. It felt good to stand again, without that weight, even with the third suitcase strapped to my back. I was thirsty. Big Uncle's water jug was on top of his cabinet and I picked it up—it was half full. I brought it to my lips and then stopped myself and poured a little onto a cupped palm first. There were gnats and moths in the water—he hadn't drunk from it in a while. I put it back, unslung the third suitcase from my back, and opened it to remove a couple cans of Coke I had brought for myself. They were warm, but the first one went down in just a few foamy gulps. I tossed the empty can behind the rock and called again, "Big Uncle!"

I would have to wait for him if he was away from camp hunting crows or something. Or maybe I had miscalculated by coming across without checking first to make sure Big Uncle wasn't at his house in the village.

"Big Uncle!" I called again. Still no answer. I was tired from the trip, and hungry now. It made no sense to go looking for him and possibly miss him if he came back to the cave from the other direction. I opened the other can of Coke and a C-ration can of pork and beans and sat down in one of the chairs to eat. When I was done I felt a crushing tiredness come over me. I could hardly keep my eyes open, and the breeze felt easy and comforting. Big Uncle kept his cot close to the entrance of the cave. I dragged it outside into the sun and, covering myself with the camouflage poncho liner I had brought for him, I lay down and fell asleep.

There were crows everywhere—in the trees, on the ground, in the air. They flew with stiff wings, like black kites, and the ones in the branches and on the ground had their wings spread wide, as if they were people with blankets stretched across their outspread arms. As they cawed and laughed, the ones on the ground strutted back and forth, turning their heads this way and that. A line of them stood in front of the cot, looking expectantly up at my sleeping body. Were they waiting to be fed? Had they asked a question and were waiting there for the answer? They pecked at the empty C-ration can, the white plastic spoon, still sticky and sweet with the pork and beans sauce. An especially large crow stood in the middle of the fire pit staring down at me; he was bundled in a green wool army blanket and looked like an Indian chief. He shifted from foot to foot, and then he said, in strangely inflected English, which sounded like German, "You do go away. Sky go away. Water go away." But I didn't want to go. I was sleeping, and I didn't want to wake up until Big Uncle showed up. "Go away," the giant crow said. "Shoo! Shoo!" It sounded like sneezing, and when I opened my eyes it was beginning to get dark. Even under the poncho liner I could feel the cool of evening carried in the breeze.

"Big Uncle!" I called, sitting up, still bundled in the camo blanket.

The wind moaned at the mouth of the cave, sounding like an unhappy ghost. It scared me to be alone out there with that sound, and I didn't want to be stuck overnight at Big Uncle's cave.

I got up, folded the blanket on top of the cot, and dragged the cot back under the lip of the cave in case it rained. Leaving the suitcases stacked neatly in a place where Big Uncle was sure to see them, I ran back to the river. It took a while to empty the boat even halfway with a coffee can I had taken from the trash pile, and by the time I launched, it was dark. The forest watched and pulled at me from behind. I had to stop myself from crying out in fear as I rowed back across, aiming for the lights of my mother's village.

VI

# Time & the River

# Time & the River

## 1975

When he went across the river that night, following the light of the moon, no one knew. Or had they not noticed, or had they not cared—or had they planned on his escape back to the cave from the beginning? His thoughts stretch in all directions, into the past and the future, into the close places and the vast directions of the present—everywhere, all at once, without effort, into the six directions of space and the two directions of time.

He remembers everything now. Memory and imagination, like the past and the future, are the same. There is no difference in the mind. He learned through long experience and long confinement, and now, inside the bowels of the cave, eyes closed, covered by three blankets of green wool, he remembers and imagines. Past and future—only the words are different, and if one disposes of them, all things become smooth and easy, the texture of fine silk, the way of a soul fortified by opium.

Outside—daylight or moonlight? He can move his vision out there like a *tokkaebi pul*—a goblin light—floating in the dark forest. There is the sun touching the distant horizon. There is the faint moon hovering over the trees, caught among the branches. And over there—the bright dot of Venus hanging in a transparent purple slate-colored sky.

There's a boy on a waterlogged boat—no, a young man—it's his youngest sister's son, Insu, and he's pulling and pushing on that oar, the one that will break last year, and the boat is moving, and the ripples in its wake have the texture of oil, and the light reflects on the water. He hears the soothing rhythm and sees the colors slowly fade, as the light of the sun continues to wane, as the moon takes its place. Sun and moon together form the Chinese character *myong*, the word meaning "bright," and later in the evening both will be gone, and instead of the white of blank paper there will be a black ink sky lit by stars like punctures of light.

He rolls over on the straw mat, smelling the distinct and familiar smell of damp rice straw. He prefers it to the odor of mildewed canvas, which distracts him when he tries to sleep on the cot. He prefers the warmth of the straw mats stacked on the ground. Soon his elements, all the components of this borrowed vessel, this ragged suit of clothes, will merge with those of the earth—and return.

Last night—or was it last month, or tomorrow—he dreamed of the fairy again, how radiant she was, how her servants watched without a word as she took his seed. Was it in the forest of her world superimposed upon this one? And he remembered Nari and her shy smile, huddling with her on the steel knuckles between the train cars. He wondered if she had mourned him—not just to maintain the pretense that he was her brother—or if she had been heartsick like him to lose the future they had imagined with each other.

Now there is that boy on the boat again, leaping onto the eastern shore, leaving deep footprints in the damp earth. He will be here once before and his spirit senses where to go, but his head is confused, full of chattering thoughts and the shrill background noise of troubled emotion. How is he to live in that way when he climbs up the giant stone mountain in the Beautiful Country and looks straight down the mile-high flat face of granite, wondering if he should jump and feel the exhilaration of life before it all turns black? And why is he not happy when he finds the arrow, and why does he let that damned shaman touch it—a thousand, ten thousand spirits, regardless.

And why did that shaman, from the place of the nine peaks, such a handsome man, become a woman and make his heart sore? Or had he been a woman all along, bringing her from a previous incarnation into this one, trapped in the body of a man now to shapeshift back and forth like a demon fox? Had he loved him like a brother? Had he desired him as a woman? And was all that youthful confusion without meaning now that they were both old, at a time when man and woman begin to lose distinction? Sagging breasts, sagging member—what's the difference now?

The boy, the young man, is trudging up the trail with a suitcase in each hand, and one rigged to carry on his back. He saw refugees like that during the war, burdened with as much as they could possibly carry—or even more—until some small mishap or some man with a weapon put an end to it all and the burden was spread across the dusty ground, picked clean of valuables, the owner dead and swollen like a pig carcass in the hot sun. And Kunsu—what of him?—dead in the war or still alive in the North, better assumed dead by the family than a traitor who would bring dishonor to the whole clan. A few simple possessions changing the course of a life. Those belongings, just like karma, weighing one down, he thinks, and here is Insu bringing them up to the cave, not knowing I am beyond accepting any more. I have all the karma I can carry. I have accumulated it over many lives. I have gathered up even more in this one, and now I wish to let it go, to release my attachments, but he will not understand, and my very wish is a desire that creates yet another attachment. He remembers the story of the young monk named Songjin, the favorite of old Master Yukgwan, who had conquered the six temptations. Poor boy, whose name means "original nature," gone to the Dragon King's palace under the mythic lake on his master's behalf. Poor boy, enticed by magic wine and unable to refuse, intoxicated and lustful upon his return, performing that embarrassing parlor trick of flowers into jewels for the eight beautiful fairies and then condemned to hell for it, only to be immediately reincarnated into the life of a golden boy, son of a Taoist immortal, a most brilliant and filial son, growing up to win the top score on the civil exam, to become the great statesman and general of the empire and to have, for himself, the eight most beautiful women in the world. And at the end, at the epitome of success, to find it all a dream when his old master walks into it and brings him back, no longer the brilliant Yang, but the humble monk Songjin upon the meditation mat. But that, too, is an illusion, after all, just a story in a book, a fantasy of the writer, and that fantasy an illusion in his life, and his life itself an illusion—illusion upon illusion, dream upon dream, into infinity.

And there is the boy now, drinking Coca Cola, eating the food of the white gods and white demons, just like he and Nari had done, with a spoon the color of bleached bone.

# The One-Eyed Cave

## 1975

When Little Uncle came down from Sambongni unannounced, he didn't even have to say anything. I knew Big Uncle was dead. His death exuded from Little Uncle like the smell of funeral incense.

Little Uncle had never been any good at telling stories. Big Uncle and the other men in the family had coached him on what to say to get out of military service, but he had been so nervous and tongue-tied with his story that he'd had to resort to cutting off his trigger finger with the feed chopper in the cowshed. Now he was telling us about how Big Uncle had been sleeping inside the cave, all the way in the back, for days, not eating any of the food they took across the river to him because someone had brought up American Army food. "We thought it was time to roll the stone in front of the entrance," he said. "Like the old days. He knew the custom. That's why we thought he was way in the back there. But he had a bunch of open cans, and animals were going in there to eat the scraps. The stink was horrible."

"How did he die?" my mother asked.

"He got all the way through the woods on the Yangsuri side somehow. Ran out into the road at night and got hit by a taxi. The driver said he ran into the middle of the road with his arms raised up."

"My goodness! He was calling a taxi?"

"No. It looked like he was surrendering is what the driver said."

I DIDN'T WANT to hear the details, but I listened from the *maru* while Little Uncle talked to my mother and Nokchon Cousin inside. As they discussed the funeral arrangements and argued about who would pay for what part, I put on my shoes and left the house.

What was I supposed to do now? Every intention had backfired somehow, as if I had thrown flour into the wind. I felt numb and empty. I wasn't even upset. It was as if the news of Big Uncle's death was something I had heard on the radio about some stranger.

I found a few crumpled one-hundred-won notes in the left pocket of my Levi's and seven dollars—two singles and a five—in the other. I also had two twenties in the secret compartment of my leather billfold. It was plenty for what I needed to do. I would return to Sambongni and find Big Uncle's missing arrow. To have it before they buried him, I had to leave right away.

THE UNPAVED STREET I took would be asphalt soon. They had already dug the sewer ditch on the two sides of the new road aimed straight at the market. I remembered when the street was ankle-deep in mud during the monsoon, so sticky in places it could suck the shoes off your feet. After the bulldozers had cleared the long stretch between the market and the road to the highway, the bleak area had become even bleaker—not a tree, not a blade of grass—just dirt and dust until the weeds and mugwort began to sprout. Soon there would be a layer of gravel thrown from the backs of row upon row of dump trucks, and then the men with their shovels would come, and then rakes, and finally the steamrollers would flatten everything and compress it before the asphalt and tar. It would happen to every dusty street eventually, if President Park had his way.

* * *

I WALKED TO the train station and occupied the twenty-minute wait by eating a bowl of noodles, then got on the train to Seoul Station. It was nearly empty that time of day, and I stretched out on one of the long seats, covering my eyes in the crook of my elbow. There is an inevitability about trains, a relentlessness. Maybe it's just their rhythm, or maybe it's their rails, leading from one station to another like the nerve fibers of a giant monster machine, or a river of steel. The sound and the motion soothed me, and soon I was drowsing in a kind of half-sleep.

And then I had what I thought was a memory: my male ancestors all gathered together inside a smoky tent at night. Through the mix of cigarette smoke and the smoke from grilled rabbit, I could see all the old men of my mother's family there—the old uncles and an intellectual-looking man I didn't recognize, with sensitive lips, who might have been my mother's father. My own father was there too, looking young and robust—the way he looked before his second tour in Vietnam. They were drinking soju and *makkolli*, eating dried squid and grilled pork, waiting for the rabbit meat, and they all began to congratulate me on the birth of my daughter. "I don't have a daughter," I said. "Ah, you do," said Big Uncle. He took my hand and shook it. My father came and patted my back, put a hand over my shoulder, and led me into the tent, where they were all sitting on long benches at the kind of table one sees in the covered-wagon eateries by the train station. I was terribly hungry from the smell of the meat.

When I opened my eyes, the train had just reached Yongdongpo. I must have been smelling the smoke from a restaurant upwind from the station. In the car where I sat, two Korean marines were eating dried squid and drinking 7-Star Cider. One of them had the leg of his pants rolled up, displaying a long scar that ran the length of his calf. "I can't wear socks," he was saying.

"How could you be so careless?" said the other marine.

"They never told us the grenades would be live, those fucking bastards."

The other marine laughed and slapped his friend on the shoulder. "Someday you become an officer and fuck some of us over, *ungh?*"

The first marine snorted and sipped his cider, looking out at the lines of telephone poles blurring by outside, the wire strung between them seeming to rise and fall like waves in a gentle sea.

THIS TIME, WHEN I reached the river, two boats were moored on the village side—the old one and one in better repair, with no sign of leakage. I considered taking the newer one at first, but then I changed my mind and took the old boat—which had the single, long oar in the back and a new wooden patch on its floor—and shoving off with the spliced oar, I slowly rowed to the other side.

When I reached Big Uncle's camp, I saw that someone had rolled the stone in front of the cave opening on the left side, and now Skullhead Cave had only one eye. The chairs and the other furnishings were gone, erasing any evidence of Big Uncle having lived there. Big Uncle had told me that the cave's two chambers were joined in the back, though only he knew about it. I found a thick branch on the ground, wrapped it tight in layers of dry grass, and then smeared it with pine sap. When I lit it with a match, it made a passable torch.

The open chamber of the cave was mostly empty, except for some garbage and a small pile of wood. Big Uncle must have used it as a toilet on cold or rainy days. The air inside was foul with the smell of piss and shit. Toward the back, a shelf had been cut into the rock, sort of like a stone bench the height of a traditional Korean kitchen stove. It was wide enough to serve as a bed platform for two, and about seven feet long. To the left of the stone shelf was a pile of twigs and leaves, oddly out of place and suspiciously neat. I put my hand in it and found a piece of rope, and when I pulled it, the whole pile came away in one piece, revealing a large hole in the wall—the entrance to the other chamber. By then all the straw had burned off of my improvised torch, and all I had was a stick with a burning tip that barely illuminated anything. But I crawled through, taking the branch with me into the other chamber, whose smell was distinctly different, still tinged with the rot of big Uncle's foot.

They had moved the chairs and other furnishings inside before they'd sealed the opening. Even the three suitcases were still there. I recognized the one in which I had packed the practical supplies and, sticking the burning branch upright into a soft patch of dirt, I knelt down and opened it. The flashlight was still inside, along with the small electric lamp. I switched on the flashlight and put it on top of the cabinet. The interior of the cave looked like the belly of a large animal.

Big Uncle's sad possessions were scattered about, even useful items like blankets that people might have wanted, and there was a small pile of what must have been his precious items laid out on top of an old pair of his pants—a broken watch, an old pen, a pair of steel-rimmed glasses cracked across one lens, a stained ivory cigarette holder. I noticed that something was wrapped in wool army socks, and when I opened the bundle I remembered a story he had told me about an old man who had given him directions to a treasure, which he had retrieved after the war. These must have been the jade eggs and the ancient hairpin, antiques I could sell in Itaewon to raise some money. I took them, thinking the villagers were afraid his ghost had attached itself to his former possessions and would bring bad luck to a new owner. That thought made me pause momentarily, but I knew somehow that Big Uncle's ghost would never come back to this cave to attach to his possessions. This was not his place. The ghosts I felt here were old ones—grandfathers and grandmothers, feeble, senile, afraid, and lonely. How could their children have brought them out here across the river to die alone? They were not buried here, but they had left enough of their blood and tears and excrement to imbue the cave with their sorrow and resentment—their *han*. Big Uncle's *han* was not here.

♦  ♦  ♦

WHY HAD I come here? There was no way, I knew, that I would be able
to find that arrow Big Uncle had shot into the night. If I had believed in
magic or sorcery—if I hadn't seen through the parlor tricks used by the
shamans and Taoists who came down from their mountain retreats every
spring to collect money from the gullible people who saw magic in their
chewing lightbulbs or bending nails or grabbing red-hot pokers and
driving knitting needles through their cheeks—maybe then I would believe in a magic that would take me to Big Uncle's arrow.

I remembered one *kut* I had witnessed when I was little, when we
lived in the house of the Japanese Colonel. The neighbor's boy, Cholsu,
had died, and in order to be sure his unhappy spirit would move on to
the next world and not abide in this one as a hungry ghost, his family
had hired a *mudang*. There was a part in the day-long ritual when the
*mudang* gave a spirit stick to one of Cholsu's male relatives—a Christian
who didn't believe in such superstition. Maybe it was a challenge, or
maybe it was a piece of drama to validate the shaman and had been secretly prearranged. Cholsu's uncle reluctantly picked up the stick, shaking his head, making it clear that he was doing it only to humor the
shaman. Something belonging to Cholsu had been lost—a spoon. He
had been attached to it in life and it would keep his spirit lingering in
death. It had to be found and burned or exorcised, and now Cholsu's
uncle was the one who would find it by letting the spirit stick guide him.
Cholsu's uncle had laughed. The entire family had been searching for
days—not just in Cholsu's house but at three of the relatives' in case he
had taken it there during a visit.

The shaman told the uncle to hold the stick upright in both hands,
and when he did, she began jumping up and down, chanting as reed *p'iri*
pipes, cymbals, and drums played frenetically. The top of the stick tilted,
as if it were tipping over, and Cholsu's uncle quickly moved the bottom
to keep it straight. It twitched, and though he looked like he was trying

to resist, the stick pulled him first one way, then the other, as he struggled with it, grinning out of embarrassment. In a few moments his muscles were straining, his expression turned grim, and he wrestled with the stick as it pulled him across the yard, around the back of the house, and into the back door of the kitchen. It led him to the edge of the stove, where trays were stacked with bowls and utensils that needed to be washed. Everyone had followed him, of course, the family, the *mudang*, the musicians. In the terrible din someone said, "We didn't need a spirit stick to find utensils in the kitchen!" There was laughter, but then the stick pulled Cholsu's uncle straight forward. He looked like he was charging with a lance, and he hit the corner where the stove met the wall so hard he knocked a piece of cement away, revealing a long, dark crack between the stove and the kitchen wall. Cholsu's uncle collapsed, his face and neck flushed and covered with beads of sweat. The *mudang* stopped. The musicians stopped. And Cholsu's mother pushed her brother-in-law aside and reached into the dark crack as if she were expecting something inside to bite off her hand. She pulled it out—a thin, long-handled silver spoon. She was crying. Cholsu's uncle huffed out of the kitchen, red-faced, and spent the rest of the day drinking. A few months later I overheard my aunt telling my mother that he had left the church to become a Buddhist.

I was going to stay in the woods until I found the arrow, and remembering what had happened to Cholsu's uncle, I decided I had to find some way to get into that same frame of mind. If Big Uncle's spirit hovered between worlds and he truly wanted to be buried where the arrow landed, he would help me find it.

Going outside was like coming out of a theater after a matinee to bright daylight when I was expecting night. I was disoriented, feeling as though I had spent the entire night inside and that it was morning. The sun on its downward course in the west looked, for a moment, like the morning sun in the east. I had come out of the right-hand chamber, and even the outside of the cave felt alien, as if I had emerged into a parallel

world where everything was subtly different. Once, my father had
dropped the cufflink to his dress blues—his fancy uniform for official
military business—and we had crawled around on the floor looking for
it with no success until, finally, he said he would try an old magic trick.
I was surprised, because he didn't believe in magic. "It's just a superstition," he said. "If you drop one cufflink and can't find it, drop the other
one, and it will find its mate for you." He made a big show of it, and
when it hit the floor we watched where it went, clattering under the table
and across the floor. It didn't find its mate, but when I crawled under the
desk to retrieve it, where it had ended up among the dust and the dried
husks of dead insects, I saw the other one in the gap between the wardrobe and the wall. I had dragged it out using a bamboo chopstick.

It was on the way down that I found an arrow. At first I thought it was
just a stray crow feather under some fallen pine needles, but then I saw
the fragment of wood from where the notch had broken on one side, and
when I uncovered it I saw that the shaft was mostly intact, but it was too
close to camp to be the one I needed to find. Big Uncle's bow hadn't
been in the cave, so I couldn't shoot this arrow to try and find its mate.
Little Uncle had probably taken the bow back home because it was valuable and he could sell it in Seoul to an antique dealer, just as I was planning to do with the jade eggs and the hairpin. But I had an arrow, and I
was determined to let it lead me to its mate, lost somewhere out in the
woods.

I stood in the spot from which Big Uncle had loosed his arrow and
looked straight up, watching the trees seem to bend into a vault above
me. He had been facing the river because that was west, the direction of
death, and the bow must have been angled slightly forward—the arrow
did not come straight down, and if it had gone toward the river, if his
angle had been shallow, it might have landed in the water. That had not
occurred to me before. And if the arrow had come down at a high angle,
it would be sticking nearly straight up like a long stalk of arrow grass.
Since Big Uncle had been able to catch crows with the bow, he must have

been a decent shot, and so, even at night the arrow would not have strayed far to the left or the right. What I needed to do was search the area shaped like a thin wedge from Skullhead Cave to the river, with the wide side of the wedge being the riverbank. If it had not gone into the water and if it had not sunk too deep into a soft patch of earth, I realized I actually might have a chance of finding it.

It didn't take long. The arrow was there. It had been there all along, stuck in a trunk just under a branch, protruding at exactly the same angle. The point had only just punctured the bark and it came out easily. I could imagine Big Uncle laughing now that I had found it. Laughing about the melodrama of his shooting it in the first place with all that gravity, asking to be buried where it landed, only to have it stick six feet up in the trunk of a pine tree. Laughing about me taking an old fool seriously enough to suffer the ordeal of the quest. Laughing to see how it had all worked out in the end because, after all, at the end of things there is nothing left to do but for one generation to die and the next to go on. Laughing because otherwise you had nothing left but tears.

And I was laughing too, as the rain drenched me and I slipped on fallen pine needles, nearly skewering myself on the arrow. I felt airy and light-headed, and as I made my way back to the cave, my feet only barely seemed to touch the ground. My body felt like a wicker frame animated by breath, the rain dripping right through me, and when I finally reached the cave, I didn't even try to light a fire. I collapsed, just inside. With my back against the wall and with the arrow stuck in the dirt by my thigh, I fell asleep.

BIG UNCLE HAD told me so much about dreams that they had become matter-of-fact for me, their world no more remarkable or mysterious than this one—at least to my dream self, who was always more composed and wiser than the waking me. Maybe in dreams a part of your usual self is missing—that part of you full of common-sense worry, since there is no common sense in dreams. So when I stood over myself and saw myself slumped over, hardly breathing, I did not worry that I might be dying or dead. I simply pulled the arrow out of the dirt and went outside into a balmy day lit by the dream light that hangs everywhere, suspended in the air. I knew it was a dream because light does not move in dreams—it is simply everywhere; it is what makes everything exist. Outside, the trees were a brighter green, with an aura that made them look like infrared photographs, and when their branches swayed in the wind, and their leaves rustled and chimed like bells, they threw trails of liquid smoke into the air.

Big Uncle had told me that dreams are your real life, and that waking life is the dream. He told me that time was elastic, like a lump of noodle dough, that you could stretch it out and fold it up and double and redouble it in dreams. The past could meet the present and the future, and then all of that could leak into your waking life. He had sounded like a madman or a shaman.

But now I remembered, and I thought of the time I had leapt from the small patch of vegetable garden at the edge of the sewer creek tended by the crazy woman who wore the overcoat all year, how I had flown through the air, feeling its smooth texture and warmth, as if it were bathwater flowing around me, and the arc I followed to the next terrace down was so slow and leisurely that I could take my time to think of things, to imagine how I might change my direction and fly upward and soar over the motor pool in ASCOM or glide even farther and look down on the airfield where the helicopters were sitting in rectangular formations like so many giant dragonflies. From that terrace to the next one below must only have been a second, but I could imagine an entire day of my future in that time, and when I finally landed, oddly light, not even feeling the stones under my feet at the edge of the creek, I thought maybe I'd been dreaming, that maybe I would wake up on the *yo* and wonder whether my mother had gotten up before me and gone to the NCO Club for pancakes and percolated coffee with cream and sugar.

In the dream I looked at the arrow in my hand and knew it was the right one. Its feathers were red, yellow, and blue; its tip was like a blade, and I could see myself finding it again in the pine tree that was both old and young, splitting into past and future with the present suspended in the middle.

When I woke up, I saw that the feathers on the arrow were black and white, and its tip was a simple fowling tip. It wasn't the one Big Uncle had shot at the moon. I had failed.

# Collateral

## 1975

When I went down the alley to find the S☉UL club again, I had a premonition. It was unclear, but not vague, a feeling that I would find something familiar and yet not recognizable. It had no image to it, but I thought of the Umbrella Seller's face, the smoothness of her skin despite her obvious age, the way she walked, as if the alleyways had become part of a habitual path memorized by her body the way you remember the lay of stones across a creek.

It didn't surprise me to see that the club was gone. In its place was another club called CW, probably for Country & Western. Through the newly enlarged front window, the interior furniture looked like it had been acquired from some U.S. Army club. The smell of the alley—stale beer, piss, and vomit—hadn't changed, and the old man who was sweeping outside the open entrance could have been sweeping in front of any or all the clubs in Itaewon. When he paused to look up at me, he recognized me right away.

"You again," he said, as if he'd been expecting me. Maybe that's the way it was with people who came looking for the Umbrella Seller. "Where's your friend?"

"I came alone, *ajoshi*." I didn't remember seeing him the last time. Maybe he'd been sitting in the shadows in the club or watching us through some secret hole in the wall. He certainly didn't look like a sweeper, with the muscles on his arms and the scars on his face.

"Did you bring money?" His question was so casual I nearly said yes, though I hadn't brought any money. Was I supposed to understand something?

"No," I said. "I just came to ask her about something."

"To ask the price of an umbrella?" He laughed, showing gold teeth.

"I came to ask about Jinju. Miklos's mother."

"What? Who sent you?"

"Nobody sent me, *ajoshi.*"

"Who told you that name?"

"The Umbrella Seller Ajuma," I lied.

He put the broom against the wall, looking at me as if something was out of kilter. He wiped his forehead and stood for a moment deciding what to do. He looked me up and down the way you look at someone before insulting them, and finally he pulled a knife from his back pocket and snapped it open. "You see this?" he said.

I didn't quite know if the butterfly blade was meant to scare me or emphasize what he was about to say. My stomach clenched momentarily, but then he pointed the blade at me, wagging it up and down, uncertain. "Wait here," he said.

When he went into the club, I put my Adidas bag down and sat on the stairs. The traffic above on the main street in Itaewon only a couple dozen yards away seemed distant and muffled. Far down the alley before it turned, I saw an old woman carrying a basin on her head. She was dressed in traditional white, with white rubber shoes, and her silver hair reflected in the sunlight before she disappeared. It made me think of Kisu's grandmother—a bad omen, I thought—and I was wondering what sort of remedy Big Uncle would have had for that when the man returned and gestured for me to follow.

He took me into the dark club and down a hall to a narrow door that led to an alleyway so cramped we had to move through it sideways, avoiding stacks of empty beer cases and aluminum kegs. Everything stank of yeast and urine, and there was a strange hint of dried mugwort. I had to hold my breath until we emerged into a small courtyard surrounded by tile-roofed houses. It wasn't the place I had been before—it looked like an old-fashioned *madang*, but with a well, and the small tree that grew next to it was twisted and old, with bare lower branches but lush at the top. Little white strips of paper dangled from the branches, swaying in a breeze and making a rustling sound as if they were substitute leaves. I couldn't tell where the wind came from, but it was cool and fresh—not the polluted air of Itaewon.

"It's a *yaksu*—a medicinal spring," said the man. He pointed to one of the buildings, which had a traditional wooden *maru* between the rooms. A few pairs of expensive shoes—both men's and women's—were laid out on the stepping-stone.

"Take your shoes off and go in there," the man said, pointing to the room on the left. When he saw me untie my Keds, he said, "If your feet smell, wash them first and leave your socks outside."

I did as he said, washing my feet in the cold well water and drying them off against the legs of my jeans before I stepped up onto the *maru*.

"When you come out, just go through that gate and go down the hill," the man told me. "That's the way to the market."

"Yes, sir," I said.

He whistled as he left back toward the narrow alleyway, and the rice-papered door slid open in its waxed wooden groove.

It was the Umbrella Seller. This time she was wearing a traditional Korean *chogori* and *ch'ima*—an expensive outfit that made me think of the New Year holiday when women would wear their best new clothes. I knew nothing about fabric, but from its sheen and the strange depth of its muted colors, I could tell she was wearing something that only a very rich or important person could afford. Her outfit reminded me of how

President Park's wife was dressed in a newsreel I had seen the year she was murdered.

"You're here," said the Umbrella Seller. "Why did you come?"

I had a feeling she knew full well why I had come and was testing me in some way. "I came to ask about Miklos's mother, *ajuma*," I answered.

She motioned for me to come into the room, and she smiled at my bare feet—how they left wet prints on the dark, polished wood floor.

It was a sitting room for meetings and doing business, though it looked like it could be out of a historical soap opera: an old folding screen covered in Chinese calligraphy, lacquered ginkgo wood tables, a floor of lacquered and polished paper as slick and tough as linoleum.

The Umbrella Seller slid the door shut on its waxed runners, then made me a cup of coffee just as she had the last time. She was treating this like a social visit or a business meeting. She peeled me a mandarin orange, filling the room with a citrus smell that wafted up with the steam from the coffee.

"What did you come to ask?" she said finally, in her perfect English. She put the mandarin sections down, neatly and symmetrically, on a little blue glass plate.

"I wanted to ask how much money she still owes you, *ajuma*." The sweet creamed coffee made the mandarin taste bitter.

"It's an amount that you or your mother or your father could never repay," she said. "Sometimes a debt isn't just dollars or won. You know that sort of thing?"

The Umbrella Seller had old hands—much older than her face. And even in the muted light I could see the crow's feet around her eyes. No amount of lotion could hide that.

I nodded.

"I could keep you here and no one would ever know."

I nodded again to show I wasn't afraid.

"So go ahead and ask me what you came to ask."

"If I pay what I have for her and we promise to keep sending you money every month, will you let her go? She needs to find her son."

"I know all about her son. A *mikuraji* like him will slip away. That's why we call it that. And the answer to what you're asking is no."

"Why, *ajuma*?"

"Because once you let a person go without some sort of collateral, you can never count on being repaid. This isn't some layaway plan you make at the PX."

"Even if I promise?"

She laughed brightly at that, as if she hadn't had a good laugh in a long time. "Even so," she said. "People promise and swear on God and their ancestors and their children and even their own lives, but you can never believe a promise—even when it's made sincerely like right now. You're sincere, aren't you? You would swear on something. I know people." When she sipped her coffee, she pointed her little finger at me.

I wished Patsy were with me then. She would have known what to say in this situation. This sort of thing was what she was good at; she knew things in a way I would never understand. Somehow, I had already known the Umbrella Seller would say no. In her world, maybe all promises were empty. Maybe the only thing you *could* count on was collateral.

I wondered if I had come so that I could tell myself—and maybe Paulie and Patsy and Miklos later—that I had tried my best, and though I didn't exactly believe in guilt or karma, I knew I would have regrets if I'd never tried.

My cheap orange Adidas bag looked out of place in the traditional décor of the room. I pulled it over to my side and opened it, drawing the large metal zipper toward me with an unexpectedly loud snarling sound. I removed the two cloth-wrapped bundles and put them on the table between the tray and the Umbrella Seller's cup.

"What are these?" she said.

"You said collateral, so I'm giving these to you. They're my Big Uncle's treasures from the 6.25 War."

She looked at me as if she expected the bundles to contain hand grenades—they were about the same size as one of those segmented metal pineapples you could buy in Itaewon as a novelty cigarette lighter. I reached into the open mouth of the Adidas bag and removed the other cloth bundle, which looked like it could be a pair of chopsticks.

"My Big Uncle told me stories about the war, so I know where these are from and how valuable they are. 'More than gold,' is what he said."

"You're a strange boy," the Umbrella Seller said, unwrapping the long bundle—the hairpin. "*More* than gold?" she repeated, looking at me quizzically. "This *is* gold. An old thing, but only white gold."

"It goes together with the other things," I explained. "They belonged to an old man who laid down and died, and my Big Uncle was told where to find it. It's some kind of treasure."

That seemed to make her curious, and she quickly unwrapped the two other cloths, revealing the jade eggs. She frowned. "Do you have any idea what these are?" she asked, pushing them suddenly away from herself as if they were tained by death and misfortune.

"Aren't they valuable antiques, *ajuma*? Like things that go in a museum? There are lots of antique shops in Itaewon."

"Who did they belong to?"

"I don't know. Just an old man. Aren't they valuable?"

"For what you want? They're not treasure—they're about as valuable as dog shit."

I looked down in shame. She might just as well have slapped me and told me I was a mongrel myself. "I'm sorry," I said. "Maybe my Big Uncle didn't walk enough paces because of his bad foot and got these instead of the real treasure." I reached across the table to gather the things up, hoping I might get some money for them later from the shop that sold brassware and fake antiques to GIs.

The Umbrella Seller held her hand out to stop me. "What did you say?"

I repeated myself.

"What's your Big Uncle's name?"

"I don't know," I said, feeling even more ashamed. I had never heard Big Uncle's given name. I wasn't in his immediate family, and I had never written him a letter. My mother didn't have a geneological record. "I only know his surname. I'm sorry."

"What is it?"

"Lee. From Sambongni."

I saw her hands tremble then, and I thought she must be furious at me now for some sort of insult I didn't understand, for wasting her precious time with my childish idea.

"Did your uncle ever tell you about being on a train to Pusan during the War?"

I nodded.

"Did he ride inside the train car?"

I shook my head—side to side in resignation. I started to get up, but the Umbrella Seller grabbed the hem of my shirt and pulled me down, jarring the table, spilling coffee as all the serving ware clattered. I hadn't been looking at her, and now I saw that her eyes were brimming with tears and her lips were quivering. She tried to say something, but her voice cracked and she began to sob, as if she were at a funeral.

"*Ajuma?*" I said.

She was kneeling sideways—I couldn't see her legs under her *ch'ima*—and tears streamed from her eyes as if she were an actress in one of those historical melodramas weeping for a lost husband or son.

"You're really Mr. Lee's nephew?" she said. "Is it true?"

"He's my Big Uncle," I said. "He's my mother's oldest brother."

"What about his family? Children? Is he healthy and living well? Did he have a good sixtieth birthday celebration?"

The Umbrella Seller seemed so excited that I couldn't bear to tell her that Big Uncle was dead. I sat there silently, my head hanging, until she understood.

"Where is his grave?" she said. "Was he cremated?"

"He died only a couple of days ago."

She turned away from me to cry some more, and when she turned back, her mascara was dark under her eyes, her face wet, and her upper lip gleaming. She smiled. "Wait," she said, and she left the room.

I tried to think of a way to give her directions to the spot where the Lee clan was buried. I knew I couldn't bear to go to the funeral, but even in the dark, I would be able to look up at the black contour of the ancestors' mountain and see the faint mist of light lingering above his grave mound. I would know it was him, though whether that would be his ghost or spirit or soul was unclear to me. Maybe it would be just my memory of him somehow projected from my mind, out of my body, to the right place.

How would I explain this to the Umbrella Seller? She would have to go to Sambongni and simply ask at the general store near the bus stop on the main road and they would tell her where the Lee clan was buried. She would have to climb up the mountain, hoping it didn't rain, and when she saw the clusters of grassy mounds, she would see that there were no headstones, no names to make out on the graves. But she would see which one was new. I realized it wouldn't be too hard, after all, to find where he was buried.

I finished my coffee. The odd quiet in the room made me uncomfortable. I wanted to get up and escape while there was still a chance. But just as I was about to stand, the Umbrella Seller returned. Her face was freshly washed and makeup-free, and it made her look both younger and older at the same time. She had a large black ledger book in her arms, and she put it on the floor by the table as she sat. "Crying makes a woman so ugly," she said. "I had to wash my face." She opened the ledger book past the middle and then flipped the yellowing pages until she found the one she wanted. I couldn't read it from where I sat, but it looked like a page listing monetary amounts, percentages, and dates. There were also notes written in Korean and English—in both pencil and pen.

"This is Jinju's contract," she said, and she tore the page out of the book. She ripped it down the middle, put the pieces on top of each other, and then ripped again, over and over until she had a pile of tiny scraps, which she spread out on the floor as if she were going to play flower cards with them. She moved the paper fragments around, sorting through them until she found the ones stamped in red *tojang* seals— what Koreans used as their signatures on official documents. She put those pieces in the ashtray and lit them with a match, and we watched them burn until they were black ash.

"You've repaid the debt with those items," she said. "I suppose they turned out to be quite valuable, like things that belong in a museum."

"Were they really that expensive?"

"I couldn't even say how valuable they are. Do you want to see Miklos's mother now?"

I shook my head. I wouldn't have known what to say to her. "No," I said. "I don't need to see her."

"I'll send her home tomorrow."

"Thank you, *ajuma*."

"You can go now," she said. "Just go out the front gate as if you'd come in that way." She reached into the pocket of her *chogori* and handed me a folded one-hundred-dollar bill. "*Ch'abi*," she said. "Buy yourself something good to eat."

"Thank you, *ajuma*," I said again. I accepted the money and gave her a little bow before I picked up my bag and left the room.

"Mr. Lee's nephew," she called as I was putting on my shoes. "When you grow up—when you become an adult—it's better if you don't come to places like this. You know that, right? This is not the place for someone with your heart. Now go."

I didn't quite know what she was saying, but I agreed and said goodbye. When I was in the alley again, making my way down to the Itaewon market by following the sound, I wondered if I had done the right thing—or, rather, if I had done it the right way.

A few days later, I heard from Nokchon Cousin that Miklos's mother had reappeared. "It's the oddest thing," she said to my mother. "Someone paid her whole debt with a couple of jewels. Jade or diamonds or something, and now she's back in Inchon looking for that son of hers."

"If only someone would pay off *my* debts like that," said my mother. "And I don't even have to go looking for *my* child."

# Paisley

## 1975

On Tuesday, when I stopped at the Chinese restaurant in Sinchon for lunch, the owner told me that Dupree wanted to see me. Something about a shirt. I went to the Graves Registration building later and walked in as usual—without knocking—and I was startled to see a different GI, a tall, lanky blond who seemed to be in the middle of some sort of exercise. His fatigues were hanging from the back of one of the gray metal chairs and he was standing on one foot, reaching for the ceiling, wearing nothing but his skivvies and green socks.

"Who the *fuck* are you?" he said.

"I got a message. Dupree wants to see me."

"He's not here, man. He's TDY up in Casey." He eyed me carefully before he decided I was okay and switched feet, standing on the other and sliding one up so the flat part rested at the side of his knee and his bent leg made him look like the number 4. "This ain't no fairy shit," he said. "I'm doin' some yoga."

"When will he be back?" I had always thought yoga was for American housewives who wanted to lose weight and skinny Indian men who looked like Mahatma Gandhi and sat on beds of nails, but the GI must have been six four and had muscles like a linebacker. I noticed pink, puckered lines of scars down his left torso from his rib cage to his hip, and a large patch where the skin was raised like a mesa from a skin graft.

The GI raised both arms straight above his head, pointing, with his hands in prayer posture, at the dangling light fixture. After a few moments he lowered his foot and looked at me.

"Buncha newbies fell at a rapelling exercise. He's prepping the stiffs. A couple days, maybe? Maybe he stretches it to a week if he likes the clubs up there better."

"A shirt," I said. "Did he say anything about a shirt?"

"Is it yours?" He walked over to the file cabinet and got himself a beer. "Coke?" he said.

When I nodded, he tossed me a can. "Thanks."

It took him a few minutes to look through some drawers, and then he remembered and brought it from the back room—a red and black paisley shirt sealed and taped inside two clear plastic bags. I recognized it right away—it was Miklos's shirt, one that Kallah had given to him. When I reached for it, the GI pulled it back.

"Well, is it yours?"

I hesitated. I should just have said yes and taken it, but I told him it was my friend's. He wouldn't give it to me. "No can do," he said.

"I'll take it and give it to him," I said. "Where did Dupree get it?"

"How the fuck would I know?" said the GI. "Probly one of his fuckee boys. You a fuckee boy?"

I didn't know what he was talking about at first, but then I realized, and my "No!" was louder than I intended. Some of the GIs had young Korean boyfriends.

"Maybe that's why he ain't back yet."

"Do you know what club he goes to in Camp Casey?"

"Off post?"

I nodded.

"Only one nigger club in the ville," he said. "All the brothers go to the Motown Club—the new one. Or check out the EM Club on post."

"Thanks," I said, motioning with the Coke can.

"Hey, if you see him, tell him I'm gonna burn this fucking thing if he doesn't get rid of it."

"That's Miklos's shirt," I said. "He'll take care of it."

"That his fuckee boy?"

I shook my head.

"You wanna see my dick or something?" He laughed out loud when that made me leave in a hurry. "Never happen!" he called out after me.

CAMP CASEY WAS named after an American Army major who was shot down in an observation plane during the Korean War. It was forty miles north of Seoul—almost at the DMZ—and the local Korean ville of Tongduchon was like an older, seedier version of Pupyong, where I lived. The Pupyong people looked down on Tongduchon people as hicks, though the prejudice was mutual, but GIs who were stationed up there or in the nearby Camp Hovey all wanted to transfer to Yongsan HQ or even ASCOM, farther from the DMZ and not in range of a surprise artillery barrage from the North.

From the Snack Bar, where I got off the army bus, I could see the ring of mountains—bleak even at this time of year. When my father had been stationed at Casey, he'd had to be out in the field a lot of the time, constantly combat-ready. And while the soldiers at Yongsan spent their time painting rocks white to keep busy, the soldiers closer to the DMZ were constantly engaged in field exercises, digging foxholes for practice, using up their required hours on the live-fire ranges.

I was glad I'd worn my satin souvenir jacket with my Levi's. A cold wind blew down from the mountains through the cluster of peeling Quonset huts, brick buildings, and sandbagged bunkers, and bare gravel and dirt roads stretched as far as the eye could see in either direction. There were trails up in the mounatins, and if you squinted, you could make out bunkers and guard posts, silhouettes of comm antennas and relay stations.

Up here, hardly anyone knew me, and I couldn't just wander around looking for Dupree on post where he must have been TDY at the morgue. One of Miklos's Korean cousins worked at the NCO Club in Casey, so I went there first. The old one, which had looked sort of like a Korean temple building with traditional tile roofs, had burned down in 1964, and I was told the new one was never as good. Everything up here was bayonet themed. There was even a big sign on the way into Casey that showed a black hourglass in a blood-red circle pierced by a bayonet. It said, WELCOME TO BAYONET LAND.

My father had told me about how scared the GIs could get up here, where the cold and the bare landscape reminded all the old-timers of the war. Because the North Koreans were constantly provoking the South, everyone up here was hypervigilant, convinced that another hot war was imminent. A soldier out in a guard post by himself had shot off the tip of his penis so he could go home, but he'd made the mistake of telling his buddies he was going to do something tricky—something FUBAR— and had ended up at the 121st for a while before being sent to the Army stockade in ASCOM. "That should teach you," my father said. "First, never shoot your dick off. Second, if you think you want to pull some tricky *dinky dau* shit, don't tell it to your buddies when you're drunk. And third, don't get fucking high on dope during guard duty." I liked the way he could turn his anecdotes into little fables for me—when he'd had enough beer to be relaxed and good-natured but not enough to become mean.

MIKLOS'S COUSIN WASN'T at the NCO Club, so I asked one of the older waitresses if she might know Dupree. I didn't recognize her, but she knew me when I introduced myself.

"I haven't seen you since you were on your cousin's back in a blanket," she said. "Do you still live in Pupyong? How is your mother doing?"

"She's doing well," I said.

"I haven't seen *her* since I had to go to the Monkey House. Tell her I thought the penicillin shots were going to kill me, but I got out and I'm healthy."

I said I would.

She couldn't pronounce the name "Dupree." Then she mumbled something and she remembered it as *"tu-ppuri"* because it sounded like "two roots" in Korean, but that was all. It was when I tried to describe the smell of formaldehyde that she remembered what he looked like and who he was.

"Take a taxi out to the New Motown Club," she said. "That's where he's likely to be if he's the type who drinks. The NCO Club here is no fun, so if he wants his Soul Brother music and the kind of girl who goes with Black men, he'll be out there."

It took only a few minutes for a taxi to appear. I shared a ride with a GI and his girlfriend, and they let me off near the mouth of the ville. The sign for the New Motown Club, unlike the ones for clubs in Seoul, wasn't in neon. A string of what must have been Christmas tree lights blinked on and off above the entrance, a pair of red doors with small blacked-out inset windows. The outside wall had been painted at one time, but now it had gone back to a patchy gray cinder block plastered with old movie posters, drug advertisements, and venereal disease notices.

I could hear the unmistakable Motown beat spilling out of the club, and when I pulled open the door, a thick cloud of cigarette smoke wafted into the street. Inside, in the blue light and the glitter of the disco ball that hung over the dance floor, it was so loud I had to hold my hands over my ears. Three GIs—sporting their off-duty Afros—danced with a middle-aged Korean woman who wore red hot pants and a white lace halter top. The tables were only sparsely occupied, and only a few GIs sat at the bar. I wondered who I should ask first, worried that I might be told to get out.

The bartender noticed me right away. He came to the corner of the bar and asked me, in English, what I wanted. We both shouted to be heard over the music.

"I'm looking for a spec 4 named Dupree," I said. "Do you know about anyone who came up here TDY from ASCOM because of the accident?"

"What accident?"

"The GIs who died when they were climbing? He was sent to take the bodies." I didn't think the bartender would know what "Graves Registration" meant, and I didn't know the Korean for "undertaker," so I described what Dupree's job was as best I could.

The bartender handed me a can of Coke and waved away my attempt to pay. "Nobody wants to be around that man," he said. "I haven't seen anyone even talk to him since he came up here. Go to the back where you smell the happy smoke." He pointed to the rear corner of the club, past the dance floor and the small stage. "You see him and then get out of here, understand?"

I thanked him, took my Coke, and quickly made my way to the back. The bartender was right—I smelled the pot right away at the periphery of the cigarette smoke. The MPs would have busted this place immediaitely if it were in Itaewon or ASCOM. Things must have been laxer up here because of the proximity to the DMZ. The Korean bouncer who guarded the back rooms let me through when the bartender signaled him. He pointed at one of the curtained doorways, and I went into it, coughing.

Dupree was alone. He lay on an old couch upholstered in the ubiquitous mottled red plastic that seemed to be on every piece of Army Club furniture. There was a small card table with a couple of empty OB beer bottles and a glass, half full, next to an open bottle of Jim Beam. The room was thick with pot smoke and lit by a single lightbulb dangling from the ceiling inside a Japanese paper lantern. Dupree didn't even see me come in.

"Dupree," I said.

He looked up at me, glassy-eyed. He took a long draw from a blue glass bong and held in the smoke as he tried to remember who I might be.

"Dupree."

"You wanna dance?" he said—"Pappa Was a Rolling Stone" was playing—and he exhaled.

"Dupree, you're all fucked up right now. I don't dance."

"I'll teach you, man. I miss Paulie. I taught *him* to dance like a *mother-fucker*, you know."

"I miss him, too."

Dupree stood up and put the bong on the table. I expected him to stagger like a drunk, but he moved smoothly, as if he were stepping right into a dance move. He was taller and looked even more gangly in his civvies with the flared, striped bell-bottoms. He just nodded his head now, dancing without dancing while he kept the beat. "How the fuck did you find me up here?" he asked suddenly, realizing we weren't in Sinchon.

"That white guy at the morgue told me you were TDY."

"Aw, fuck."

"He had Miklos's shirt," I said. "Did you see Miklos, man? Did he give you his shirt?"

Dupree was still nodding his head to the music. He closed his eyes. Maybe he wanted me not to be there.

"I can't find Miklos. *Anywhere.* And you know he disappeared, man. Did you *see* him?"

In the dim light I saw tears dripping down Dupree's cheeks, leaving shiny trails on his sweaty skin. "This is not the time," he said. "I'm fucked up, like you said, Seven. I got some Mandrax to mellow out, man. I wanna get the stink of all them fucking stiffs off me so I can just hang like every-body else. You think that's too much to ask coming from a brother?"

I had never seen Dupree like this. He seemed so weak and needy I felt like hugging him to give comfort and—at the same time—I wanted to slap him and tell him to stop being such a pussy. I knew it must have been the pot and Mandrax and the alcohol that made him like that. How horrible must those bodies be to make him have to get so wasted? I won-dered. How mangled could they be from falling off some cliff?

I put my Coke down and hugged him the way I might have hugged Paulie or Miklos—tight, no space between us—I could smell the formaldehyde on him—and then a few slaps on the back. He slapped my back, too, and when we drew apart he looked a bit more sober.

"This is not the time," he said again. "This is not the place. This is all fucked, but now you're here, so we gotta do what we gotta do, man. I'm gonna have another drink and you gonna have one too." He pulled two of the chairs up to the table and spilled the flat beer onto the floor before he poured out a third of the Jim Beam into the glass and handed it to me. "Korean style."

The glass was dirty, but I accepted it with both hands. Dupree lifted the bottle and knocked the neck against the glass as a toast and we each took a long drink. I coughed when the whiskey burned my throat. I poured some Coke into what was left over, and while it foamed, Dupree added more whiskey.

"There's some stuff I gotta tell you, man. You ain't gonna like it. I say drink up." He knew I wouldn't take it, but he even offered me one of his pills.

"I know what you're gonna tell me."

"Yeah? Then why you up here, man?"

I took another drink—whiskey and Coke that tasted like cleaning fluid, chemical, toxic. I drank again, and I felt the heat go up the sides of my neck to my cheeks and ears. "You're gonna tell me Paulie was your fuckee boy. That's what the GI said. You're a fucking homo."

"I ought to whup your ass," Dupree said. "You *better* than that, man. You afraid of me now?"

I shook my head.

"Then how can you say that shit after what Paulie wrote you?"

I felt a terrible guilt, and all I could do was finish my drink. "I never read the letters," I said. "I finally got them, and I can't read them."

"You sorry motherfucker, Seven. Paulie poured his guts out and you didn't even fucking read 'em. What's the matter with you?"

I wanted to be angry at Dupree, but now I felt guilty, instead, like I was a criminal sitting at an interrogation table in one of those awful noir films. My face was already pounding from the alcohol and my stomach had gone all sour.

"Why didn't you read the letters, man?"

"I don't *know!*" I said, looking away. "I don't know. Why did he have to leave?"

"You know why."

"Why did he have to keep a secret from me? Why couldn't he just say?"

"*Say?* Say what?" Dupree took another swig from the bottle. "Would it change anything, man? Would it? Everything? Nothing?"

I glared at him, my eyes burning.

"You think Paulie be any different if he had his dick in my mouth or my dick in his ass? You think that makes a difference and you afraid of that?"

I hid my face in my hands and shook my head. I didn't want to imagine what Dupree was saying, but I couldn't help it. Paulie could never have told me those things, at least not until just before he left. Maybe he'd wanted to tell me in Itaewon after we saw the Umbrella Seller. Maybe he had to write it to me because he was too afraid to look at my face. What if I had been angry with him and told his mother? What would she have done to him—or to herself? What would her church have done?

"Paulie and me got plans," Dupree said. "I got me *beaucoup* money and I'm gonna be legit when I get out. *Totally* legit. Paulie gonna go to college to learn about business and taxes and investments and all that shit, and I'm gonna start my own company. Be my own fucking boss after I'm home. He told you all that in his letter, man, and you didn't fucking bother."

"I'm sorry."

"No sweat. Read your mail. Now I know for sure why you came up here."

"Yeah?"

"Miklos is dead, man."

DUPREE TOLD ME HOW a cleaning crew had found a body in the rafters of the shower house by the Crafts Shop. They had sent up the Korean cleaners, thinking it was dead rats again because of the stink that had begun to permeate the whole building. What they found, instead, looked like a squatter's hideout, complete with rope beds and a stash of C-rations. In the heat, and with the flies and rats, the body had decomposed so badly that it couldn't be identified. When Dupree saw it the next day he was on duty, all he recognized, as he cleaned off the maggots and liquefied tissue, was the shirt. He guessed it must be Miklos's because the hair was light brown and then, when he saw the switchblade comb in the bag of possessions that had been retrieved, he knew for sure the body was Miklos.

I didn't want to believe it, and I tried to imagine Miklos grinning as he flipped back his hair with his switchblade comb. Why would he be dead up there? Maybe he just left his shirt—we left stuff up there all the time—and someone else was wearing it when they died. We knew that other people used the Fort. Maybe he'd combed his hair and left the comb in the shirt pocket?

When Dupree told me the body had a chipped front tooth, I couldn't remember. Did *Miklos* have one? I knew his teeth were crooked when he smiled. I could *see* him with a chipped front tooth. But was I just imagining it because of Dupree's question? I couldn't be sure. Did Miklos wear a silver ring? I knew he wore a punching ring sometimes, but we wore rings and took them off or traded them all the time just like we did with watches. It didn't matter if the body had a Timex with a cammo strap on its wrist—plenty of Koreans could get a watch just like that on the black market. And brown hair? Maybe another mixed-blood kid had come down from Seoul and died up there after going up with Miklos, and maybe Miklos had felt guilty about that and run away. Or maybe he just wanted everyone to *think* he was dead because of all the money he owed and he was hiding out until he had it. Maybe he was sick of this shitty life he'd gotten himself into and took the other guy's identity so he could be someone else.

"Miklos would've had his ID card in his wallet," I told Dupree. "He had a picture of us in there too. We used to have it taped to a beam up in the Fort, but that might give us away, so he kept it."

"The fort?" Dupree didn't know about the Fort. Paulie must have kept our secret.

"That's what we call that place inside the roof," I said. "We used to spend the night up there all the time."

"You little motherfuckers," Dupree said. He was asking me whether I wanted Miklos's stuff as I passed out.

WHEN I WOKE UP, I couldn't tell what time it was. I smelled mildewed canvas and heard a thrumming sound that made the pounding in my head feel even worse. There was a foul taste in my mouth, which I recognized as the remnants of my own puke. I was lying on an army cot covered in a green wool blanket, still in my clothes. Someone had taken my shoes off.

I sat up. I was in a large tent, the kind used for temporary housing, and that meant I must be on post. Dupree must have sneaked me into the barracks. It was nine thirty according to my Timex. Morning. No lights were on; the washed-out light that gave me a headache was coming in through the opaque plastic windows. Now I remembered a few things: Dupree and another GI debating whether they should cut my hair and put me in a uniform to get past the gate guards. Their wheezy laughter. Being lifted and tossed into the back seat of a taxi. A bumpy ride with someone singing—could that heart-wrenching voice have been Dupree's?

My sneakers were on the floor at the foot of the bunk. Someone had sprayed water on them and they were still wet when I put them on. I hated tying wet laces.

I remembered sobbing, and Dupree sitting by the bunk with his hand on my brow telling me it was okay, though he and I both knew that nothing was okay now. I wondered how he could be so sober when he, and not I, had been the one all fucked up at the beginning of the night. I needed to know if Miklos had killed himself. I remembered there was rat poison up in the Fort, and he could have taken it if he'd been alone in one of his moods. And now I couldn't quite remember what Dupree had told me. Miklos was all tangled in parachute cord or something. They found him on one of the rope beds with the cord caught around his neck, and they thought maybe he was so drunk that he'd rolled over in his sleep and stuck his head through the cords. He must have struggled in the dark when he woke up and gotten all tangled up like a bug in a spider's web. But they couldn't really say, and Dupree hadn't been up there, and the body was too far gone even to have much flesh on the neck to examine. Dupree wasn't even a medical examiner anyway.

I checked for my wallet—it was there. Dupree had said there was no wallet with Miklos's body. Someone—probably one of the cleaning crew that found him—had stolen it for the ID card. It was nine thirty. Dupree was on duty by now, and I didn't want to go looking for him on an unfamiliar post. I went outside into the cool, too-bright morning and found the bathroom, where I washed my oily face and scrubbed my teeth with a finger. There was a ten-thirty bus back to Yongsan, so I forced myself to eat something at the Snack Bar and had a cup of coffee while I waited. And I remembered the last thing Dupree had said before I fell asleep— Paulie had told him that Miklos didn't just steal all that money from his mother for himself. He was planning to give half his dog winnings to me so I could help Big Uncle. Dupree said that was probably in one of the letters I couldn't bring myself to read.

I bought another cup of coffee and drank it on the bus, but I still fell asleep. The GI sitting behind me tapped me awake when we arrived at the main depot in Yongsan. The next ASCOM/Inchon bus would be leaving in ten minutes—just enough time for me to make it to the bathroom and get on with another cup of coffee. I fell asleep again and woke up just before we got to the main ASCOM gate.

On the last step getting off the bus, I paused and looked out at the gatehouse and the beginning of the obstacle course—the tire run and the monkey bars—just beyond, along the inside of the barbed-wired wall. And farther on was the jump tower with its cables still up. I had walked off the Yongsan bus so many times—just like this—with Paulie and Miklos. It felt like they were just behind me. We would joke about something, Miklos would check if his bike was still chained to the bus stop sign, Paulie would wonder if Dupree was on duty at the morgue, and then we would all go to the bowling alley for Cokes and hot dogs even if we were headed up the hill later to the main Snack Bar. When my feet touched the sidewalk and the folding door huffed shut behind me, I caught myself turning around to see if my friends were there. The bus released its air brake with a spit-hiss and pulled away, and I was left in a cloud of diesel exhaust. I could almost make out the impression of Miklos's bike in the patch of clover.

It seemed a long way to the Graves Registration building walking by myself. I could hear traffic on the other side of the base's main wall, faint voices, laughter, yelling, cars honking. The heat of the late afternoon sun bore down on me, and I felt grimy sweat under my clothes. Halfway to the building, I stopped and lay down in the middle of the tarmac as if I were stretched across a railroad track waiting for a train. I closed my eyes and let the heat from the black tar rise into me to mingle with the heat of the sun, to cook me, as I listened for the rumble of an Army truck or a jeep. But I only heard the pulse in my ears telling me I was alive, felt the rise and fall of my belly to know I was drawing breath. I lay there for a long time, until a cloud passed in front of the sun, and then I got up, brushed myself off, and walked the rest of the way to the morgue.

Yogi Bear—that was what Dupree called his sub because the white GI had said he wanted to be a devoted yogi. He gave me Miklos's shirt and the switchblade comb—though he wasn't supposed to—but he wouldn't let me see the body. I knew he could have just lied and told me it was cremated, or shipped stateside according to some army regulation, but he told me, instead, that Dupree had made him promise not to show it to me.

"He tells me to tell your ass the draw's locked and he took the keys up to Casey with him, right? He calls me this morning at oh-eight-hundred sharp and tells me that shit, but I ain't lyin' to you, man. That would be bad karma for *my* ass *and* my yoga."

I told him I wasn't actually sure I wanted to see Miklos's body but was just asking. What if it was so gruesome that I had nightmares for the rest of my life? What if his ghost latched on to me or the smell got into my lungs and never left and I had the smell of his death on me all the time? And why couldn't he lie for his friend and still do his fancy yoga poses?

"Man," he said. "Yoga ain't just making a pretzel outta your body. It's a whole *philosophy,* dig? You figure it out for yourself someday." Instead of taking me back to the storage room, Yogi Bear took me to Dupree's unlocked locker, pulled the rattly green metal door open, and said, "Here, man. Dupree said you look at this."

And there it was, Scotch-taped to the inside, just under the vents. A color Polaroid of Paulie, Miklos, and me, standing with our arms across each other's shoulders in our *chebi* Kallah shirts.

Miklos was smiling at the camera, his mouth open to reveal his chipped front tooth.

# Meetings & Farewells

### 1975

My mother had gone up to Sambongni for three days with An-na for Big Uncle's funeral, but we never spoke about it until years later when she would tell me how An-na had seen hungry ghosts in the village and scared everyone—even the Christians—into taking Kubong Manshin more seriously. They had been dismissive of the old shaman, and it was An-na who made them first consider a *kut* to placate the spirits. I could not get myself to attend the funeral, but Phillips went up for the photo op and brought back pictures of the funeral procession.

Phillips and I were at the old helipad overlooking what was left of the 121st Hospital after the fire years ago. From up there I could see that the charred buildings had still not been rebuilt or demolished, and the rows of Quonset huts still stretched out toward the perimeter fences of ASCOM. Phillips had folded the cracked windshield of his jeep down onto the hood and we were sitting on it, smoking Marlboros.

"Thanks for the tip," Phillips said. "It was good. I'm sorry it had to be your uncle, man."

Plumes of smoke. I thought of cremation. That's what a Buddhist family would have done. A Christian family, these days, would have saved the money that a traditional burial and funeral cost—since the government was discouraging them anyway—and had a simpler Western ceremony with black suits and not sack cloth, a hearse and not a half-mile-long procession of mourners, with family carrying spirit banners and symbolic long poles of bamboo and paulownia, and a fancy bier painted in all the auspicious colors. In the photos I recognized some of my country uncles in their sack cloth hats, shaped like brown paper grocery bags and bound with straw rope. My aunts wore circlets of twisted straw low on their foreheads—the same kind used for making cheap traditional sandals. Phillips had printed a dozen black-and-white five-by-seven glossies for me. He had taken another set of color slides with his Nikon, and he said he could show me those sometime and I could order Kodak prints of them if I wanted.

"Think I could make *National Geographic* with those?" he said.

I nodded, letting out a long lungful of smoke. In one of the pictures I could make out a black limousine in the background, just visible because of a curve in the road. Standing outside the limo with the door open was a woman in sunglasses wearing an elegant black dress and holding a black umbrella to shade herself from the sun. I pointed her out.

"It's the Umbrella Seller," I said.

I couldn't see his eyes, but I knew Phillips was squinting behind his gold-framed aviator shades. "You know the Umbrella Seller? No shit? I didn't even know she was in the shot."

"Why would she come to see Big Uncle's funeral?" I said, more to myself than him.

"All those people were blocking the road. That limo driver was pissed, man, honkin' like fuck-all to get by, not stoppin' to watch. How come *you* know her? Bitch got goods on the Commanding General of Eighth Army, man." He pulled his shades down as if to get a better look at me—as if he had never seen me properly before.

"I paid her for Miklos's mom."

"You *met* the Umbrella Seller? *Nobody* meets that woman. We just pay our taxes like good little citizens, man. She *owns* people, you know what I mean?"

When I told him how Paulie and I had found her, and how I'd gone to see her again, Phillips made a mock kowtow. "You got bigger balls than me now," he joked. "You know why they call her that?"

I thought it must have been because she had once actually sold um-brellas, but Phillips thought that was funny, and he laughed out a cloud of smoke and lit another Marlboro from his hard pack. An army truck—a deuce-and-a-half—rumbled up the hill, spewing diesel smoke from its vertical exhaust pipes, driven by a KATUSA with a Black GI riding shotgun. It was what we'd been waiting for, me keeping Phillips com-pany so he could show me the pictures while we talked—his days were full of these rendezvous at odd places and times, and he seemed always to be waiting for something, the next thing, the thing after that, even when his appointment arrived. Phillips waved at the GI and the truck pulled alongside the jeep and stopped. I could feel the rumbling of its idle in my belly.

"Bingo," Phillips said.

The truck, I already knew, was loaded with full-sized refrigerators. Now that electricity had become more reliable and you didn't need to have a transformer to run one, refrigerators had become even more in demand. Soon every family would have one—and another, smaller one to store their kimchi in so the smell wouldn't get into everything.

"So why do they call her that?"

Phillips looked confused for a moment. He had been thinking of something else. "It's 'cause the Eighth Army patch looks like a beach umbrella from up top. A red-and-white beach umbrella."

"She sells that umbrella?"

"Like I said, the fucking Commanding General, man. I don't know why she would even want to stay in this shithole of a country when she could live anywhere. I wonder about that sometimes."

"What about you?"

"I love this shithole, baby-san," Phillips said. "This shithole's gonna make me rich and famous."

"I'm leaving soon," I said. "Most skosh."

He squinted at me again. He looked happy for me. "Send me a fucking postcard. Where'd your old man get stationed?"

"Fort Ord."

"He coulda done worse. Ord's a nice place. Monterey. Carmel. Beach, but too cold in the water."

"He's going to the hospital there."

"You don't worry now, Seven. Your old man is *beaucoup* tough and nothin' but a Claymore's gonna take him out. Lifers like him don't croak in no hospital." Phillips scooted off the hood of the jeep and into the driver's seat. He signaled the truck and started his engine. "Can I drop you somewhere on the way out? We're headed up the MSR toward Sosa."

"Can I keep the pictures?" I got into the passenger seat and tossed my cigarette down onto a patch of grass.

"They're for you."

I asked Phillips if he could take a roundabout route and drop me off near the entrance to the temple at Yaksan. "No sweat," he said.

As we drove over the hill and toward the front gate, with the deuce-and-a-half following us, the sky cleared, and the sun, a bright white disk behind the overcast, broke through with a sharp golden light. The wind felt brisk against my face as I clutched the stack of pictures and put them back in the manila envelope.

Shipjong-dong, the neighborhood after Sinchon, looked alien to me—everything too bright and new. I recognized the *t'aeguk*-painted gate of my old judo teacher's house as we drove by, the little hole-in-the-wall store where his wife had bought the *ramyon* noodles to cook for me and Miklos when we had paid a surprise visit. Middle-school boys with their heads freshly buzzed were playing with wooden tops—the kind with bullets for points. I could feel Phillips noticing all this, how his intention seemed to send an electrical current to the new Nikon on the floor at my feet.

Phillips had been to the temple at Yaksasa. He knew where to stop to let me off. "Take it easy," he said.

"You, too."

"I'm gonna miss you, but I ain't sayin' goodbye."

I gave him a mock salute and hopped out of the jeep in front of the turnoff. "Bye," I said.

He winked. "We never know where we're gonna meet again, Seven. But we always do." He popped the clutch, and the jeep roared off with the deuce-and-a-half on its tail, the canvas flapping over the bed of the truck.

I made my way past the temple entrance, the curio shops, the stores, and the restaurant and got a few things at the little grocery before I started up the mountain. The owner insisted I buy two bottles of soju instead of one—so I did.

The photos felt heavy in the manila envelope with its two red buttons fastened by string. By the time I reached the ridge and started down the other side, toward the public cemetery, the sweat from my hand had created a soggy patch on the envelope, and when I shifted my grip the paper peeled away like old skin and I saw part of the glossy photo underneath: the back of Big Uncle's funeral bier, his vessel to what Koreans called *chosaesang—that* world.

By the time I reached the old man's grave mound, I was winded. It had taken longer than I'd expected to find the grave—things had changed. There were more grave mounds, a tree missing, and then there was the grave itself: it had been tended by the family, and I knew, finally, that I had found it from the telltale signs of previous erosion—a swatch of pebbles—and the palpable feeling that rose from my gut when the wind shifted and I smelled the dirt.

"I should be doing this at *your* grave, Big Uncle," I said out loud. "I know you'll understand."

I opened the paper package of the soju and apples. With my Swiss Army knife I sliced the tops and bottoms off the four apples and stacked them—three in a triangle and one on top—Confucian style. And with my head bowed, I pried the cap off the bottle and made three circular pours of the clear soju onto the grassy mound. As the sharp alcohol bit into my nose, I thought apologetic thoughts. I felt sorrow and remorse as I took the photos out of the envelope and set them aflame one by one with my Zippo lighter, coughing at the acrid smoke. One corner to the other, the paper curling, crinkling, turning to black ash, which I dropped on top of Old Man Heaven's grave.

When all the photos were gone, I burned the envelope and the wrapping paper too, and left all the ashes in a single pile. Over that, I poured the remaining soju, saving a small amount to dash westward toward the Western Paradise, where good Buddhists were said to reincarnate before their final enlightenment.

I felt as if I had completed something, but no sense of completion. A cycle, maybe. Or the motion of an invisible worm in my stomach, a momentary nausea like a sudden dropping sensation. I felt saliva thick in my mouth, and I remembered how I'd had motion sickness the first weeks after I'd started school in Yongsan, how that thickening in my mouth came before I had to throw up, how the smell of perfume or body odor or a whiff of hair gel would be the last straw, and how much better I would feel afterward—purged, pure, clean. Airy.

I knew what was wrong then—Old Man Heaven's *chang'gi* pieces were missing. I dug around in the dirt and grass until I found them, the general and his two small protectors, and put them back on top of the grave mound. There was a rustling sound then, in the tall grass on the slope above me by the plum trees, and when I looked up I saw the gray form of the monk, standing as if he had been there all along, the whole time we had been digging down into Old Man Heaven's grave, and afterward, waiting for us to return. I expected him to say something, but he remained silent until I acknowledged him with a wave of the empty soju bottle in my hand. Then he jerked his head in a motion for me to follow him and disappeared up the slope.

I followed quickly with the remaining bottle of soju, leaving everything else behind to clean up later, realizing that it meant I planned to return to the grave again. The monk was supernaturally quick—I would have said he was as fast as a ghost if I were speaking Korean. Quick as a *kwishin*. "Mumyong Sunim!" I called after him. "*Sunim*, wait for me!" But he said nothing and continued up the mountain in his rubber shoes.

"Mumyong Sunim!" I called again, and by that time he was at the top of the ridge where Paulie, Miklos, and I had made our camp. When I reached the flat area, the monk led me to the mouth of the shallow cave and sat there, legs crossed, on the rock by the entrance.

When he finally spoke, it was something I didn't understand. "The wheel of samsara is kept in motion by karma," he said. "There is nothing you can do about it."

I knew, at least, that wheels spun in a circle, so I asked, "Do you mean I had no choice but to come back, *sunim*?"

"There is always choice," he said. "What we think of as a willful choice is sometimes just an illusion, but there is always choice for us in this incarnation. It's a privilege."

"I came back because my Big Uncle died," I said. "I didn't go to his funeral or his burial. I didn't know what to do."

"He will be on his way to the Westward Land. I will pray for him."

"I don't think he was a Buddhist, *sunim*. How could he go to the Buddhist paradise? His family is Christian."

The monk pointed at the ground, then at the sky. "It makes no difference," he said. "We all go to the same places in the end. Did I tell you I'm also going to the West? But I'm flying *east* to get there. Just like you." He laughed.

"Is that a Buddhist riddle?" I asked.

"When I spoke to you last, I recall I told you the story of the great master Wonhyo. You asked me something that *was* a Buddhist puzzle then—about the water in a skull."

I felt a sudden flush of guilt and shame. Had he seen us then? Was it the monks from the temple who had repaired Old Man Heaven's grave mound? I wanted to confess to him, but I suspected he already knew everything, that all of what I had done was transparent to him, or apparent, written on my face and in the posture of my body, exuding from me in my breath.

"There's part of the story I didn't tell you," he said when I was silent. "While Wonhyo and Uisang were asleep in the cave on their way to China, a *tokkaebi* came to them. A hideous creature they did not see because they were asleep in the dark."

"So then it was a goblin that tricked him into drinking out of the skull?" I said. *Tokkaebi* often lived in graveyards and they could be terrible pranksters. I had heard enough stories about them to figure out this new puzzle.

"Not many people know this part of the story," he said. "I'm telling you because I see that you came up here today with a good intention—to do the right thing. But you also came up in ignorance."

"Do you mean I don't know what I'm doing?" He was right, of course. If the emptiness and helplessness I felt was born of ignorance, I wondered if all I had to do was learn my way out of it. But what was I supposed to learn? If I didn't know, then how would I know what I needed to learn?

"We think we know what we're doing most of the time," said Mumyong Sunim. "That is the greatest part of our ignorance, because even when we believe we know the causes and conditions of things, our knowledge is limited. We are not all buddhas yet, and we cannot know the outcomes of our actions."

"If I drop a rock, I know it will hit the ground," I said. "That's a simple thing."

"But you don't know whether someone will trip on that rock tomorrow and sprain his ankle."

I remembered our conversation from the last time about the possible outcomes of his having eaten the spoiled rice I had given to him. "My uncle once told me a story about a boy who moved a rock out of the road so no one would trip on it, and underneath he found a pot of gold. It was a reward because he thought of other people and not just himself."

"That's a good story. It could just as well have been a poison snake under that rock."

"But not in that story."

"You're good at this," he said. "You learned something from our last conversation." He chuckled and gestured at the landscape. "No, this is all a story," he said. "Stories inside stories inside stories. We just haven't heard them all, and we don't have the time in our incarnations even to understand the one we happen to be in. My master told me that's why he liked to watch sentimental movies—because then you could see all the meaning and feelings in a life—forward and backward—with all of it in your memory, and you could learn from it."

"So what happened in the story of Wonhyo?" I asked.

"You would assume that it was the *tokkaebi*'s trick that got him to drink out of that skull, thinking it was a gourd of fresh water. And you would be right. But why did the *tokkaebi* do that? Was it a malicious trick? Was it a simple prank he expected to enjoy? Did he do it because he wanted to help Wonhyo see the truth? You see, we can't know that goblin's intention. But what we thought was a bad thing had a good outcome. Just like that person who tripped on the rock you dropped, then sprained his ankle—but then it slowed him down and he was delayed in getting to the bridge, only to learn, when he got there, that it had collapsed and everyone on it had died."

"Then you're saying ignorance might be a good thing sometimes?"

"Ignorance is ignorance. Knowledge of one's ignorance—awareness of it—now, that can be a good thing."

"I don't know whether I did the right things, *sunim*. But I tried to. I wish I knew more so I could make the right decisions. It isn't even just for me. It's for the people who are important to me, but every time I do something, the thing that happens isn't what I wanted."

"You can only do what you understand in your ignorance is right," he said. "Try not to want particular outcomes, because your desire will cause disappointment and suffering. But if you listen to what your heart tells you, you might discover that you actually know more than you think regarding outcomes." When he said "heart," he touched his chest to distinguish that part of the mind from the brain.

"Were you waiting for me here, *sunim*? To teach me a lesson? Like last time?"

He shook his head. "I came up here for some fresh air—to breathe—and then to smoke a cigarette. Isn't it funny how things work out?"

"I'm glad it worked out this way."

"You're going to America soon," he said.

"Yes."

"I will see you there in the future. Maybe it will be you who steps out for some fresh air and a cigarette. Maybe after you see a sentimental movie or after a funeral you didn't want to go to. And I will be there."

I didn't know whether to believe him, and I didn't know how to reply. It could have been him adding the final twist to the lesson he had taught me—a trick, a test—to see if I had actually learned anything.

Mumyong Sunim pointed at the bottle of soju I still carried. "Were you tricked?" he said. "The store owner down there can be very persuasive. Who is that one for?" He smiled, and I laughed with him.

"I think it must be for you, *sunim*," I said. "The store owner said the soju was such a good brand I might as well buy two while I was at it. I said I didn't need two, but he told me that there was no way to know whether I might need another one. He was right."

"You know a monk is not supposed to drink," he said.

"But you smoke, *sunim*. Aren't monks not supposed to smoke?"

"We are followers of the Middle Path," he said when I handed him the bottle. "The path between extremes, as the Buddha discovered through his own experience. Before he could starve to death, he ate a bowl of rice milk given to him by a lowly girl named Sujata. His followers left him for that, but then, eventually, they came back. Imagine if he had been a stubborn acetic and starved himself until he died. Where would all this be?"

I imagined the Buddha starving to death. I had seen a picture of a sculpture—Siddhartha not yet the Buddha, sitting with legs crossed and looking like a skeleton. But if he had died, everything would still be here—at least the mountain and the sky, but perhaps no temple, no monk.

Mumyong Sunim had a look at the label on the soju bottle. "This is a good brand," he said. "Not what they usually sell. No wonder the store *ajoshi* made you buy a second bottle. Do you have an opener?"

I handed him my Swiss Army knife and he folded out the bottle opener, admiring it, his eyes twinkling as the light reflected off the metal. He popped the cap open in one quick movement and caught it before it fell to the ground, and before he took a swig, he held the clear bottle up like an offering to the mountain. The liquid looked almost blue. "*Kaah!*" he said, wiping his mouth with the back of a sleeve. "To think this is one of the things I gave up to become a monk. Would *you* ever take a vow not to smoke or drink or womanize? Lying, stealing, killing—those are easy things to give up, if you think about it. They're not exactly necessary things, are they?"

I didn't answer because I suspected he was using me to justify his breaking of those vows. "You're drinking soju I brought up for Old Man Heaven," I said. "Are you stealing from his ghost? Does that make a difference?"

"I suppose it could, but only time will tell. Years from now, when you're old and white-haired like Old Man Heaven, maybe you'll remember something about today, and then you'll realize it was inside you, and you'll appreciate your past, with all the unanswered questions and the suffering. That is one of the ways you grow older and wiser and become a better human being who helps others end the suffering the world is so full of." He took another swallow of the soju, offered it to me, and then snatched it back to return my knife instead. "My, I talk too much for a

monk. Tonight I'll have to sit a while longer, and when I do that, I'll remember the terrible things you made me eat when you were a kid and I
will smile. Now go back down before it's dark, and I'll see you in America someday. That is where the Dharma is going—like a tide—and I am
just a fleck of sea foam."

I thanked him and turned to leave.

"Your Big Uncle. Old Man Heaven. They are here," he said, touching
his temple with the bottle. "And they are here." He touched the middle
of his chest. "Where are *you*?"

He did not even turn to go. Mumyong Sunim stood up in a swift
motion and seemed to glide off the boulder and disappear over the
ridge. I folded my knife, put it in my pocket, and started down the mountain. I did not want to go back to Old Man Heaven's grave to clean up,
but I remembered what I had to do and I did it.

# River of Light

## 1975

In the days before our departure, things happened one after the other in a kind of collage, and I often could not remember what came first or what happened next. It was as if I wanted to cram my brain full of memories and sensations because I felt that I would never see Korea again. When we flew, I knew that the land would be pulled out from under us, and if we ever did return, it would not be the same place that had received us. That was the curse brought on by the clash of time, and change, and memory.

My father's official orders were cut, with a specific date by which he would have to check in with his unit at Fort Ord. He told me it would be an easy trip—not like his last transfer to Germany—because we would be landing at Travis Air Base near San Francisco and the drive south was only a few hours. "We'll take the slow and scenic route along the coast," he said. "Highway One will be beautiful this time of year. We can stop at a beach or look at some giant redwood trees that will blow your mind."

He had never said that before—*blow your mind*—and I wondered if he was trying to sound younger, to use what he thought was *my* language. The last time I had visited him at the hospital he was reading a paperback western and he had shown me the bookmark, a playing card with a red heart and a black horsehead silhouette followed by an *S*-shaped snake. "This must have belonged to some grunt in the First Calf," he said. "But why do *this* when you could just use the Ace of Spades or a Suicide King to mark a kill?"

I realized it was Phillip's card, and I was confused. When I asked him what the card had to do with a kill, he explained that it was a practice among some units in Vietnam to leave a *calling card.* "Scare the shit out of Charlie," he said. "Or at least that was the idea. Maybe it was just their own delusion or something they did for their fucking trophy pictures." He had shown me some of those by accident one time when I had visited him at Panmunjom. They weren't even his, but ones he had confiscated from soldiers in his unit, along with illegal knives, dope, and pornography. All I remembered was the necklace of ears that looked like dried pear slices.

We hadn't decided yet whether we would all fly together. If my father was well enough, the plan was that he would fly out first, report to his new unit, procure the house on post—where we would live—buy a car—a station wagon, something large and maybe with wood paneling—and then come get us when we arrived. That would make it far easier, since we wouldn't all have to be living in the temporaries and then endure the onerous ritual of having to clean the place and pass a corrupt inspection as we moved out to our permanent quarters. When my mother asked him how long that might be, he said a week, or a month—or two. He would be taking a MAC flight to Travis, but if the policy had changed, dependents would have to take a commercial flight from Kimpo to San Francisco. The timing would all depend on when permanent quarters were available. She was happy with that—probably much happier than he'd expected—and that left him in a good mood.

After her fight with Busy-Busy, my mother was finally able to scrounge up a third refrigerator and sold it on the black market. She had claimed one was stolen, as instructed by the CID, and we had one—running on the *maru* with an old-fashioned transformer—between the bedroom and sunken kitchen. When its condenser kicked in at night, the wooden floor would suddenly vibrate, and sometimes a frightened rat would run out from somewhere, flash across the living room, and leap down onto the concrete of the veranda where all the old *hangari* storage jars stood full of the salty Korean soy sauce and the bricks of dried, fermented soy. That is what I recalled, for some reason, when Nokchon Cousin told me that Mahmi had been *stabbed,* and the CID had come to our house. It was obvious who had turned her in, since Busy-Busy made it no secret when she reported others. Even among GIs who didn't know her by that name, it was rumored that she was a snitch. No one with any experience would deal with the woman with the red "bracelets" where she had sliced her wrists.

The CID had come to our house while Mahmi was out at the NCO Club, and they had taken Nokchon Cousin for her at first because she had been using my mother's passport when she went with me to the foreigners' stores in Seoul. The Korean policeman who came with them wanted to arrest her—the connection was close enough for him—but the CIDs wanted the right person even if *all gooks look alike* as far as they were concerned. Nokchon Cousin knew a little English and she remembered the phrase they used.

Nokchon Cousin said she had kept my identity a secret at first. She told the Korean cop my name was "Ketchupson," and he had translated it for the Americans, much to their amusement. That made the Korean policeman mad, and through his subsequent questioning, they learned that my mother was the real "Insu's Mother." She showed me the bruises where the Korean had hit her just to show off to the CIDs, who apparently had no respect for him. She was told to raise at least a million won if she wanted to avoid a "penalty," and she had been asking around to borrow it while my mother hid out in Inchon at a *yogwan.* "But the strangest thing happened," she said. "The CID came to the house again without that bastard policeman. They parked their big green sedan right outside the gate and out came your mother! They caught her!

"But she looked *happy*. Glowing! Like she was pregnant! I thought they'd brought her home to get clothes for prison or something, but she came in with her big handbag and a paper sack full of fried chicken and hamburgers. She told us the *yogwan* owner had turned her in. The Korean police came, but before they took her, the CID arrived and saved her. They took her to the NCO Club.

"When they were eating, the sweaty bastard with the curly red hair gave her a strange American flower card. It had a heart and a horse on it. A bloody red heart and a horse as black as a *yontan* briquette. And a black snake! They said it was like a pass card. It would get her out of prison without having to pay anyone off. Isn't that strange?"

"Did they say something about getting out of jail free?" I asked. I tried to explain what that meant, but it only confused her.

"Mahmi didn't have to use it. She keeps it, just in case."

"Show it to me," I said. But I already knew. The CIDs had given her Phillips's calling card to show her who had saved her—the "get out of jail free" card.

A few days later, we got word that Busy-Busy and seven other black marketeers had been caught by the Korean National Police for selling refrigerators and color TVs. Their arrest was aired on TV on MBC News, their heads bowed and faces obscured by newspapers, but their wrists—with handcuffs gleaming in the lights—were prominently displayed for the camera and all of Korea to see.

LITTLE UNCLE CAME DOWN unexpectedly from the country late one Sunday, and so we knew that something important was happening in Sambongni again. It was warm, and the adults talked through the night while An-na and I tried to sleep out on the *maru* with the mosquito coil burning, emitting its white wisp of poisonous smoke. I lay on the *yo*, telling my little sister what it would be like in the States when she was older, how she would have a locker at school and how the day would be

different, migrating from class to class as the periods and subjects
changed, how she could hang out with her friends instead of having to
get in line for class. She didn't remember much about our year in Germany, but she knew she hadn't liked school there, where she had been
singled out in her class as the Jap girl or the Chink girl or the Gook
girl—whichever Oriental nationality suited the mood of the kids who
taunted her. In Korea the mixed-blood girls all stuck together—like a
gang—and they were often the ones who got in trouble for terrorizing
their white classmates.

When An-na fell asleep, I listened to Little Uncle's story about how
Big Uncle's Christian family was now haunted by his restless ghost. "Terrible things keep happening," he said. "And everyone in the whole village is having only bad luck." They were playing flower cards as usual as
they talked, and I could hear the steady and irregular slapping sound of
the little plastic cards hitting the mat. "Damn!" he said. "I lost again. Do
you see what I mean?"

I heard my mother or Nokchon Cousin chuckle. "So you came down
to collect money for a *kut* or something?" Nokchon Cousin said. She
thought all shamans were frauds, so she must have been joking.

There was a long silence, and my mother asked, "How much will you
need?"

"You're having bad luck too?" Little Uncle asked.

"*Ungh.* Me too."

"You're the youngest. I would have thought his ghost might spare you
because he liked your son so much."

"*What* ghost? She's having *good* luck!" Nokchon Cousin said. "I'd say
it was good luck what happened with the CID."

"I was almost taken by the police."

"The carp are dying downstream. A little boy drowned in the river at
the wide part near the dam where the restaurants are supposed to come.
People on the other side are afraid to go into the woods or drive at night
on the road where Big Brother was killed. They say they see lights."

"That's just a bunch of stories, like hometown legends," Nokchon Cousin said. "You hardly have to tell us that ridiculous stuff if all you want is to borrow some money."

"He was my oldest brother, and for a while he had to be like a father to all of us," my mother said.

"Every *kye* collective is busted, and people are running off with the money and disappearing somewhere in Pusan or Taegu," Little Uncle said. "Nobody in the village is going to have money to get through the year even with those investors and speculators who keep coming up from Seoul."

"So you'll waste your money on a charlatan *mudang*." *Slap*. I heard the sound of Nokchon Cousin scraping her winnings toward herself.

"I'll come up," my mother said. "My dreams have been bad too."

"Oh, you and your dreams! What was it this time? Some one-legged *tokkaebi* chasing you down the street?"

"Calm down." *Slap*. There was the sound of coins, dull collisions of metal.

"I dreamed there was a pig from the country in your old house in Nokchon. You moved back there after we went to America."

"Well, a pig dream is *good*! You don't even know good luck from bad luck anymore with those dreams of yours. No wonder you never win at slot machines!"

My mother's tone was quiet. "The pig was dead with a knife through its heart."

"*Ayu!*"

That settled it. We would have to go back up to my mother's village practically on the eve of our departure from Kimpo International Airport.

WE LEFT FOR Sambongni late in the morning on the day of Big Uncle's *kut*. My mother and Nokchon Cousin and I took a taxi from Pupyong to Yongsan and then switched to a different Arirang taxi driven by Specialist Ajoshi, who remembered me from Kimpo and played old Lee Mija cassettes for us. He said he'd wanted to see an authentic shamanic ritual of exorcism for a long time. My mother told him it wasn't an exorcism but a *shikkim kut*, a ritual of cleansing to help Big Uncle's spirit go to its next incarnation, but Nokchon Cousin said it was all the same. "The *mudang* is going to jump up and down, and there will be a big racket and babbling in voices and sobbing and crying, but it's all just for the money." She was the one who thought it best that An-na stay home because the *kut* might frighten her and fill her head with superstition. My mother agreed, though the real reason was different. She didn't want An-na seeing too much into the next world. They talked about it enough when An-na described her dreams.

It was the middle of the afternoon when we passed the Paldang Dam, and we saw all the sluices open, the water thundering out on the downstream side. "They must be getting ready for a flood on the North Han," the driver said. The *kut* had been going since dawn, and only a few minutes farther upstream, we could hear it as we approached Sambongni on the riverside road. The sounds of the gongs and drums carried over the water from more than a mile away. They had set up a canopy and screens near the boat landing, and the entire village—and others—must have been assembled there like a crowd gathered to watch a traveling medicine show. Mechanical cultivators and their attached carts, bicycles, and even a car were parked along the path to the water.

The driver parked the taxi near the cinder block toilet building and asked where he could go and pee before watching the *kut*. He already knew the building was just a show for New Community money. My mother pointed out one of the village outhouses as we got out.

"Go on ahead," said the driver. "I'll follow the noise." When my mother and Nokchon Cousin started down the path, the driver called me over and handed me a small pink envelope.

"What is it, Specialist Ajoshi?"

"It's from Oduri," he said. "She told me to give it to your mother for you, but since you're here . . ."

I thanked him, and when he had jogged off toward the outhouse, I ripped the envelope open. There was a black-and-white postcard inside: Audrey Hepburn in her black dress and sunglasses holding a cup of to-go coffee and a paper bag in her hand. My hands trembled so badly I could barely read what was written on the back:

> *Wish you could be there for the wedding, 7.*
> *We could use the lucky number. Write me!*
>
> *Love,*
> *Patsy*

She had signed it with a large heart with a cigarette holder where the arrow should have been, and at the very bottom was her new address. I felt as if my heart had just been pierced by that cigarette holder, and there was no place to sit down. I didn't want to collapse onto the path, so I stood there, doubled over as if I had just been on a long run, tears dripping onto my shoes.

After a few moments I looked up and saw that my mother was right. It was a *shikkim kut*. I had never seen one before, but I knew from the white costumes and banners—everything white—that it was the cleansing ritual. I felt uneasy in the belly realizing this—they were cleaning up Big Uncle's ghost the same way they had exiled him across the river because of the smell from his foot. As I walked past the vegetable gardens and approached the canopy and the screens, where I caught up to my mother and Nokchon Cousin, I could feel the drums in my pulse and the raspy reed flutes and gongs pounding from inside my head. The last sound that carried into my body was the jangling bells—like a mixer stirring all thought into a jumble of impressions. Even my vision seemed to change, becoming narrower and sharper, and when I heard Nokchon Cousin exclaim, "It's him!" and my mother said, "Kubong Manshin!" I could almost hear my thoughts as words outside my head. *Of course, it's him!*

"He's wearing a *kaat* on his head!"

The black horsehair gentleman's hat did not go with the white woman's *ch'ima* and *chogori* Kubong Manshin wore as he leaped up and down in his *poson* socks, chanting. Even from this distance, through the heads of the crowd, I could see he was flushed and covered in sweat.

"What is he doing?" I asked.

My mother paused on the path to let someone by. "He's acting out Big Brother's life story, but he's mixing it with stories about other people—all the Sambongni people, suffering."

Nokchon Cousin went ahead when she saw some of our relatives. "I'll be over there by Country Sister," she said.

When Nokchon Cousin was out of earshot, my mother turned to me with a hopeless look. I hadn't seen that look since I was little and she was going to the hospital for her radiation treatments for her thyroid. "Insu-ya," she said, "Daeri isn't going to live very long."

I wanted to blurt out that I had already known that for a long time—that I wasn't a child anymore, that my father had made it clear to me without having to say so—but instead, I just stood there, silent, letting the sound of the ritual wash over us.

"I shouldn't have taken the money," she said, and I realized what she was telling me. She believed Big Uncle's ghost was bringing her bad luck as revenge. "It was wrong of me."

I wanted to scream at her, "Now you want to appease his fucking *ghost*? Why didn't you just do the right thing at the right time instead of wasting all your time and money on the slot machines?" But all I could say was, "Why are you telling me *now*?" The appropriate time would never come back no matter what we did now—the causes and conditions, as the monk had told me, were forever changed.

"I'm going to ask Big Uncle to let Daeri live longer. What will we do in America if he leaves us all alone?" I could hear the quaver in her voice.

I was going to turn away when I thought I heard Kubong Manshin's chant suddenly change, the cadence shifting to that of normal speech.

He spoke only three syllables like that—*Ro Bing Ho*—before he resumed
the frenetic pace of the chant, which I couldn't follow through the cacophony of the music. But that name shot a chill through my body. How
could he have known that name? Or was I mistaken just now and those
were just three random syllables I'd heard in a lull in the music? I remembered what Big Uncle had said about Robin Hood and how he
wanted to be buried where the arrow landed. I had not found that arrow,
and Big Uncle was buried up on the ancestral mountain near his mother
and father.

"Mahmi," I said. "I have something I need to do right now. For Big
Uncle." Before she could even ask me what it was or where I was going,
I ran down to the river and found one of the old boats on the bank.

When I heard those words—maybe the crazy *mudang* had known I
was here and meant them for me—I knew immediately that I would
have to find the lost arrow. Nothing would work without it. Kubong
Manshin would sing Big Uncle's life, right up to the part where he says,
"Insu-ya, bury me where this arrow lands. Swear you'll do it." And I
would swear, but there was no arrow and his grave would be in the
wrong place. Big Uncle would return as a hungry ghost with his frightening *han*—all his grievous longing and his harbored resentment—just
like in those historical dramas that were so popular in the theaters these
days, all about unfulfilled *han* and the tragic sorrow it carried into the
next generation—and even to the entire nation. Nobody really talked
about things that way, but the shamans knew—they watched the movies
like everyone else and understood that people secretly wanted their lives
to be like movies anyway. The grievous longing of an ancestor's *han*
could ruin a family for generations, and I would be the one who'd failed
to find the arrow. I would be the one to take the *han* of that failure to my
own grave.

All this knowledge flashed through my mind instant by instant in
time to the rhythmic pounding of the drums and the harsh metallic res-
onance of the gong. My mind couldn't follow all the images—trying

made me terribly anxious—but if I relaxed and let them flash by like movement under an Itaewon club's disco strobe light, I thought I could see everything—even backward and forward in time.

I was standing in one of the old boats, breathing too quickly. The boat creaked as I propelled it from side to side in the green-tinted water, and moving slowly forward, I felt as if I were performing an ancient dance. I imagined there must be some song to sing with that dance—a song about Big Uncle's life, like what Kubong Manshin was chanting—but the only song that came to me was "Red Scarf," the theme song in the movie about the heroic squadron of Korean Sabre jet pilots. I sang that as I rowed, with the line of the refrain stuck in my head—

> *With a red scarf wrapped around my neck*
> *Flowing with the clouds, I am flowing too*

—and I repeated those lines over and over until I saw the water in the boat rising, sloshing up under my feet with each stroke of the oar, until I was standing in the river, sinking, until I began to swim, my water-logged clothes dragging me down so I could barely draw breath with my head above water, the music on the shore pounding in my ears, until, when I feared I might drown, I felt the bottom and waded ashore.

An unearthly amount of water dripped off me as I walked up the muddy bank of the other side. My sneakers squelched with each step. I did not even pause to take them off because I knew I had to find the arrow while the music still sounded from across the river. Then I heard other sounds too—the pounding of my heart, what seemed to be the squeaking of my pulse, the groaning and creaking of tree trunks in the wind, the variegated rustling of leaves. My wet shoes slipped and I fell again and again, and when I finally reached the familiar site of Big Uncle's camp in front of the blocked eye socket of the cave, I was covered in mud and twigs, pine needles and leaves.

Some other shaman must have been there earlier—the low branches of all the trees around the cave were covered in strips of white and yellow paper inscribed with Buddhist prayers and Taoist talismans. The black calligraphy and the strange red symbols had already begun to fade, and the strips of paper quivered in the wind like aspen leaves showing their pale undersides.

This was where Big Uncle had stood when he fired the arrow. I was standing where he had been standing and I could retrace its flight now—I felt it in my body, the texture of air rushing past my face. The cadence of the drumming and the gong changed across the river. I couldn't hear the reedy *p'iri* or the bells, but I could feel the duller vibration of the *manshin*'s voice in my gut. My vision was suddenly clearer now—everything sharper, brighter, more colorful, buzzing with a strange energy that created jittering afterimages. When I heard the caw of a crow I saw the zigzag of its *ki* flash blue-white through the air. I could feel it on my skin, itching through my wet clothes like a swarm of insects crawling from my groin up to my heart. I slapped my pants, my shirt, but the sensation persisted, so intense that I tore off all of my clothes and threw them onto the ground where the old fire pit used to burn. Plumes of luminous mist rose from the ground like steam, and I breathed them in. Now I was cold. I hugged myself and shivered, but my mind felt calm and attentive, and I could tell now where it was—the thing in my thoughts—the image of the arrow with the steel hunting tip and the red cock's feather. I heard a fluttering sound, felt its vibration, saw its trail, and I bolted into the woods, surprising myself by how quickly I could run barefoot through the forest, oddly detached from the pain in my feet, which were soon torn and bleeding.

I rise and descend, following the arrow past an ancient oak that might once have been a village holy tree, brushing by so quickly I scrape a patch of flesh from my shoulder, leaping through a hedge of thorns without feeling them puncture and rip my arms, my thighs, my cheeks. Blood dribbles down my forehead and into my eyes. I am breathing too quickly, panting like a small animal as I look, confused, at the blood that covers my palms when I wipe what I think is sweat from my face. I stand under an old white pine that must have been struck long ago by lightning. The trunk has split, and twelve feet up in the crack, which has accumulated dirt and bird droppings, moss, and fungus over the years, there grows another tree, another white pine. Its needles are fresher, brighter, greener than those of the old tree. I hear the crow call again, see the multicolored flash of its feathers in the sun like a rainbow oil slick in water, and just at the base of the small pine I see it—the cock's feather in a swatch of moss, its faded red stark against the cool green in the shadow of the big tree. The old pine's trunk is straight, with no low branches, all the way from the split to the ground. There is no time. I have to return across the river before the ritual ends, and the sun is already on its downward arc.

I take a breath—a slow, deep one, then another. After the third breath I am calm. My body turns to my mind, and I project my intention, pointed at the spot where the red feather seems to glow in its bed of moss. Before I know it, I am sprinting toward the tree, hardly touching the ground as I let gravity take me. I do not have to push against the ground with my feet—I merely move in cadence to let the Earth receive me with each step, as if I were leaning forward, suspended, and it is the Earth that moves under me. When I do push against the ground it is to leap up—higher than I could have imagined—until I am dangling from a branch that allows me to swing my entire body up and over, onto the patch of moss in the crotch of the split branches. I am afraid it is just the feather, but when I touch it I feel the wood of the arrow's shaft, the still-intact lacquered threads that reinforce the notch. I pull it, slowly, firmly, but it is lodged too deep. I break off the end of a dry branch and dig into the moss, gouging a hole, clawing at the dirt and debris and rotting insect carcasses until I have freed the arrow and it comes up, with a sudden jerk, knocking me off balance. I fall, hitting the branch of another tree, another, and then the duff-covered ground, where the back of my head slams into an exposed root and I see a flash of light, stars, blackness.

The world comes back quickly. I am lying on my back on the forest floor, the smell of metal in my nose, a dull pain and a pounding in my head, which I quickly recognize as the drums of the *kut* echoing from across the river. I sit up. My left hand is sticky with blood. When I look down at myself I see the gash in my ribs from where the blade of the arrowhead cut me before burying itself into a tree root, where it now stands upright in a small patch of brassy light. The arrow's shaft is dirty and covered with scratches, but it is not broken. I pull it out of the root and stand up. I feel a burning pain in my side. I spit some blood and sway unsteadily for a moment before I move. It is still light—I can see the angle of the sun from the shadows in the forest, and I know I can make it to the other side of the river. There is no sense of urgency or feeling of panic, just a calm and matter-of-fact knowledge that I will run to the river and swim across. I run without hesitation, though my wound opens and my feet burn with each step. I run without looking at the ground—it feels as if I am gliding on a layer of flame, and when I finally crash through the thorny underbrush and reach the water, I pause for only a moment to get my bearings.

THE SHADOWS OF the trees stretched all the way to the water now as the sun hung only a few degrees over the western horizon. I walked into the river, waded several steps, and plunged in, holding the arrow up in my right hand. The water felt cool at first, then icy, and then warm as I swam sidestroke, scissoring my legs, pushing with my left arm, the top of my head breaking the water. I swam to the beat of the gong whose sound was loud and dull by turns each time my head dipped under the water. I could feel my self beginning to dissolve as the river cleansed my naked body, flaps of my torn skin opening up like tiny gills leaking blood. My lungs pumped and my throat was both dry and wet as I spat out mouthfuls of water, coughing, when I breathed out of time with the wave that formed in front of my head. I could not brush the hair out of my face with the hand that held the arrow up in the air, and so I was blind until I managed to blink the wet strands out of my burning eyes.

I was still only halfway across when I felt the thickness in my limbs. The river was warm and cold by turns, but in the middle, where the current was strongest, it remained icy, and my muscles began to cramp. I swam lower and lower in the water, and I began to sink, struggling—not to swim, but to get enough air as I tried to lose the current's grip.

I swam faster, cramping my neck and swallowing water, but the faster I swam, the farther away the *kut* seemed to be. After a while I stopped to tread water and look back at the riverbank. It was only a couple dozen yards away, but I knew now that I couldn't make it, so I waved the arrow at people on the shore and called out to them to help me. They just gave me encouraging waves back. When I called to them again, they held their hands to their ears as if they couldn't make out what I was saying.

My arms and legs grew leaden, and after another minute I began to sink. But I wasn't at all concerned about drowning. It never occurred to me to be afraid. The river was deep, and as I sank I could see the bright shimmer of the surface and then progressively darker water. I continued to kick and flap my arms to go up, but it was no use, and I felt the urgency of running out of air. The panicky feeling of having to breathe became a different kind of pressure in my chest, and everything turned a velvety black. Then something in my head burst—like ears popping with a change of altitude—and I inhaled *light*. It filled my chest and turned my entire body luminous, and the capacity of my body was immense—the light rushed in with a loud roaring sound like a waterfall, and my body grew larger and larger until I was a giant floating in the middle of space. I could see the periphery of darkness all around me. An incredibly beautiful sound permeated everything, and I felt at ease and full of wonder—not so much an ecstasy as an amazement—at how profoundly beautiful everything was. And there *was* everything: in the time it took for me to inhale the light, I recalled everything. It wasn't at all like my life flashing before my eyes; it was as if every instant in my life before and after my drowning existed simultaneously and could be perceived and recalled simultaneously, and the memory went back to before my birth and after my death, and when I finished inhaling, when my body became light, I *was* everything and yet I had also ceased to exist except to see: my father, young, sunburned, standing at the edge of a white sand beach in Nha Trang, smiling at a little boy who looks like he could be my brother, the two of them are smiling, and the water is a shocking shade of blue, as if the sky had come down into the sea, and my father's smile is gap-toothed because he has forgotten his partial plate; I see my mother in a beehive hairdo, wearing a cream-colored miniskirt, standing with her beaded white purse in front of the Bolero Tea Room, and her front teeth are wide, just like her portrait with my father, painted from a photo by some artist at the Friendship Arcade in Yongsan; I see a girl who looks like my sister, but I know it is Patsy, and she is in her white lace wedding dress, crying, waiting for a man to walk her up the aisle of the Catholic church, and behind her I see the body of Christ in his crown of thorns, his palms and feet pierced by real nails and the blood painted to look like real human blood, and Patsy is looking down the aisle, into the distance, thinking of a Beatles song that will play at her reception; I see Miklos, his body tangled so tight in the webbing of parachute cord it is cutting into his bloated, purple flesh, and his younger self is smiling proudly at the first "S" he received on his Seoul American Middle School report card, and he is spitting through his front teeth just like his brother; I see Paulie sitting at a picnic table in the sun, a day with blue sky and puffy clouds, writing a letter—it is hard for him, and he concentrates, his tongue protruding from the side of his mouth as he stains his fingers with ink from his cheap Korean fountain pen, and he will go to college and become a businessman in Macon, Georgia; and I see my sister in a cap and gown giving a valedictorian's speech, and the crowd cheers her

and she has newspaper articles written about her, and then she is proud
of her children as a huge island erupts in flames; and I see a boy trying
to swim across the river, and the current is too strong for him and he
gives up—releases himself into the river's flow—and he is filled with
water, and he must breathe it now to live; and there are crows and cranes
and jets and egrets flying, black wings, white wings, rainbow wings, all
the colors of the sun and moon, and then, suddenly, people pull me up
in terrible pain onto the shore.

The light seemed to break in half as if something were pinching a
sphere in the middle, and then I could see blurry images and feel my hair
poking my right eye. I was coughing up water, my lungs were burning,
and my body was pierced everywhere with hot needles. Every time I
coughed up more water, there was a brightening and dimming in my
vision, and my point of view shifted back and forth from inside my body
to many feet above myself, looking down at the people who stood around
me from above and behind, and past them I could see the pained expression on my own face and the water coming from my mouth. At first I
wondered who it was they had fished out of the river—I looked so
strange, naked and pale, covered in pink gashes. After a few more
coughs, my vision stayed in my body, but I still felt very distant, watching
a slow-motion movie with muffled sound, and that feeling would stay
with me for days. As the rhythm of my breath returned and people exclaimed, I could hear the gong and the clashing cymbals grow frenetic—
the ritual was coming to its conclusion—and I could not let it end
without the arrow. Frantically, I rose to my knees and looked around
me—it was still clutched in my hand, which was bleeding again. I pushed
people away against their objections and stood up. I seemed to tower
above them, and when one of them gave me a shirt to cover my naked-
ness, I slapped it away and ran toward the canopy in the direction of the
sound. I could hear the pleading tone in Kubong Manshin's voice,
though it was not his. The cadence was different—it was a woman's

voice—and I wondered who it must be to sound so bereft and anguished when Big Uncle's relatives seem to have no feelings of that sort.

As I ran I heard people saying, "Who is that?" "Is he crazy?" "Is he a deaf-mute?" "Is he Hwasuni's son?" "What sort of *tokkaebi* came out of the river?" "Is it the ghost of the drowned boy?"

Kubong Manshin had come out from under the canopy where the offerings of food were laid out on a long table with Big Uncle's black-banded portrait between the stacks of apples and spiral pillars of multi-colored rice cakes and candies. The folding screen behind the table was covered in grass-style calligraphy, two of the panels discolored pink from the watery blood of a pig's head, which lay on its side, mouth stuffed with money, a short-shafted trident sticking out of its neck stump. It had fallen over—the ritual was inauspicious.

A woman who could have been one of my relatives screamed and pointed at me, and all heads turned my way. Someone had just declared the whole thing a fraud—"He's a fake woman and he's even a fake *mudang*!"—but now, as they all saw me, they grew quiet. The drums and *p'iri* and gong were suddenly louder. The rhythm surged. "He's covered in blood!" someone shouted. I saw the taxi driver staring at me, eyes wide, mouth ajar in the middle of calling out to my mother.

There was a long piece of white fabric held by six people on each side, leading down into the river. Two of the people carrying it were already knee-deep in the water as they waded in, holding the cloth between them, its end submerged. The cloth sagged in the middle with the weight of money—coins and bills—that had been thrown onto it, and on the near end on shore was Kubong Manshin, now wearing a white Buddhist nun's hat over her white clothes, beating the gong, her eyes glazed, sweat dripping down her flushed face. She called out Big Uncle's name and asked him to follow the road into the next world. Big Uncle's Christian daughter and son-in-law, who should have been at the front of the crowd, were standing in the middle, their faces hidden in shame and embarrassment.

"Stop the bitch!" shouted a drunken voice. "He'll ruin the fortunes of your whole clan!"

Someone grabbed the drum and kicked the *p'iri* player, interrupting the music, but Kubong Manshin still pounded the gong. The white cloth it dangled from was gray with dirt and sweat from his hand. "*Go!*" he shouted.

> You were born into this world of dust
> You lost your mother to harsh disease
> You lost your father—he broke taboo
> You lost your birthplace to civil war
> All taken away
>
> A *tokkaebi* took your foot away
> You could not run, you could not leap
> You could not dance, you could not walk
> When you crawled like a little babe
> They sent you to die in Skullhead Cave!
>
> This world of red dust is full of sorrow,
> They took the house, they took your land
> They took the money out of your hand
> They took the food right out of your mouth
> They took your dignity out of your heart
>
> Sorrow upon sorrow
> This world of red dust, full of sorrow
> Go now! Go! To your ancestors, go!
> To the Westward Land, to the Lotus Land,
> To the land of bodhisattvas, go!
>
> *Go!*

With a glance in my direction, Kubong Manshin leaped up with the last "*Go!*" and smacked the end of the stretched fabric with a folded fan.

I could see the twelve carriers straining, pulling the fabric tight so it would rip down the middle—but nothing happened.

The crowd murmured, and a woman's voice cried out, "He doesn't want to go!" Everything was louder now because the music had died out. Kubong Manshin had put down the gong so he could use the fan.

"His ghost is still here!" someone shouted.

"*Go!*" cried Kubong Manshin. He struck the fabric again, and all that happened was the sound of the fan—a woody *clack*—as it bounced off the fabric. People started to shout in anger and fear. Kubong Manshin's assistants held back the drunken villager who'd lurched forward.

Then the *manshin* saw me. He had noticed me already, but now he looked at me with the full force of his attention, and there was a dead silence as everyone suddenly saw me at once—naked, dripping, my flesh torn all over. My hand and ribs were bleeding again, and fresh blood— startlingly red—dripped from me onto the grass. In my bleeding hand, I held Big Uncle's arrow.

"*Wat-ta!*" cried Kubong Manshin. "He's here!"

The crowd stepped away from me. I heard my mother shouting for someone to bring some clothes for me. Big Uncle's second daughter burst into tears.

"Who's here?" Kubong Manshin said, staring into my eyes. His were bloodshot, radiating a strange heat that made my own eyes tingle and tear up. I wiped them with the back of my left hand, sniffling. "*Who's* here?" he cried again, and I shouted out, "Big Uncle!"

It wasn't my voice. It was too deep and too raspy, wet sounding, like the voice of someone who smoked too much, who would have a wet cough like a man dying of tuberculosis. What I said wasn't an answer, it was me calling out to a different place. "Big Uncle!" I cried, and lurching forward, just as Kubong Manshin shouted "*Go!*" for the last time, I touched the stretched white fabric with the tip of the arrow, the slightest touch, as if the arrow were a flame and the fabric a fuse, and after a momentary interruption—everything seemed to stop—there came a loud tearing sound as the fabric split neatly down the middle, like a huge zipper opening. As the two sides parted like a pair of egret's wings, outspread, all the money showered to the ground, and Big Uncle's spirit followed the path and flew into the river. The fabric ripped so quickly the twelve people who held it all fell backward, four of them into the water, splashing and flailing their arms, as the last part of the cloth tore under the surface, and a single swell pushed its way downstream into the current in the middle of the North Han.

I dropped the arrow. Kubong Manshin caught me before I could fall on it and impale myself. He called me by Big Uncle's name as he embraced me, and then by my own name as he lowered me to the ground, and my mother covered me with a flower-patterned blanket as I watched the sun sinking into the west, into the tops of the tall trees across the water.

# Forsythia

## 1975

The late September air is thick with humidity and the bitter fragrance of mugwort. She makes her way up the mountain along the narrow trail, wearing a plain dress, an old military ruck slung on her back, and even under her umbrella she can feel the force of the sun. She is sweating, already a little out of breath, surprised to feel her age for a change. *Am I really this old?* she thinks. How swiftly the years have flown—so fast she hardly had time to notice—and now she endures the sharp bands of pain in her joints and the brittleness in her bones.

From here she can see the road, and then the river, dark green and shimmering below. It grows wider, westward toward Seoul, and she knows now why the resorts are moving in this direction, away from the congestion of the city. In the milky blue sky the clouds are pulled apart in tufts like raw cotton batting and spread across the horizon.

It isn't hard to find the grave. There are no headstones among the several grassy mounds of varying size, but she can tell which is his from the new grass, not yet a season old, growing on top. She puts down the umbrella, leaving it open, and unpacks the offerings she has brought—tangerines, apples—all the typical things, and Chivas Regal instead of soju, because he had so much wanted to try it. When she has laid everything out, she pokes three incense sticks upright into a small bowl of dried rice and lights them *with a Zippo lighter, which she then snaps shut and leaves with the other offerings.*

*"All these years I thought you were dead," she says. "All these years, and now here you are, you old fool." A breeze catches the umbrella, and the red-and-white panels spin, momentarily, like a propeller before the ribs catch in the earth and it is still again. Smoke from the incense wafts up in the wind, burning her eyes, but she does not cry as she takes a small hand spade from the rucksack.*

*She digs a hole at the base of the grave, on the back side, and buries a small box there, tamping the earth down when she is done. "There," she says. "Your promise." She unwraps a cloth bundle of forsythia cuttings that she knows will root easily and plants them in a circle along the midrift of the mound. The bright yellow flowers will come up in the spring. She will visit again to see, and perhaps then, all the tears she has dammed up for a quarter century, she will release in a single flood, the tears she has yet to shed for him and for herself, a woman still haunted by dreams.*

# A Note on the Hexagrams
# & Pictograms

THE HEXAGRAMS THAT designate the sections of *Skull Water* are from the *I Ching*, the ancient Chinese *Book of Changes* (易 經 , called the *Yeokgyeong* in Korean), which is still used today as an oracle. The hexagrams, which are constructed out of a stack of six broken (yin) or whole (yang) lines, are accompanied by a textual explication in verse form and in prose commentary to help the users of the *I Ching* determine the answers to the questions they pose. Westerners are most familiar with the Wilhelm/Baynes translation of the *I Ching*, which also includes an introduction by Carl Jung.

For *Skull Water*, I used the older form of the *I Ching*, generally known as the *Zhou Yi*, which does not include the later commentaries and was used much more specifically for oracular purposes. My oldest maternal uncle (on whom the character Big Uncle is based) had memorized all the hexagrams and accompanying Chinese characters, but in their old pictographic forms. He used a small pouch, with four black and four white *baduk* (*go*) stones inside, which he would draw three at a time in order to form each line. While most people (including experts) who consult the *I Ching* will use an intersecting chart of eight by eight trigrams to look up the sixty-four hexagrams, my uncle would simply scratch the hexagram into the dirt with a stick and then draw the accompanying pictogram while he chanted, under his breath, the short verse that went with it. The pictographic form of consultation (which I think is likely to be the oldest method, since it is most concrete) is special; it not only lends a Rorschach-like quality to the reading, it is also linked to the very origins of Chinese writing via its connection to the ancient practices of scapulomancy and plastromancy (the reading of cracks in sheep scapula bones and turtle shells for divination).

There are many Western writers and artists who have used the *I Ching* in their work, most notably John Cage in his music and Philip K. Dick in his classic science fiction work, *The Man in the High Castle.* For *Skull Water,* I have used my uncle's method, casting hexagrams and reading their accompanying pictograms before or during most of my writing sessions. Much of the structure of *Skull Water* is thus woven together out of the associative synchronicities of the *Zhou Yi* and their intersection with my memories of 1970s Korea, the world in which the character Insu grows up. I have used the technique throughout *Skull Water* in order to maintain a Taoist undercurrent parallel to Big Uncle's interest in Taoist alchemy. The principle of the five Taoist elements was maintained by writing in ink (water & earth) in a notebook with a wooden cover (wood) with a fountain pen (metal). The fire element is implicit in the construction of the metal pen nib and the manufacture of ink out of ash; it is also present, via its association with electricity, in the fact that the handwritten manuscript was then typed on a computer.

The pictograms I've used as chapter heads come from a wonderful resource, the Chinese Etymology website (*hanziyuan.net*), based on the work of Richard Sears, or "Uncle Hanzi."

# Acknowledgments

One doesn't usually begin by thanking places, but *Skull Water* happens in a lost landscape of history, so I salute my old neighborhood in Bupyeong and the two U.S. military bases, ASCOM and the former Yongsan Garrison, that exist now only in bittersweet memory. I wrote most of this novel at my favorite table in the basement of the Thompson Memorial Library at Vassar College during a sabbatical awarded by my home institution, the State University of New York, New Paltz—my appreciative thanks to those places as well.

I would like to thank my many colleagues—especially Fred Carriere, Bruce Fulton, Ted Hughes, Minsoo Kang, Kwon Youngmin, Kun Jong Lee, Young-Jun Lee, David McCann, Chan Park, Mark Peterson, and Michael Robinson—whose interest in my work over the years helped me to see it in a broader context and gave me additional reasons to finish this project. Thanks to Terry Hong for inviting me to the Smithsonian, where my participation in the centennial celebration of Korean immigration made me see both my academic and creative work in a new light. Thanks to my old friend Howard Yellen for humoring my writerly activities in my naïve college days and for his patience in seeing it mature; I am also grateful to him and Allison Kozak for support that came at a crucial time. Thanks also to fellow writers Marie Myung-Ok Lee, Yongsoo Park, and Lee Chang-dong, whose comments gave me new resolve to depict a usually unseen aspect of Korean history.

The Buddhist themes in *Skull Water* were much influenced by Musan Cho Oh-hyun, whose Zen poetry challenged and inspired me, and I humbly bow to him for the dream advice I carry with me to this day. Thanks to Lee Manjoo for bringing to my attention the little-known story of the *tokkaebi* in Wonhyo's cave and to Walter Lew for his incisive semiotic analysis of Wonhyo's writing.

Many thanks to my wonderful agent, Rob McQuilkin, who brought the manuscript to Spiegel & Grau, to Cindy Spiegel for her masterful editing, and to Aaron Robertson for his many insights. There are also other editors I wish to thank for their work with me on stories that eventually became part of this novel: Cressida Leyshon, Deborah Treisman, and David Remnick at *The New Yorker*; Jenny Ryun Foster and Frank Stewart, my co-editors for *The Century of the Tiger*; and Cerrissa Kim, Katherine Kim, Sora Kim-Russell, and Mary-Kim Arnold, editors of the *Mixed Korean* anthology.

And, finally, my heartfelt appreciation to Bella, for her fresh and penetrating insights into symbolism, theme, and structure, and Anne, my first and last reader extraordinaire who labored until the long lunar eclipse to help me see this project through. Words fail me because there are not enough of them in any language to express all the thanks you deserve!

# About the Author

**Heinz Insu Fenkl** was born in 1960 in Bupyeong, Korea, and grew up in Korea, Germany, and the United States. His autobiographical novel *Memories of My Ghost Brother* was named a PEN/Hemingway Award finalist and a Barnes & Noble "Discover Great New Writers" selection. His fiction and translations have been published in the *New Yorker*. A member of the editorial board for Harvard University's *AZALEA: Journal of Korean Literature and Culture* from its inception until 2017, he is also the translator of the classic seventeenth-century Korean Buddhist novel *The Nine Cloud Dream* by Kim Man-jung, published in 2019 as a Penguin Classic.

Fenkl received his BA in English from Vassar College and his MA in Creative Writing from the University of California, Davis. He was a Fulbright scholar in South Korea, where he studied literary translation and began a project collecting narrative folktales, which led to his book *Korean Folktales*. He was codirector of the Fulbright Summer Seminar in Korean History and Culture, and he studied in the PhD Program in Cultural Anthropology at the University of California, Davis, specializing in the areas of shamanism, narrative folklore, and ethnographic theory.

He has taught a wide array of creative writing, folklore, literature, and Asian and Asian American studies courses at Vassar College, Eastern Michigan University, and Sarah Lawrence College. He was also a core faculty member for the Milton Avery MFA program at Bard College and has taught at Yonsei University in Korea. He currently teaches creative writing and Asian studies courses at the State University of New York, New Paltz. He lives in the Hudson Valley with his wife and daughter.